Curl up ...
Caroline Anderson and Cara ...
this Christmas, and share the warmth,
wonder—and of course romance—
as two families' holiday wishes are granted!

Enjoy our new 2-in-1 editions of stories
by your favourite authors—

*for double the romance!*

with

**THEIR CHRISTMAS FAMILY MIRACLE**
by Caroline Anderson

**SNOWBOUND BRIDE-TO-BE**
by Cara Colter

**Dear Reader**

Isn't it amazing how quickly Christmas comes round? How wonderfully, reliably, *relentlessly* often? And it's so expensive, too. Expectations are unrealistically high, emotions are near the surface, and there's nothing quite like it for underlining not only the joys but the tragedies and disappointments of our lives too.

So imagine you've suddenly been made homeless and your life is in total chaos. Or that Christmas is the worst time in the world for you and the only way you can deal with it is to pretend it doesn't happen. Then imagine what happens when these two people are thrown together at Christmastime—and put three children and a dog into the mix. Stir well and make a wish...

I cried buckets writing this, so a word of warning—if you're a softie, put on your waterproof mascara! And I hope you have a wonderful Christmas.

With love

*Caroline*

# THEIR CHRISTMAS
# FAMILY MIRACLE

BY
CAROLINE ANDERSON

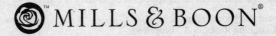

All the characters in this book have no existence outside the imagination of the author, and have no relation whatsoever to anyone bearing the same name or names. They are not even distantly inspired by any individual known or unknown to the author, and all the incidents are pure invention.

First published in Great Britain 2009
Harlequin Mills & Boon Limited,
Eton House, 18-24 Paradise Road, Richmond, Surrey TW9 1SR

© Caroline Anderson 2009

ISBN: 978 0 263 86983 5

Set in Times Roman 13 on 15 pt
02-1209-48777

Harlequin Mills & Boon policy is to use papers that are natural, renewable and recyclable products and made from wood grown in sustainable forests. The logging and manufacturing process conform to the legal environmental regulations of the country of origin.

Printed and bound in Spain
by Litografia Rosés, S.A., Barcelona

**Caroline Anderson** has the mind of a butterfly. She's been a nurse, a secretary, a teacher, run her own soft-furnishing business and now she's settled on writing. She says, 'I was looking for that elusive something. I finally realised it was variety, and now I have it in abundance. Every book brings new horizons and new friends, and in between books I have learned to be a juggler. My teacher husband John and I have two beautiful and talented daughters, Sarah and Hannah, umpteen pets and several acres of Suffolk that nature tries to reclaim every time we turn our backs!'

Caroline also writes for the Mills & Boon® Medical™ Romance series.

# CHAPTER ONE

'WE NEED to talk.'

Amelia sat back on her heels and looked up at her sister with a sinking heart. She'd heard them arguing, heard her brother-in-law's harsh, bitter tone, heard the slamming of the doors, then her sister's approaching footsteps on the stairs. And she knew what was coming.

What she didn't know was how to deal with it.

'This isn't working,' she said calmly.

'No.' Laura looked awkward and acutely uncomfortable, but she also looked a little relieved that Amelia had made it easy for her. Again. Her hands clenched and unclenched nervously. 'It's not me—it's Andy. Well, and me, really, I suppose. It's the kids. They just—run around all the time, and the baby cries all night, and Andy's tired. He's supposed to be having a rest over Christmas, and instead—it's not their fault,

Millie, but having the children here is difficult, we're just not used to it. And the dog, really, is the last straw. So—yes, I'm sorry, but—if you could find somewhere as soon as possible after Christmas—'

Amelia set aside the washing she was folding and got up, shaking her head, the thought of staying where she—no, where her *children* were not wanted, anathema to her. 'It's OK. Don't apologise. It's a terrible imposition. Don't worry about it, we'll go now. I'll just pack their things and we'll get out of your hair—'

'I thought you didn't have anywhere to go?'

She didn't. Or money to pay for it, but that was hardly her sister's fault, was it? 'Don't worry,' she said again. 'We'll go to Kate's.'

But crossing her fingers behind her back was pointless. Kate lived in a tiny cottage, one up one down, with hardly room for her and her own daughter. There was no way the four of them and the dog could squeeze in, too. But her sister didn't know that, and her shoulders dropped in relief.

'I'll help you get their things together,' she said quickly, and disappeared, presumably to comb the house for any trace of their presence while Amelia sagged against the wall, shutting her eyes hard against the bitter sting of tears and fighting down the sob of desperation that was rising in her throat. Two and a half days to Christmas.

Short, dark, chaotic days in which she had no hope of finding anywhere for them to go or another job to pay for it. And, just to make it worse, they were in the grip of an unseasonably cold snap, so even if they were driven to it, there was no way they could sleep in the car. Not without running the engine, and that wasn't an option, since she probably only had just enough fuel to get away from her sister's house with her pride intact.

And, as it was the only thing she had left, that was a priority.

Sucking in a good, deep breath, she gathered up the baby's clothes and started packing them haphazardly, then stopped herself. She had to prioritise. Things for the next twenty-four hours in one little bag, then everything else she could sort out later once they'd arrived at wherever they were going. She sorted, shuffled, packed the baby's clothes, then her own, then finally went into the bedroom Kitty and Edward were sharing and packed their clothes and toys, with her mind firmly shut down and her thoughts banished for now.

She could think later. There'd be time to think once they were out of here. In the meantime, she needed to gather up the children and any other bits and pieces she'd overlooked and get them out before she totally lost it. She went down with the bags hanging like bunches of grapes from her fingers, dumped them in the hall and went into the euphemistically entitled family room, where her children were lying on their tummies watching the TV with the dog between them.

Not on the sofa again, mercifully.

'Kitty? Edward? Come and help me look for all your things, because we're going to go and see Kate and Megan.'

'What—now?' Edward asked, twisting round, his face sceptical. 'It's nearly lunch time.'

'Are we going to Kate's for lunch?' Kitty asked brightly.

'Yes. It's a surprise.' A surprise for Kate, at least, she thought, hustling them through the house and gathering up the last few traces of their brief but eventful stay.

'Why do we need all our things to go and see Kate and Megan for lunch?' Kitty asked, but Edward got there first and shushed her. Bless his heart. Eight years old and she'd be lost without him.

They met up with Laura in the kitchen, her face strained, a bag in her hand.

'I found these,' she said, giving it to Amelia. 'The baby's bottles. There was one in the dishwasher, too.'

'Thanks. Right, well, I just need to get the baby up and fold his cot, and we'll be out of your hair.'

She retreated upstairs to get him. Poor Thomas. He whimpered and snuggled into her as she picked him up, and she collapsed his travel cot one-handed and bumped it down the stairs. Their stuff was piled by the door, and she wondered if Andy might come out of his study and give them a hand to load it into her car, but the door stayed resolutely shut throughout.

It was just as well. It would save her the bother of being civil.

She put the baby in his seat, the cold air bringing him wide awake and protesting, threw their things into the boot and buckled the other two in, with Rufus on the floor in the front, before turning to her sister with her last remnant of pride and meeting her eyes.

'Thank you for having us. I'm sorry it was so difficult.'

Laura's face creased in a mixture of distress and embarrassment. 'Oh, don't. I'm so sorry, Millie. I hope you get sorted out. Here, these are for the children.' She handed over a bag of presents, all beautifully wrapped. Of course. They would be. Also expensive and impossible to compete with. And that wasn't what it was supposed to be about, but she took them, her arm working on autopilot.

'Thank you. I'm afraid I haven't got round to getting yours yet—'

'It doesn't matter. I hope you find somewhere nice soon. And—take this, please. I know money's tight for you at the moment, but it might give you the first month's rent or deposit—'

She stared at the cheque. 'Laura, I can't—'

'Yes, you can. Please. Owe me, if you have to, but take it. It's the least I can do.'

So she took it, stuffing it into her pocket without looking at it. 'I'll pay you back as soon as I can.'

'Whenever. Have a good Christmas.'

How she found that smile she'd never know. 'And you,' she said, unable to bring herself to say the actual words, and getting behind the wheel and dropping the presents into the passenger footwell next to Rufus, she shut the door before her sister could lean in and hug her, started the engine and drove away.

'Mummy, why *are* we taking all our Christmas presents and Rufus and the cot and everything to

Kate and Megan's for lunch?' Kitty asked, still obviously troubled and confused, as well she might be.

Damn Laura. Damn Andy. And especially damn David. She schooled her expression and threw a smile over her shoulder at her little daughter. 'Well, we aren't going to stay with Auntie Laura and Uncle Andy any more, so after we've had lunch we're going to go somewhere else to stay,' she said.

'Why? Don't they like us?'

Ouch. 'Of course they do,' she lied, 'but they just need a bit of space.'

'So where *are* we going?'

It was a very good question, but one Millie didn't have a hope of answering right now...

It was an ominous sound.

He'd heard it before, knew instantly what it was, and Jake felt his mouth dry and his heart begin to pound. He glanced up over his shoulder, swore softly and turned, skiing sideways straight across and down the mountain, pushing off on his sticks and plunging down and away from the path of the avalanche that was threatening to wipe him out, his legs driving him forward out of its reach.

The choking powder cloud it threw up engulfed

him, blinding him as the raging, roaring monster shot past behind him. The snow was shaking under his skis, the air almost solid with the fine snow thrown up as the snowfield covering the side of the ridge collapsed and thundered down towards the valley floor below.

He was skiing blind, praying that he was still heading in the right direction, hoping that the little stand of trees down to his left was now above him and not still in front of him, because at the speed he was travelling to hit one could be fatal.

It wasn't fatal, he discovered. It was just unbelievably, immensely painful. He bounced off a tree, then felt himself lifted up and carried on by the snow—down towards the scattered tumble of rocks at the bottom of the snowfield.

Hell.

With his last vestige of self-preservation, he triggered the airbags of his avalanche pack, and then he hit the rocks…

'Can you squeeze in a few more for lunch?'

Kate took one look at them all, opened the door wide and ushered them inside. 'What on earth is going on?' she asked, her concerned eyes seeking out the truth from Millie's face.

'We've come for lunch,' Kitty said, still sounding puzzled. 'And then we're going to find somewhere to live. Auntie Laura and Uncle Andy don't want us. Mummy says they need space, but I don't think they like us.'

'Of course they do, darling. They're just very busy, that's all.'

Kate's eyes flicked down to Kitty with the dog at her side, to Edward, standing silently and saying nothing, and back to Millie. 'Nice timing,' she said flatly, reading between the lines.

'Tell me about it,' she muttered. 'Got any good ideas?'

Kate laughed slightly hysterically and handed the three older children a bag of chocolate coins off the tree. 'Here, guys, go and get stuck into these while Mummy and I have a chat. Megan, share nicely and don't give any chocolate to Rufus.'

'I *always* share nicely! Come on, we can share them out—and Rufus, you're not having *any*!'

Rolling her eyes, Kate towed Amelia down to the other end of the narrow room that was the entire living space in her little cottage, put the kettle on and raised an eyebrow. 'Well?'

She shifted Thomas into a more comfortable position in her arms. 'They aren't really child-orientated. They don't have any, and I'm not sure if it's because they haven't got round to it or because they really don't like them,' Millie said softly.

'And your lot were too much of a dose of reality?'

She smiled a little tightly. 'The dog got on the sofa, and Thomas is teething.'

'Ah.' Kate looked down at the tired, grizzling baby in his mother's arms and her kind face crumpled. 'Oh, Amelia, I'm so sorry,' she murmured under her breath. 'I can't believe they kicked you out just before Christmas!'

'They didn't. They wanted me to look for somewhere afterwards, but…'

'But—?'

She shrugged. 'My pride got in the way,' she said, hating the little catch in her voice. 'And now my kids have nowhere to go for Christmas. And convincing a landlord to give me a house before I can get another job is going to be tricky, and that's not going to happen any time soon if the response to my CV continues to be as resoundingly successful as it's being at the moment, and anyway the letting agents aren't going to be able to find us anything this close to Christmas. I could *kill* David for cutting off the maintenance,' she added under her breath, a little catch in her voice.

'Go ahead—I'll be a character witness for you in court,' Kate growled, then she leant back, folded her arms and chewed her lip thoughtfully. 'I wonder…?'

'What?'

'You could have Jake's house,' she said softly. 'My boss. I would say stay here, but I've got my parents and my sister coming for Christmas Day and I can hardly fit us all in as it is, but there's tons of room at Jake's. He's away until the middle of January. He always goes away at Christmas for a month—he shuts the office, gives everyone three weeks off on full pay and leaves the country before the office party, and I have the keys to keep an eye on it. And it's just sitting there, the most fabulous house, and it's just made for Christmas.'

'Won't he mind?'

'What, Jake? No. He wouldn't give a damn. You won't do it any harm, after all, will you? It's hundreds of years old and it's survived. What harm can you do it?'

What harm? She felt rising panic just thinking about it. 'I couldn't—'

'Don't be daft. Where else are you going to go? Besides, with the weather so cold it'll be much better for the house to have the heating on full and the fire lit. He'll be grateful when he finds out, and besides, Jake's generous to a fault. He'd want you to have it. Truly.'

Amelia hesitated. Kate seemed so convinced he wouldn't mind. 'You'd better ring him, then,' she said in the end. 'But tell him I'll give him money for rent just as soon as I can—'

Kate shook her head. 'No. I can't. I don't have the number, but I know he'd say yes,' she said, and Amelia's heart sank.

'Well, then, we can't stay there. Not without asking—'

'Millie, really. It'll be all right. He'd die before he'd let you be homeless over Christmas and there's no way he'd take money off you. Believe me, he'd want you to have the house.'

Still she hesitated, searching Kate's face for any sign of uncertainty, but if she felt any, Kate was keeping it to herself, and besides, Amelia was so out of options she couldn't afford the luxury of scruples, and in the end she gave in.

'Are you sure?'

'Absolutely. There won't be any food there, his housekeeper will have emptied the fridge, but I've got some basics I can let you have and bread and stuff, and there's bound to be something in the freezer and the cupboards to tide you over until you can replace it. We'll go over there the minute we've had lunch and settle you in. It'll be great—fantastic! You'll love it.'

'Love what?' Kitty asked, sidling up with chocolate all round her mouth and a doubtful expression on her face.

'My boss's house. He's gone away, and he's going to let you borrow it.'

'Let?' Millie said softly under her breath, but Kate just flashed her a smile and shrugged.

'Well, he would if he knew… OK, lunch first, and then let's go!'

It was, as Kate had said, the most fabulous house.

A beautiful old Tudor manor house, it had been in its time a farm and then a small hotel and country club, she explained, and then Jake had bought it and moved his offices out here into the Berkshire countryside. He lived in the house, and there was an office suite housing Jake's centre of operations in the former country club buildings on the far side of the old walled kitchen garden. There was a swimming pool, a sauna and steam room and a squash court over there, Kate told her as they pulled up outside on the broad gravel sweep, and all the facilities were available to the staff and their families.

Further evidence of his apparent generosity.

But it was the house which drew Amelia—old mellow red brick, with a beautiful Dutch gabled porch set in the centre, and as Kate opened the huge, heavy oak door that bore the scars of countless generations and ushered them into the great entrance hall, even the children fell silent.

'Wow,' Edward said after a long, breathless moment.

Wow, indeed. Amelia stared around her, dumbstruck. There was a beautiful, ancient oak staircase on her left, and across the wide hall which ran from side to side were several lovely old doors which must lead to the principal rooms.

She ran her hand over the top of the newel post, once heavily carved, the carving now almost worn away by the passage of generations of hands. She could feel them all, stretching back four hundred years, the young, the old, the children who'd been born and grown old and died here, sheltered and protected by this beautiful, magnificent old house, and ridiculous though it was, as the front door closed behind them, she felt as if the house was gathering them up into its heart.

'Come on, I'll give you a quick tour,' Kate said, going down the corridor to the left, and they all trooped after her, the children still in a state of awe. The carpet under her feet must be a good inch thick, she thought numbly. Just how rich *was* this guy?

As Kate opened the door in front of her and they went into a vast and beautifully furnished sitting room with a huge bay window at the side overlooking what must surely be acres of parkland, she got her answer, and she felt her jaw drop.

Very rich. Fabulously, spectacularly rich, without a shadow of a doubt.

And yet he was gone, abandoning this beautiful house in which he lived alone to spend Christmas on a ski slope.

She felt tears prick her eyes, strangely sorry for a man she'd never met, who'd furnished his house with such love and attention to detail, and yet didn't apparently want to stay in it at the time of year when it must surely be at its most welcoming.

'Why?' she asked, turning to Kate in confusion. 'Why does he go?'

Kate shrugged. 'Nobody really knows. Or nobody talks about it. There aren't very many people who've worked for him that long. I've been his PA for a little over three years, since he moved the business here from London, and he doesn't talk about himself.'

'How sad.'

'Sad? No. Not Jake. He's not sad. He's crazy, he has some pretty wacky ideas and they nearly always work, and he's an amazingly thoughtful boss, but he's intensely private. Nobody knows anything about him, really, although he always makes a point of asking about Megan, for instance. But I don't think he's sad. I think he's just a loner and he likes to ski. Come and see the rest.'

They went back down the hall, along the squishy pile carpet that absorbed all the sound of their feet, past all the lovely old doors while Kate opened them one by one and showed them the rooms in turn.

A dining room with a huge table and oak-panelled walls; another sitting room, much smaller than the first, with a plasma TV in the corner, book-lined walls, battered leather sofas and all the evidence that this was his very personal retreat. There was a study at the front of the house which they didn't enter; and then finally the room Kate called the breakfast room—huge again, but with the same informality as the little sitting room, with foot-wide oak boards on the floor and a great big old refectory table covered in the scars of generations and just made for family living.

And the kitchen off it was, as she might have expected, also designed for a family—or entertaining on an epic scale. Vast, with duck-egg blue painted cabinets under thick, oiled wood worktops, a gleaming white four-oven Aga in the inglenook, and in the middle a granite-topped island with stools pulled up to it. It was a kitchen to die for, the kitchen of her dreams and fantasies, and it took her breath away. It took all their breaths away.

The children stared round it in stunned silence, Edward motionless, Kitty running her fingers reverently over the highly polished black granite, lingering over the tiny gold sparkles trapped deep inside the stone. Edward was the first to recover.

'Are we really going to stay here?' he asked, finally finding his voice, and she shook her head in disbelief.

'I don't think so.'

'Of course you are!'

'Kate, we can't—'

'Rubbish! Of course you can. It's only for a week or two. Come and see the bedrooms.'

Amelia shifted Thomas to her other hip and

followed Kate up the gently creaking stairs, the children trailing awestruck in her wake, listening to Megan chattering about when they'd stayed there earlier in the year.

'That's Jake's room,' Kate said, turning away from it, and Amelia felt a prickle of curiosity. What would his room be like? Opulent? Austere? Monastic?

No, not monastic. This man was a sensualist, she realised, fingering the curtains in the bedroom Kate led them into. Pure silk, lined with padding for warmth and that feeling of luxury that pervaded the entire house. Definitely not monastic.

'All the rooms are like this—except for some in the attic, which are a bit simpler,' Kate told her. 'You could take your pick but I'd have the ones upstairs. They're nicer.'

'How many are there?' she asked, amazed.

'Ten. Seven en suite, five on this floor and two above, and three more in the attic which share a bathroom. Those are the simpler ones. He entertains business clients here quite often, and they love it. So many people have offered to buy it, but he just laughs and says no.'

'I should think so. Oh, Kate—what if we ruin something?'

'You won't ruin it. The last person to stay here knocked a pot of coffee over on the bedroom carpet. He just had it cleaned.'

Millie didn't bother to point out that the last person to stay here had been invited—not to mention an adult who presumably was either a friend or of some commercial interest to their unknowing host.

'Can we see the attic? The simple rooms? It sounds more like our thing.'

'Sure. Megan, why don't you show Kitty and Edward your favourite room?'

The children ran upstairs after Megan, freed from their trance now and getting excited as the reality of it began to sink in, and she turned to Kate and took her arm. 'Kate, we can't possibly stay here without asking him,' she said urgently, her voice low. 'It would be so rude—and I just know something'll get damaged.'

'Don't be silly. Come on, I'll show you *my* favourite room. It's lovely, you'll adore it. Megan and I stayed here when my pipes froze last February, and it was bliss. It's got a gorgeous bed.'

'They've all got gorgeous beds.'

They had. Four-posters, with great heavy carved posts and silk canopies, or half testers with

just the head end of the bed clothed in sumptu-
ous drapes.

Except for the three Kate showed her now. In
the first one, instead of a four-poster there was a
great big old brass and iron bedstead, the whole
style of the room much simpler and somehow
less terrifying, even though the quality of the furnishings was every bit as good, and in the adjoin-
ing room was an antique child-sized sleigh bed
that looked safe and inviting.

It was clearly intended to be a nursery, and
would be perfect for Thomas, she thought wistfully, and beside it was a twin room with two
black iron beds, again decorated more simply,
and Megan and Kitty were sitting on the beds and
bouncing, while giggles rose from their throats
and Edward pretended to be too old for such
nonsense and looked on longingly.

'We could sleep up here,' she agreed at last.
'And we could spend the days in the breakfast
room.' Even the children couldn't hurt that old
table…

'There's a playroom—come and see,' Megan
said, pelting out of the room with the other children
in hot pursuit, and Amelia followed them to where
the landing widened and there were big sofas and
another TV and lots and lots of books and toys.

'He said he had this area done for people who came with children, so they'd have somewhere to go where they could let their hair down a bit,' Kate explained, and then smiled. 'You see—he doesn't mind children being in the house. If he did, why would he have done this?'

Why, indeed? There was even a stair gate, she noticed, made of oak and folded back against the banisters. And somehow she didn't mind the idea of tucking them away in what amounted to the servants' quarters nearly as much.

'I'll help you bring everything up,' Kate said. 'Kids, come and help. You can carry some of your stuff.'

It only took one journey because most of their possessions were in storage, packed away in a unit on the edge of town, waiting for the time when she could find a way to house them in a place of their own again. Hopefully, this time with a landlord who wouldn't take the first opportunity to get them out.

And then, with everything installed, she let Rufus out of the car and took him for a little run on the grass at the side of the drive. Poor little dog. He was so confused but, so long as he was with her and the children, he was as good as gold, and she felt her eyes fill with tears.

If David had had his way, the dog would have been put down because of his health problems, but she'd struggled to keep up the insurance premiums to maintain his veterinary cover, knowing that the moment they lapsed, her funding for the dog's health and well-being would come to a grinding halt.

And that would be the end of Rufus.

She couldn't allow that to happen. The little Cavalier King Charles spaniel that she'd rescued as a puppy had been a lifeline for the children in the last few dreadful years, and she owed him more than she could ever say. So his premiums were paid, even if it meant she couldn't eat.

'Mummy, it's lovely here,' Kitty said, coming up to her and snuggling her tiny, chilly hand into Millie's. 'Can we stay for ever?'

Oh, I wish, she thought, but she ruffled Kitty's hair and smiled. 'No, darling—but we can stay until after Christmas, and then we'll find another house.'

'Promise?'

She crossed her fingers behind her back. 'Promise,' she said, and hoped that fate wouldn't make her a liar.

He couldn't breathe.

For a moment he thought he was buried despite

his avalanche pack, and for that fleeting moment in time he felt fear swamp him, but then he realised he was lying face down in the snow.

His legs were buried in the solidified aftermath of the avalanche, but near the surface, and his body was mostly on the top. He tipped his head awkwardly, and a searing pain shot through his shoulder and down his left arm. Damn. He tried again, more cautiously this time, and the snow on his goggles slid off, showering his face with ice crystals that stung his skin in the cold, sharp air. He breathed deeply and opened his eyes and saw daylight. The last traces of it, the shadows long as night approached.

He managed to clear the snow from around his arms, and shook his head to clear his goggles better and regretted it instantly. He gave the pain a moment, and then began to yell into the silence of the fading light.

He yelled for what seemed like hours, and then, like a miracle, he heard voices.

'Help!' he bellowed again, and waved, blanking out the pain.

And help came, in the form of big, burly lads who broke away the snow surrounding him, dug his legs out and helped him struggle free. Dear God, he hurt. Everywhere, but most particularly his left arm and his left knee, he realised. Where he'd hit the tree. Or the rocks. No, he'd hurt them on the tree, he remembered, but the rocks certainly hadn't helped and he was going to have a million bruises.

'Can you ski back down?' they asked, and he realised he was still wearing his skis. The bindings had held, even through that. He got up and tested his left leg and winced, but it was holding his weight, and the right one was fine. He nodded and, cradling his left arm against his chest, he picked his way off the rock field to the edge, then followed them slowly down the mountain to the village.

He was shipped off to hospital the moment they arrived back, and he was prodded and poked and tutted over for what seemed like an age. And then, finally, they put his arm in a temporary cast, gave him a nice fat shot of something blissful and he escaped into the blessed oblivion of sleep…

# CHAPTER TWO

SHE refused to let Kate turn up the heating.

'We'll be fine,' she protested. 'Believe me, this isn't cold.'

'It's only on frost protection!'

'It's fine. We're used to it. Please, I really don't want to argue about this. We have jumpers.'

'Well, at least light the woodburner,' Kate said, relenting with a sigh. 'There's a huge stack of logs outside the back door.'

'I can't use his logs! Logs are expensive!'

Kate just laughed. 'Not if you own several acres of woodland. He has more logs than he knows what to do with. We all use them. I throw some into the boot of my car every day and take them home to burn overnight, and so does everyone else. Really, you can't let the kids be cold, Millie. Just use the wood.'

So she did. She lit the fire, stood the heavy

black mesh guard in front of it and the children settled down on the rug with Rufus and watched the television while she made them something quick and simple for supper. Even Thomas was good, managing to eat his supper without spitting it out all over the room or screaming the place down, and Amelia felt herself start to relax.

And when the wind picked up in the night and the old house creaked and groaned, it was just as if it was settling down, turning up its collar against the wind and wrapping its arms around them all to keep them warm.

Fanciful nonsense.

But it felt real, and when she got up in the morning and tiptoed downstairs to check the fire before the children woke, she found Rufus fast asleep on the rug in front of the woodburner, and he lifted his head and wagged his tail. She picked him up and hugged him, tears of relief prickling her eyes because finally, for the first time in months, she felt—even if it would only be for a few days—as if they were safe.

She filled up the fire, amazed that it had stayed alight, and made herself a cup of tea while Rufus went out in the garden for a moment. Then she took advantage of the quiet time and sat with him by the fire to drink her tea and contemplate her next move.

Rattling the cage of the job agencies, of course. What choice was there? Without a job, she couldn't hope to get a house. And she needed to get some food in. Maybe a small chicken? She could roast it, and put a few sausages round it, and it would be much cheaper than a turkey. Just as well, as she was trying to stretch the small amount of money she had left for as long as possible.

She thought of the extravagant Christmases she'd had with David in the past, the lavish presents, the wasted food, and wondered if the children felt cheated. Probably, but Christmas was just one of the many ways in which he'd let them down on a regular basis, so she was sure they'd just take it all in their stride.

Unlike being homeless, she thought, getting to her feet and washing out her mug before going upstairs to start the day. They were finding that really difficult and confusing, and all the chopping and changing was making them feel insecure. And she hated that. But there was Laura's cheque, which meant she might be able to find somewhere sooner—even if she would have to pay her back, just for the sake of her pride.

So, bearing the cheque in mind, she spent part of the morning on the phone trying to find somewhere to live, but the next day would be Christmas Eve and realistically nobody wanted to show her anything until after the Christmas period was over, and the job agencies were no more helpful. Nobody, apparently, was looking for a translator at the moment, so abandoning her search until after Christmas, she took the kids out for a long walk around the grounds, with Thomas in his stroller and Rufus sniffing the ground and having a wonderful time while Kitty and Edward ran around shrieking and giggling.

And there was nobody to hear, nobody to complain, nobody to stifle the sound of their childish laughter, and gradually she relaxed and let herself enjoy the day.

'Mummy, can we have a Christmas tree?' Edward asked as they trudged back for lunch.

More money—not only for the tree, but also for decorations. And she couldn't let herself touch Laura's money except for a house. 'I don't know if we should,' she said, blaming it on the unknown Jake and burying her guilt because she was sick of telling her children that they couldn't have things when it was all because their unprincipled and disinterested father refused to pay up. 'It's not our house, and you know how they drop needles. He might mind.'

'He won't mind! Of course he won't! *Everyone* has a Christmas tree!' Kitty explained patiently to her obviously dense mother.

'But we haven't got the decorations, and anyway, I don't know where we could get one this late,' she said, wondering if she'd get away with it and hating the fact that she had to disappoint them yet again.

They walked on in silence for a moment, then Edward stopped. 'We could make one!' he said, his eyes lighting up at the challenge and finding a solution, as he always did. 'And we could put fir cones on it! There were lots in the wood—and there were some branches there that looked like Christmas tree branches, a bit. Can we get them after lunch and tie them together and pretend they're a tree, and then we can put fir cones on it, and berries—I saw some berries, and I'm sure he won't mind if we only pick a few—'

'Well, he might—'

'No, he won't! Mummy, he's lent us his *house*!' Kitty said earnestly and, not for the first time, Millie felt a stab of unease.

But the children were right, everybody had a tree, and what harm could a few cut branches and some fir cones do? And maybe even the odd sprig of berries…

'All right,' she agreed, 'just a little tree.' So after lunch they trooped back, leaving the exhausted little Rufus snoozing by the fire, and Amelia and Edward loaded themselves up with branches and they set off, Kitty dragging Thomas in the stroller backwards all the way from the woods to the house.

'There!' Edward said in satisfaction, dropping his pile of branches by the back door. 'Now we can make our tree!'

The only thing that kept him going on that hellish journey was the thought of home.

The blissful comfort of his favourite old leather sofa, a bottle of fifteen-year-old single malt and—equally importantly—the painkillers in his flight bag.

Getting upstairs to bed would be beyond him at this point. His knee was killing him—not like last time, when he'd done the ligaments in his other leg, but badly enough to mean that staying would have been pointless, even if he hadn't broken his wrist. And now all he could think about was lying down, and the sooner the better. He'd been stupid to travel so soon; his body was black and blue from end to end, but somehow, with Christmas what felt like seconds away and everyone down in the village getting so damned excited about it, leaving had become imperative now that he could no longer ski to outrun his demons.

Not that he ever really managed to outrun them, although he always gave it a damn good try, but this time he'd come too close to losing everything, and deep down he'd realised that maybe it was time to stop running, time to go home and just get on with life—and at least here he could find plenty to occupy himself.

He heard the car tyres crunch on gravel and cracked open his eyes. Home. Thank God for that. Lights blazed in the dusk, triggered by the taxi pulling up at the door, and handing over what was probably an excessive amount of money, he got out of the car with a grunt of pain and walked slowly to the door.

And stopped.

There was a car on the drive, not one he recognised, and there were lights on inside.

One in the attic, and one on the landing.

'Where d'you want these, guv?' the taxi driver asked, and he glanced down at the cases.

'Just in here would be good,' he said, opening the door and sniffing. Woodsmoke. And there was light coming from the breakfast room, and the sound of—laughter? A child's laughter?

Pain squeezed his chest. Dear God, no. Not today, of all days, when he just needed to crawl into a corner and forget—

'There you go then, guv. Have a good Christmas.'

'And you,' he said, closing the door quietly behind the man and staring numbly towards the breakfast room. What the hell was going on? It must be Kate—no one else had a key, and the place was like Fort Knox. She must have dropped in with Megan and a friend to check on the house—but it didn't sound as if they were checking anything. It sounded as if they were having fun.

Oh, Lord, please, not today…

He limped over to the door and pushed it gently open, and then stood transfixed.

Chaos. Complete, utter chaos.

Two children were sitting on the floor by the fire in a welter of greenery, carefully tying berries to some rather battered branches that looked as if they had come off the conifer hedge at the back of the country club, but it was the woman standing on the table who held his attention.

Tall, slender, with rather wild fair hair escaping from a ponytail and jeans that had definitely seen better days, she was reaching up and twisting another of the branches into the heavy iron hoop over the refectory table, festooning the light fitting with a makeshift attempt at a Christmas decoration which did nothing to improve it.

He'd never seen her before. He would have recognised her, he was sure, if he had. So who the hell—?

His mouth tightened, but then she bent over, giving him an unrestricted view of her neat, shapely bottom as the old jeans pulled across it, and he felt a sudden, unwelcome and utterly unexpected tug of need.

'It's such a shame Jake isn't going to be here, because we're making it so pretty,' the little girl was saying.

'Why *does* he go away?' the boy asked.

'I don't know,' the woman replied, her voice soft and melodious. 'I can't imagine.'

'Didn't Kate say?'

Kate. Of course, she'd be at the bottom of this, he thought, and he could have wrung her neck for her abysmal timing.

Well, if he had two good hands…which at the moment, of course, he didn't.

'He goes skiing.'

'I hate skiing,' the boy said. 'That woman in the kindergarten was horrible. She smelt funny. Here, I've finished this one.'

And he scrambled to his feet and turned round, then caught sight of Jake and froze.

'Well, come on then, give it to me,' the woman said, waving her hand behind her to try and locate it.

'Um…Mum…'

'Darling, give me the branch, I can't stand here for ever—'

She turned towards her son, followed the direction of his gaze and her eyes flew wide. 'Oh—!'

'Mummy, do I need more berries or is that enough?' the little girl asked, but Jake hardly heard her because the woman's eyes were locked on his and the shock and desperation in them blinded his senses to anything else.

'Kitty, hush, darling,' she said softly and, dropping down, she slid off the edge of the table and came towards him with a haphazard attempt at a smile. 'Um…I imagine you're Jake Forrester?' she asked, her voice a little uneven, and he hardened himself against her undoubted appeal and the desperate eyes.

'Well, there you have the advantage over me,' he murmured drily, 'because I have no idea who you are, or why I should come home and find you smothering my house in bits of dead vegetation in my absence—'

Her eyes fluttered briefly closed and colour flooded her cheeks. 'I can explain—'

'Don't bother. I'm not interested. Just get all that—*tat* out of here, clear the place up and then leave.'

He turned on his heel—not a good idea, with his knee screaming in protest, but the pain just fuelled the fire of his anger and he stalked into the study, picked up the phone and rang Kate.

'Millie?'

'So that's her name.'

'*Jake*?' Kate shrieked, and he could hear her collecting herself at the other end of the line. 'What are you doing home?'

'There was an avalanche. I got in the way. And I seem to have guests. Would you care to elaborate?'

'Oh, Jake, I'm so sorry, I can explain—'

'Excellent. Feel free. You've got ten seconds, so make it good.' He settled back in the chair with a wince, listening as Kate sucked in her breath and gave her pitch her best shot.

'She's a friend. Her ex has gone to Thailand, he won't pay the maintenance and she lost her job so she lost her house and her sister kicked her out yesterday.'

'Tough. She's packing now, so I suggest you

find some other sucker to put her and her kids up so I can lie and be sore in peace. And don't imagine for a moment that you've heard the end of this.'

He stabbed the off button and threw the phone down on his desk, then glanced up to see the woman—Millie, apparently—transfixed in the doorway, her face still flaming.

'Please don't take it out on Kate. She was only trying to help us.'

He stifled a contemptuous snort and met her eyes challengingly, too sore in every way to moderate his sarcasm. 'You're not doing so well, are you? You don't seem to be able to keep anything. Your husband, your job, your house— even your sister doesn't want you. I wonder why? I wonder what it is about you that makes everyone want to get rid of you?'

She stepped back as if she'd been struck, the colour draining from her face, and he felt a twinge of guilt but suppressed it ruthlessly.

'We'll be out of here in half an hour. I just need to pack our things. What do you want me to do with the sheets?'

Sheets? He was throwing her out and she was worrying about the *sheets*?

'Just leave them. I wouldn't want to hold you up.'

She straightened her spine and took another step back, and he could see her legs shaking. 'Right. Um…fine.'

And she spun round and walked briskly away in the direction of the breakfast room, leaving him to his guilt. He sighed and sagged back against the chair, a wave of pain swamping him for a moment. When he opened his eyes, the boy was there.

'I'm really sorry,' he said, his little chin up, just like his mother's, his eyes huge in a thin, pale face. 'Please don't be angry with Mummy. She was just trying to make a nice Christmas for us. She thought we were going to stay with Auntie Laura, but Uncle Andy didn't want us there because he said the baby kept him awake—'

There was a baby, too? Dear God, it went from bad to worse, but that wasn't the end of it.

'—and the dog smells and he got on the sofa, and that made him really mad. I heard them fighting. And then Mummy said we were going to see Kate, and she said we ought to come here because you were a nice man and you wouldn't mind and what harm could we do because the house was hundreds of years old and had survived and anyway you liked children or you wouldn't have done the playroom in the attic.'

He finally ran out of breath and Jake stared at him.

Kate thought he was that nice? Kate was dreaming.

But the boy's wounded eyes called to something deep inside him, and Jake couldn't ignore it. Couldn't kick them all out into the cold just before Christmas. Even he wasn't that much of a bastard.

But it wasn't just old Ebenezer Scrooge who had ghosts, and the last thing he needed was a houseful of children over Christmas, Jake thought with a touch of panic. And a baby, of all things, and—a dog?

Not much of a dog. It hadn't barked, and there was no sign of it, so it was obviously a very odd breed of dog. Or old and deaf?

No. Not old and deaf, and not much of a dog at all, he realised, his eyes flicking to the dimly lit hallway behind the boy and focusing on a small red and white bundle of fluff with an anxiously wriggling tail and big soulful eyes that were watching him hopefully.

A little spaniel, like the one his grandmother had had. He'd always liked it—and he wasn't going to be suckered because of the damn dog!

But the boy was still there, one sock-clad foot

on top of the other, squirming slightly but holding his ground, and if his ribs hadn't hurt so much he would have screamed with frustration.

'What's your name?'

'Edward. Edward Jones.'

Nice, honest name. Like the child, he thought inconsequentially. Oh, damn. He gave an inward sigh as he felt his defences crumble. After all, it was hardly the boy's fault that he couldn't cope with the memories… 'Where's your mother, Edward?'

'Um…packing. I'm supposed to be clearing up the branches, but I can't reach the ones in the light so I've got to wait for her to come down.'

'Could you go and get her for me, and then look after the others while we have a chat?'

He nodded, but stood there another moment, chewing his lip.

Jake sighed softly. 'What is it?'

'You won't be mean to her, will you? She was only trying to look after us, and she feels so guilty because Dad won't give us any money so we can't have anything nice ever, but it's really not her fault—'

'Just get her, Edward,' he said gently. 'I won't be mean to her.'

'Promise?'

Oh, what was he doing? He needed to get rid of them before he lost his mind! 'I promise.'

The boy vanished, but the dog stayed there, whining softly and wagging his tail, and Jake held out his hand and called the dog over. He came, a little warily, and sat down just a few feet away, tail waving but not yet really ready to trust.

Very wise, Jake thought. He really, really wasn't in a very nice mood, but it was hardly the dog's fault. And he'd promised the boy he wouldn't be mean to his mother.

Well, any more mean than he already had been. He pressed his lips together and sighed. He was going to have to apologise to her, he realised— to the woman who'd moved into his house without a by-your-leave and completely trashed his plans for crawling back into his cave to lick his wounds.

Oh, damn.

'Mummy, he wants to talk to you.'

Millie lifted her head from the bag she was stuffing clothes into and stared at her son. 'I think he's said everything he has to say,' she said crisply. 'Have you finished clearing up downstairs?'

'I couldn't reach the light, but I've put everything else outside and picked up all the bits off the floor. Well, most of them. Mummy, he really does want to talk to you. He asked me to tell you and to look after the others while you have a chat.'

Well, that sounded like a quote, she thought, and her heart sank. It was bad enough enduring the humiliation of one verbal battering. The last thing she needed was to go back down there now he'd drawn breath and had time to think about it and give him the opportunity to have a more concerted attack.

'Please, Mummy. He asked—and he promised he wouldn't be mean to you.'

Her eyes widened, then she shut them fast and counted to ten. What on *earth* had Edward been saying to him? She got to her feet and held out her arms to him, and he ran into them and hugged her hard.

'It'll be all right, Mummy,' he said into her side. 'It will.'

If only she could be so sure.

She let him go and made her way downstairs, down the beautiful old oak staircase she'd fallen so in love with, along the hall on the inches-thick carpet, and tapped on the open study door, her heart pounding out a tattoo against her ribs.

He was sitting with his back to her, and at her knock he swivelled the chair round and met her eyes. He'd taken off the coat that had been slung round his shoulders, and she could see now that he was wearing a cast on his left wrist. And, with the light now shining on his face, she could see the livid bruise on his left cheekbone, and the purple stain around his eye.

His hair was dark, soft and glossy, cut short round the sides but flopping forwards over his eyes. It looked rumpled, as if he'd run his fingers through it over and over again, and his jaw was deeply shadowed. He looks awful, she thought, and she wondered briefly what he'd done.

Not that it mattered. It was enough to have brought him home, and that was the only thing that affected her. His injuries were none of her business.

'You wanted to see me,' she said, and waited for the stinging insults to start again.

'I owe you an apology,' he said gruffly, and she felt her jaw drop and yanked it up again. 'I was unforgivably rude to you, and I had no justification for it.'

'I disagree. I'm in your house without your permission,' she said, fairness overcoming her shock. 'I would have been just as rude, I'm sure.'

'I doubt it, somehow. The manners you've drilled into your son would blow that theory out of the water. He's a credit to you.'

She swallowed hard and nodded. 'Thank you. He's a great kid, and he's been through a lot.'

'I'm sure. However, it's not him I want to talk to you about, it's you. You have nowhere to go, is this right?'

Her chin went up. 'We'll find somewhere,' she lied, her pride rescuing her in the nick of time, and she thought she saw a smile flicker on that strong, sculpted mouth before he firmed it.

'Do you or do you not have anywhere else suitable to go with your children for Christmas?' he asked, a thread of steel underlying the softness of his voice, and she swallowed again and shook her head.

'No,' she admitted. 'But that's not your problem.'

He inclined his head, accepting that, but went on, 'Nevertheless, I do have a problem, and one you might be able to fix. As you can see, I've been stupid enough to get mixed up with an avalanche, and I've broken my wrist. Now, I can't cook at the best of times, and I'm not getting my housekeeper back from her well-earned holiday to wait on me, but you, on the other hand, are here, have nowhere else to go and might therefore be interested in a proposition.'

For the first time, she felt a flicker of hope. 'A proposition?' she asked warily, not quite sure she liked the sound of that but prepared to listen because her options were somewhat limited. He nodded.

'I have no intention of paying you—under the circumstances, I don't think that's unreasonable, considering you moved into my house without my knowledge or consent and made yourselves at home, but I am prepared to let you stay until such time as you find somewhere to go after the New Year, in exchange for certain duties. Can you cook?'

She felt the weight of fear lift from her shoulders, and nodded. 'Yes, I can cook,' she assured him, hoping she could still remember how. It was a while since she'd had anything lavish on her table, but cooking had once been her love and her forte.

'Good. You can cook for me, and keep the housework under control, and help me do anything I can't manage—can you drive?'

She nodded again. 'Yes—but it will have to be my car, unless you've got a big one. I can't go anywhere without the children, so if it's some sexy little sports car it will have to be my hatchback.'

'I've got an Audi A6 estate. It's automatic. Is that a problem?'

'No problem,' she said confidently. 'David had one.' On a finance agreement that, like everything else, had gone belly-up in the last few years. 'Anything else? Any rules?'

'Yes. The children can use the playroom upstairs on the landing, and you can keep the attic bedrooms—I assume you're in the three with the patchwork quilts?'

She felt her jaw sag. 'How did you guess?'

His mouth twisted into a wry smile. 'Let's just say I'm usually a good judge of character, and you're pretty easy to read,' he told her drily. 'So— you can have the top floor, and when you're cooking the children can be down here in the breakfast room with you.'

'Um…there's the dog,' she said, a little unnecessarily as Rufus was now sitting on her foot, and to her surprise Jake's mouth softened into a genuine smile.

'Yes,' he said quietly. 'The dog. My grandmother had one like him. What's his name?'

'Rufus,' she said, and the little dog's tail wagged hopefully. 'Please don't say he has to be outside in a kennel or anything awful, because he's old and not very well and it's so cold at the moment and he's no trouble—'

'Millie—what does that stand for, by the way?'

'Amelia.'

He studied her for a second, then nodded. 'Amelia,' he said, his voice turning it into something that sounded almost like a caress. 'Of course the dog doesn't have to be outside—not if he's housetrained.'

'Oh, he is. Well, mostly. Sometimes he has the odd accident, but that's only if he's ill.'

'Fine. Just don't let him on the beds. Right, I'm done. If you could find me a glass, the malt whisky and my flight bag, I'd be very grateful. And then I'm going to lie down on my sofa and go to sleep.'

And, getting to his feet with a grunt of pain, he limped slowly towards her.

'You really did mess yourself up, didn't you?' she said softly, and he paused just a foot away from her and stared down into her eyes for the longest moment.

'Yes, Amelia. I really did—and I could do with those painkillers, so if you wouldn't mind—?'

'Right away,' she said, trying to remember how to breathe. Slipping past him into the kitchen, she found a glass, filled it with water, put the kettle on, made a sandwich with the last of the cheese and two precious slices of bread, smeared some chutney she found in the fridge onto the cheese and took it through to him.

'I thought you might be hungry,' she said, 'and there's nothing much else in the house at the moment, but you shouldn't take painkillers on an empty stomach.'

He sighed and looked up at her from the sofa where he was lying stretched out full length and looking not the slightest bit vulnerable despite the cast, the bruises and the swelling under his eye. 'Is that right?' he said drily. 'Where's the malt whisky?'

'You shouldn't have alcohol—'

'—with painkillers,' he finished for her, and gave a frustrated growl that probably should have frightened her but just gave her the urge to smile. 'Well, give me the damned painkillers, then. They're in my flight bag, in the outside pocket. I'll take them with the water.'

She rummaged, found them and handed them to him. 'When did you take the last lot? It says no more than six in twenty-four hours—'

'Did I ask you for your medical advice?' he snarled, taking the strip of tablets from her and popping two out awkwardly with his good hand.

Definitely not vulnerable. Just crabby as hell. She stood her ground. 'I just don't want your family suing me for killing you with an overdose,' she said, and his mouth tightened.

'No danger of that,' he said flatly. 'I don't have a family. Now, go away and leave me alone. I haven't got the energy to argue with a mouthy, opinionated woman and I can't stand being fussed over. And find me the whisky!'

'I've put the kettle on to make you tea or coffee—'

'Well, don't bother. I've had enough caffeine in the last twenty-four hours to last me a lifetime. I just want the malt—'

'Eat the sandwich and I'll think about it,' she said, and then went out and closed the door, quickly, before he changed his mind and threw them all out anyway…

# CHAPTER THREE

EDWARD was waiting for her.

He was sitting on the top step, and his eyes were full of trepidation. 'Well?'

'We're staying,' she said with a smile, still not really believing it but so out of options that she had to *make* it work. 'But he'd like us to spend the time up here unless we're down in the break-fast room or kitchen cooking for him, so we don't disturb him, because he had an accident skiing and he's a bit sore. He needs to sleep.'

'So can I unpack my things again?' Kitty asked, appearing on the landing, her little face puzzled and a bulging carrier bag dangling from her fingers.

'Yes, darling. We can all unpack, and then we need to go downstairs very quietly and tidy up the kitchen and see what I can find to cook us for supper.'

Not that there was much, but she'd have to

make something proper for Jake, and she had no idea how she'd achieve that with no ingredients and no money to buy any. Maybe there was something in his freezer?

'I'll be very, very quiet,' Kitty whispered, her grey eyes serious, and tiptoed off to her room with bag in hand and her finger pressed over her lips.

It worked until she bumped into the door frame and the bag fell out of her hand and landed on the floor, the book in the top falling out with a little thud. Her eyes widened like saucers, and for one awful minute Millie thought she was going to cry.

'It's all right, darling, you don't have to be that quiet,' she said with an encouraging smile, and Edward, ever his little sister's protector, picked up his own bag and went back into the bedroom and hugged her, then helped her put her things away while Millie unpacked all the baby's things again.

He was still sleeping. Innocence was such a precious gift, she thought, her eyes filling, and blinking hard, she turned away and went to the window, drawn by the sound of a car. Looking down on the drive as the floodlights came on, she realised it was Kate.

Of course. Dear Kate, rushing to her rescue, coming to smooth things over with Jake.

Who was sleeping.

'Keep an eye on Thomas, I'm going to let Kate in,' she said to Edward and ran lightly down the stairs, arriving in the hall just as Kate turned the heavy handle and opened the door.

'Oh, Millie, I'm so sorry I've been so long, but Megan was in the bath and I had to dry her hair before I brought her out in the cold,' she said in a rush. 'Where are the children?'

'Upstairs. It's all right, we're staying. Megan, do you want to go up and see them while I make Mummy a coffee?'

'I don't have time for a coffee, I need to see Jake. I've got to try and reason with him—what do you mean, you're staying?' she added, her eyes widening.

'Shh. He's asleep. Go on, Megan, it's all right, but please be quiet because Jake's not well.'

Megan nodded seriously. 'I'll be very quiet,' she whispered and ran upstairs, her little feet soundless on the thick carpet. Kate took Millie by the arm and towed her into the breakfast room and closed the door.

'So what's going on?' she asked in a desperate undertone. 'I thought you'd be packed and leaving?'

Amelia shook her head. 'No. He's broken his

wrist and he's battered from end to end, and I think he's probably messed his knee up, too, so he needs someone to cook for him and run round after him.'

Kate's jaw dropped. 'So he's *employing* you?'

Millie felt her mouth twist into a wry smile. 'Not exactly employing,' she admitted, remembering his blunt words with an inward wince. 'But we can stay in exchange for helping him, so long as I keep the children out of his way.'

'And the dog? Does he even *know* about the dog?'

She smiled. 'Ah, well, now. Apparently he likes the dog, doesn't he, Rufus?' she murmured, looking down at him. He was stuck on her leg, sensing the need to behave, his eyes anxious, and she felt him quiver.

When she glanced back up, Kate was staring at her openmouthed. 'He likes the dog?' she hissed.

'His grandmother had one. He doesn't go a bundle on the Christmas decorations, though,' she added ruefully with a pointed glance at the light fitting. 'Come on, let's make a drink and take it upstairs to the kids.'

'He was going to put a kitchen up there,' Kate told her as she boiled the kettle. 'Just a little one, enough to make drinks and snacks, but he hasn't got round to it yet. Pity. It would have been handy for you.'

'It would. Still, I only need to bring the children down if I'm actually cooking. We're quite all right up in the playroom, and at least it'll give us a little breathing space before we have to find somewhere to go.'

'And, actually, it's a huge relief,' Kate said, sagging back against the worktop and folding her arms. 'I was wondering what to do about Jake— I mean, I couldn't leave him here on his own over Christmas when he's injured, but my house is going to be heaving and noisy and chaotic, and I would have had to run backwards and forwards— so you've done me a massive favour. And, you never know, maybe you'll all have a good time together! In fact—'

Amelia cut her off with a laugh and a raised hand. 'I don't think so,' she said firmly, remembering his bitterly sarcastic opening remarks. 'But if we can just keep out of his way, maybe we'll all survive.'

She handed Kate her drink, picked up her own mug and then hesitated. No matter how rude and sarcastic he'd been, he was still a human being and for that alone he deserved her consideration, and he was injured and exhausted and probably not thinking straight. 'I ought to check on him,' she said, putting her mug back down. 'He was talking about malt whisky.'

'So? Don't worry, he's not a drinker. He won't have had much.'

'On top of painkillers?'

'Ah. What were they?'

'Goodness knows—something pretty heavy-duty. Nothing I recognised. Not paracetamol, that's for sure!'

'Oh, hell. Where is he?'

'Just next door in the little sitting room.'

'I'll go—'

'No. Let me. He was pretty cross.'

Kate laughed softly. 'You think I've never seen him cross?'

So they went together, opening the door silently and pushing it in until they could see him sprawled full length on the sofa, one leg dangling off the edge, his cast resting across his chest, his head lolling against the arm.

Kate frowned. 'He doesn't look very comfortable.'

He didn't, but at least there was no sign of the whisky. Amelia went into the room and picked up a soft velvety cushion and tucked it under his bruised cheek to support his head better. He grunted and shifted slightly and she froze, waiting for those piercing slate grey eyes to open and stab her with a hard, angry glare, but then he relaxed, settling his face down against the pillow with a little sigh, and she let herself breathe again.

It was chilly in there, though, and she had refused to let Kate turn the heating up. She could do it now but, in the meantime, he ought to have something over him. She spotted a throw over the back of the other sofa and lowered it carefully over him, tucking it in to keep the draughts off until the heat kicked in.

Then she tiptoed out, glancing back over her shoulder as she reached the door.

Did she imagine it or had his eyelids fluttered? She wasn't sure, but she didn't want to hang around and provoke him if she'd disturbed him, so she pushed Kate out and closed the door softly behind them.

'Can you turn the heating up?' she murmured to Kate, and she nodded and went into his study and fiddled with a keypad on the wall.

'He looks awful,' Kate said, sparing the door of the room another glance as she tapped keys and reprogrammed the heating. 'He's got bruises all over his face and neck. It must have been a hell of an avalanche.'

'He didn't say, but he's very sore and stiff. I expect he's got bruises all over his body,' Millie said, trying not to think about his body in too much detail but failing dismally. She stifled the little whimper that rose in her throat.

Why?

Why, of all the men to bring her body out of the freezer, did it have to be Jake? There was no way he'd be interested in her—even if she hadn't upset and alienated him by taking such a massive liberty with his house, to all intents and purposes moving into his house as a squatter, she'd then compounded her sins by telling him what to do!

And he most particularly wouldn't be interested in her children. In fact it was probably the dog who was responsible for his change of heart.

Oh, well, it was just as well he wouldn't be interested in her, because there was no way her life was even remotely stable or coherent enough at the moment for her to contemplate a relationship. Frankly, she wasn't sure it ever would be again and, if it was, it *certainly* wouldn't be with another empire builder. She'd had it with the entrepreneurial type, big time.

But there was just something about Jake Forrester that called to something deep inside her, something that had lain undisturbed for years, and she was going to have to ignore it and get through these next few days and weeks until they could find somewhere else. And maybe then she'd get her sanity back.

'Come on, let's go back up and leave him to sleep,' she said, crossing her fingers and hoping that he slept for a good long while and woke in a rather better mood…

He was hot.

He'd been cold, but he'd been too tired and sore to bother to get the throw, but someone must have been in and covered him, because it was snuggled round him, and there was a pillow under his face and the lingering scent of a familiar fragrance.

Kate. She must have come over and covered him up. Hell. He hadn't meant her to turn out on such a freezing night with little Megan. He should have rung her back, he realised, after he'd spoken to Amelia, but he'd been high as a kite on the rather nice drugs the French doctor had given him and he hadn't even thought about it.

Damn.

He rolled onto his back and his breath caught. Ouch. That was quite a bruise on his left hip. And his knee desperately needed some ice, and his arm hurt. Even through the painkillers.

He struggled off the sofa, eventually escaping from the confines of the throw with an impatient tug and straightening up with a wince. The gel pack was in the freezer in the kitchen. It wasn't far.

Further than he thought, he realised, swaying slightly and pausing while the world steadied. He took a step, then another, and blinked hard to clear his head.

Amelia was right, he shouldn't have too many of those damn painkillers. They were turning his brain to mush. And it was probably just as well he hadn't taken them with whisky either, he thought with regret. Not that she'd been about to give him any, the bossy witch.

Amelia. Millie.

No, Amelia. Millie didn't suit her. It was a little girl's name and, whatever else she was, she was all woman. And damn her for making him notice the fact.

He limped into the breakfast room and saw that Edward had done a pretty good job of removing the branches and berries from the floor in front of the fire. He felt his brow pleat into a frown, and stifled the pang of guilt. It was his house. If he didn't want decorations in it, it was perfectly reasonable to say so.

But had he had to be so harsh?

No, was the simple answer. Especially to the kids. Oh, rats. He made his way carefully through to the kitchen, took the pack out of the freezer and wrapped it in a tea towel, then went back to the breakfast room and sat down in the chair near the fire and propped the ice pack over his knee. Better.

Or it would be, in about a week. It was only a bruise, not a ligament rupture, thankfully. He'd done that before on the other knee, and he didn't need to do it again, but he realised he'd been lucky not to be smashed to bits on the tree or the rock field.

Very lucky.

He eased back in the chair cautiously and thought with longing of the whisky. It was a particularly smooth old single malt, smoky and peaty, with a lovely complex aftertaste. Or was that afterburn?

Whatever, it was in the drinks cupboard in the drawing room, and he wasn't convinced he could summon up the energy to walk all the way to the far end of the house and back again, so he closed his eyes and fantasised that he was on Islay, sitting in an old croft house with a peat fire at his feet, a collie instead of a little spaniel leaning on his leg and a glass of liquid gold in his hand.

He could all but taste it. Pity he couldn't. Pity it was only in his imagination, because then he'd be able to put Amelia and her children out of his mind.

Or he would have been able to, if it hadn't been for the baby crying.

'Oh, Thomas, sweetheart, what's the matter, little one?'

She couldn't believe he was doing this. She'd fed him just before Jake had arrived home, but now he was awake and he wouldn't settle again and he was starting to sob into her chest, letting fly with a scream that she was sure would travel all the way down to Jake.

He couldn't be hungry, not really, but he obviously wanted a bottle of milk, and that meant going back down to the kitchen and heating it, taking the screaming baby with her, and by the time she'd done that, he would certainly have disturbed her reluctant host. Unless she left him with Edward?

'Darling, could you please look after him for a moment while I get him his bottle?' she asked, and Edward, being Edward, just nodded and held his arms out, and carried Thomas off towards the bedroom and closed the door.

She ran lightly downstairs to the sound of his escalating wails. As she hurried into the breakfast room, she came face to face with Jake sitting by the fire, an ice pack on his knee and the dog at his side.

She skidded to a halt and his eyes searched her face. 'Is the baby all right?'

She nodded. 'Yes—I'm sorry. I just need to make him a bottle. He'll settle then. I'm really sorry—'

'Why didn't you bring him down?'

'I didn't want to wake you.' She chewed her lip, only too conscious of the fact that he was very much awake. Awake and up and about and looking rumpled and disturbingly attractive, with the dark shadow of stubble on his firm jaw and the subtle drift of a warm, slightly spicy cologne reaching her nostrils.

'I was awake,' he told her, his voice a little gruff. 'I put a gel pack on my knee, and I was about to make some tea. Want to join me?'

'Oh—I can't, I've left the baby with Edward.'

'Bring them all down. Maybe I should meet them—since they're staying in my house.'

Oh, Lord. 'Let me just make the bottle so it can be cooling, and then we'll get a little peace and I can introduce you properly.'

He nodded, his mouth twitching into a slight smile, and she felt relief flood through her at this tiny evidence of his humanity. She went into the kitchen and spooned formula into a bottle, then poured hot water from the kettle on it, shook it and plonked it into a bowl of cold water. Thankfully there had been some water in the kettle so it didn't have to cool from boiling, she thought as she ran back upstairs and collected the children, suddenly ludicrously conscious of how scruffy they looked after foraging in the woods, and how apprehensive.

'Hey, it's all right, he wants to meet you,' she murmured reassuringly to Kitty, who was clinging to her, and then pushed the breakfast room door open and ushered them in.

He was putting wood on the fire, and as he closed the door and straightened up, he caught sight of them and turned. The smile was gone, his face oddly taut, and her own smile faltered for a moment.

'Kids, this is Mr Forrester—'

'Jake,' he said, cutting her off and taking a step forward. His mouth twisted into a smile. 'I've already met Edward. And you must be Kitty. And this, I take it, is Thomas?'

'Yes.'

Thomas, sensing the change of atmosphere, had gone obligingly silent, but after a moment he lost interest in Jake and anything except his stomach and, burrowing into her shoulder, he began to wail again.

'I'm sorry. I—'

'Go on, feed him. I gave the bottle a shake to help cool it.'

'Thanks.' She went into the kitchen, wondering how he knew to do that. Nieces and nephews, probably—although he'd said he didn't have any family. How odd, she thought briefly, but then Thomas tried to lunge out of her arms and she fielded him with the ease of practice and tested the bottle on her wrist.

Cool enough. She shook it again, tested it once more to be on the safe side and offered it to her son.

Silence. Utter, blissful silence, broken only by a strained chuckle.

'Oh, for such simple needs,' he said softly, and she turned and met his eyes. They were darker than before, and his mouth was set in a grim line despite the laugh. But then his expression went carefully blank and he limped across to the kettle. 'So—who has tea, and who wants juice or whatever else?'

'We haven't got any juice. The children will have water.'

'Sounds dull.'

'They're fine with it. It's good for them.'

'I don't doubt it. It's good for me, too, but that doesn't mean I drink it. Except in meetings. I get through gallons of it in meetings. So—is that just me, or are you going to join me?'

'Oh.' Join him? That sounded curiously—intimate. 'Yes, please,' she said, and hoped she didn't sound absurdly breathless. It's a cup of tea, she told herself crossly. Just a cup of tea. Nothing else. She didn't want anything else. Ever.

And if she told herself that enough times, maybe she'd start to believe it.

'Have the children eaten?'

'Thomas has. Edward and Kitty haven't. I was going to wait until you woke up and ask you what you wanted.'

'Anything. I'm not really hungry after that sandwich. What is there?'

'I have no idea. I'll give the children eggs on toast—'

'Again?' Kitty said plaintively. 'We had eggs on toast for supper last night.'

'I'm sure we can find something else,' their host was saying, rummaging in a tall cupboard with pull-out racking that was crammed with tins and jars and packets. 'What did you all have for lunch?'

'Jam sandwiches and an apple.'

He turned and studied Kitty thoughtfully, then his gaze flicked up to Amelia's and speared her. 'Jam sandwiches?' he said softly. 'Eggs on toast?'

She felt her chin lift, but he just frowned and turned back to the cupboard, staring into its depths blankly for a moment before shutting it and opening the big door beside it and going systematically through the drawers of the freezer.

'How about fish?'

'What sort? They don't eat smoked fish or fish fingers.'

'Salmon—and mixed shellfish. A lobster,' he added, rummaging. 'Raw king prawns—there's some Thai curry paste somewhere I just saw. Or there's probably a casserole if you don't fancy fish.'

'Whatever. Choose what you want. We'll have eggs.'

He frowned again, shut the freezer and studied her searchingly.

She wished he wouldn't do that. Her arm was aching, Thomas was starting to loll against her shoulder and if she was sitting down, she could probably settle him and get him off to sleep so she could concentrate on feeding the others—most particularly their reluctant host.

After all, she'd told him she could cook—

'Go and sit down. I'll order a takeaway,' he said softly, and she looked back up into his eyes and surprised a gentle, almost puzzled expression in them for a fleeting moment before he turned away and limped out. 'What do they like?' he asked over his shoulder, then turned to the children. 'What's it to be, kids? Pizza? Chinese? Curry? Kebabs? Burgers?'

'What's a kebab?'

'Disgusting. Anyway, you're having eggs, Kitty, we've already decided that.'

Over their heads she met his eyes defiantly, and saw a reluctant grin blossom on his firm, sculpted lips. 'OK, we'll have eggs. Do we have enough?'

We? Her eyes widened. 'For all of us?'

'Am I excluded?'

She ran a mental eye over the meagre contents of the fridge and relaxed. 'Of course not.'

'Good. Then we'll have omelettes and oven-baked potato wedges and peas, if that's OK? Now, for heaven's sake sit down, woman, before you drop the baby, and I'll make you a cup of tea.'

'I thought I was supposed to be looking after you?' she said, but one glare from those rather gorgeous slate grey eyes and she retreated to the comfort of the fireside, settling down in the chair he'd been using with a sigh of relief. She'd have her tea, settle Thomas in his cot and make supper.

For all of them, apparently. So—was he going to sit and eat with them? He'd been so anti his little army of squatters, so what had brought about this sudden change?

Jake pulled the mugs out of the cupboard and then contemplated the lid of the tea caddy. Tea bags, he decided, with only one useful hand, not leaves and the pot, and putting the caddy back, he dropped tea bags into the mugs and poured water on them. Thank God it was his left arm he'd broken, not his right. At least he could manage most things like this.

The stud on his jeans was a bit of a challenge, he'd discovered, but he'd managed to get them on this morning. Shoelaces were another issue, but he'd kicked his shoes off when he'd got in and he'd been padding around in his socks, and he had shoes without laces he could wear until the blasted cast came off.

But cooking—well, cooking would be a step

too far, he thought, but by some minor interven-
tion of fate he seemed to have acquired an answer
to that one. A feisty, slightly offbeat and rather de-
lightful answer. Easy on the eye. And with a voice
that seemed to dig right down inside him and tug
at something long forgotten.

It was the kids he found hardest, of course, but it
was the kids he was most concerned about, because
their mother was obviously struggling to hold
things together. And she wasn't coping very well
with it—or maybe, he thought, reconsidering as he
poked the tea bags with the spoon, she was coping
very well, against atrocious odds. Whatever, a staple
diet of bread and eggs wasn't good for anyone and,
as he knew from his experience with the cheese
sandwich, it wasn't even decent bread. Perfectly nu-
tritious, no doubt, but closely related to cotton wool.

He put the milk down and poured two glasses
of filtered water for Edward and Kitty. 'Hey, you
guys, come and get your drinks,' he said, and
they ran over, Edward more slowly, Kitty skip-
ping, head on one side in a gesture so like her
mother's he nearly laughed.

'So—what *are* kebabs, really?' she asked,
twizzling a lock of hair with one forefinger, and
he did laugh then, the sound dragged out of him
almost reluctantly.

'Well—there are different kinds. There's shish kebab, which is pieces of meat on skewers, a bit like you'd put on a barbecue, or there's doner kebab, which is like a great big sausage on a stick, and they turn it in front of a fire to cook it and slice bits off. You have both in a kind of bread pocket, with salad, and your mother's right, the doner kebabs certainly aren't very healthy—well, not the ones in this country. In Turkey they're fantastic.'

'They don't *sound* disgusting,' Kitty said wistfully. 'I like sausages on sticks.'

'Maybe we can get some sausages and put sticks in them,' Edward said, and Jake realised he was the peacemaker in the family, trying to hold it all together, humouring Kitty and helping with Thomas and supporting his mother—and the thought that he should have to do all that left a great hollow in the pit of Jake's stomach.

No child should have to do that. He'd spent years doing that, fighting helplessly against the odds to keep it all together, and for what?

'Good idea,' he said softly. 'We'll get some sausages tomorrow.' He gathered up the mugs in his right hand and limped through to the breakfast room and put them down on the table near Amelia. She looked up with a smile.

'Thanks,' she murmured, and he found his eyes drawn down to the baby, sleeping now, his chubby little face turned against her chest, arm outflung, dead to the world. A great lump in his throat threatened to choke him, and he nodded curtly, took his mug and went back to the other room, shutting the door firmly so he couldn't hear the children's voices.

He couldn't do this. It was killing him, and he couldn't do it.

He'd meant to sit with her, talk to her, but the children had unravelled him and he couldn't sit there and look at them, he discovered. Not today. Not the day before Christmas Eve.

The day his wife and son had died.

# CHAPTER FOUR

WELL, what was that about?

He'd come in, taken one look at her and gone.

Because she'd sat in his chair?

No—and he'd been looking at Thomas, not her. And had she dreamed it, or had there been a slight sheen in his eyes?

The glitter of tears?

No. She was being ridiculous. He just wanted to be alone. He always wanted to be alone, according to Kate, and they'd scuppered that for him, so he was making the best of a bad job and keeping out of the way.

So why did he want to eat with them? Or was he simply having the same food?

She had no idea, and no way of working it out, and knowing so little about him, her guesswork was just a total stab in the dark. But there had been *something* in his eyes…

'I'm just going to put Thomas to bed, then I'll cook you supper,' she told the children quietly and, getting up without disturbing the baby, she took him up to the attic and slipped him into his cot. She'd change his nappy later. She didn't want to risk waking him now—not when he'd finally settled.

And not when Jake had that odd look about him that was flagging up all kinds of warning signals. She was sure he was hurting, but she had no idea why—and it was frankly none of her business. She just needed to feed the children, get them out of the way and then deal with him later.

'Right, kids, let's make supper,' she said, going back in and smiling at them brightly. 'Who wants to break the eggs into the cup?'

Not the bowl, because that was just asking for trouble, and she sensed that crunchy omelettes wouldn't win her any Brownie points with Jake, but one at a time was all right. She could fish for shell in one egg.

She looked out of the window at the herb garden and wondered what was out there. Sage? Rosemary? Thyme? It was a shame she didn't have any cheese, but she could put fresh herbs in his, and she remembered seeing a packet of pancetta in the fridge.

She cooked for herself and the children first, then while she was eating she cooked his spicy potato wedges in a second batch, then sent the children up to wash and change ready for bed.

'I'll come up and read to you when I've given Jake his supper,' she promised, kissing them both, and they went, still looking a little uncertain, and she felt another wave of anger at David for putting them in this position.

And at herself, for allowing him to make them so vulnerable, for relying on him even after he'd proved over and over again that he was unreliable, for giving him the power to do this to them. He'd walked out on them four years ago, and letting him back again two years later had been stupid in the extreme. It hadn't taken her long to realise it, and she'd finally taken the last step and divorced him, but their failed reconciliation had resulted in Thomas. And, though she loved Thomas to bits, having him didn't make life easier and had forced her to rely on David again. Well, no more. Not him, not any man.

Never again, she thought, vigorously beating the last two eggs for Jake's omelette while the little cubes of pancetta crisped in the pan. No way was she putting herself and her family at risk again. Even if Jake was remotely interested in her, which he simply wasn't. He couldn't even bear to be in the same room as her—and she had to stop thinking about him!

She went out and picked the herbs by the light from the kitchen window, letting Rufus out into the garden for a moment while she breathed deeply and felt the cold, clean air fill her lungs and calm her.

They'd survive, she told herself. They'd get through this hitch, and she'd get another job somehow, and they'd be all right.

They had to be.

She went back in with Rufus and the herbs, made Jake's omelette and left it to set on the side of the Aga while she called him to the table.

She tapped on the door of what she was beginning to think of as his cave, and he opened it almost instantly. She stepped back hastily and smiled. 'Hi. I was just coming to call you for supper.'

He smiled back. 'The smell was reeling me in—I was just on my way. Apparently I'm hungrier than I thought.'

Oh, damn. Had she made enough for him?

He followed her through to the breakfast room and stopped. 'Where are the other place settings?'

'Oh—the children were starving, so I ate with them. Anyway, I wasn't sure—'

She broke off, biting her lip, and he sighed softly.

'I'm sorry. I was rude. I just walked out.'

'No—no, why should you want to sit with us? It's your house, we're in your way. I feel so guilty—'

'Don't. Please, don't. I don't know the ins and outs of it, and I don't need to, but it's quite obvious that you're doing your best to cope and life's just gone pear-shaped recently. And, whatever the rights and wrongs of your being here, it's nothing to do with the children. They've got every right to feel safe and secure, and wanted, and if I've given you the impression that they're not welcome here, then I apologise. I don't do kids—I have my reasons, which I don't intend to go into, but—your kids have done nothing wrong and—well, tomorrow I'd like to fix it a bit, if you'll let me.'

'Fix it?' she said, standing with the plate in her hand and her eyes searching his. 'How?' How on earth could he fix it? And why didn't he do kids?

'I'd like to give the children Christmas. I'd like to go shopping and buy food. I've already promised them sausages, but I'd like to get the works—a turkey and all the trimmings, satsumas, mince pies, Christmas cake, a Christmas pudding and cream, and something else if they don't like the heavy fruit—perhaps a chocolate log or something? And a tree. They ought to have a tree, with real decorations on it.'

She felt her eyes fill with tears, and swallowed hard.

'You don't have to do that,' she said, trying to firm her voice. 'We don't need all that.'

'I know—but I'd like to. I don't normally do Christmas, but the kids have done nothing to deserve this hideous uncertainty in their lives, and if I can help to make this time a little better for them, then maybe—'

He broke off and turned away, moving slowly to the table, his leg obviously troubling him.

She set the plate down in front of him with trembling hands. 'I don't know what to say.'

'Then just say yes, and let me do it,' he said gruffly, then tilted his head and gave her a wry look. 'I don't suppose I'm allowed a glass of wine?'

'Of course you are.'

'You wouldn't let me have the whisky.'

She gave a little laugh, swallowing down the tears and shaking her head. 'That was because of the painkillers. I thought you should drink water, especially as you'd been flying. But—sure, you can have a glass of wine.'

'Will you join me?'

'I thought you wanted to be alone?' she said softly, and he smiled again, a little crookedly.

'Amelia, just open the wine. There's a gluggable Aussie Shiraz in the wine rack in the side of the island unit, and the glasses are in the cupboard next to the Aga.'

'Corkscrew?'

'It's a screwtop.'

'Right.' She found the wine, found the glasses, poured his and a small one for herself and perched a little warily opposite him. 'How's the omelette?'

'Good. Just right. What herbs did you use? Are they from the garden?'

'Yes. Thyme and sage. And I found some pancetta—I hope it was OK to use it.'

'Of course. It's really tasty. Thanks.'

He turned his attention back to his food, and then pushed his plate away with a sigh when it was scraped clean. 'I don't suppose there's any pud?'

She chuckled. 'A budget yogurt?'

He wrinkled his nose. 'Maybe not. There might be some ice cream in the freezer—top drawer.'

There was. Luxury Belgian chocolate that made her mouth water. 'This one?' she offered, and he nodded.

'Brilliant. Will you join me?'

She gave in to the temptation because her omelette had only been tiny—elastic eggs, to make sure he had enough so she didn't fall at the first hurdle—and she was still hungry. She dished up and took it through, feeling a pang of guilt because she could feed her children for a day on the cost of that ice cream and in the good old days it had been their favourite—

'Stop it. We'll get some for the children tomorrow,' he chided, reading her mind with uncanny accuracy, and she laughed and sat down.

'How did you know?'

His mouth quirked. 'Your face is like an open book—every flicker of guilt registers on it. Stop beating yourself up, Amelia, and tell me about yourself. What do you do for a living?'

She tried to smile, but it felt pretty pathetic, really. 'Nothing at the moment. I was working freelance as a technical translator for a firm that went into liquidation. They owed me for three months' work.'

'Ouch.'

'Indeed. And David had just run off to Thailand with the receivers in hot pursuit after yet another failed business venture—'

'David?'

'My ex-husband. Self-styled entrepreneur and master of delusion, absent father of my children and what Kate describes as a waste of a good skin. He'd already declined to pay the maintenance when I left him for the second time when I was pregnant with Thomas, so I'd already had to find a way to survive for over a year while I waited for the courts to tell him to pay up. And then I lost my job, David wasn't in a position to help by then even if he'd chosen to, and my landlord wanted out of the property business so the moment I couldn't pay my overdue rent on the date he'd set, he asked me to leave. As in, "I want you out by the morning".'

Jake winced. 'So you went to your sister.'

'Yes. We moved in on the tenth of December—and it lasted less than two weeks.' She laughed softly and wrinkled her nose. 'You know what they say about guests being like fish—they go off after three days. So twelve wasn't bad. And the dog does smell.'

'So why don't you bath him?'

'Because they wouldn't let me. Not in their pristine house. I would have had to take him to the groomer, which I couldn't afford, or do it outside under the hose.'

'In December?' he said with a frown.

She smiled wryly, remembering Andy's blank incomprehension. 'Quite. So he still smells, I'm afraid.'

'That's ridiculous. Heavens, he's only tiny. Shove him in the sink and dry him by the fire.'

'Really?' She put down her ice cream spoon and sat back, staring at him in amazement. 'You're telling me I could bath him in your lovely kitchen?'

'Why not? Or you could use the utility room. Wherever. It doesn't matter, does it? He's only a dog. I can think of worse things. You're all right, aren't you, mate?' he said softly, turning his head and looking at the hearth where Rufus was lying as close to the woodburner as the fireguard would let him. He thumped his tail on the floor, his eyes fixed on Jake as if he was afraid that any minute now he'd be told to move.

But apparently not. Jake liked dogs—and thought it was fine to wash him in the kitchen sink. She stood up and took their bowls through to the kitchen, using the excuse to get away because her eyes were filling again and threatening to overflow and embarrass her. She put all the plates into the dishwasher and straightened up and took a nice steadying breath.

Rufus was at her feet, his tail waving, his eyes hopeful.

She had to squash the urge to hug him. 'Do you think I'm going to give you something? You've had supper,' she told him firmly. 'Don't beg.'

His tail drooped and he trotted back to Jake and sat beside him, staring up into his eyes and making him laugh.

'He's not looking convinced.'

'Don't you dare give him anything. He's not allowed to beg, and he's on a special diet.'

'I don't doubt it. I bet he costs more to run than all the rest of you put together.'

She laughed and shook her head. 'You'd better believe it. But he's worth every penny. He's been brilliant.' She bit her lip. 'I don't mean to be rude, but I did promise the children I'd read to them, and I need to change Thomas's nappy and put him into pyjamas.'

He nodded. 'That's fine. Don't worry. I'll see you later. In fact, I might just go to bed.'

'Can I get you anything else?'

He shook his head. 'No. I'm fine, don't worry about me. I'll see you in the morning. If you get a minute before then, you could dream up a shopping list. And thank you for my supper, by the way, it was lovely.'

She felt the cold, dead place around her heart warm a little, and she smiled. 'My pleasure,' she said, and took herself upstairs before she fell any further under his spell, because she'd discovered during the course of a glass of wine and a bowl of ice cream that Jake Forrester, when it suited him, could be very, very charming indeed.

And that scared the living daylights out of her.

His bags were missing.

The cabbie had stacked them by the front door, and they were gone. Kate, he thought. She'd been over while he was sleeping earlier, he knew that, and he realised she must have taken them up to his room. Unless Amelia had done it?

Whatever, he needed to go to bed. Lying on the sofa resting for an hour was all very well, but he needed more than that. And it was already after ten. He'd sat and had another glass of wine in front of the fire in the breakfast room, with Rufus keeping him company and creeping gradually closer until he was lying against his foot, and eventually it dawned on him that he was hanging around in the vain hope that Amelia would come back down and sit with him again.

Ridiculous. And dangerous. They both had far too much baggage, and it would be dicing with disaster, no matter how appealing the physical package. And there was no way he wanted any other kind of relationship. So, although he was loath to disturb the dog, he'd finally eased his toes out from under his side and left the room.

And then had to work out, in his muddled, tired mind, what had happened to his bags.

He detoured into the sitting room and picked up his painkillers, then made his way slowly and carefully up the stairs. He was getting stiffer, he realised. Maybe he needed a bath—a long, hot soak—except that he'd almost inevitably fall asleep in it and wake up cold and wrinkled in the middle of the night. And, anyway, he hated baths.

A shower? No. There was the difficulty of his cast to consider, and sealing it in a bag was beyond him at the moment. He'd really had enough. He'd deal with it tomorrow.

Reluctantly abandoning the tempting thought of hot water sluicing over his body, he eased off his clothes, found his wash things in the bag that had indeed arrived in his room, cleaned his teeth and then crawled into bed.

Bliss.

There was nothing like your own bed, he thought, closing his eyes with a long, unravelling sigh. And then he remembered he hadn't taken the painkillers, and he needed to before he went to sleep or his arm would wake him in the night.

He put the light back on and got out of bed again, filled a glass with water and came back to the bed. He'd thrown the pills on the bedside chest, and he took two and opened the top drawer to put them in.

And there it was.

Lying in the drawer, jumbled up with pens and cufflinks and bits of loose change. Oh, Lord. Slowly, almost reluctantly, he pulled the little frame out and stared down at the faces laughing back up at him—Rachel, full of life as usual, sitting on the grass with Ben in between her knees, his little hands filled with grass mowings and his eyes alight with mischief. He'd been throwing the grass mowings all over her, and they'd all been laughing.

And six months later, five years ago today, they'd been mown down by a drunk driver who'd just left his office Christmas party. They'd been doing some last-minute shopping—collecting a watch she'd bought him, he discovered when he eventually went through the bag of their things he'd been given at the hospital. He'd worn it every day for the last five years—until it had been shattered, smashed to bits against an alpine tree during the avalanche.

An avalanche that had brought him home—to

a woman called Amelia, and her three innocent and displaced children.

Was this Rachel's doing? Trying to tell him to move on, to forget them both?

He traced their faces with his finger, swallowing down the grief that had never really left him, the grief that sent him away every Christmas to try and forget the unforgettable, to escape the inescapable.

He put the photo back in the drawer and closed it softly, turned off the light, then lay back down and stared dry-eyed into the night.

She couldn't sleep.

Something had woken her—some strange sound, although how she could know the sounds of the house so well already she had no idea, but somehow she did, and this one was strange.

She got out of bed and checked the children, but all of them were sleeping, Thomas flat out on his back with his arms flung up over his head, Edward on his tummy with one leg stuck out the side, and Kitty curled on her side with her hand under her cheek and her battered old teddy snuggled in the crook of her arm.

So not them, then.

Jake?

She looked over the banisters, but all was quiet and there was no light.

Rufus?

Oh, Lord, Rufus. Did he want to go out? Was that what had woken her, him yipping or scratching at the door?

She pulled on a jumper over her pyjamas—because, of course, in her haste she'd left her dressing gown on the back of the door at her sister's—and tiptoed down the stairs, glancing along to Jake's room as she reached the head of the lower flight.

She'd brought his luggage up earlier while he was sleeping and put it in there, because he couldn't possibly manage to lug it up there himself, and she'd had her first look at his room.

It was over the formal drawing room, with an arched opening to the bathroom at the bay window end, and a great rolltop bath sat in the middle, with what must be the most spectacular view along the endless lawn to the woods in the distance. She couldn't picture him in it at all, there was a huge double shower the size of the average wetroom that seemed much more likely, and a pair of gleaming washbasins, and in a separate little room with its own basin and marble-tiled walls was a loo.

And at the opposite end of the room was the bed. Old, solid, a vast and imposing four-poster, the head end and the top filled in with heavily carved panelling, it was perfect for the room. Perfect for the house. The sort of bed where love was made and children were born and people slipped quietly away at the end of their lives, safe in its arms.

It was a wonderful, wonderful bed. And not in the least monastic. She could picture him in it so easily.

Was he lying in it now? She didn't know. Maybe, maybe not—and she was mad to think about it.

There was no light on, and the house was in silence, but it felt different, she thought. There was something about it which had changed with his arrival, a sort of—rightness, as if the house had relaxed now he was home.

Which didn't explain what had woken her. And the door to his room was open a crack. She'd gone down to let the dog out and tidy up the kitchen after she'd settled the children and finished unpacking their things and he must have come upstairs by then, but she hadn't noticed the door open. Perhaps he'd come out again to get something and hadn't shut it, and that was what had woken her, but there was no sign of him now.

She went down to the breakfast room, guided

only by the moonlight, and opened the door, and she heard the gentle thump of the dog's tail on the floor and the clatter of his nails.

'Hello, my lovely man,' she crooned, crouching down and pulling gently on his ears. 'Are you all right?'

'I take it you're talking to the dog.'

She gave a little shriek and pressed her hand to her chest, then started to laugh. 'Good grief, Jake, you scared me to death!' She straightened up and reached for the light, then hesitated, conscious of her tired old pyjamas. 'Are you OK?'

'I couldn't sleep. You?'

'I thought I heard a noise.'

He laughed softly. 'In this house? Of course you heard a noise! It creaks like a ship.'

'I know. It settles. I love it—it sounds as if it's relaxing. No, there was something else. It must have been you.'

'I stumbled over the dog—he came to see me and I hadn't put the light on and I kicked him by accident and he yelped—and, before you ask, he's fine. I nudged him, really, but he seemed a bit upset by it, so I sat with him.'

'Oh, I'm so sorry—he does get underfoot and—well, I think he was kicked as a puppy. Has he forgiven you?'

The soft sound of Jake's laughter curled round her again, warming her. 'I think so. He's been on my lap.'

'Ah. Sounds like it, then.' She hesitated, wondering if she should leave him to it and go back to bed, but sensing that there was something wrong, something more than he was telling her. 'How's the fire?'

'OK. I think it could do with more wood.'

'I'll get some.'

She went out of the back door and brought in an armful of logs, putting on the kitchen light as she went, and she left it on when she came back, enough to see by but hopefully not enough to see just how tired her pyjamas really were, and the spill of yellow light made the room seem cosy and intimate.

Which was absurd, considering its size, but everything was in scale and so it didn't seem big, just—safe.

She put the logs in the basket and opened the fire, throwing some in, and as the flames leapt up she went to shut it but he stopped her.

'Leave it open. It's nice to sit and stare into the flames. It helps—'

Helps? Helps what? she wanted to ask, but she couldn't, somehow, so she knelt there on the hearthrug in the warmth of the flames, with Rufus snuggled against her side, his skinny, feathery tail wafting against her, and waited.

But Jake didn't say any more, just sighed and dropped his head back against the chair and closed his eyes. She could see that his fingers were curled around a glass, and on the table behind him was a bottle. The whisky?

'What?'

She jumped guiltily. 'Nothing.'

He snorted. 'It's never nothing with women. Yes, it's the whisky. No, it doesn't help.'

'Jake—'

'No. Leave it, Amelia. Please. If you want to do something useful, you could make us a cup of tea.'

'How about a hot milky drink?'

'I'm not five.'

'No, but you're tired, you're hurt and you said you'd had enough caffeine today—it might help you sleep.'

'Tea,' he said implacably.

She shrugged and got to her feet, padded back through to the kitchen and put the kettle on, turning in time to see him drain his glass and set it down on the table. He glanced up and met her eyes, and sighed.

'I've only had one. I'm not an alcoholic, Amelia.'

'I never suggested you were!' she said, appalled that he'd think she was criticising when actually she'd simply been concerned for his health and well-being.

'So stop looking at me as if you're the Archangel Gabriel and I'm going off the rails!'

She gave a soft chuckle and took two mugs out of the cupboard. 'I'm the last person to criticise anyone for life choices. I'm homeless, for heavens' sake! And I've got three children, only one of whom was planned, and I'm unemployed and my life's a total mess, so pardon me if I pick you up on that one! I just wondered...'

'Wondered what? Why I'm such a miserable bastard?'

'Are you? Miserable, I mean? Kate thought—' She broke off, not wanting him to think Kate had been discussing him, but it was too late, and one eyebrow climbed autocratically.

'Kate thought—?' he prompted.

'You were just a loner. You are, I mean. A loner.'

'And what do you think, little Miss Fixit?'

She swallowed. 'I think you're sad, and lonely. She said you're very private, but I think that's because it all hurts too much to talk about.'

His face lost all expression, and he turned back to the fire, the only sign of movement from him the flex of the muscle in his jaw. 'Why don't you forget the amateur psychology and concentrate on making the tea?' he said, his voice devoid of emotion, but she could still see that tic in his jaw, the rhythmic bunching of the muscle, and she didn't know whether to persevere or give up, because she sensed it might all be a bit of a Pandora's box and, once opened, she might well regret all the things that came out.

So she made the tea, and took it through and sat beside the fire in what started as a stiff and unyielding silence and became in the end a wary truce.

He was the first to break the silence.

'I don't suppose you've made the shopping list?'

She shook her head. 'Not yet. I could do it now.'

'No, don't worry. We can do it over breakfast. I have no doubt that, no matter how little sleep we may have had, the kids will be up at the crack of dawn raring to go, so there'll be plenty of time.'

She laughed a little unsteadily, feeling the tension drain out of her at his words. 'I'm sure.' She got to her feet and held out her hand for his mug, then was surprised when he reached up his left hand, the one in the cast, and took her fingers in his.

'Ignore me, Amelia. I'll get over it. I'll be fine tomorrow.'

She nodded, not understanding really, because how could she? But she let it go, for now at least, and she squeezed his fingers gently and then let go, and he dropped his arm and held out the mug.

'Thanks for the tea. It was nice.'

The tea? Or having someone to sit and drink it with?

He didn't say, and she wasn't asking, but one thing she knew about this man, whatever Kate might say to the contrary—he wasn't a loner.

'My pleasure,' she murmured and, putting the mugs in the sink, she closed the doors of the fire and shut it down again. With a murmured, 'Good night,' she went upstairs to bed, but she didn't sleep until she heard the soft creak of the stairs and the little click as his bedroom door closed.

Then she let out the breath she'd been holding and slipped into a troubled and uneasy sleep.

# CHAPTER FIVE

IT WAS the first time in years he'd been round a supermarket, and Christmas Eve probably wasn't the day to start—not when they even had to queue to get into the car park, and by the time they'd found a space Jake was beginning to wonder why on earth he'd suggested it.

It was going to be a nightmare, he knew it, rammed to the roof with festive goodies and wall-to-wall Christmas jingles and people in silly hats—he was dreading it, and it didn't disappoint.

The infuriatingly jolly little tunes on the in-store speakers were constantly being interrupted with calls for multi-skilled staff to go to the checkouts—a fact that didn't inspire hope for a quick getaway—and the place was rammed with frustrated shoppers who couldn't reach the shelves for the trolleys jamming the aisles.

'I have an idea,' he said as they fought to get

down the dairy aisle and he was shunted in the ankle by yet another trolley. 'You know what we need, I don't want to be shoved around and Thomas needs company, so why don't I stand at the end with him and you go backwards and forwards picking up the stuff?'

And it all, suddenly, got much easier because he could concentrate on amusing Thomas—and that actually was probably the hardest part. Not that he was hard to entertain, quite the opposite, but it brought back so many memories— memories he'd buried with his son—and it was threatening to wreck him. Then, just when he thought he'd go mad if he had to look at that cheerful, chubby little smile any longer, he realised their system wasn't working.

The trolley wasn't getting fuller and, watching her, he could see why. She was obviously reluctant to spend too much of his money, which was refreshing but unnecessary, so he gave up and shoved the trolley one-handed into the fray while she was dithering over the fresh turkeys.

'What's the matter?'

'They're so expensive. The frozen ones are much cheaper—'

'But they take ages to defrost so we don't have a choice. Just pick one. Here, they've got nice free-range Bronze turkeys—get one of them,' he suggested, earning himself a searching look.

'What do you know about Bronze turkeys?' she asked incredulously.

He chuckled. 'Very little—but I know they're supposed to have the best flavour, I'm ethically comfortable with free range and, anyway, they're the most expensive and therefore probably the most sought after. That's usually an indicator of quality. So pick one and let's get on.'

'But—they're so expensive, Jake, and I feel so guilty taking your money—'

He gave up, reached over and single-handedly heaved a nice fat turkey into the trolley. 'Right. Next?'

'Um—stuffing,' she said weakly, and he felt a little tug at his sleeve.

'You said we could have sausages and cook them and have them on sticks,' Kitty said hopefully.

'Here—traditional chipolatas,' he said, and threw three packets in the trolley, thought better of it and added another two for good measure. 'Bacon?'

'Um—probably.' She put a packet of sausage-meat stuffing in the trolley and he frowned at it, picked up another with chestnuts and cranberries, which looked more interesting, and put that in, too.

'You're getting into this, aren't you?' she teased, coming back with the bacon.

So was she, he noticed with relief, seeing that at last she was picking up the quality products and not the cheapest, smallest packet she could find of whatever it was. They moved on, and the trolley filled up. Vegetables, fruit, a traditional Christmas pudding that would last them days, probably, but would at least be visible in the middle of the old refectory table in the breakfast room, and a chocolate log for the children. Then, when they'd done the food shopping and filled the trolley almost to the brim, they took it through the checkout, put it all in the car and went back inside for 'the exciting stuff', as Kitty put it.

Christmas decorations for the tree they had yet to buy, little nets of chocolate coins in gold foil, crackers for the table, a wreath for the door—the list was nearly as long as the first and, by the time they got to the end of it, the children were hungry and Thomas, who'd been as good as gold and utterly, heart-wrenchingly enchanting until that point, was starting to grizzle.

'I tell you what—why don't you take the kids and get them something to eat and drink while I deal with this lot?' he suggested, peeling a twenty pound note out of his wallet and giving it to her.

She hesitated, but he just sighed and shoved it at her, and with a silent nod she flashed him a smile and took the children off to the canteen.

Which gave him long enough to go back up the aisles and look for presents for them all. And, because it had thinned out by that point, he went to the customer services and asked if there was anyone who could help him wrap the presents for the children. He brandished his cast pathetically and, between that and the black eye, he charmed them into it shamelessly.

There was nothing outrageous in his choices. There was nothing outrageous in the shop anyway but, even if there had been, he would have avoided it. It wasn't necessary, and he didn't believe in spoiling children, but there was a colouring book with glue and glitter that Kitty had fingered longingly and been made to put back, and he'd noticed Edward looking at an intricate construction toy of the sort he'd loved as a boy, and there was a nice chunky plastic shape sorter which he thought Thomas might like.

And then there was Amelia.

She didn't have any gloves, he'd noticed, and he'd commented on it on the way there when she was rubbing her hands and blowing on them holding the steering wheel.

'Sure, it's freezing, but I can't do things with gloves on,' she'd explained.

But he'd noticed some fingerless mitts, with little flaps that buttoned back out of the way and could be let down to tuck her fingers into to turn them into mittens. And they were in wonderful, ludicrously pink stripes with a matching scarf that would snuggle round her neck and keep her warm while she walked the dog.

He even bought a little coat for Rufus, because he'd noticed him shivering out on their walk first thing.

And then he had to make himself stop, because they weren't his family and he didn't want to make them—or, more specifically, Amelia—feel embarrassed. But he chucked in a jigsaw to put on the low coffee table in the drawing room and work on together, just because it was the sort of thing he'd loved in his childhood, and also a family game they could play together.

And then he really *did* stop, and they were all wrapped and paid for, together with the decorations, and someone even helped him load them into the car and wished him a merry Christmas, and he found himself saying it back with a smile.

Really?

He went into the canteen and found them

sitting in a litter of sandwich wrappers and empty cups. 'All set?'

She nodded. 'Yes. We were just coming to find you. Thank you so much—'

'Don't mention it. Right, we'd better get on, because we need to take this lot home and then get a tree before it's too late, and at some point today I need to go to the hospital and have a proper cast put on my arm.'

'Wow! Look at the tree. It's *enormous!*'

It wasn't, not really, but it was quite big enough—and it had been a bit of a struggle to get it in place with one arm out of action in its new cast, but just the look on the children's faces made it all worth it—and, if he wasn't mistaken, there was the sheen of tears in Amelia's eyes.

They'd put it in pride of place in the bay window in the drawing room, and lit the fire—a great roaring log fire in the open hearth, with crackling flames and the sweet smell of apple-wood smoke—and, between the wood smoke and the heady scent of the tree, the air just smelled of Christmas. All they had to do now was decorate the tree, and for Jake it was a step too far.

'I'm going to sit this out,' he said, heading for the door, but Kitty shook her head and grabbed his good hand and tugged him back, shocking him into immobility.

'You *can't*, Jake! You have to help us—we're all too small to reach the top, and you *have* to put the *lights* on and the *fairy* and all the tinsel and *everything*!'

Why was it, he wondered, that children—especially earnest little girls—always talked in italics and exclamation marks? And her eyes were pleading with him, and there was no way he could walk away from her. From any of them.

'OK. I'll just go and put the kettle on—'

'No! Lights first, because otherwise we can't do *anything* until you get back, and you'll be *ages*!'

Italics again. He smiled at her. 'Well, in that case, I'll put the *lights* on *first*, but *just* the lights, and then we'll have a *quick* cup of tea and we'll finish it off. OK?'

She eyed him a little suspiciously, as if she didn't trust his notion of quick and wasn't quite sure about the emphasis on the words, because there was something mildly teasing in them and he could see she was working it out, working out if he *was* only teasing or if he was being mean.

And he couldn't be mean to her, he discovered. Not in the least. In fact, all he wanted to do was gather her up into his arms and tell her it would all be all right, but of course it wasn't his place to do that and he couldn't make it right for her, couldn't make her father step up to the plate and behave like a decent human being.

If he was the man he was thinking of, Jake knew David Jones, had met him in the past, and he hadn't liked him at all. Oh, he'd been charming enough, but he'd talked rubbish, been full of bull and wild ideas with no foundation, and at one point a year or two ago he'd approached him at a conference asking for his investment in some madcap scheme. He'd declined, and he'd heard later, not unexpectedly, that he'd gone down the pan. And it didn't surprise him in the least, if it *was* the same David Jones, that he'd walked out on his family.

So he couldn't make it right for David's little daughter. But he could help her with the tree, and he could make sure they were warm and safely housed until their situation improved. And it was all he needed to do, all his conscience required.

It was only his heart that he was having trouble with, and he shut the door on it firmly and concentrated on getting the lights on the tree without either knocking it over or hurting any more of the innumerable aches and pains that were emerging with every hour that passed.

'Are you OK doing that?'

He turned his head and smiled down at Amelia ruefully. 'I'll live. I'm nearly done.'

'I'll put the kettle on. You look as if you could do with some more painkillers.'

'I'll be fine. It's just stretching that hurts—'

'And bending over, and standing, and—'

'Just put the kettle on,' he said softly, and she opened her mouth again, closed it and went out.

He watched her walk down the hall, watched the gentle sway of her hips, the fluid grace of her movements, the lightness in her step that hadn't been there yesterday, and he felt a sharp stab of what could only be lust. She was a beautiful, sensuous woman, intelligent and brave, and he realised he wanted to gather her up in his arms, too, and to hell with the complications.

But he couldn't, and he wouldn't, so with a quiet sigh he turned back to the tree and finished draping the string of lights around the bottom, then turned them on and stood back.

'How's that?'

'*Really* pretty!' Kitty whispered, awed.

'It's a bit crooked,' he said, wondering if there was any way he could struggle in under the tree and right it, but Edward—typically—rushed in with reassurance.

'It doesn't show,' he said quickly, 'and it looks really nice. Can we put the rest of the things on now?'

'We have to wait for Mummy!' Kitty said, sounding appalled, and so Jake sent them off to the kitchen to find out what she was doing and to tell her to bring biscuits with the tea. He lowered himself carefully on to the sofa and smiled at Thomas, who was sitting on the floor inside a ring of fat cushions with a colourful plastic teething ring in his mouth.

'All right, little man?' he asked, and Thomas gave him a toothy grin and held out the toy. It was covered in spit, but it didn't matter, he was only showing it to Jake, not offering it to him, so he admired it dutifully and tried oh, so hard not to think about Ben.

'That's really nice,' he said gruffly. 'Does it taste good?'

'Mumum,' he said, shoving it back in his mouth with a delicious chuckle, and Jake clenched his teeth and gave a tiny huff of laughter that was more than halfway to a sob.

What was it about kids that they got through your defences like nothing else on earth?

'You're going to be a proper little charmer, aren't you?' he said softly, and was rewarded with another spitty little chuckle. Then he threw down the toy and held out his hands, and it was beyond Jake to refuse.

He held out his hands, hoping his broken wrist was up to it, and Thomas grabbed his fingers and pulled himself up with a delighted gurgle, taking Jake's breath away.

'Are you all right?'

'Not really,' he said a little tightly, massively relieved to see Amelia reappear. 'Um—could you take him? My hand—'

'Oh, Jake! Thomas, come here, darling.'

She gently prised his fingers off Jake's, and the pull on the fracture eased and he sank back with a shaky sigh, because it hadn't only been the fracture, it had been that gummy, dribbly smile and the feel of those strong, chubby little fingers, and he just wanted to get the hell out. 'Thanks. That was probably a stupid thing to do, but—'

'You couldn't refuse him? Tell me about it. Look, I've brought you something lovely!'

'I don't really want a cup of juice,' he said softly, and she laughed, the sound running through him like a tinkling stream, clean and pure and sweet.

'Silly. Your tea's there, with the painkillers.'

He found a smile. Actually, not that hard, with

the warmth of her laughter still echoing through him. 'Thanks.'

'And chocolate biscuits, and shortbread!' Edward said, sounding slightly amazed.

'Goodness. Anyone would think it was Christmas,' he said in mock surprise, and Kitty giggled and then, before he could react or do anything to prevent it, she climbed onto his lap and snuggled up against his chest with a smile.

'It *is* Christmas, silly—well, it is tomorrow,' she corrected, and squirmed round to study the tree. 'We need to put everything else on it.'

'Biscuits first,' he said firmly, because he needed his painkillers, especially if Kitty was going to bounce and fidget and squirm on his bruises. And his arm was really aching now after all the silly things he'd done with it that day.

So they ate biscuits, and Kitty snuggled closer, and he caught the anguished look in Amelia's eye and felt so sad for them all that it had all gone wrong, because Kitty's father should have been sitting somewhere else with her on his lap instead of hiding from his responsibilities in Thailand, and he should have been there with Rachel and Ben, and none of them had deserved it—

'Right. Let's do the tree,' he said and, shunting

Kitty off his lap, he got stiffly to his feet and put the baubles where he was told.

He was being amazing.

She couldn't believe just how kind he'd been all day. He'd been so foul to her yesterday, so sarcastic and bitter, but somehow all that was gone and he was being the man Kate had talked about, generous to a fault and the soul of kindness.

He was so gentle with the children, teasing them, humouring them, putting up with their enthusiastic nonsense, and then, when the tree was done and she'd swept underneath it to pick up the needles that had fallen out of it while they'd decorated it, they went into the kitchen and she cooked supper while she danced around the kitchen with tinsel in her hair, singing along with the Christmas songs on the radio and making Thomas giggle.

And then she'd looked up and seen Jake watching her with an odd look on his face, and she'd felt the breath squeeze out of her lungs. No. She was misreading the signals. He couldn't possibly want her—not a destitute woman with three children and a smelly, expensive little dog.

So she pulled the tinsel out of her hair and tied it round the dog's neck, and concentrated on cooking the supper.

Sausages on sticks for Kitty, with roasted vegetable skewers in mini pitta pockets so she could pretend she was having kebabs, followed by the sort of fruit Millie couldn't afford to buy, cut into cubes and dunked into melted chocolate. He'd put little pots on the top of the Aga with squares of chocolate in, and they'd melted and made the most fabulous sauce.

And the children had loved every mouthful of it. Even Thomas had sucked on a bit of sausage and had a few slices of banana and some peeled grapes dipped in chocolate and, apart from the shocking mess, it was a huge success.

'Right, you lot, time for bed,' she said.

'Oh, but it's Christmas!'

'Yes, and it'll come all the earlier if you're in bed asleep,' she reasoned. 'And Father Christmas won't come down the chimney if you're still awake.'

'But he won't come anyway, because of the fire,' Kitty said, looking suddenly worried, but Jake rescued the situation instantly.

'Not a problem,' he said promptly. 'There's another chimney in the dining room, and he'll come down that.'

'But he won't know where to put the presents!' she argued.

'Yes, he will, because he knows everything,' Edward said with an air of patient indulgence that made Millie want to laugh and cry all at once. 'Come on, let's go up to bed and then he'll come.'

'Promise?' Kitty said, staring at her hopefully.

Oh, Lord, there was so little for them. They were going to be horribly disappointed. 'Promise,' she said, near to tears, but then the doorbell rang, jangling the ancient bell over the breakfast room door, and Jake got to his feet.

'I'll get it, it's probably Kate,' he said, and she followed him, meaning to say hello if it *was* Kate or take the children up to bed if not, but as he reached for the door they heard the unmistakable sound of a choir.

'Carol singers,' he said in a hollow voice, rooted to the spot with an appalled expression on his face.

'I'll deal with them,' she said softly, and opened the door, meaning to give them some change for their tin and send them away. But he was still standing there in full view and the vicar, who was standing at the front, beamed at him.

'Mr Forrester! We heard you were back and that you'd been injured, so we thought we'd come and share some carols with you on the way back from evensong—bring you a little Christmas cheer.'

Jake opened his mouth, shut it again and smiled a little tightly. 'Thank you,' he said, and he probably would have stood there with that frozen smile on his face if Amelia hadn't elbowed him gently out of the way, opened the door wide and invited them in, because after all there was no choice, no matter how unhappy it might make him.

'You'll freeze,' she said with a smile. 'Come inside and join us.' And Jake would just have to cope, because anything else would have been too rude for words. And apparently he realised that, because he found another smile and stepped back.

'Yes—of course, come on in by the fire,' he said, and led them to the drawing room, where they gathered round the fire and sang all the old favourites—*Silent Night*, *Away In A Manger* and *O Come All Ye Faithful*, and then the vicar smilingly apologised for not having a chorister to sing *Once In Royal David's City*, and beside her Amelia felt Edward jiggle and she squeezed his shoulder in encouragement.

'Go on,' she murmured, and he took a step forwards.

'I could do it,' he offered, and the vicar looked at him and smiled broadly.

'Well—please do. Do you need the words?'

He shook his head, went over to them and started to sing.

Jake was speechless.

The boy's voice filled the room, pure and sweet, and he felt his throat close. It brought so much back—the pain of his childhood, the respite that music had brought him, the hard work but the immense rewards of being a chorister.

And when Edward got to the end of the first verse and everyone joined in, he found himself singing, too, found the voice he'd grown into as a man, rusty with lack of use and emotion, but warming up, filling him with joy again as he sang the familiar carol. And Edward looked at him in astonishment and then smiled, as if he'd just discovered something wonderful.

And maybe he had.

Maybe Jake had, too, because Edward had a truly beautiful voice and it would be a travesty if he didn't get the opportunity to develop and explore this musical gift. And if there was anything he could do to help with that, he wanted to do it, even if it was just to encourage him to join the school choir.

But in the meantime he sang, and the choir

launched into *God Rest Ye Merry Gentlemen*, which was perfect for his baritone, and so for the first time in years he dragged the air deep down into his lungs and let himself go, and the old house was filled with the joyful sound of their voices.

And Edward grinned, and he grinned back, and beside him he could see Amelia staring up at him in astonishment, her eyes like saucers, and Kitty too. When they got to the end they all smiled and laughed, and Amelia ran down to the kitchen and came back with a tray of mince pies she'd made earlier, and he offered them a drink to wash them down but they all refused.

'Sorry, we'd love to, but we have to get home,' was the consensus, and of course they did. It was Christmas Eve, and he'd been fitted in as a favour. A favour by people he didn't know, who'd heard he'd been hurt and had come to bring Christmas to him, and deep down inside, the fissure that was opening around his heart cracked open a little further, letting the warmth seep in.

'Thank you so much for coming,' he said with genuine feeling as he showed them out. 'The children have really enjoyed it. It was extremely kind of you, and I can't thank you enough.'

'Well, there's always the church roof,' the

vicar joked, and he laughed, but he made a mental note to send him a cheque. 'And if the boy wants to join us…'

'Ah, they're only visiting,' he said, and the words gave him a curious pang, as if somehow that was wrong and vaguely unsettling. 'But— yes, I agree. He could be a chorister.'

'As you were once, I would imagine. You could always join us yourself. The choir's always got room for a good voice.'

He smiled a little crookedly. 'My choir days are over—but thank you. Have a good Christmas, all of you. Good night.'

They left in a chorus of good-nights and merry Christmases, and he closed the door and turned to see Edward standing there staring at him.

'Did you really sing in a choir?' he asked warily, and Jake nodded.

'Yes, I did. When I was about your age, and a little older. My voice started to break when I was twelve, which rather put a stop to singing for a couple of years, and I never really got back into it after that, but—yeah, I went to choir school. What about you? Do you sing in a choir?'

'We didn't really have a choir at the school, but the music teacher said I ought to have a voice test somewhere. I was supposed to sing in the school

carol concert last week, but we had to move to
Auntie Laura's and it was too far away, so I
couldn't. And I'd been practising for weeks and
weeks.'

'I can tell. What a shame. Still, you did it for
us, and it was great. You did really well. Here,
come with me. I've got something to show you.'

'Is it a picture?'

'No. It's a film of me when I was in the choir.
I had to sing *Once In Royal David's City* myself
at the start of the carol service when I was twelve,
just before my voice broke.'

And it had been televised, but he didn't
mention that because it was irrelevant, really. He
took Edward into his sitting room, found the
DVD he'd had the old video copied onto, and
turned it on.

'Wow,' Edward said at the end of his solo, his
voice hushed. 'That was amazing. You must have
been so scared.'

He laughed. 'I was pretty terrified, I can tell
you. But it was worth it, it was fantastic. It was a
good time all round. Hard work, but lots of fun,
too, and I wouldn't have swapped it for the
world.'

He told him more about it, about the fun, about
the pranks he'd got up to and the trouble he'd got

in, and about the hard work and the gruelling schedule of rehearsals, but also about the amazing thrill and privilege of singing in the cathedral.

'I'd love to do that,' the boy said wistfully.

'Would you? It's a big commitment. I had to go to boarding school, but then I wasn't very happy at home, so actually I enjoyed it,' he found himself admitting.

'Why weren't you happy?' Edward asked.

'Oh—my parents used to row a lot, and I always seemed to be in the way. So it was quite nice when I wasn't, for all of us, really. But you are happy, aren't you?'

He nodded. 'And I couldn't leave Mummy, because she needs me.'

'Of course she does—but, you know, she also needs you to be happy, and if it made you happy—anyway, you don't have to go away to school. Most schools have a choir, and certainly the bigger churches do. I'm sure they'd be delighted to have you. You've got a good voice.'

'But we don't live anywhere properly, so we don't have a church or a school,' he said, and Jake's heart ached for the poor, uprooted child.

'You will soon,' he consoled him, hoping it was true, and he turned off the television and got to his feet. 'Now, you'd better run up to bed or I'm going to be in trouble with your mother. You sleep well, and I'll see you in the morning. Good night, Edward.'

'Good night,' Edward said, and then without warning he ran over to Jake, put his arms round him and hugged him before running out of the door. And Jake stood there, rooted to the spot, unravelled by the simple spontaneous gesture of a child.

Amelia stood in the shadows of the hall, scarcely able to breathe for emotion.

The sound of his voice had been exquisite, the sort of sound that made your hair stand on end and your heart swell, and she'd stood there and listened to it, then to his gentle and revealing conversation with her son, and her eyes had filled with tears. Poor little boy, to have felt so unwanted and unloved. And thank God for a choir school which had helped him through it, given him something beautiful and perfect to compensate in some small way for the disappointments of his young life.

She'd taken Kitty and Thomas upstairs when she'd seen Edward deep in conversation with Jake, knowing he missed the influence of a man in his life, and she'd bathed them quickly, tucked them up and gone back down—and heard the pure, sweet sound of a chorister coming from Jake's sitting room.

She hadn't known it was him until she'd heard him talking to Edward, but she wasn't surprised. It had been obvious when he'd joined in with the carol singers that he'd had some kind of voice training, as well as a beautiful voice, deep and rich and warm. It had shivered through her then, and it had done the same thing now, hearing him as a child.

And he was talking to Edward about it, treating him as an equal, encouraging him, giving him hope—

But too much hope, and it was pointless doing that, because there was no way she could afford any lessons or anything for him, so it was cruel of Jake to encourage him. It was easy if you had money. Everything was easier, and it wasn't fair to Edward to build him up. She'd have to talk to Jake, to stop him—

She dived into the kitchen and scrubbed the tears away from her eyes while she cleared up the aftermath of their supper, and then she took the presents she'd brought downstairs with her through to the drawing room—the few things she'd bought the children, and the ones from Kate, and of course the beautiful and inevitably expensive ones from her sister—and, by the time she got there, there were some others waiting.

They must be Jake's, she thought. Presents from friends, if not family, and people like Kate, who was bound to have given him a present.

But they weren't. They were for the children, and for her, and, of all things, for Rufus. Her eyes flooded with tears, and she sat back on her heels and sniffed.

Damn him, how could he do this? Squandering money on them all because it was so easy for him, not realising how much worse it made it all, how much harder it would be when it was all over and they came down to earth with a bump. He was even spoiling the wretched dog—

'Amelia?'

'What are these? You shouldn't—' she began, but he just shook his head.

'They're nothing—'

'No. They're not nothing,' she corrected tautly. 'They're nothing to you, but believe me, you have no idea what nothing's like. Nothing is not having anywhere for your children to live, having to take them away from school just before the carol concert your son's been practising for for weeks, having to tell them that Daddy doesn't have any money and he's not even here to see them because he's run away from the law—except of course I can't tell them that, can I, because it wouldn't be fair, so I have to pretend he's just had to go away and lie to them, and I'm sick of lying to them and struggling and the last—absolutely the *last* damn thing I need is you telling Edward he should go to choir school. I'll never be able to afford it and you'll just build his hopes up and then they'll be dashed and it's just another disappointment in his life—'

She couldn't go on, tears streaming down her cheeks, and he gave a ragged sigh and crouched awkwardly down beside her, his hand gentle on her shoulder, his eyes distressed. 'Amelia—Millie—please don't,' he murmured softly. 'It wasn't like that. I didn't build his hopes up, but he's good, and there are places—'

'Didn't you *hear* what I said?' she raged. '*We have no money!*'

'But you don't need money. He could get a scholarship, like I did. My parents didn't pay. If someone's got talent, they don't turn them away—and there are other things. It doesn't have to be choir school. Just because I went there doesn't mean it's right for everyone. It's very hard, and the hours are really long, and you work every Sunday, Christmas Day, Easter—you have to be dedicated, it's a massive commitment, and it's not for everybody—'

'No, it's not, but even if it was for him, it's not for you to decide! He's my son, Jake—*mine*! It's none of your business! You have no right to take him off like that and fill his head with ideas—'

'It wasn't like that! He was asking…I just thought…'

'Well, don't! If you want a son to follow in your footsteps, then get your own, Jake, but leave mine out of it! And we don't need your flashy presents!'

And, without giving him a chance to reply, she scrambled to her feet and ran into the kitchen, tears pouring down her face and furious with herself as well as him because, whatever he'd done, whatever he'd spent or said, they were in his house against his wishes, and he'd busted a gut today to make their Christmas Day tomorrow a good one, and now she'd gone and ruined it for all of them…

# CHAPTER SIX

IF YOU want a son…

His legs gave way and he sat down abruptly on the rug in front of the tree, her words ringing in his ears.

It had never occurred to him he was doing any harm by talking to Edward, showing him the recording. He was just sharing an interest, taking an interest—and not because he wanted a son to follow in his footsteps. He'd been there, done that, and lost everything. She thought he didn't know what nothing meant? Well, he had news for her.

Nothing meant waking up every morning alone, with nobody to share your day with, nobody to help you live out your dreams, nobody to love, nobody to love you in return.

Nothing meant standing in a cold and lonely churchyard staring at a headstone bearing the names of the only people in the world you cared about and wondering how on earth it had happened, how one minute they'd been there, and the next they'd been gone for ever.

If you want a son…

Pain seared through him. *Oh, Ben, I want you. I want you every day. What would you have been like? Would you have loved singing, like me, or would you have been tone-deaf like your mother? Tall or short? Quiet or noisy? I would have loved you, whatever. I'll always love you.* He glanced out of the window and saw a pale swirl of snow, and his heart contracted. *Are you cold tonight, my precious son, lying there in the churchyard?*

Oh, God.

A sob ripped through him and he stifled it, battening it down, refusing to allow it to surface. She hadn't meant to hurt him. She hadn't known about Ben, hadn't realised what she was saying. And maybe she was right. Maybe he'd overstepped the mark with Edward.

He needed to talk to her, to go and find her and apologise—but not yet. Not now. Now, he needed to get himself under control, to let the pain recede a little.

And then he became aware of Rufus, standing just a few inches away from him, his tail down, his eyes worried, and when he held out his hand, the dog's tail flickered briefly.

'Oh, Rufus. What's happened to us all?' he murmured unsteadily, and Rufus came and sat down with his side against Jake's thigh, and rested his head in his lap and licked his hand.

'Yeah, I know. I need to talk to Amelia. I need to tell her I'm sorry. But I can't—'

He bit his lip, and Rufus licked him again, and he ruffled his fur and waited a little longer, until his emotions were back under control, because he owed Amelia more than just an apology. He owed her an explanation, and it would mean opening himself to her, to her pity, and he never ever did that. It was just too damned hard.

But eventually he couldn't leave it any longer, so he got stiffly to his feet, found the whisky and limped down the hall to the breakfast room and pushed open the door.

She was sitting in front of the fire, her legs drawn up and her arms wrapped round her knees, and he could tell she'd been crying. Her face was ravaged with tears, her eyes wide with distress. He went over to her, poured two hefty measures of spirit and held one out to her.

'I'm sorry,' he said. 'I should have thought— should have asked you before showing it to him.'

'No. You were only being kind. I was so rude—'

'Yes, you were, but I'm not surprised, with everything going on in your life. You're just fighting their corner. I can't criticise you for that.'

And then, before his courage failed him and he chickened out, he said, 'I had a son.'

She lifted her head and stared at him.

'Had?' she whispered in horrified disbelief.

'Ben. He died five years ago—five years yesterday, just a month after his second birthday. He'd been Christmas shopping with my wife, Rachel, and they were by the entrance to the car park when someone mounted the kerb and hit them. They were both killed instantly.'

'Oh, Jake—'

Her voice was hardly more than a breath, and then she dragged in a shuddering sob and pressed her hand against her lips. Dear God, what had she said to him? If you want a son…then get your own. And all the time—

'Oh, Jake, I don't know what to say—'

'Don't say anything. There's nothing you can say. Here, have a drink. And please don't worry about the presents, they really are nothing. It was just a gesture, nothing more. They aren't lavish,

I promise, so you don't have to worry. I wouldn't do that to you. I just…it's Christmas, and I'd expect to give something small to any child who was staying here. And I promise not to say anything more to any of them that might give you a problem later on. So come on, drink up and let's go and stuff the turkey, otherwise we'll be eating at midnight.'

She hauled in a breath, sniffed and scrubbed her cheeks with her hands. 'You're right. We've got a lot to do.' And just then she couldn't talk to him, couldn't say another word or she really would howl her eyes out, and so she sipped the whisky he pressed into her hand, feeling the slow burn as it slid down her throat, letting the warmth drive out the cold horror of his simple words.

No wonder he didn't do children. No wonder he hadn't been pleased to see them in his house, on the very anniversary…

She took a gulp and felt it scorch down her throat. What had it done to him, to come home and find them all there? His words had been cruel, but not as cruel as their presence must have been to him. And her own words—they'd been far more cruel, so infinitely hurtful, and there was nothing she could do to take them back.

'What I said—'

'Don't. Don't go there, Amelia. You weren't to know. Forget it.'

But she couldn't, and she knew she never would. She couldn't bear the thought that she'd hurt him with her words, that their presence in his house must be tearing him apart, but there was nothing she could do about it now—the words were said, the children were sleeping upstairs, and all she could do was make sure it all went as well and smoothly as possible, and kept the children away from him so they didn't rub salt in his wound.

'I'm going to get on,' she said, and she set the glass down and stood up, brushed herself off mentally and physically, and headed for the kitchen.

'We still haven't dealt with the decorations in here,' he said from behind her, and she looked up at their makeshift decorations in the light fitting over the breakfast table, still half-finished and looking bedraggled and forlorn.

Damn. 'I'm sorry, I meant to take them down,' she said, tugging out a chair, but he just shook his head.

'No. Leave them. The children made them.'

She stopped, one foot on the chair, the other on the table, and looked down at him.

'But—you said it was tat. And you were right, it is.'

'No. I'm sorry. I was just feeling rough and you took me by surprise,' he said, master of the understatement. 'Please, leave them. In fact, weren't there some more bits?'

She nodded and climbed slowly down off the chair. 'Edward put them out of the back door.'

'Get them and put them in—finish it off. And I'll put the wreath we bought on the front door. And then we ought to do the things you need help with, and then I'm really going to have to turn in, because I'm bushed, frankly. It's been a long day, and I've had enough.'

She felt another great wave of guilt. 'Oh, Jake—sit down, let me get you another drink. I can do everything. Please—just sit there and rest and keep me company, if you really want to help, or otherwise just go to bed. I can manage.'

He smiled wryly. 'I'm sure you can. I get the feeling there's not a lot you can't manage. But I'm OK.'

And he helped her, even though he must be feeling pretty rough, because she got the distinct impression that he didn't give up easily. So she made them both a cup of tea, and finished off the decorations in the light fitting while he put the wreath on the door. Then he sat down in the chair to drink his tea while she stuffed the turkey and wrapped the sausages in bacon, and the next time she looked he'd leant back and closed his eyes, with Rufus curled up on his lap and his legs stretched out in front of the fire. She made another batch of mince pies and peeled potatoes and carrots and trimmed the sprouts while they cooked, and then she woke him up and sent him to bed.

It was almost Christmas Day, she thought as she tiptoed into the children's room and hung their stockings on the end of their beds. Nothing like what they'd had last year or the year before, but they were good kids and they understood, in their way, and thanks to Jake they had tiny oranges and chocolates and little bits of this and that to add to her offerings.

And at least they were alive, unlike Jake's little boy.

She stared down at Edward. He was a little older than Ben would have been, she realised with a pang. How painful it must be for Jake, knowing that. How could she have said what she did? How did he cope with the terrible loss? How did anyone?

Edward's face blurred, and she kissed him lightly on the cheek, snuggling the quilt up round him, then tucked Kitty in and went to check on Thomas. He didn't have a stocking, but he was only eight months old, he didn't even know what Christmas was yet. And at least he was in a warm, comfortable house.

They were so lucky. They could have been anywhere, and instead they were here, warm and safe—and, without Jake, it would have been so much worse. He'd done so much for them, and she'd repaid him by throwing his kindness back in his face. And not just his kindness.

*If you want a son...*

Tears scalded her cheeks, and she scrubbed them away. She could never take those words back, but she owed him more than she could ever repay, and she vowed to do everything in her power to make it right.

Starting with giving him a Christmas to remember...

'Mummy—Mummy, it's snowing!'

She opened her eyes a crack, but it was still dark—except for a strange light that filtered through the gap in the curtains.

'Kitty, whatever's the time?' she whispered.

'It's nearly six—Mummy, get up and come and *see*! It's so pretty!'

She let Kitty drag her out of bed and over to the window, and sure enough, the garden was blanketed with snow, thick and crisp and brilliant white, eerie in the moonlight.

Whatever time was it? The last thing she wanted was for the children to disturb Jake in the middle of the night! She peered at her watch anxiously. 'Kitty, it's only half past five!'

'No, it's not, it's after, 'cos I waited! And we've got stockings! Come and see!'

'Is Edward awake?'

'Of course I'm awake,' her sleepy, rumpled son said as he came in. 'She's been whispering at me for hours! Happy Christmas, Mummy,' he added with a smile and went into her arms, hugging her hard.

She bent her head and pressed a kiss to his hair, knowing the time for such liberties was probably numbered and enjoying it while she could, and then she scooped Kitty up and kissed her, too, and carried her back into their bedroom, closing the door to keep the noise down.

She snuggled into Amelia's side for a moment, but then wriggled down and ran to her bed. 'Can we open our stockings now?' she asked excitedly.

'All right,' she agreed reluctantly. 'But just the

stockings. Nothing under the tree until later.'
Much later!

'Are there presents under the tree? Did you see
them?' Kitty asked, wide-eyed and eager, and
Millie could have kicked herself for mentioning
it.

'I expect there might be,' she said. *Unless
there have been burglars.* 'But you can't go
down and look until much, much later, in case
you disturb Jake.'

And that wasn't going to happen if she had
anything to do with it.

'How much later?' Kitty asked, persistent to
the last, and she rolled her eyes and laughed
softly.

'Half past eight,' she said, 'and that's only if
Jake's awake. And if you wake him by making
too much noise, then you'll have to wait till ten,'
she added, trying to look stern.

'Ten?' Kitty wailed softly, and scrambled onto
the bed. 'I'll be very, very quiet,' she vowed.
'Edward, don't make a noise!'

'I haven't said a thing!' he whispered indig-
nantly, climbing onto his own bed and sliding a
hand down inside his stocking. 'You're the one
making all the noise—'

'Stop that, or the stockings go.'

There was instant silence, broken only by the tiny squeals of excitement from Kitty and the murmured, 'Oh, brilliant!' from Edward when he found a page-a-day diary. He flashed her a huge smile, and she felt a lump in her throat. It was such a little thing, but since David had left he'd kept a diary every day, and she knew he was using it as a way of working through his feelings.

He was such a good kid—and Jake was right, he deserved every chance. She'd look into getting him that voice test, but she was so afraid of tempting fate, of dangling something under his nose and then having it snatched away yet again.

'A chocolate Father Christmas!' Kitty said in delight, delving deeper. 'And a satsuma! Can I eat them now? Pretty please with a cherry on top?'

She sat down with a chuckle on the end of the bed and watched as her children found innocent pleasure in the simplest things. Then Edward looked up with hopeful eyes and said, 'Can we make a snowman?'

It was on the tip of her tongue to say, Of course, when she remembered it wasn't her garden, and she smiled ruefully.

'We'll have to ask Jake,' she said.

Edward nodded and went back to his orange, peeling it meticulously and savouring it segment by segment. He was so thorough, so methodical in everything he did. So very unlike his father, who rushed into everything without thought. And out of it again. Like marriage. And fatherhood.

No, she wasn't going to think about that now. She could hear Thomas starting to stir, and she went back and scooped him out of his cot and gave him a hug. 'Hello, my little man!' she crooned softly. 'Happy Christmas. Look, Thomas—it's snowing!'

And, lifting the curtain aside, she looked out into the garden and saw Jake standing out there with Rufus, racing around in the snow and barking his head off as he tried to bite the snow-flakes, while Jake laughed at him.

She chuckled and stood there for a moment watching them. Then, as if his eyes had been drawn to hers, Jake turned and looked up and waved.

She waved back and went in to the children. 'Jake's awake,' she said, 'so I'm going to go down and make a cup of tea and get a bottle for Thomas. Why don't you try and get back to sleep?'

'But we have to say Happy Christmas to Jake!' Kitty said, and ran for the stairs before Amelia could stop her. Edward followed, the two of them thundering and whooping down through the house, and she trailed after them with Thomas, hoping that the onslaught of the children wouldn't prove to be too much for him. Especially now that she knew—

She felt the shadow of his grief fall over the day, and paused a moment to think of a little boy she'd never known and would never have the chance to meet, and the woman who should have been greeting her husband and son here in this house this morning.

'I'm so sorry,' she whispered. 'So, so sorry.'

And then she followed the others downstairs to the kitchen.

It was freezing outside, but there was something wonderful about standing in the snow while Rufus raced round like a puppy and chased the snowflakes.

And as he went back in, the children tumbled into the kitchen, eyes sparkling with excitement, and Kitty ran over to him and reached up. He bent and hugged her, feeling the warm, damp kiss land on his cheek. 'Happy Christmas,' she said, her arms tight around his neck for a second, then she let him go and laughed, and he looked up and met her brother's eyes and remembered last night's spontaneous hug and smiled at him.

'Happy Christmas, Kitty. Happy Christmas, Edward,' he said.

His reply was drowned out by Kitty, plucking at his sleeve and giggling. 'You're all snowy!' she said. 'Like a snowman! Can we make a snowman?'

She was jumping up and down, her enthusiasm infectious, and he grinned down at her. 'Sure. It's great snow for that. It'll stick together. We can do it after we've opened the presents and had breakfast. Well, if that's all right with your mother—'

He looked up and met her eyes, and felt warmth uncurl deep inside him at her smile.

'Of course it's all right. It'll be fun. We can do it whenever you like. But maybe we need to get dressed first.'

'Oh, I don't know, it might be fun for the little cats on your pyjamas to play in the snow,' he teased, and a soft wash of colour swept her cheeks.

'Don't be silly,' she said, a trifle breathlessly, and he felt a totally inappropriate surge of longing.

'Can we make a really huge one?' Edward was asking, and Jake nodded, touched at the grin that blossomed on his usually serious young face.

'The biggest.'

'In the *world*?' Kitty said, her eyes like saucers, and he laughed.

'Well—maybe not *quite*.'

'He'll need a hat.'

'I might have a ski hat he can borrow,' Jake suggested. 'And a scarf.'

'And some coal for his eyes and a carrot for his nose—Mummy, have we got a carrot?'

Amelia threw up her hands and laughed. 'Kitty, slow down! Yes, we've got a carrot. You watched me buy them.'

'Awesome,' she said. 'So can we open the presents now? You said we had to wait till Jake was awake, but he's awake already, so can we go and do it now, and then we can get dressed and go and build our snowman?'

Catching the look on her face, Jake intervened rapidly. 'No, it's too early. Let your mother have a cup of tea and feed the baby. I tell you what,' he went on, watching their faces fall, 'why don't you go and see if you can guess what they are? We'll come through in a minute.'

And, as they ran excitedly out of the room, he met Amelia's eyes and they both let out their breath on a soft laugh.

'Kids,' he said, and she nodded, her smile

touched with sadness. On his behalf, he realised, and wanted to hug her. Nothing to do with those crazy cat pyjamas under a baggy old jumper that made him want to peel it off over her head and unwrap her as his very own Christmas present.

He cleared his throat. 'Right, how about that tea?'

'Sounds great. What on earth are you doing up this early, by the way?' she added as he went over to the kettle, and she sounded slightly amazed.

'Making tea, letting the dog out.'

'I'm sorry, I didn't hear him.'

'He didn't make a sound, but I was awake and I wanted to see the snow.'

'You surprise me. I wouldn't have thought you were best friends with snow at the moment.'

He chuckled. 'It wasn't the snow's fault. It was the idiot skiing up above me, but we were well off piste and if I hadn't had an avalanche kit with airbags to help me float on the snow cloud, it would have been very different. So, not the snow at fault, just someone who didn't know what they were doing, and anyway, it isn't often we have a white Christmas. Besides, I was already awake.'

She made a soft sound of sympathy. 'Couldn't you sleep?'

'On the contrary,' he told her, pouring their tea.

'I didn't think I'd sleep, but actually I slept better than I have for ages.'

'It must have been the whisky.'

'Maybe,' he agreed, but he knew it wasn't.

It had been the warmth—the human warmth from having a family in a house so obviously built with families in mind. And the fact that it had been a good day, and he'd enjoyed it. Well, most of it. The supermarket had been pretty hellish, but even that had had its high points. 'Here—' he said, handing her some tea, 'and there's a bottle for the baby cooling by the sink.'

'Oh, you star, thank you,' she said softly, sounding stunned. 'You didn't have to do that.'

'I knew he'd be awake soon. I made it according to the directions, so I hope it's all right and not too weak or strong. And it might still be a bit hot.'

'No, it's fine,' she said with a smile that threatened to send him into meltdown. Damn. Last night she was ripping him to shreds, and today he just wanted to undress her and carry her off to bed.

He took a step away and pretended to check the temperature on the Aga. 'What time do you want to put the turkey in?'

'It needs four hours in a moderate oven.'

He frowned at her. 'What does that mean?' he asked, and she laughed, the soft sound running through him like teasing fingertips.

'It means not too hot and not too cold. I'm sure it'll be fine. We've got ages. Why don't we go and see what the children are doing before they "accidentally" tear the paper?'

He chuckled and followed her, the dog trotting between them, not sure if he should be with the woman who fed him and loved him, or this new friend who'd taken him out in the magical white stuff and played with him. It occurred to Jake that he was having a good time—that, although he'd thought this would be his worst nightmare, in fact he was enjoying himself.

And that, in itself, was an amazing Christmas present.

He'd been wrong.

His presents weren't nothing. They were thoughtfully chosen, simple but absolutely perfect. Laura's had been extravagant, as she'd guessed, and just made her feel guilty and inadequate, and Kate's were very simple and sweet, the children's handmade by Megan, and an outrageous pair of frivolous lacy knickers for her to cheer her up, apparently—only she'd opened

them in front of Jake and turned bright red with
embarrassment and stuffed them in her pocket.

Her presents to the children had been things
they needed, because there simply wasn't the
money for anything else, but his—they were just
fun, and the children were delighted.

'Oh, Mummy, look! It's that book I wanted!'
Kitty said, eyes sparkling, and Millie looked up
and met Jake's wary eyes and smiled apologeti-
cally.

'So it is. You'll have to be careful with the
glitter, it goes everywhere. Say—'

But she didn't need to finish, because Kitty
had thrown herself at Jake and hugged him hard.
Very hard—hard enough to make him wince, but
he was smiling, so she didn't think he minded.

'Edward, what's that?' she asked, watching her
meticulous son peel away the last bit of wrapping
and reveal his present.

'It's a kit to build all sorts of things—it's brilliant. Thank you, Jake!' her son said, and although
he didn't hug him, his eyes were shining and she
could see Jake was pleased that he'd got it right.

So very, very right. 'Thomas, look at this!' she
exclaimed, unwrapping the shape sorter and
giving it to him, and he picked it up and shook it
and laughed happily.

'Tull!' he said, and Jake's face creased in bewilderment.

'Tull?'

'He thinks it's a rattle,' Edward explained. 'Look, Thomas, it opens, and you can put these bits in. See this one? It's a square. Look!'

And Thomas stared, fascinated, as the little shape went into the hole as if by magic, and Jake stared, just as fascinated, it seemed, and Millie blinked away the tears and looked back under the tree. There were still two presents there, and Kitty dived under and pulled them out.

'This is for Rufus, and this one's for you,' she said, handing Millie a soft, squashy parcel.

'Me?' she said, horribly conscious that she hadn't bought him anything, or made him anything or in fact done anything except make his already difficult life even harder.

She swallowed and met his eyes, and he smiled tentatively. 'Go on, open it. It's only silly.'

'I haven't—'

'Shh. Open it.'

So she did, and when she saw the fingerless mitts that could turn into proper mittens, her eyes filled. He'd listened to what she'd said about not being able to do anything with gloves on, and he'd found her a solution.

A silly, crazy pink solution, with a matching scarf that was soft and cosy and gorgeous, and her eyes flooded with tears that she could no longer hold back.

'You've made Mummy cry,' Kitty said, staring at her, and Edward looked at her worriedly, but she dredged up a smile and scrubbed her cheeks with the heels of her hands and met Jake's eyes.

'I'm fine, really. Thank you, Jake. Thank you for everything.'

'My pleasure,' he said. 'What about the dog's?'

'I hope it's not food.'

'It's not food. Here, open it,' he said, handing it to her, and she knelt up beside him and tore off the paper and her eyes filled again.

'It's a coat!' she said, choked. 'Oh, thank you, he's been miserable in the cold and he hates the rain. Oh, that's lovely.'

And then, because she couldn't hold back any longer, she leant over and hugged him. Not as hard as Kitty, careful of his bruises, but hard enough that he would know she really meant it.

And he hugged her back, his arms warm and hard and strong around her, and it would have been so easy to sink into them and stay there for the rest of the day.

The rest of her life.

No!

She straightened up, blinking away fresh tears and scrambling to her feet. 'Right, let's put all this paper in the bin and tidy up, and then we need to get dressed, and come back down and have breakfast, and then we've got the world's biggest snowman to build!'

# CHAPTER SEVEN

IT WAS the most magical day.

They'd all gone upstairs to wash and dress, and Jake had called her back and asked her to help him.

'I could do with a shower, but I don't want to get the new cast wet and I didn't do so well yesterday. Could you tape this bag over my arm?'

'Of course,' she said, putting Thomas on the floor, and he handed her the bag and some tape, and then shucked off his robe so he was standing in front of her in nothing more than snug-fitting jersey boxers that sent her heart rate rocketing. Until she saw his bruises, and they took her breath away.

'Oh, Jake—you're black and blue!'

He smiled wryly. 'Tell me about it. Still, I'm alive. It could have been worse. And it's better today.'

She wasn't convinced, but she stuck the bag on his arm and stood back, trying not to look at him and not really succeeding, because her eyes were relentlessly drawn to his taut, well-muscled chest with its scatter of dark curls, to the strong, straight legs with their spectacular muscles and equally spectacular bruises. 'Can you manage now?' she asked, trying to sound businesslike and obviously failing, because his right eyebrow twitched.

'Why?' he asked, his voice low and his eyes dancing with mischief. 'Are you offering to wash my back?'

'On second thoughts,' she said and, scooping Thomas up, she left him to it and concentrated—barely—on dressing her children and making breakfast for them all before she put Thomas down for a nap and they wrapped up warmly and went out into the snow.

The snowman was huge—probably not the biggest in the world, but huge for all that—and Jake had found his old ski hat and scarf and they'd raided the fridge for a carrot—and two sprouts for his eyes, 'because,' Kitty said, 'they're too disgusting to eat.' Edward found a twig that looked like a pipe to stick in his mouth. Then, when the snowman was finished, standing in pride of place outside the breakfast room window so he could watch them eat, they came back inside, hung their coats in the boiler room to dry, and settled down by the fire in the drawing room to watch a film while they warmed up.

She flitted between the film and the kitchen, making sure everything was set in motion at the right time like a military operation and laying the table in the breakfast room, because, as Jake said, the dining room was too formal for having fun in. Not to mention too beautiful for Thomas to hurl his dinner across the room or for Kitty to 'accidentally' shoot peas off the edge of her plate for the dog to find, and anyway, it was a long way from the kitchen.

So she put out the crackers and the cutlery and the jolly red and green paper napkins with reindeer on, and a big white pillar candle they'd bought in the supermarket standing on a red plate. In between doing that and checking on the meal, she sat with her family and Jake, squeezing up next to Edward, while Thomas sat wedged between him and Jake, and Kitty had found herself a little place on Jake's lap, with his arm round her and her head on his shoulder and her thumb in her mouth. The next time she came in he had Thomas on his lap instead, standing on his leg and trying to climb over the arm of the sofa.

'I think he's bored,' Jake said softly, and Thomas looked up at her and beamed and held up his arms, and she scooped him up and hugged him.

'Hungry too, probably.'

'Is it lunchtime yet?' Kitty asked hopefully. 'I'm *starving*!'

'Nearly.'

'Can I help?'

Could he? Could she cope with him in the kitchen, that strong, hard, battered body so close to hers in the confined space?

She nearly laughed. What was she thinking about? It wasn't confined, it was huge—but it had seemed confined this morning, while he was making her tea and she was in the pyjamas he'd teased her about and he was in a robe with melted snow on the shoulders and dripping off his hair and those curiously sexy bare feet planted squarely on the tiled floor.

And now she knew what had been under that robe, it would be all the harder...

'I don't really know what you can do,' she said, but he followed her anyway, and he managed one-handed to make himself very useful. He helped lift the turkey out of the dish, entertained Thomas while she warmed his lunch, and then blew on it and fed him while she made the gravy and put everything out into the serving dishes he'd found for her.

'Lunch!' she called, sticking her head round the door, and they came pelting down the hall and skidded into the breakfast room.

'Oh, it looks really pretty!' Kitty said. Jake lit the candle and she carried in the turkey and knew how Tiny Tim's mother must have felt when Scrooge gave them the goose.

The food was delicious, and the children piled in, eating themselves to a standstill, and still there was enough there to feed an army.

'I hope you've got a nice line in leftover recipes,' Jake murmured as he carried it out to the kitchen and put it on the side, making her laugh.

'Oh, I have. I can turn anything into a meal. Have you got any brandy to put over the pudding?'

'I have—and holly. I picked it this morning. Here.'

He turned off the lights, and she carried in the flaming pudding by candlelight, making the children ooh and aah. Then, when they couldn't manage another mouthful, they cleared the table and put on their warm, dry coats and went back out in the garden for a walk, with Rufus in his smart new tartan coat and Thomas snuggled on her hip in his all-in-one suit. When the children had run around and worked off their lunch and the adults had strolled all down the long walk from the house towards the woods, they turned back.

And, right in the middle of the lawn outside the bay window, Kitty stopped.

'We have to make snow angels!' she said. 'Come on, everybody!'

'Snow angels?' Jake said, his voice taut, and Millie looked at him worriedly. Was this another memory they were trampling on? Oh, dear lord—

'Yes—all of us! Come on, Jake, you're the biggest, you can be the daddy angel!'

And, oblivious to the shocked reluctance on his face, she dragged him by the arm, made him lie down, and lay down beside him with her arms and legs outstretched and fanned them back and forth until she'd cleared the snow, and then she got up, laughing and pulled him to his feet.

'Look! You're so big!' she said with a giggle. 'Mummy, you lie down there on the other side, and then Edward, and Thomas, too—'

'Not Thomas, darling, he's too small, he doesn't understand.'

'Well, Jake can hold him while you and Edward make your snow angels,' she said, bossy and persistent to the last. She looked into Jake's eyes and saw gentle resignation.

'I'll take him,' he said softly and, reaching out, he scooped him onto his right hip and held him firmly, one-handed, while she and Edward carved out their shapes in the snow, and then she took her baby back and they went inside to look, shedding their wet clothes all over again, only this time their trousers were wet as well, and they had to go up and change.

'Hey, you guys, come and look,' Jake called from his room, and they followed him in and stood in the bay window looking down on the little row of snow angels.

'That's so pretty!' Kitty said. 'Jake, take a picture!'

So he got out his phone and snapped a picture, then went along the landing and took another of the snowman. Afterwards they all went downstairs again and Kitty got out her book, and Edward got out the construction kit, and they set them up at the far end of the breakfast table and busied themselves while she loaded the dishwasher and cleared up the pots and pans.

There was no sign of Jake, but at least Thomas in his cot had stopped grizzling and settled into sleep.

Or so she thought, until Jake appeared in the doorway with her little son on his hip.

'He's a bit sorry for himself,' Jake said with a tender smile, and handed him over. 'Why don't you sit down and I'll make you a cup of tea?'

'Because I'm supposed to be looking after you and all you've done is make me tea!'

'You've been on your feet all day. Go on, shoo. I'll do it. Anyway, I can't sit, I'm too full.'

She laughed at that, and took Thomas through to the breakfast room, put him in his high chair with his shape sorter puzzle and sat down with the children while she waited for her tea.

'Mummy, I can't do this. I can't work it out,' Edward said, staring at the instructions and the zillions of pieces he was trying to put together. It was complicated—more complicated than anything he'd tackled yet, but she was sure he'd be able to do it.

And how clever of Jake to realise that he was very bright, she thought, as she saw the kit was for older children. Bright and brave and hugely talented in all sorts of ways, and yet his father couldn't see it—just saw a quiet child with nothing to say for himself and no apparent personality.

Well, it was his loss, she thought, but of course

it wasn't—it was Edward's, too, that he was so undervalued by the man who should have been so proud of him, should have nurtured and encouraged him. It wouldn't have occurred to David to look into choir school. He would have thought it was sissy.

But there was nothing—*nothing*—sissy about Jake. In fact he was a lot like Edward—thorough, meticulous, paying attention to detail, noticing the little things, fixing stuff, making it right.

The nurturer, she realised, and wondered if he'd spent his childhood trying to stick his family back together again when clearly, from what she'd overheard, it had been broken beyond repair. How sad that when he'd found his own, it had been torn away from him.

And then he came out and sat down with them all, on the opposite side of the table, and slid the tea across to her. Edward looked up at him and said, 'Can you give me a hand?'

'Sure. What's the problem?' he asked, and bent his head over the instructions, sorted through the pieces and found the missing bit. 'I think this needs to go in here,' he said, and handed it to Edward. Didn't take over, didn't do it for him, did just enough to help him on his way and then sat back and let him do it.

He did, of course, bit by bit, with the occasional input from Jake to keep him on the straight and narrow, but there was a worrying touch of hero worship in his voice. She only hoped they could all get through this and emerge unscathed without too many broken hopes and dreams, because, although Jake was doing nothing she could fault, Edward was lapping up every moment of his attention, desperate for a father figure in his life, for a man who understood him.

And she was dreading the day they moved out, to wherever they ended up, and she had to take him away from Jake.

She doubted Jake was dreading it. He was putting up with the invasion of his privacy with incredible fortitude, but she had no doubts at all that he'd be glad when they left and he could settle back into his own routine without all the painful reminders.

Sadly, she didn't think it would be any time soon, but all too quickly reality was going to intervene and she'd have to start sending out her CV again and trying to get another job. Maybe Jake would let her use the Internet so she could do that.

But not now. It was Christmas, and she was

going to keep smiling and make sure everyone enjoyed it.

Jake included.

He thought the day would never end.

It had been fun—much more fun than he could have imagined—but it was also painful. Physically, because he was still sore from his encounter with the trees and the rocks in France, and emotionally, because the kids were great and it just underlined exactly what he'd lost.

And until that day, he'd avoided thinking about it, had shut his heart and his mind to such thoughts.

But he couldn't shut them out any more; they seeped in, like light round the edges of a blind, and while Millie was putting the children to bed he went into his little sitting room and closed the door. There was a video of them all taken on Ben's second birthday, and he'd never watched it again, but it was there, tormenting him.

So he put it on, and he watched his little son and the wife he'd loved to bits laughing into the camera, and he let the tears fall. Healing tears—tears that washed away the pain and left bittersweet memories of happier days. Full days.

Days like today.

And then he took the DVD out and put it away again, and lay down on the sofa and dozed. He was tired, he realised. He'd slept well last night, but not for long, and today had been a long day. He'd go to bed later, but for now he was comfortable, and if he kept out of the way Amelia wouldn't feel she had to talk to him when she'd rather be doing something—probably anything—else.

She'd done well. Brilliantly. The meal had been fabulous, and he was still full. Maybe he'd have a sandwich later, start on the pile of cold turkey that would be on the menu into the hereafter. Turkey and cold stuffing and cranberry sauce.

But later. Not now. Now, he was sleeping…

'That was the *best* day,' Edward said, snuggling down under the quilt and smiling at her. 'Jake's really cool.'

'He's been very kind,' she said, wondering how she could take Jake gently off this pedestal without shattering Edward's illusions, 'but we are in his way.'

'He doesn't seem to mind.'

'That's because he's a very kind man, very generous.'

'That's what Kate said—that he was generous.'

He rolled onto his back and folded his arms under his head. 'Did you know he went to choir school?'

'Yes—I heard him tell you,' she said. 'I'd just come downstairs.'

'He said it was great. Hard work, but he loved it there. He was a boarder, did you know that? He had to sleep there, but he said his mum and dad used to fight, and he was always in the way, so it was good, really.'

She was just opening her mouth to comment when Edward went on diffidently, 'Were we in the way? Was that why Dad left?'

Her heart aching, she hugged him. 'No, darling. He left because he realised he didn't love me any more, and it wouldn't have been right to stay.'

He hadn't loved the children either, but there was no way she was telling Edward that his father had used them as a lever to get her to agree to things she wouldn't otherwise have countenanced. Things like remortgaging their house so riskily, because otherwise, he said, they'd be homeless.

Well, they were homeless now, and he'd had to flee the country to escape the debt, so a lot of good it had done to prolong it. And why on earth she'd let him back last year so that she'd ended up pregnant again, she couldn't imagine. She must have been insane, and he'd gone again long before she'd realised about the baby.

Not that she'd send Thomas back, not for a moment, but life had become infinitely more complicated with another youngster.

She'd have to work on her CV, she thought, and wondered what Jake was doing and if he'd let her use the Internet to download a template so she could lay it out better.

'You need to go to sleep,' she said softly, and bent over and kissed Edward's cheek. 'Come on, snuggle down.'

'Can we play in the snow again tomorrow?' he asked sleepily, and she nodded.

'Of course—if it's still there.'

'It will be. Jake said.'

And if Jake had said…

She went out and pulled the door to, leaving the landing light on for them, and after checking on the sleeping baby she went back downstairs, expecting to find Jake in the breakfast room or the drawing room.

But he wasn't, and his study door was open, and his bedroom door had been wide open, too.

Which left his little sitting room. His cave, the

place to which he retreated from the world when it all became too much.

She didn't like to disturb him, so she put her laptop in the breakfast room and tidied up the kitchen. The children had had a snack, and she was pretty sure that Jake would want something later, so she made a pile of sandwiches with freshly cut bread, and wrapped them in cling film and put them in the fridge ready for him. Then she put Rufus's new coat on and took him out into the snow for a run around.

He should have been used to it, he'd been outside several times today, but still he raced around and barked and tried to bite it, and she stood there feeling the cold seep into her boots and laughed at him as he played.

And then she turned and saw Jake standing in the window of his sitting room, watching her with a brooding expression on his face, and she felt her heart miss a beat.

Their eyes locked, and she couldn't breathe, frozen there in time, waiting for—

What? For him to summon her? To call her to him, to ask her to join him?

Then he glanced away, his gaze caught by the dog, and she could breathe again.

'Rufus!' she called, and she took him back inside,

dried his paws on an old towel and took off her snowy boots and left them by the Aga to dry off. And as she straightened up, he came into the kitchen.

'Hi. All settled?'

She nodded. 'Yes. Yes, they're all settled. I wasn't sure if you'd be hungry, so I made some sandwiches.'

'Brilliant. Thanks. I was just coming to do that, but I wasn't sure if I could cut the bread with one hand. It's all a bit awkward.'

'Done,' she said, opening the fridge and lifting them out. 'Do you want them now, or later?'

'Now?' he said. 'Are you going to join me? I thought maybe we could have a glass of wine and a little adult conversation.'

His smile was wry, and she laughed softly, her whole body responding to the warmth in his eyes.

'That would be lovely,' she said, and found some plates while he opened the bottle of red they'd started the night before last and poured two glasses, and they carried them through to the breakfast room, but then he hesitated.

'Come and slum it with me on the sofa,' he suggested, to her surprise, and she followed him through to the other room and sat down at one end while he sprawled into the other corner, his sore leg—well, the sorer of the two, if the bruises were anything to go by—stretched out so that his foot was almost touching her thigh.

And they ate their sandwiches and talked about the day, and then he put his plate down on the table beside him and said, 'Tell me about your work.'

'I don't have any,' she reminded him. 'In fact, I was going to ask you about that. I need to write a CV and get it out to some firms. I don't suppose you've got wireless broadband so I can go online and do some research?'

'Sure. You can do it now, if you like. I'll help you—if you want.'

She flashed him a smile. 'That would be great. Thanks.'

'Any time. Have you got a computer or do you want to use mine?'

'My laptop—it's in the breakfast room. I'll get it.'

He'd sat up by the time she got back in there, so she ended up sitting close to him, his solid, muscled thigh against hers, his arm slung along the back of the sofa behind her. As she brought up her CV, he glanced at it and sat back.

'OK, I can see a few problems with it. It needs more immediacy, it needs to grab the attention.

You could do with a photo of yourself, for a start. People like to know who they're dealing with.'

'Really? For freelance? It's not as if I'd have to disgrace their office—'

'Disgrace? Don't be ridiculous,' he said, leaving her feeling curiously warm inside. 'And anyway, it's about how you look at the camera, if you're open and straightforward and decent.'

'Or if you have tattoos or a ton of shrapnel in your face,' she added, but he laughed and shook his head.

'That's irrelevant unless you're talking front of house and it's the sort of organisation where it matters. In some places it'd be an asset. It's much more about connecting with the photo. Stay there.'

And he limped out stiffly, drawing her attention to the fact that he was still sore, despite all he'd done today for her and her children. He should have been lying down taking it easy, she thought uncomfortably, not making snowmen and snow angels and construction toys. And now her CV.

He came back with another laptop, flipped it open and logged on, and then scrolled through his files and brought up his own CV. 'Here—this is me. I can't show you anyone else's, it wouldn't be fair, but this is the basic stuff—fonts, the photo size and so on.'

She scanned it, much more interested in the personal information than anything else. His date of birth—he was a Cancerian, she noticed, and thirty-five this year, five years older than her—and he'd been born in Norwich, he had three degrees, he was crazily clever and his interests were diverse and, well, interesting.

She scanned through it and sat back.

'Wow. You're pretty well qualified.'

'So are you. How come you can't find a job? Is it that they don't get beyond the CV?'

She laughed. 'What, a single woman with three young children and one of them under a year?'

'But people aren't allowed to ask that sort of thing.'

'No, but they ask about how much time you're able to commit and can you give weekends and evenings if necessary, are you available for business trips—all sorts of sly manoeuvring to get it out of you, and then you can hear the gates slam shut.'

'That's crazy. Lots of my key people are mothers, and they tend to be well-organised, efficient and considerate. And OK, from time to time I have to make concessions, but they don't pull sickies because they've drunk too much the night before, and they don't get bored and go off travelling. There are some significant advantages. I'd take you on.'

She stared at him, not sure if he'd meant that quite how it sounded, because Kate had said in the past that it was a shame he had someone and didn't need her. So it was probably just a casual remark. But it might not have been…

'You would?' she asked tentatively, and he nodded.

'Sure. I could do with a translator. It's not technical stuff, it's more business contract work, but I farm it out at the moment to someone I've used for years and she told me before Christmas that she wants a career break. What languages have you got?'

'French, Italian, Spanish and Russian.'

He nodded slowly. 'OK. Want to try? Have a look at some of the things I need translating and see if you've got enough of the specific vocabulary to do it?'

'Sure,' she said slowly, although she wasn't sure. She wasn't sure at all if it would be a good thing to do, to become even more involved with a man who her son thought had hung the moon and the stars, and on whose lap her daughter had spent a good part of the day cuddled up in front of the fire.

A man whose heart was so badly broken that he had to run away every Christmas and hide from the pain.

A man, she realised, who she could very easily come to love…

He must be crazy.

It was bad enough having them all descend on him without a by-your-leave, taking over his house and his life and his mind. It was only a step from lunacy to suggest a lasting liaison.

Not that it need be anything other than strictly professional, he realised. It could all be done online—in fact, it could be Kate who dealt with all the communications. He didn't have to do anything other than rubber-stamp payment of her invoices. It would solve her financial problems, give her independence from the scumbag of an ex-husband who'd trashed her life so comprehensively with his lousy judgement and wild ideas, and give the children security.

And that, he discovered, mattered more to him than he really wanted to admit. It would give them a chance to find a house, to settle into schools—and that in itself would give Edward a chance to join a choir, church or school, or maybe even apply to choir schools for a scholarship. They could live anywhere they chose, because she wouldn't have to come into the office, and so if he did end up in a choir school he wouldn't necessarily have to board if she was close enough to run around after him.

And she could afford to look after Rufus.

He glanced down at the dog, snuggled up between their feet, utterly devoted to his mistress.

Hell, he'd miss the dog when they moved. Miss all of them. He'd have to think about getting a dog. He'd considered it in the past but dismissed it because of his business visitors who stayed in the house from time to time, but maybe it was time to think about himself, to put himself first, to admit, perhaps, that he, too, had needs.

And feelings.

'Think about it, and we'll go over some stuff tomorrow, maybe,' he said, shutting his laptop and getting to his feet. 'I'm going to turn in.'

'Yes, it's been a long day.' She shut her own laptop and stood up beside him, gathering up their glasses with her free hand. Then, while she put the dog out, he put his computer back in the study and went back to the kitchen, looking broodingly out over the garden at the snowman staring back at him with slightly crooked Brussels sprout eyes, and he wondered if his feelings could extend to a relationship.

Not sex, not just another casual, meaningless affair, a way to scratch an itch, to blank out the emptiness of his life, but a relationship.

With Amelia.

She was calling Rufus, patting her leg and encouraging him away from a particularly fascinating smell, and then the door shut and he heard the key turn and she came through to the breakfast room and stopped.

'Oh! I thought you'd gone upstairs.'

'No. I was waiting for you,' he said, and something flickered in her eyes, an acknowledgement of what he might have said.

He led her to the landing by his bedroom and turned to her, staring wordlessly down at her for the longest moment. It was crazy. He didn't know her, he wasn't ready, he was only now starting to sift through the raft of feelings left behind by losing his family—but he wanted her, her and her family, and he didn't know how to deal with that.

Sex he could handle. This—this was something else entirely. He lifted his right hand and cradled her cheek. 'Thank you for today,' he said softly, and her eyes widened and she shook her head.

'No—thank *you*, Jake. You've been amazing— so kind I don't know how to start. It could have all been unimaginably awful, and instead—it's been the best Christmas I can remember. And it's all down to you. So thank you, for everything you've done, for me, for the children, even for Rufus. You're a star, Jake Forrester—a good man.'

And, going up on tiptoe, she pressed a soft, tentative kiss to his lips.

The kiss lingered for a second, and then her heels sank back to the floor, taking her away from him, and he took a step back and let her go with reluctance.

There was time, he told himself as he got ready for bed. There was no hurry—and maybe this was better not hurried, but given time to grow and develop over time.

He opened the bedside drawer and took out his painkillers, and the photo caught his eye. He lifted it out and stared at them. They seemed like strangers now, distant memories, part of his past. He'd never forget them, but they were gone, and maybe he was ready to move on.

He opened his suitcase and pulled out the

broken remains of the watch, and put it with the photograph in a box full of Rachel's things in the top of his wardrobe.

Time to move on, he told himself.

With Amelia?

## CHAPTER EIGHT

'Isn't it time we bathed the dog? We've been talking about it for days, and we still haven't got round to it.'

She looked up at Jake and bit her lip to stop the smile. 'He is pretty smelly, isn't he?'

'You could say that. And right now he's wet and mucky from the snow, so it seems like a good time. And he's got all night to dry by the fire.'

'I'll get my shampoo and conditioner and run the water in the sink,' she said, getting to her feet from the hearthrug and running up to her bathroom, then coming back to the utility room—because even she drew the line at bathing the dog in the kitchen sink—and a moment later Jake appeared with the dog at his heels and an armful of towels from the cupboard in the boiler room.

'Here—old towels. I tend to use them for swimming, but I'm sure the dog won't object.'

They were better than her best ones, she thought, but she didn't comment, just thanked him, picked Rufus up and stood him in the water and ladled it over him with a plastic jug she'd found in the cupboard under the sink.

'He's very good,' Jake said, leaning against the worktop and watching her bath him. 'Not that that surprises me. Did you have time to look at any of that stuff I gave you, by the way?'

'Yes. It doesn't look too bad. Do you want me to have a go?'

'Could you?'

'Sure. I'll do it while Rufus dries, if you like.' She lathered him from end to end, drenched him in conditioner to get the tangles out, then rinsed him again even more thoroughly and lifted the plug out and squeezed the water off him and then bundled him up in the towels and carried him back to the fire.

'Have you got a comb?'

'I'll brush him,' she said, and gently teased the tangles out while he stood and shivered.

'Is he cold?'

'No, he just hates it. He's a wuss and he doesn't like being brushed. He'll get over it.'

'Is she being mean to you, sweetheart?' he crooned, and Rufus wafted his skinny little tail, looking pleadingly at his hero for rescue.

'Forget it, big-eyes, you're getting brushed,' she said firmly, but she kissed him to take the sting out of it. It was over in a moment, and then he shook wildly and ran round the room, scrubbing his face on the rug and making them laugh.

'Right, those documents,' she said. 'Shall I do it on my computer?'

'It's probably easier.'

So she sat at the table, and he sat in the chair by the fire, and Rufus settled down on a towel and let Jake brush him gently until he was dry, and she thought how nice it was, how cosy—and she couldn't imagine what she was doing getting herself sucked into La-La Land like this.

So she forced herself to concentrate, and after a while she sat back and blew out her cheeks.

'OK, I've done it.'

'What, the first one?'

'No, all three.'

'Really?'

He sat next to her, produced the translations he'd already apparently had done and scanned the two side by side, and then sat back and met her eyes.

'They're excellent. Better. Better English—cleaner, clearer. So—do you want the job?'

She laughed a little breathlessly. 'Do I—I don't

know. That depends on what you pay, and how.' And how much contact I'll have to have with you, and whether it's going to do my head in trying to be sensible—

'Word count, normally. I'm not sure what we pay without looking, but I'm sure it's fair, and if you don't agree with it, I'll match what you've been getting. That's on top of a retainer, of course. I can check for you. I'll have a look through the accounts. We can go over to the office tomorrow—in fact, do you think the kids would like to swim? The pool's there doing nothing, and you'll have it to yourselves unless any of the staff come over to use it, but I would have thought they're unlikely to do so this soon after Christmas. It's up to you.'

'Oh. They'd love to swim,' she said ruefully, contemplating the idea of being on a retainer because her last job had been much more hit and miss than that, 'but they haven't got any costumes. Swimwear wasn't top of my list of priorities when I was packing things up to go into storage. I have no idea where they'd be, either.'

'It doesn't matter. They can swim in pants. So can you. Bra and pants is only what a bikini is, and I promise I won't look.'

She felt her cheeks heat and looked away from

his teasing eyes. Since she'd kissed him last night, she'd scarcely been able to think about anything else, and for the whole day it had been simmering between them. It wasn't just her, she was sure of it, but he didn't seem to be about to take it any further, and goodness knows she shouldn't be encouraging him to.

The last thing—well, almost the last thing, anyway—she needed was to get involved in a complicated relationship with the first person to offer her work in months. And she needed a job more than she needed sex.

Except it wasn't that, or it didn't feel like it. It felt like—help, it felt dangerously like love, and that was so scary she couldn't allow herself to think about it. She'd had it with rich, flashy, ruthless men.

Not that he was flashy, not in the least, but he was certainly rich, and however generous he might have been to her, she was sure that Jake could be ruthless when it suited him or the occasion demanded it. Heavens, she knew he could, she'd been on the receiving end of his ruthless tongue on the first night!

But that had been him lashing out, sore and tired and a little desperate, at someone who'd come uninvited into his home, his retreat, his sanctuary. No wonder.

Nevertheless, it was there, that ruthless streak, and David's ruthlessness had scarred her and her children in a way that she was sure would never completely fade.

'It's not such a hard question, is it?' he murmured, jerking her back to the present, and she met his eyes in confusion.

'What isn't?'

'Swimming,' he reminded her gently. 'What did you think I was talking about?'

She had no idea. She'd been so far away, reliving the horror of David's heartless and uncaring defection, that she'd forgotten all about the swim he'd talked of.

She tried to smile. 'I'm sorry, I was wool-gathering. No, it's not hard. I'm sure the children would both love to swim, but you can't, can you, with the cast on?' And there was no way she was swimming in pants—most especially not the pants Kate had given her!

'No. No, of course not, but it's sitting there. I just thought they might enjoy it. And I'd like to show you the office. Not that you'll be working there necessarily, but you might find it interesting to see the place.'

She would. She found everything about him interesting, and that was deeply worrying. But she accepted, telling herself that it would give her a better insight into his business operation and help her make a more informed decision about whether to take the job or not.

In fact, maybe she should talk to Kate, and she vowed to do that as soon as she had a chance. But, in the meantime, she'd have a look at his offices, let the kids have a swim and think about it.

The following morning, after the children were washed and dressed and she'd taped up Jake's cast so he could shower, and once they'd had breakfast and walked the squeaky-clean Rufus in his smart little coat, they went over to the old country club site and he let them into the offices hidden away behind the walls of the old kitchen garden.

'Sorry, it's a bit chilly. The heating's turned down but we won't be in here long and the pool area's warm,' he said, and pushed open a door into what had to be his office. There was a huge desk, a vast window and the same beautiful view down the long walk that the drawing room and his bedroom enjoyed. A long, low sofa stretched across one wall, and she guessed he sprawled on it often when he was working late, a coffee in his hand, checking emails on his laptop or talking on the phone.

She pictured him pacing, gesturing, holding everything in his head while he negotiated and wrangled until he was satisfied that he'd got the best deal. She'd seen David do it, seen the way he worked, the way he pinned people down and bullied them until he got his way, and a chill ran over her.

Was Jake like that? The iron hand in the velvet glove? She didn't like to think so, but even a pussycat had claws, and Jake was no pussycat. He could be tough and uncompromising, she was sure, and that made her deeply uneasy. But then wasn't everyone who'd survived in business in these difficult times? And she needed that job.

'Come on, kids, more to see and then there's the pool,' he was saying. They scrambled off his sofa and ran back to the door, and she followed them, Thomas in the stroller so she could have her hands free to help the children when they had their swim.

'This is the main office, this is Kate's office, this is reception—I brought you in the back way, but visitors come in via this door from the garden,' he explained, opening it so that the children could go out and run around in the snow, and she looked out over a pretty scene of snow-covered lawn surrounded by what looked like roses climbing up against the mellow brick walls. In the centre was a little fountain. The children were chasing each other round it, giggling and shrieking and throwing snowballs, and she smiled, relieved to see them so happy after such a difficult year.

'It's beautiful. It must be lovely in the summer.'

'It is. The staff sit out there for their coffee and lunch breaks. It's a lovely place to work, and I knew it would be. I saw it just before—' He broke off, then went on, 'I saw it five and a half years ago, and I was committed to it, so I just shifted my plans a little and went ahead anyway, and it's been a good move—and the right one, although I had no choice because the house was sold and we'd started work on this already.'

'That must have been hard,' she said softly, and he shrugged.

'Not really. We'd made the decision. It was the house that was so hard to deal with. We got the builders in and started at the top. We'd planned to live in the rooms up there at first, so that was already commissioned, and then—well, I got an interior designer in to do the rest, but I wouldn't let her interfere with that bit. It went ahead as planned, and I made it the place where people with children stay, because that was always the idea. We were going to put a kitchen up there as a temporary measure but of course that never happened and I lived somewhere else while it was all done and concentrated on the offices at first.'

He was standing staring at the house, visible over the top of the garden wall, his hands in his pockets, a brooding expression on his face, and she turned away, giving him privacy. Why on earth was she imagining he'd be interested in a relationship with her? Of course he wasn't. He was still in love with his wife—the wife with whom he'd planned the rooms she and her family were living in now.

Of all the rooms for them to have chosen—but maybe it was a good thing. It showed that the plans had been right, and Kate, who didn't know about his wife and son, loved the rooms, too, and had stayed there. And he'd designated it the area for families, so maybe she was just being oversensitive.

What was she thinking? Did she like the set-up, or was she just being polite? Or did she genuinely like it but didn't want to work with him?

Too complicated, too much baggage for both of them?

'We need to talk terms,' he said, hoping that he could coax her into it and that, once coaxed, she would have time to get used to him, to find out the kind of man he was, to learn to trust him. Because she must have trust issues after a bastard like David Jones had messed so comprehensively with her life.

But he couldn't rush her, he knew that. All he could do was make it possible for her to live again, to give her time to draw breath, to get back on her feet. And maybe then—

His phone rang and he pulled it impatiently out of his pocket and glanced at the screen. Kate. He felt a flicker of guilt but dismissed it and answered the call.

'Well, hello there. Had a good Christmas?'

'Yes…Jake, can we talk?'

'Why? What's wrong?' he asked, suddenly concerned that something might have happened to her.

She just gave a strangled laugh. 'What's wrong?' she exclaimed. 'You told me I hadn't heard the end of it, and I haven't heard a thing from you since, and the last time I spoke to you, you were injured and hopping mad. I didn't know if you were all right, if you'd forgiven me, if I'd even got a job to come back to. So of course I didn't have a good Christmas, you idiot! Oh, I'm sorry, I didn't mean to say that, but—really, Jake, I've been so worried and you didn't return my call, and you always do.'

Damn. He should have rung her. He'd meant to, so many times, but his eye had been so firmly off the ball—

'I'm sorry. I meant to ring. Of course you've got a job. Look, why don't you bring Megan over for a swim and have a chat and a coffee? In fact, swing by a sports shop and pick up some swimming things for Amelia and the kids on the way here. Theirs are in store. See you in—what? An hour?'

'Less—much less. I've got a costume Millie can use, and one of Megan's that Kitty can borrow, so I only need to get something for Edward and I might be able to find something here of his he left behind in the summer. I'll see you soon,' she said, and hung up.

He put the phone back in his pocket and turned to Amelia. 'That was Kate,' he said unnecessarily. 'She's coming over now with swimming things for all of you.'

'I gathered. Did she really think she might not have a job?' Amelia asked, frowning worriedly. 'Sorry, I didn't mean to eavesdrop, but I couldn't help overhearing your remark. I've been meaning to ring. I had a missed call from her on my phone, and I meant to ring her back, but—'

'Ditto. We've been dealing with other things. Don't worry, she's fine. She's far too valuable for me to lose, and she knows that. Or I hope she knows that.'

'I don't know that she does. She certainly doesn't take you for granted. I think she feels you're a bit of a miracle.'

'Me?' He gave a startled laugh and thought about it. 'I'm no miracle. I'm a tough boss. Make no mistake about that, Amelia. I don't pull punches. I expect my staff to work hard, but no harder than I do, and if they give me their best, I'll defend them to the hilt. But I don't suffer fools.'

Fools like her husband. Correction—*ex*-husband. Thank God he was in Thailand, it'd save him the effort of driving him out of the country.

'Jake? Does she know? About your family?'

He shook his head. 'No. Hardly anybody does. A few who've known me for years, but they don't talk about it and neither do I, we all just get on with it.'

'OK. Just so I know not to say anything. I thought she probably didn't because we talked about you and she didn't mention it, but I don't want to put my foot in it and you've obviously got your reasons for not telling everyone.'

He shrugged. 'It's just never come up. Work is work. I don't talk about myself.'

'But you talk about them. Kate said you always ask about Megan, and about other people's families, and you give very generous maternity deals and so on, and you send flowers when people are sick, and when Kate's pipes froze you put them up in the house—so it's only yourself you keep at arm's length,' she pointed out— probably fairly, now he thought about it.

He gave her a smile that felt slightly off-kilter. 'It's just easier that way. I don't want sympathy, Amelia. I don't need it. I just want to be left alone to live my life.'

Except suddenly that wasn't true any more, he acknowledged, feeling himself frown. He didn't want to be left alone. He wanted—

'Can we see the pool now?'

Kitty was under his nose, covered in snow, her cheeks bright and glowing with health, her eyes sparkling, and behind her Edward was stamping snow off his boots and shutting the door and watching him hopefully.

'Sure. Kate rang. She's bringing Megan over

and some swimming things for you all. She'll be here in a minute.'

'Yippee, yippee, we're going in the pool!' Kitty sang, and Edward was laughing.

'That's amazing. We've just had a snowball fight and now we're going swimming! That's so weird. Are you coming in?'

He shook his head. 'I can't—my cast,' he explained, lifting up his arm. 'I can't get it wet. But I can't wait. I swim every day at six before everyone gets here, and I really miss it. So you won't mind if I don't watch you, because I'll just get jealous. You guys go ahead and have a really good time, OK?'

And then Kate arrived with Megan, to the children's delight, and he took one look at her and went over and hugged her.

'Hey, smile for me,' he said, holding her by the shoulders and looking down into her eyes. To his surprise, they filled with tears.

'I felt so awful, but I didn't know what to do, and I didn't think you'd mind. You weren't even supposed to be here—'

'Hey, it's fine. And you're right, I wouldn't have minded and you did absolutely the right thing, so stop worrying. I'd probably be more cross if you hadn't done what you did, so forget it. Anyway,' he said, changing the subject, 'the kids are dying to get in the pool, and I'd like a minute to talk to Amelia, so if you wouldn't mind keeping an eye on them. Amelia, is that OK with you?'

'Sure.' Amelia nodded, and Kate shot her a curious look.

'Right—sort yourselves out, and come and find me, Amelia. I'll be in my office.'

And he left them to it, turned up the heating in his office and checked his emails. Grief. There were loads, and he scrolled through them, deleting the majority without a second glance, saving a few, answering a couple.

And then she was there, standing in the doorway looking a little uneasy, and he switched off his machine and stood up.

'Come on in, I was just doing my email. Coffee?'

'Oh—thanks. Will you have any milk or should I go and get some?'

'Creamer. Is that OK?'

'Fine.' She crossed over to the window and stood staring down the long walk. 'How do you get any work done?' she asked softly, and he chuckled.

'It helps. There's nothing going on—well,

apart from the odd squirrel. So my mind's free to think. It's good. No distractions, no diversions—it works for me. And it's peaceful. I love it best when there's nobody here, first thing in the morning and last thing at night.'

'And the house?' she asked, turning to face him.

'What about the house?'

'I get the feeling you sleep there.'

'And eat. Sometimes. And entertain. And I do spend time there, in my study or the sitting room. I don't use the rest of it much, it's a bit formal really.'

And lonely, but he didn't add that, because he didn't want to think about it, about how it hadn't been lonely for the last few days, and how empty and desolate it would feel when they were gone.

'I don't suppose you've thought about the job any more overnight?' he asked, handing her a coffee, and she took it and nodded, following him to the sofa and sitting down.

'Yes, but I need to know if it will be enough, if you can offer me enough work to live on. I don't want to be rude, and I'm not trying to push the rate up or anything, but I do need to earn a living and because my time's limited I need to maximise. And I am good, I know that. So I need to do the best I can for my family. I've been thinking about what you said about Edward, too, wondering if I could get him a voice test or singing lessons, but I need financial security before I even consider that. It's a juggling act, work time and quality time, although without the work the quality's pretty compromised so what am I talking about? But I do have to think about this and I know you're shut over Christmas and New Year, so I don't know when you're thinking of me starting—'

'Whenever,' he said, cutting her off before she talked herself out of it. 'I can find you a pile of stuff. Judith—my translator—has been doing less recently, and there's a bit of a backlog, so if you want to start on that, I'd be very grateful. Some of it's probably getting a bit urgent.'

'So—would I submit an invoice when you're happy?'

'Or I can give you a cheque now,' he said. 'Just an advance, to start you off.' Which would give her enough money to find a rented house and move out, he realised with regret, but he couldn't hold her hostage, even if he wanted to.

'Don't you want references?' she was asking incredulously, and he laughed.

'No. You're a friend of Kate's, I've met your children, I've met your husband—'

'David? When did you meet David?' she asked, her voice shocked.

He shrugged. 'Last year? I believe it was him. He came to me with an idea he wanted to float for a coffee shop chain.'

'Oh, that's him. It was a crazy idea. I had no idea he'd approached you about it. I expect the fact Kate works for you put the idea into his head. Funny she didn't mention he'd been to see you.'

'She didn't know. I met him at a conference.'

'Oh. So what did you say?'

'I turned him down. It was ill-considered, risky and I didn't want to put my money there.' And he'd disliked the man on sight, but he didn't say that, because it was irrelevant and, after all, presumably she'd loved him once, although what came next made him wonder.

'Wise move,' she said, and smiled ruefully. 'Who knows what I saw in him, but by the time I realised what he was like it was too late, we were married and our second child was on the way. And when I tackled him about some things I'd found out, he walked.'

'And Thomas?'

'I let him come back. Don't ask me why, I have

no idea. Maybe I felt I owed it to the children to give it another chance. It didn't last, and then when he'd gone—my idea, not his, because I realised he was relying on my income to support him—I discovered I was pregnant again. And that time I did divorce him. But what's David got to do with my job?'

'Just that I know the mess your life's in isn't your fault. I can imagine you trying to hold it all together, and I can imagine him selling it all out from under you without you realising. So I know you aren't in this position because you're incompetent, and you're right, you are good at your job. Quick and accurate. I need that—particularly the accuracy. The exact meaning of a contract is massively important, and although a lot of the stuff is standard, there are some sneaky little clauses. I like those dealt with, and I need to know what they are. So—I'm more than happy to take you on. My HR people will sort out the fine print when they get back, but in the meantime I'll give you the same rate Judith was on plus a twenty per cent enhancement and increase the retainer by forty per cent—I can find out exactly what that translates to in a minute, and you can start as soon as you like.'

She nodded slowly. 'OK. I need to see how the

figures stack up. I might need to take on other work from somewhere else—'

'Don't do that,' he said, cutting her off. 'There's plenty of communication with foreign companies on a daily basis that we might need help with, as well as the really important stuff. French and Italian aren't too much of a problem—I speak them well enough for most things and so do a couple of others—but we struggle with Russian and our Spanish is on the weak side, so if you find you aren't earning enough, just shout. I could probably use you getting on for full-time, even maybe phone calls, that sort of thing. We do so much work abroad now and it would be really handy.'

She nodded thoughtfully. 'OK. Let me see the figures, and we'll talk again,' she said with a smile, and he felt the tension go out of his shoulders.

Good. He wasn't going to lose her—not entirely. He'd make sure of that, make sure the money was so tempting she would be mad to turn it down. She might move out once she'd got some financial security, but he could still phone her, ask her to explain something, find excuses to keep in touch personally—and now he was being ridiculous.

'Go and swim with your children. I'll look up the figures, find some material for you to start on and we'll go from there.'

He just hoped he could convince her…

## CHAPTER NINE

'SO WHAT was that all about?'

She swam over to Kate and propped her arms on the edge of the pool. 'He's offered me a job. Apparently his translator wants to take a career break.'

'Judith? I didn't know that. Wow. Well, you've obviously made a good impression. I'm so sorry you ended up in that difficult situation with him before Christmas, by the way. I've been feeling so guilty, but you've obviously survived it. How did it go?'

How did it go? Between the tears and the heart-searching—

'OK. It was OK. Fun. He was brilliant. We went to the supermarket and bought loads of food, and I cooked Christmas lunch, and he bought the children little presents—he even got the dog a coat.'

'Good grief,' Kate said faintly. 'Still, it shouldn't really surprise me—when he does something, he usually does it well. He's a stickler for detail.'

'Hmm, that's what worries me about taking this job on. What if I'm not good enough?'

'You will be,' Kate said instantly. 'Of course you will be. He's only got to look at your references to know that. Is he taking them up?'

'He says not.'

Kate's eyes widened, and then she started to laugh. 'Oh, my. Still, it's not the first time, he's a very good judge of character, but...Millie, I have a feeling he really likes you. As in, *likes* you.'

She shook her head. 'No. No way, Kate, it's too complicated. He isn't in the market for that sort of thing and neither am I.'

'How do you know? That he isn't, I mean? Did he say something?'

Damn. 'Well, he wouldn't be, would he?' she said, going for the obvious in the interests of preserving his privacy. 'Three kids and a dog? You'd be insane to want to take that on. And besides, what would I want with another entrepreneur? I've had it with living my life on a knife-edge, waiting for the next roll of the stock market dice to see if I'll be homeless or not. I want security,

Kate, and I don't need a man for that. But I will take his job, and as soon as I can I'll find a house and get out of his hair and get our life back on track. Get the kids enrolled in a new school, and start again. And hopefully, this time it'll last longer than a few months.'

'So what's for supper?' he asked, coming up behind her and peering over her shoulder as she stirred the pan on the stove.

'Would you believe a variation on the theme of turkey?' she said with a laugh, and he chuckled.

'Smells good, whatever it is. Sort of Moroccan?'

'Mmm. A tagine. I found all the ingredients in the cupboard—I hope you don't mind?'

'Of course I don't mind. Use what you like. There doesn't look very much there, have you done enough for us all?'

'Oh. I'm feeding the children earlier. This is just for you.'

She caught his frown out of the corner of her eye. 'What about you?'

'I'll eat with the children—'

'Why?'

She turned and looked at him, not knowing what her role was any longer, not sure what he expected of her.

So she said so, and his brow pleated in a frown.

'I thought…I don't know. We seem to have all eaten together since Christmas Day. Breakfast, lunch, variation on a theme of turkey—I rather thought that was the way it was now.'

'But I'm supposed to be looking after you, helping you with the things you can't do, cooking for you—that's all.'

'Does that mean you can't eat with me?'

'Well…no, of course not, but I thought you might want to be alone—'

'No,' he said emphatically. 'Eat with me—please? Or, if there isn't enough, do something else—throw a bit more turkey in, or make a starter, but—no, I don't want to eat alone. And anyway, I thought we could talk about the job.'

The job. Of course. Nothing to do with wanting her company—and she shouldn't want him to, shouldn't be contemplating intimate little dinners *à deux*, or cosy drinks by the fire with the lights off and only the flickering flames to see by.

But that was what they ended up doing that evening, eating alone together after the children were in bed, opening a bottle of wine and then carrying the rest of it through to the drawing room, because they'd been in there during the day with Kate and Megan, doing a jigsaw by the fire while Thomas alternately slept or tried to haul himself up and eat the pieces.

Jake threw another log on, sat down at one end of the sofa at right angles to the fireplace and patted the seat beside him. 'Come and sit with me and talk,' he said. 'I've got some figures for you.'

And so she sat, hitching her feet up under her bottom and turning half towards him, studying him over her wine glass. 'Figures?'

He told her what he was prepared to pay, and she blinked. 'That's generous,' she said, and he shrugged.

'I expect a lot for my money.'

'And if I can't deliver?' she said with a shiver of dread. She hated to miss deadlines, hated letting people down, but— 'What if the children are sick, or Thomas won't sleep—what then?'

He shrugged. 'Then I expect you to let me know, to do the best you can and be upfront with me. Don't tell me you're doing it if you can't. Tell me if you've got a problem and I'll find another way round it. It's not impossible. We do it all the time. I'm not asking for an unbreakable commitment, just a promise to do your best to fulfil your side of the bargain. That's all any of us can ever do.'

'And if you don't think my work's up to scratch?'

'I know it will be. I know Barry Green. I've phoned him. He's gutted he had to let you down, but he's made some investments that have collapsed and it's not his fault. He really didn't have the money to pay you. In fact, he was relieved that I was going to be able to give you a job because he's been feeling really guilty. So—all I need to know is, will you take the job or do I need to look for someone else?'

Still she hesitated. So many reasons to take it—and so many not to.

'You don't have to deal with me, if that's what's troubling you,' he said softly. 'If you're worried about it all getting a bit too cosy, you can deal with Kate or my contracts manager. And it doesn't have to be for ever. If something better comes along, you can go. And Judith only wants a career break, she hasn't said she's stopping for ever—well, not yet. So it's only for the foreseeable future.'

He was making it so easy to say yes, so hard to say no. And the silly thing was, she didn't want to say no, but she was still afraid of getting involved. But she could deal with Kate, he said. That would be all right. Less complicated.

And so she nodded, her heart pounding as she said, 'Yes. OK. I'll take it. Thank you.'

He let out his breath on a soft huff of laughter. 'Good. Welcome to the team,' he said, lifting his glass and clinking it gently against hers, and she felt the smile spread over her face until it felt as if her whole body was glowing with relief.

'Thank you,' she said, and then as she lowered her glass, their eyes met and a breathless silence descended over them, broken only by the sharp crackling of the logs in the grate.

Oh, Lord. She could hardly breathe. Her eyes locked with his, the heat in them searing her to her soul. He reached out and took her glass and set it down beside his, and then his fingers curled around her jaw, his thumb grazing her bottom lip, dragging softly over the moist skin, the gentle tug bringing a whimper to her throat.

His fingertips traced her face, seeking out the fine lines around her eyes, the crease by her nose, the pulse pounding in the hollow of her throat.

'Come to bed with me,' he said softly, his voice gruff but gentle, and she felt her whole body responding to his touch, to his voice, to the need she could feel vibrating through his hand as it lay lightly against her collarbone.

'Is that wise?' she asked, with the last vestige of common sense, and gave a soft huff of laughter and he smiled.

'Probably not,' he said, but he stood up, holding out his hand to her and waiting, and after an endless pause she put her hand in his and let him draw her to her feet.

Her heart was pounding as he led her upstairs, his hand warm and firm around hers, his fingers sure. He closed the door with a soft click and pressed a switch, and the lights came on, soft and low, barely enough to see by.

'I'm not on the Pill,' she said, remembering in time another reason why this was a bad idea and why the last time it had been such a bad idea, too, but he shook his head.

'It's all right, I'll take care of it. Come here.'

And he drew her gently into his arms, folding her against his heart and just holding her for the longest time. Then she felt his warm breath against her neck, the soft touch of his hand easing the hair aside so he could press his lips to the skin, and she arched her neck, giving him access, desperate for the feel of his lips all over her body, the touch of his hand, the feel of his heart beating against hers.

She slid her hands under his cashmere sweater, so soft, and laid them against the heated satin of his skin. Hot skin, smooth, dry, taut over bones and muscles. She ran her palms up his spine, feeling the solid columns tense, the breath jerk in his lungs.

His hand cupped her jaw, tilting her head back, and his lips found hers, firm and yet yielding, his tongue coaxing her lips apart so that she opened for him with a tiny sound of need that brought an answering groan from low in his chest.

She could feel his hands at her waist, but her camisole was tucked into her jeans and his fingers plucked at it, a growl of frustration erupting from his lips. 'Too many clothes,' he muttered. 'I want to touch you, Amelia. I want to feel your skin against mine.'

Her legs buckled slightly and he caught her against him. 'I need you. This is crazy. Come to bed.'

And, moving away from her, he stripped off his clothes—the soft jumper, which was easy, then the jeans, harder, the stud exasperating him so that she took over and helped him, her knuckles brushing the taut, hard plane of his abdomen so that he sucked his breath in with a sharp hiss and seared her with his eyes.

They were like coals now, the slate-grey gone, banished by the inky-black of his flared pupils burning into her. The stud undone, he reached for her, peeling the sweater over her head, then the camisole, wrenching it out from her jeans with a grunt of satisfaction and then slowly sliding it up over her breasts, his eyes darkening still further as he let them linger on her.

And she'd never felt more wanted, had never felt more beautiful. He hadn't said a word, not a single compliment or facile remark, just the look in his eyes, which was turning her blood to rivers of fire.

He reached for her bra, giving her a moment of unease because after three children...but he unclipped it and eased it away, and his lids fluttered briefly before his eyes met hers. 'I need you,' he breathed.

'I need you, too. Jake, make love to me.'

'Oh, I intend to,' he said gruffly, then smiled a little off-kilter. 'Once you've undone the stud on your jeans.'

She laughed, releasing the tension that held her, and then he tugged them down once she'd undone the stud, and she stepped out of them and bent to pick them up, dragging another groan from his throat.

'That was my first view of you,' he said almost conversationally. 'When I walked into the breakfast room and you bent over to pick something off the table.' His hand stroked over her bottom, catching her hip with his fingertips and easing her back against his groin. She straightened up and saw their reflection in a mirror, his hand curled around her hip, his fingertips toying with the hem of her little lace shorts—the ones Kate had given her for Christmas.

Breathlessly she watched as his hand slid round, his fingers inside the edge tangling with the soft, damp curls and bringing a tiny gasp to her lips. He rocked against her, hard and solid and urgent, and she could see the tension in his face, the taut jaw, the parted lips, the dark, burning eyes.

His other arm was round her waist, the cast holding her firmly against him, the fingertips trailing over her skin.

And she couldn't play any more, she couldn't wait, couldn't hold on another moment. She needed him. She'd needed him all her life, and she didn't want to waste another second.

She turned in his arms, sliding her hands down inside his jeans and boxers, pushing them down just far enough, and he lifted her with one arm and carried her to the bed, dropping her on the edge and stripping away the scrap of lace before rummaging in the bedside table.

'Damn, can you help me? I can't do this with

one hand,' he growled, and she took over, her fingers shaking as she touched him so intimately for the first time. His breath hissed in sharply, and then he paused, dragging in a ragged breath, his eyes closed, slowing his breathing until finally he opened his eyes and stared down at her body.

'Jake, please,' she breathed, and with a tortured sigh he went into her arms.

'Are you OK?'

She laughed softly. 'I don't know. I'll tell you in a minute,' she said, and he propped himself up on his elbow and stared down at her.

'You've got glitter in your hair,' she murmured, reaching up to touch it and testing the soft, silky strands between her fingers.

'Mmm. That would be your daughter,' he said, laughter in his voice. 'She thought it would be funny to sprinkle it on me—apparently it's fairy dust. It's going to make me rich.'

'Oh, well, that'll be handy,' she said with a chuckle.

He smiled at the irony. 'Do you have any idea how lovely you are?' he murmured, the fingertips of his left hand trailing slowly over her breasts. He brushed the knuckles over her nipple and it peaked for him obligingly, so he bent and took it in his mouth, suckling it hard and making her gasp.

'How is it I've fed three babies and yet that's so erotic?' she asked in wonder.

'I don't know. How about the other one?' he asked, bending over it. 'We ought to be fair and do a proper survey of both, just in case.'

'Idiot,' she said, but then his mouth closed over her and she forgot to speak, forgot her name almost—and forgot the reason why this was such a dangerous idea, such a silly thing to do as she gave herself up once more to the touch of his hands, the warmth of his lips, the solid, masculine body that could drive her to madness...

For the next week, while the office was still closed and the housekeeper was on her annual leave, they fell into a routine.

In the morning they had breakfast together, and then after they'd walked the dog and Thomas was back in his cot for his nap, Jake would go over to the office and she'd work on the laptop in the playroom upstairs while the children were amusing themselves, something they were very good at and which she encouraged.

And then Jake would come back and they'd have lunch, and Thomas would nap again, and when he woke they'd have a swim while Jake worked again, and then she'd cook supper for all of them and after the children were in bed she'd fit in another couple of hours before he'd come and shut down her laptop, give her a glass of wine and then take her up to bed.

She didn't sleep with him, because of the children, but every night she went upstairs with him and he made love to her, slowly, tenderly, until her nerves were stretched to breaking point and she was pleading with him to end it.

But it couldn't go on like this, and they both knew it.

'I need to find a house,' she said, as they were standing in the attic on New Year's Eve watching the fireworks in the distance at midnight. 'New Year, new start. And now I've got a job, I can contact the agents and see what they've got—'

'You don't have to go,' he said quietly. 'You could stay—you and the children. Move in properly.'

'Live with you?'

'Yes.'

'No.' She shook her head. 'No, Jake, I can't,' she said, feeling the fear close in round her. 'I can't put us in anyone else's hands, ever again. I can't do that to myself, never mind my children.

They've been through enough, and I can't ask it of them. I can't—' She broke off and shook her head again. 'I just can't. I'm sorry. Anyway, it's really sweet of you, but you don't mean it—'

'Sweet?' he said, his voice stunned. 'There's nothing sweet about it, Amelia. I want you. I need you. And I thought…hell, we were getting on so well.'

'We are—but that doesn't mean I can give up my independence, Jake—or theirs. I thought you understood that. I swore I'd never let another man have that much power over me.'

'How do I have power over you? You'd be sharing my life. I'd have no more power over you than you'd have over me.'

'But you would, because it's your house, and my only money is from you, and—it's called having all your eggs in one basket. Not a good idea.'

'It's OK if it's the right basket. Most of us do that, emotionally, at least, if not financially. Get another job if that's what's worrying you, although I have to say I'd be extremely reluctant to lose you. Don't walk away just because there's a chance it may not be right, because there's a much bigger chance, from where I'm standing, that it *is* right.'

'And how do I know? How do I know if it's right, Jake?'

He cradled her shoulders in his hands and met her eyes searchingly. 'You have faith,' he said softly. 'You have faith, and you give it your best shot, and if you're lucky, and you work at it, then all's well.'

'And if it's not? If we find out it's no good, that we aren't the people we thought we were?'

He sighed and dropped his hands. 'OK. It's too soon, I'm rushing you. But think about it. Don't dismiss it. Get somewhere else to live, and give us time. We can still see each other, have dinner, take the kids out—'

She shook her head. 'No. I don't want the kids coming to think of you as part of their life. This is different, we're staying here for a short time, you're doing us a favour. But if we move in properly, if it all gets too cosy and then it goes wrong—bang! Another rug out from under their feet. And I can't do it. I'm sorry.'

She felt tears clog her throat, and turned away. 'I'm sorry, Jake. It's been wonderful, but it ends when I leave. Or now. It's your choice.'

'Then come to bed with me,' he said, his voice rough with emotion. 'If I've only got you for a short while longer, I want to savour every moment.'

* * *

He thought it would tear him apart. Making love to her, knowing she was going, knowing he was losing her— It nearly broke him, but he needed to hold her, to love her, to show her without words just how infinitely sweet and precious she was to him.

He'd been a fool, imagining he could win her. She'd been so hurt, so damaged by her life with David and all its tortured twists and turns that it was no surprise she found it hard to trust. But he wouldn't give up. Somehow he'd find a way to convince her. He had to.

But then a week later, just before his housekeeper was due to return, she told him she'd found a house.

'Where?'

'About ten miles away—so I can still come in and see you if I need to for work.'

'Where is it?'

'In Reading.'

'Whereabouts?'

She sighed. 'Does it matter?'

He wanted to tear his hair out. 'Yes! Yes, it matters. What's it like? What's the area like?'

She wouldn't look at him, and that worried the hell out of him. 'Fine.'

He didn't believe her for a minute.

'Have you signed?'

'No. I'm going to see him tomorrow. I looked round it today.'

'And?'

She swallowed. 'It'll be perfectly all right.'

Damn it! He paced across the kitchen, then came back to her. 'I have an alternative—'

'I'm not living here, Jake!'

'Not here. Another house. You remember I said I lived somewhere else while this place was being done? It's empty. I was going to sell it, put it on the market in the spring. It's got four bedrooms, it's detached, the furniture's reasonable—it needs a clean, the tenant left yesterday, but it's close to Kate, it's in a good school catchment area, it's got a nice garden… Can you have pets in this house you've found?'

She sighed. 'I had to convince the letting agent he was all right. He's going to talk to the landlord.'

He stopped pacing and leant back against the worktop, his arms folded across his chest. 'And if he says no?'

She stared at him. 'Then I try again—Jake, why do you *care*?'

'Because I do,' he said honestly, and to hell with giving her time and not rushing her and letting her learn to trust him, because if she was going to go and live in some vile little house in a horrible area and send her kids to a grotty school, he was damned if he was going to stand back and let her do it. 'Because I love you, dammit!' And then his voice softened, his throat clogging. 'I love you, Amelia, and I can't make you stay here, but I can still keep you safe, and make you more secure. Take my rental house—I'll put it in your name, and you can have it. And you can work for me, or not. Your choice. But don't take your kids to some horrible area and put them in a ghastly school just—'

'Just what? Just what, Jake? Just because it's the best I can afford to do? Some of us don't have your options—'

'But I'm trying to *give* you options, and you're turning them down!'

'Because they're not options, Jake. They're just a honey trap—and I can't let you do this for us.'

'Then let me do it for the children. Let me put the house in their names, not yours. Let me give you the freedom to choose whether or not you want me, whether or not you can trust me enough to take my love at face value, and marry me. No strings, no ultimatums. The house is yours. The job is yours. And I'm yours—if you want me.

Think about it. I'll get my solicitor on it in the morning. Let me have their full names.'

And he walked out of the room before he said anything else that might prejudice her against him, because he felt so close to losing her this time, and he didn't know what he'd do if he couldn't win her back.

# CHAPTER TEN

'RIGHT, that's everything. Time to say goodbye. Say thank you to Jake.'

'I don't want to say goodbye,' Kitty wailed, wrapping her arms around his hips and hanging on for dear life.

'Nor do I,' Edward said, his chin wobbling, and Jake could understand that. His own chin was less than firm, and he had to clench his teeth to stop himself from saying something stupid, like, Stay.

'Jake, don't,' she said, and for a moment he thought he'd said it out loud, but she was just pre-empting him, her voice little more than a breath, and he nodded understanding.

No. Compliance. Not understanding. He couldn't understand for the life of him how she could tear herself away from him when it was going to leave him in tatters and he was pretty sure it would do the same for her, and for the children. But it was her choice, her decision, her life.

And she'd chosen to go. He peeled Kitty's arms away from his hips and lifted her up, hugging her gently and posting her into the car. 'Take care, sweetheart. Let me know how your new school is.'

She sniffed and nodded, and he kissed her wet little cheek and felt the lump in his throat grow larger. 'Take care, Tiger,' he said to Thomas, who just grinned at him, and then he ducked out of the car and turned and Edward was standing there. He dredged up a smile.

'Hey, sport. You'll be all right. Let me know about your voice test.'

'I don't want to go.'

'Yes, you do. Nothing might come of it anyway, but you might get a scholarship. You don't know unless you try. And you wouldn't have to be a boarder. Give it a go,' he encouraged, and then, because he could see Edward needed the reassurance, he held out his arms and hugged him.

'I want to stay here,' he mumbled into Jake's chest.

'I know, but you've got your own house now,' he told him, fighting down the emotion, making himself let go of a boy so like him it could have been him at the same age, with all the same emotional turmoil, the need to do the right thing. And that need was still with him, which was the only reason he could do what he did then, to let the boy go, to unwind his arms and push him gently towards the car and turn away.

To find Amelia there, standing awkwardly, twisting the keys in her hands and biting her lip. As he looked at her, her eyes welled with tears. 'Jake…I can't thank you…'

'Don't. Just go, if you have to. I can't do goodbyes.'

She nodded and got into the car, calling Rufus, but he refused to go. He sat down beside Jake and whined, and stupidly, that was the thing that brought tears to his eyes.

He blinked them savagely away, scooped the dog up and put him into the front footwell.

'Can I ring you?' Edward asked.

'Ask your mother. She's got my number. Take care, now—and good luck.'

He shut the door and stepped back, willing the engine to fail, but it started first turn and she drove away. He watched her until they reached the end of the drive and turned onto the road, and then he went back inside and shut the door.

It was so empty.

The house felt as if the very soul had been ripped out of it, and he wandered, lost, from room to room, the silence echoing with their laughter and tears, the squabbles of the children, the baby's gurgling laugh, the dog's sharp, excited bark, Amelia's warm, sexy chuckle, her teasing glances, the tenderness of her loving.

Gone, all of it, wiped out by her stubborn insistence on being independent.

And, hell, he could understand that. He'd grabbed his independence as soon as he could— as a child first at boarding school, then, with valuable life lessons learned, in senior school, and then in life itself, out there in the real world, cutting himself adrift from parents who'd never stopped bickering for long enough to understand him.

But he'd never walked away from love for fear of being hurt. If he had, he might never have married Rachel, never have known the joy of having a child, and for all it had been snatched away from him, he wouldn't have missed a second of it just because it hurt to lose it.

Better to have loved and lost...

But losing Amelia was so unnecessary! He wasn't *like* David. She didn't need to be cautious, because he wouldn't let them down, he wouldn't fail them with his lousy judgement or turn his back or walk away. He'd cut his own heart out before he'd hurt them, any of them. Even the damn dog.

He went into the sitting room, his sanctuary, and saw the recording of him singing. He'd never be able to listen to it again without thinking of Edward standing by the fire with the carol singers and filling the house with that sweet, pure sound.

He looked out of the window at the lump of slush on the lawn that was the remains of the snowman. The sprouts lay haphazard in the scarf, the carrot on the ground, and his hat had slid off sideways and was lying in a soggy heap.

They'd had such fun that day. They'd made snow angels as well, and eaten mountains of delicious food, and they'd played with their toys. Kitty had made him a picture with glitter, and then she'd sprinkled it in his hair.

Fairy dust.

And Amelia had found it that night, in bed, and teased him. The night he'd made love to her for the first time. He'd be finding glitter all over the house for months. Years, probably—

'Jake?'

There was a tap on the door, and it swung in and Kate stood there.

'Are you all right?'

'Why shouldn't I be?'

'I don't know. Why don't you tell me? You look like hell.'

'Thanks. What can I do for you?'

'I've got George Crosbie on the phone. I've been calling your mobile and you haven't had it switched on. He's been trying to get you since yesterday.'

'Sorry. Switch it through to my study, I'll take it there. On second thoughts, I'll come over.'

Anything—even George—was better than sitting in the house on his own and listening to the echoes of the children.

He might have to stay over there all night.

'I hate it here.'

'It'll be lovely, Kitty, I promise. We'll soon make it nice. I'll get all our things out of store in the next few days, and we'll get settled in and it'll be home then.'

'Rufus isn't happy. He doesn't like it.'

He didn't. He sat by the front door and howled the whole time, as if he was hoping Jake would come. Amelia knew how he felt. She could have sat there and howled herself.

Edward was just quiet, retreating into himself as he'd done when David left. Not even the upcoming voice test in a week's time seemed to mean anything to him, and Millie didn't know what to do to help.

Apart from ring Jake and tell him it had all been a big mistake, but how could she? What if it all went wrong again? What if he got bored with the idea of another man's family? Your own was one thing, somebody else's was quite another. And David hadn't even wanted his own, so she didn't hold out hope for anyone else.

'Come on, it's time for bed.'

'I don't like my bed. It's lumpy.'

Hers wasn't. There wasn't a lump in it. Nothing so supportive. It was just saggy, saggy and uncomfortable and maybe even slightly damp. And there was a definite musty aroma that came off it, even through the sheets.

But she'd taken the house because the landlord hadn't demanded a huge deposit or dozens of references, he hadn't minded about the dog, and it was in budget. Just. She wanted to put by a good chunk of her money every month, just in case—

That was going to be carved on her headstone. 'Here lies Amelia Jones—Just In Case.'

'Come on, school tomorrow,' she said brightly. 'You need to get to bed.'

'I don't like the new school,' Edward said. 'I asked about a choir and they laughed.'

Oh, no. How much worse could it get?

'Heard anything from Amelia?'

'Yes. She says they're fine. She's done lots of work for you.'

'Yes. She's good.' Missing, but good. And how he missed her. Missed them all. 'Any news of Edward's voice test?'

She sighed and sat back on the sofa and met his eyes. 'Why don't you just ring them?'

'Because it's none of my business.'

She propped her elbows on her knees and planted her chin in her hands. 'You're in love with her, aren't you?'

'Do I pay you for this?'

'Yes. I'm your personal assistant—and, just now, I think you need a little personal assistance, so, yes, you do.'

He grunted. 'I could do with another coffee, if you want to assist me,' he said bluntly, flicking open a file and scanning the contents.

'He doesn't want to go.'

'What?'

'Edward. He doesn't want to go to the voice test.'

Jake shut the file and stared at her searchingly. 'Why not?'

She shrugged. 'He wouldn't say, apparently. Just announced that he wasn't going, it was rubbish and he didn't want to sing any more, and that was it.'

'Well, maybe he doesn't,' he said slowly, although he didn't believe it for a moment. He'd been really fired up, keen to go, keen to find out all he could, and he'd been really excited when the invitation to attend the test had come through so quickly. So why—?

'I'm going to see her on Sunday. Any message?'

He slammed the door on temptation. 'No. She knows where to find me.'

'You give up easily.'

'No, I don't. But I'm not going to hound her. I gave her the choice, and she went. Her decision. I'm not going to beg.'

'I didn't ask you to beg, just not to give up—'

'Oh, for God's sake, Kate, I poured out my heart to her, told her things I've never told another soul! And she walked away. What else do you expect me to do?' he raged, jack-knifing to his feet and slamming his hand so hard against the window frame that the wood bit into the skin.

'Jake?' Kate's voice was tentative, her hand gentle on his shoulder. 'I'm sorry. I didn't mean to pry. But I can see you're unhappy, and…well, she is, too.'

He stared down the long walk, remembering the children running about having fun, throwing snowballs. 'There's nothing I can do about that. I haven't got the right or the power to do anything about that. Did she tell you I offered her the house in the village?'

'No. Could she afford it? I thought her rent budget was lower than that.'

'No—I mean, I offered to give it to her. Said I'd put it in her name. She said no, so I told her to give me the names of the children so I could put it in their names, and she refused. I thought— if she had a house, if she had independence—'

'But it wouldn't be, would it? It would be like being a concubine. Maybe you should have offered to marry her.'

He turned his head and met her eyes. 'I did. She said no.'

Kate's jaw dropped, and he pushed it up with his finger and smiled tiredly. 'Leave it now. I can't do this any more. I've told her I love her, I've asked her to marry me, I've offered her a house, I've given her a job—and the only thing she's taken is the job, which is her escape route from me. So I've taken the hint,' he said, his voice cracking. He cleared his throat. 'Right, I've done enough today, I'm going home. I'll see you on Monday.'

And he walked out of the office without a backward glance, went over to the house, shut the door of his sitting room, dropped into the sofa with a hefty glass of malt whisky and dedicated the next five hours to drowning his sorrows.

It didn't work.

'Jake looks awful.'

'Does he?'

'Yes—much like you. He told me he asked you to marry him and you said no. And he said you refused the house.'

'He talks too much,' she said tightly, closing the kitchen door so the children couldn't hear, and Kate laughed.

'I don't think so. Are you crazy? If a man like that asked me to marry him, I'd say yes like a shot.'

'What—because he's rich? It's meaningless.'

'No—because he's *nice*, Millie. He's a lovely guy. I can't understand why he's never been married before—although, come to think of it, he's never said that,' she went on thoughtfully. 'I wonder if he's divorced?'

'Don't ask me,' Amelia said, ignoring Kate's searching look, so Kate gave up and leant back against the worktop, her coffee cradled in her hands.

'He seemed shocked that Edward didn't want to do his voice test.'

Oh, *hell.* 'And how did he know that?'

'I told him.'

Millie sighed abruptly and stared at Kate in frustration. 'Do you and Jake do *nothing* at work except talk about me?'

'Oh, we fit in the odd bit—the occasional company takeover, a little asset-stripping, pruning out the dead wood, rolling the stock market dice—'

'Stop it! I don't want to hear it!'

Kate sighed. 'Millie, he's not like David. He doesn't do that. Yes, he buys companies, but he's considered, thoughtful, and he takes risks, sure, but only calculated ones—and here's the difference, he has a better calculator than David. He knows what he's doing, and he doesn't hurt innocent people along the way. If he did, I wouldn't work for him.'

No, she wouldn't, Amelia thought, staring

down the bleak, scruffy little garden at the back of the house. Kate was too intrinsically decent to work for someone who wasn't. But that didn't mean that he was a safe bet personally. Maybe he was just lonely and thought they'd do to fill the gap in his life left by Rachel and Ben. Maybe he thought he could turn Edward into the son he'd lost, the son who could never grow up.

And her boy didn't deserve to be anybody's substitute. Even if that person was his hero—

'Give him another chance. At least see him. I'll babysit for you—you can tell the children you have to work, and they can come to me for a sleep-over.'

Oh, she was so tempted. To see him again—it had only been a week, and she was missing him with every passing second. The rest of her life seemed like an eternity, stretching out in front of her without him.

A safe, dull, boring eternity.

'He hasn't contacted me. If he wanted to see me, he could ring.'

'You told him you didn't want him. Don't expect him to grovel. He said you know where to find him.'

So the ball was in her court.

Tough.

'I can't talk about this now. Not with the children here,' she said as their raised voices filtered through the door. 'Come on, we need to supervise this, it sounds a bit lively.'

Which made a change, because all week they'd been quiet and sad. Oh, damn.

'So—aren't you going to ask how they are?'

Oh, hell. He'd promised himself he wouldn't, but Kate would have known that, and she'd waited all day, keeping him in suspense, keeping him dangling.

'No,' he said bluntly. 'I'm not.'

'They're miserable. They were thrilled to see Megan, and Millie said it was the first time they'd laughed since they'd moved. And the dog sat by the door all day and whined.'

'Not my problem,' he said, his heart contracting into a tight ball in his chest. 'I've done all I can, Kate. I can't do more.'

But then later that week Kate came into his office looking worried.

'I've had a call from Millie. She can't finish that work you sent her—there's a problem.'

He leant back in his chair and looked up at her. 'What sort of a problem?'

'Rufus is ill. He's collapsed. She's taken him

to the vet, but he's got to go to a referral centre. She's got Thomas with her and the children don't know—they need picking up from school. She's asked me if I can have Thomas and keep the children overnight—Jake, what are you doing?'

'Coming with you. She can't face this alone. I'll take my car and follow you.'

'What about your arm?'

'It's fine. She can drive from the vet's. Are you meeting her there?'

'Yes.'

'Right, let's go.'

He stuck his head into Reception on the way past. 'Clear my diary, and Kate's. We're going out,' he said, and followed Kate to the veterinary surgery.

She was standing by the door, pushing Thomas backwards and forwards in the stroller, trying to stop him crying while she watched the car park entrance for Kate's car.

'Come on, come on,' she muttered, and then she saw it turn in and her eyes flooded with tears of relief. 'Look, Thomas, it's Kate! You like Kate! You're going to stay with her—'

'How is he?'

She jerked upright. 'Jake?' she whispered, and

then his arms were round her, and he was folding
her against his heart and holding her tight.

'He's on a drip. They've sedated him—they
think he might have had a stroke. They get them,
apparently. I have to take him to a place miles
away and I haven't got any petrol in the car—'

'I've got mine. You can drive it, I probably
shouldn't with a cast on. Leave yours here, I'm
sure they won't mind. Let's go and talk to them.'

'Where's Kate? I saw her car—'

'I'm here, sweetheart. I'll take Thomas. Give
me your house keys. I'll pick up his stuff and
some things for the others, and you can come
and see me when you get back, OK?'

'OK,' she said, fumbling for her keys with
nerveless fingers. 'Thank you.'

Her eyes flooded again, and Kate hugged her
hard—difficult, because Jake still had one arm
round her, holding her up—and then she was
gone and Jake was steering her into Reception
and talking to the staff.

Rufus was ready to go—the referral centre was
expecting him—and she drove with one eye on
the rear-view mirror, where she could see Jake
sitting with Rufus beside him, still on the drip, the
bag suspended above him clipped to the coat
hook on the edge of the roof lining, his hand

stroking the dog gently and murmuring soothingly to him.

He'd set the sat-nav to direct her, but although
it took the stress out of finding the way, it left her
nothing to worry about but Rufus. And the
journey was interminable.

'Thank you so much for coming with me,' she
said, what seemed like hours later as they sat
outside waiting for news.

'Don't be silly,' he said, his voice gruff. 'I
couldn't let you do this alone.'

'You always did like the stupid dog,' she said,
her voice wobbling, and he put his arm round her
shoulders and squeezed gently.

Not nearly as much as he liked the stupid
owner, he thought, and then the door swung open
and the vet who'd admitted Rufus came out to
them.

'Mrs Jones?'

She leapt to her feet, but her legs nearly gave
out and he held her up, his arm firmly round her
waist, holding her tight as they waited for the
news.

'We've done an MRI, and he has had a stroke,'
the vet said, and he felt a shudder go through her.
'It's in the back of his brain, the cerebellum,

which controls balance. It's quite common in Cavaliers. Their skulls are a little on the small side and the vessels can get restricted, and he's got a little bleed, but we're going to keep him quiet and watch him, and hopefully it will heal and he'll recover. He's still very heavily sedated and we'll keep him like that for a while. The first few hours are obviously critical, and he's got through them so far, but until we can get this settled down and reduce the sedation we won't know if there's any lasting damage. I expect the unsteadiness he was showing will be worse, and he might stagger around in circles or hold his head on one side or just be unable to sort his feet out—it may be temporary, it may be permanent, or there may be a degree of permanent deficit, which is what I would expect. Do you have any questions?'

'Yes—how long will he be in?' she asked, her voice tight.

'Maybe a week. Possibly more.'

'Oh, no. Um…my insurance cover is only for three thousand pounds—'

'Don't worry about that,' Jake said firmly. 'Just do what you have to do and we'll sort it out later.'

She turned her face up to him, pale and shocked, the hideous, unpalatable decision clouding her lovely eyes. 'Jake, you can't do that—'

'Don't argue, Amelia,' he said firmly. 'Not about this. Will you keep in touch?' he added to the vet.

'I can't go—'

'There's nothing you can do here, Mrs Jones,' the vet said gently but firmly. 'Go home. We'll ring you if there's any change, and we'll ring you at seven in the morning and seven in the evening every day for an update.'

'Can I see him?'

'Of course. And you can come and visit him later in the week if he's progressing well, but we want him kept as quiet as possible for now.'

She nodded, and they were led through to see him. He was in a cage, flat on his side on a sheepskin blanket, with drips and oxygen and a heat lamp, and he looked tiny and vulnerable and very, very sick.

Jake felt his eyes prickle, and beside him Amelia was shaking like a jelly.

'Come on, I'm taking you home,' he said firmly, and led her out to the car park. He drove— he probably shouldn't have, with the cast on, but she certainly wasn't fit to drive, so he buckled her in beside him and set off. He could see her knotted hands working in her lap out of the corner of his eye, and her head was bent; he thought she was probably crying.

She lifted her head as they crunched onto the gravel drive, and looked around. 'Why are we here?'

'Because Kate's got your house keys, and I think you need a little TLC in private for a while,' he said, and cut the engine. 'Come on.'

He led her inside, and as soon as the door closed behind them, she collapsed against his chest, sobbing.

'I can't lose him,' she wept. 'I can't—how can I tell the children? I can't take him away from them as well—'

'Shh. Come and sit down, I'll get you a drink.'

'I don't want a drink, I want Rufus,' she said, abandoning all attempt at courage, and he steered her into his sitting room, pushed her down onto the sofa and dragged her into his arms.

She cried for ages, not only for the dog, he suspected, but for all the things she'd lost, the things that had gone wrong, the agonies and disappointments and bitter regrets of the past several years.

And then finally she hiccupped to a halt, her eyes puffy and red-rimmed, her cheeks streaked with drying tears, her mouth swollen. And he'd never seen anything more beautiful in his entire life.

'Better now?'

She nodded, sniffing again, and he hugged her and stood up. 'Come on, let's get something to eat and tell Kate what's happening,' he said gently, and she let him pull her up and lead her through to the kitchen.

There was a note on the island from his housekeeper.

CASSEROLE IN FRIDGE. TOP OVEN, HALF AN HOUR. VEG IN MICROWAVE. FIVE MINUTES.

'Hungry?' he asked. She shook her head, but he didn't believe her, so he put the casserole in the top oven anyway and put the kettle on, then rang Kate.

'Hi. He's doing all right, but the next few hours are critical, so I've got her at home. I don't want her by herself. Can you keep the kids?'

'Of course. I won't be in tomorrow, then.'

'No, I know. Nor will I. I'll keep in touch. Thanks, Kate. I think Amelia wants to talk to you.'

He handed the phone over and listened as she tried hard to be brave and upbeat—talking to the children, he guessed, because she said the same thing three times—to Kate, then to Kitty, then to Edward—and then she turned to him. 'Edward wants to talk to you.'

Oh, hell. He took the phone out of her hand. 'Hi, Edward. How are things?'

'Horrible. Is Rufus really going to be OK?'

'I hope so,' he said, refusing to lie to the child. 'They're very skilled, and if he can get through this, he'll do it there, but we're all thinking about him, and if thinking can help, then he'll make it for sure.'

'Thinking doesn't help,' he said. 'I keep thinking about living with you, but it hasn't helped at all.'

'We can't always have what we want,' he said gently. 'You have to change the things you can, and find the strength to deal with the things you can't. Like this voice test. Kate said you didn't want to go.'

'But what's the point? We can't afford it—and anyway, if Rufus dies, I can't leave Mummy, can I?'

'OK. One thing at a time. You have to be offered a place first, and see if you'd like to do it.

Then you worry about paying. There might be a way—a scholarship, for instance. That was how I got there. My parents didn't have any money, and the choir school paid my fees. And Rufus hasn't died, and there's every chance he'll live and get better, although it may take a while. And you could probably go to the school as a day boy, so you wouldn't have to leave your mother.'

There was a silence at the end of the line.

'Edward?' he prompted.

'Mmm.'

'Don't shut doors until you know what's on the other side. It might be what you're looking for, it might not. But you owe it yourself to find that out. Do you want to talk to your mum again?'

'No, it's OK. Tell her I love her.'

'OK. We'll be in touch. Don't worry. He's in the best place.'

He turned off the phone and set it down. 'I have to give you a message,' he said, turning towards her. 'I love you.'

She looked up into his eyes, startled. 'What did you say?'

'I love you.'

Something—hope?—flared in her eyes, and then died. 'That's the message?'

'Yes. So does Edward. That's his message.'

He saw the hope dawn again, then saw her fight it, not allowing herself the luxury of his love, because she didn't dare to trust him—and there was nothing more he could do to prove to her that he loved her, that she and her family and her dog had a home with him, a place in his heart for ever.

He stepped back. 'I'll make the tea,' he said gruffly, and turned away, the pain of knowing he would never have her in his life too great to stand there in front of her and make civilised conversation about her son and her dog and—

'Jake?'

He paused and put the kettle down. 'What?'

'I'm sorry. I've been so stupid. I've kept thinking you were like David, that under it all you were the same kind of person, pursuing the same goals, but you're not, are you? You're just in the same line of business. He always wanted to get rich quick, but you've got where you are by doing what you can to the best of your ability, by working hard, paying attention to detail, doing it right. And you've been successful, not lucky, because you're good at what you do and you do what you're good at.

'And you're good at being a father, Jake. You've been more of a father to my children in the last few weeks than their own father ever has, and a better man to me than he could ever be. And, as for Rufus—there's no *way* David would have done everything you've done for him. He would have told the vet to put him down, because he didn't realise how important he was to the children, how much he's given them. Not that he would have cared. He never gave them anything without considering it first, but you— when your heart was breaking, you gave us Christmas, even though it must have hurt you unbearably, because it was the right thing to do. And you do that, don't you? The right thing. Always.

'So, if the offer's still open—if you really meant it, if you really do love me and want to marry me—then nothing would make me prouder than to be your wife—'

She broke off, her voice cracking, and he turned slowly and stared at her. Her eyes were downcast, her lip caught between her teeth, and he reached out gently and lifted her chin.

'Was that a yes?' he asked softly, hardly daring to breathe, and she laughed, her eyes flooding with tears.

'Yes, it was a yes,' she said unsteadily. 'If you'll still have me—'

'Stuff the tea,' he said. 'I've got a better idea.'

And, scooping her up in his arms, he carried her upstairs to bed.

'What's that smell?'

'The casserole. Damn.'

He got up and walked, still naked, out of the bedroom and down to the kitchen. She pulled on his shirt and followed him, arriving in the kitchen as he set the casserole dish down on the island. 'Oops.'

'Oops, indeed. Never mind. We'll grab something on the way to Kate's.'

'Kate's?'

'Mmm. I think we need to tell the children— and then we've got wedding plans to make. How do you fancy a January wedding?'

She blinked. 'Two weeks, max? That's tight.'

'Why? We've got the venue. We'll get married in the church, and we'll come back here and celebrate. It's not like it's going to be a huge affair. Your family, our friends—twenty or so? The people from work are my family, really—so more than twenty. OK. It's getting bigger,' he admitted with a laugh, and she hugged him.

'And two weeks isn't long enough to be legal.

I don't care when I marry you, or where, just so long as I can be with you.'

It was May, in the end.

Her brother-in-law gave her away—Andy, who'd apologised for the way he and Laura had treated her at Christmas. He had finally told her that they were unable to have children, which was why they'd found it so hard to have the children there. Kate was her matron of honour, with Kitty and a slightly wobbly Rufus in a brand-new collar as her attendants.

And Edward, who'd been practising for weeks with the choir master at his new school, sang an anthem which reduced them both to tears, and then after the service they walked back to the walled garden where the fountain was playing, and in a pause in the proceedings Jake turned to her and smiled.

'All right, my darling?'

'Much better than all right. Have I ever told you that I love you?'

He laughed softly. 'Only a few thousand times, but it took you long enough, so I'm quite happy to hear it again.'

'Good,' she said, squeezing his arm, 'because I intend to keep telling you for the rest of my life…'

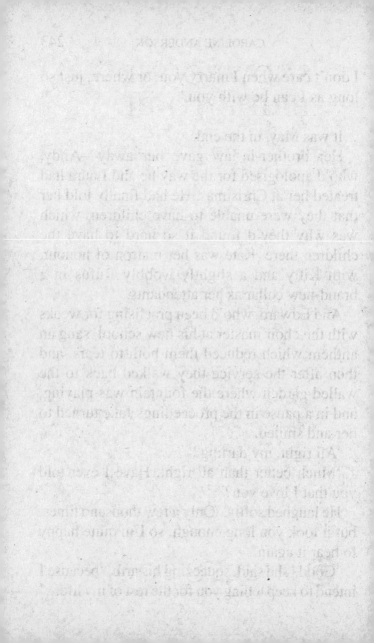

# SNOWBOUND
# BRIDE-TO-BE

BY

## CARA COLTER

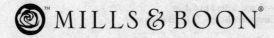

To Alice Sonntag, who gave me a Christmas wreath
with the word *believe* peeking out of fragrant boughs.

First published in Great Britain 2009
Harlequin Mills & Boon Limited,
Eton House, 18-24 Paradise Road, Richmond, Surrey TW9 1SR

© Cara Colter 2009

ISBN: 978 0 263 86983 5

Set in Times Roman 13 on 15 pt
02-1209-51114

Printed and bound in Spain
by Litografia Rosés, S.A., Barcelona

**Dear Reader**

This story is about choices: the choice to run away from love, with all its potential for pain, or to embrace it with all its potential to give life extraordinary richness and fullness. That choice is huge—one of the biggest and most life-altering choices any of us will ever make—and it is at the heart of every romance novel.

But buried in the pages of this story is another choice, and I don't want you to overlook it as insignificant. A man makes a choice to disconnect his smoke detector, and sets in place a series of tragic and unforeseen consequences.

And so, if you are looking for a special gift to give yourself this Christmas, do not overlook the one that may seem insignificant but could in fact be life-altering. Check your smoke detector and make sure it is working. If you don't have one, buy one today. It is truly one of the most wonderful gifts you could ever give yourself and your family.

With warmest wishes for a safe and happy holiday, from my home to yours,

*Cara Colter*

**Cara Colter** lives on an acreage in British Columbia with her partner, Rob, and eleven horses. She has three grown children and a grandson. She is a recent recipient of the *RT Book Reviews* Career Achievement Award in the 'Love and Laughter' category. Cara loves to hear from readers, and you can contact her or learn more about her through her website: www.cara-colter.com

# CHAPTER ONE

TWENTY-TWO gallons of hot chocolate.

Ten of mulled wine.

Four hundred and sixty-two painstakingly decorated Christmas cookies.

And no one was coming.

The storm battering the windows of the White Pond Inn—Emma White had rechristened it the White Christmas Inn just this morning—was being compared by the radio announcer to the Great Ice Storm of 1998 that had wreaked havoc on this region of Atlantic Canada, not to mention Quebec, Ontario, New York and New England.

Christmas was clearly going to be ruined.

"Just like always," Emma murmured out loud to herself, her voice seeming to echo through the empty inn.

Her optimism was not in the least bolstered by the fire crackling cheerfully in the hearth, by her exquisite up-country holiday decorations in the great room, or by her bright-red Santa hat and her lovely red wool sweater with the white angora snowflakes on its front.

In fact, speaking the thought out loud—that Christmas was going to be ruined, just like always—invited a little girl, the ghost of herself, to join her in the room.

The little girl had long, dark wavy hair and was staring at an opened package that held a doll with jaggedly cut hair and blue ink stains on its face, clearly not Clara, the doll she had whispered to Santa that she coveted, but rather a cast-off of one of the children her mother cleaned houses for.

"Shut up," Emma ordered herself, but for some reason the little ghost girl wanted her to remember how she had pretended to be happy. For her mother.

Her mother, Lynelle, who had finally agreed to come for Christmas. Emma could not wait to show her the refurbished house that Lynelle had grown up in but not returned to since she was sixteen, not even when Grandma had died.

Emma tried not to think that her mother had sounded backed into a corner rather than enthused about spending Christmas here. And she had agreed to come only on Christmas Eve, taking a miss on the seasonal celebrations at the inn: the ten-day pre-Christmas celebration, Holiday Happenings. But still Lynelle would be here for the culmination of all Emma's hard work and planning, Christmas Day Dream.

Lynelle's lack of enthusiasm probably meant she was distracted. In Emma's experience that usually meant a new man.

It was probably uncharitable—and unChristmas-like—but when Emma sent the bus ticket, she was sending fare for a single passenger.

The radio cut into her thoughts, but only to add to her sense of unease and gloom. "This just in, the highway closed at Harvey all the way through to the U.S. border."

Emma got up and deliberately snapped off the radio, thoughts of her mother and her memories. She tried to focus on the facts, to be pragmatic, though the inn was plenty of evidence that prag-matism did not come naturally to her. The inn was the project of a dreamer, not a realist.

Okay, she told herself, visitors would not be making the scenic drive up from Maine tonight. Maybe it was just as well. Her aging neighbor, Tim Fenshaw, had already called to say he couldn't bring the horses out in this, so there would be no sleigh rides. The phone line had gone dead before he had said good-bye.

And just before the last light had died in the evening sky, Emma had looked out her back window at her pond and seen that it was being covered with snow faster than she could hope to clear it. So, no skating, either.

"Holiday Happenings is not happening," Emma announced to herself. Or at least not happening tonight, which was to have been the opening night of ten days of skating and sleigh rides right up until Christmas Eve.

It was all adding up to a big fat zero. No sledding, no sleigh rides, no skating, no admission fees, no hot dog sales, no craft sales, no cookie sales. All the things Emma had counted on *finally* to bring the inn firmly into the black.

And to finance her Christmas Day Dream.

"Would one little miracle be so much to ask for?" she asked out loud, sending an irritated look heavenward.

The Christmas Day Dream was Emma's plan to provide a very special Christmas for those who did not have fantasy Christmases. The disappointments of her childhood had not all occurred at Christmas. But somehow, at that time of year in particular, she had waited for the miracle that didn't come.

Last year she'd thought she had left all of that behind her. She was an adult now, and she had looked forward, finally, to the best Christmas of all. Her then fiancé, Dr. Peter Henderson, had invited her to spend Christmas with his family. The very memory tasted of bitterness. Was it possible last year had been worse than all the rest combined?

Emma had learned her lesson! She was not putting her expectations in the hands of others, not her mother, and not a man!

This year she was in charge. She was devoted to eradicating Christmas disappointments. She was determined to make Christmas joyous, not just for herself, but for a world she knew from personal experience was grimly in need of a dose of true Christmas spirit.

In collusion with several area churches and a homeless shelter, a dozen of the neediest families in this region had received invitations to spend Christmas Day at the inn.

The invitations targeted families with nothing to hope for, families who could not have Christmas, or could not have it as they dreamed it should be.

On Christmas Day Emma was throwing open the doors to fifty-one confirmed guests who would arrive on a chartered bus.

Emma *knew* the people coming: the oldest a
seventy-six-year-old grandmother who was the
sole guardian of her three grandchildren, one of
whom was the youngest, a nine-month-old baby
whose two siblings were under age five. The
largest group was a family of eight whose father
had been hurt in an accident early last year, and
had not been able to work since; the smallest was
a single mother and her handicapped son.

And, of course, her mother, who understood
Christmases with nothing—one year they had
not even had a tree—would be there to share in
the joy. There would be gifts for everyone. Brand-
new. No hairless ink-stained dolls. But more than
gifts, the *feeling* would be there. Emma had been
collecting skates, and having them sharpened in
anticipation of skating, Tim was hooking up the
Clydes to give sleigh rides.

His daughter-in-law, Mona, and two granddaughters, Sue and Peggy, who were staying with
him while Tim, Jr., served with the Canadian
Armed Forces overseas, had practically been
living here preparing for Holiday Happenings
and the Christmas Day Dream.

Not even last year, anticipating Christmas
with the Hendersons, had filled Emma with this
sense that by giving this gift to others, she would

know the secret of the season, would share in its universal peace.

Now, her dreams felt precarious. *Naive.* She could hear Peter's voice as if he stood next to her.

"How am I going to pay for everything?" she whispered. How was she going to pay the Fenshaws for all the time they had given her? And, indeed, for Christmas Day Dream? And the stacks of wonderful brand-new gifts she'd been foolish enough to put on credit, her optimism had been so high? She hadn't been able to see how Holiday Happenings could possibly fail. She'd been having a dozen calls a day about it since she'd put the posters up in mid-November.

The St. Martin's Church youth group had sent her the admissions in full for thirty-two kids—who were supposed to come tonight. She remembered how gleeful she had been when she had used their money to make a deposit on the chartered bus for her Christmas-Day guests.

Emma could feel a familiar headache pulling between her eyebrows, knotting above the bridge of her nose.

She'd inherited White Pond, the neglected house and overgrown eighteen acres from her grandmother last spring. It had quickly become apparent to her she couldn't afford to keep it.

By then Emma was committed to keeping it. There was something here of her family and her history that Lynelle had scorned, but that Emma *needed*. So, she'd used her life savings, not huge on her wage as a medical receptionist, given permanent notice to the job she had taken temporary leave from, and risked her engagement, which had already been on the rocks since last Christmas, and which had well and truly washed up on shore when she'd made the decision to come home and care for the grandmother who had been a virtual stranger to her.

And then on a shoe-string budget, with endless determination and elbow grease, Emma had done her best to refurbish the house. She had opened as a bed and breakfast last summer.

It had soon been woefully obvious to her that the B and B business was as tricky and as full of pitfalls as her old house. Still, she had hoped to repair all the foibles of her first summer season with Holiday Happenings.

Again, Emma could sense her former fiancé and boss, Dr. Peter Henderson, his thin face puckered with disapproval, his arms folded over the narrowness of his chest. "Emma," he was saying, "you don't have any idea what you are getting into."

She hated it that with each passing day, his predictions of doom and gloom seemed to be just a little closer to coming true.

*And if I had known the full extent of what I was getting into, would I have—* She wasn't allowing herself to think like that.

Emma turned an eye to the inn's tree, a Fraser fir, magnificent in completely white ribbons and ornaments and lights, the angel's wings brushing the ten-foot ceiling. Emma let her eyes rest on that angel for a moment.

"One miracle," Emma said quietly. "I wanted a perfect Christmas. I wanted to give the best gift of all, hope."

The angel gazed back at her with absolute serenity.

"Oh," Emma said, annoyed, "you aren't even a real angel. If I had glass eyes, and paper wings I could look serene, too!"

But then she cast her gaze around the room and her heart softened. The great room of the White Pond Inn had been turned into a picture out of a Christmas fairy tale. This scene was the payoff for all her hard work, and worth the crush of bills, the exhaustion that had become her constant companion.

A fire roared and crackled in the river-rock

hearth, colorful woolen socks hung at the solid-slab oak mantle. Garlands of real holly were tacked to crown molding. White poinsettias shone like lights in the dark corners of the room.

Parcels wrapped in shades of white and festooned with homemade bows, containing brand-new dolls and fire trucks were already piled high under that tree, though she had to admit they didn't look quite as pretty when she wasn't sure how she was going to pay for them!

She forced her mind away from that, and finished her inventory of the room. Red-and-white cushions had replaced the ordinary ones on the sofas and chairs, vases held candy canes, the glowing dark planks of the hardwood floors were covered with white area rugs.

The room held a delicious aroma because of the continuous baking that had been happening in the house. The sweet comforting scents of cinnamon and nutmeg and pumpkin and apples had mixed with the smell of the occasional back puff of wood smoke to create a scent that could have been labeled and sold, *Christmas*.

*Another great money-making idea from Emma White,* she told herself sarcastically, but then she sighed, unable not to enjoy the pleasure of what she had done.

The inn was a vision of Christmas. It was going to bring great joy to many people. When her mother saw it, it would erase every bad Christmas they had ever spent together.

"Holiday Happenings and the Christmas Day Dream will still happen," Emma told herself stubbornly, but details from the ice storm of 1998 insisted on crowding into her head.

The six-day storm had caused billions of dollars in damage, left millions of people without power for periods that had varied from days to weeks. Roads had been closed, trees destroyed, power lines had snapped under the weight of rain turning to ice.

"I could not be so unlucky to have a six-day storm shut down Holiday Happenings completely," she muttered, but then she whispered, "Could I?"

The storm threw shards of ice up against her window and howled under her eaves in answer.

And then, above the howl of the wind, her doorbell chimed its one clanging, broken note, but still an answer to her question about her luck!

Emma's eyes flew to her grandfather clock. Eight o'clock! Just when people were supposed to arrive. They had come anyway! The miracle had happened! How was it she had not heard cars, slamming doors, voices?

She tried to rein in her happiness. Of course, it could just be Tim, checking to make sure she was all right in the storm.

The Fenshaws had invited her into the fold of this lovely small community as if she belonged here, as if she was one of them. Tim had been interested in the White Pond property for his son when he returned from overseas, but when Emma had told him she had decided to keep it, he and his daughter-in-law Mona had seemed genuinely pleased, as if they had waited all their lives for her to come home to them.

Now, what if she couldn't pay them after the hours and hours they had devoted to making her dreams become a reality? She couldn't have operated the inn for one day without their constant help and support.

A shiver went down her spine. Worse, what if all these dreams, her foolishness as Peter had called it, cost her the inn?

She went and opened the door, and despite the rush of ice-cold air, her heart beat hopefully in anticipation of guests, maybe locals from Willowbrook who had braved the weather.

Only it wasn't locals.

And it wasn't Tim.

A stranger stood there, the glow from the string

of white Christmas lights that illuminated the porch nearly totally blocked by his size. He was tall and impossibly broad across the shoulders. The sense of darkness was intensified by the absolute black of a knee-length wool coat, black gloves, dark, glossy hair, shot through with snow-flakes.

His features were shadowed, but even so, Emma could see the perfect cast of his nose, the thrust of high cheekbones, the strength in the jut of his chin.

The stranger was astonishingly, heart-stop-pingly handsome, even though the set of his firm mouth was grim, and his eyes were dark, intense and totally forbidding.

Emma shivered under his scrutiny, felt the sweep of his cool gaze take her in from red socks to ridiculous hat, and saw his mouth tighten into an even grimmer line.

It felt to Emma as if the devil himself had decided to pay her an early Christmas visit. In an instant she went from being an independent woman, operating her own business, to one who wished she could strip off her shapeless sweater and the added bulk of the long johns she had put on earlier in prepara-tion for skating and sleigh-riding.

She became a woman who would have given

up just about anything to take back the recent disastrous haircut. In an effort to make her life simpler—or maybe to assert it was *her* life—she had cut her long glossy black hair, one of the few things about her that Peter had approved of. In rebellion, set free, heavy waves had turned to impossible, crazy curls. At least the Santa hat would be hiding the worst of it, though Emma wished she wasn't wearing that, too.

There was something alarmingly intriguing in the to-die-for features of the stranger who blocked the light from her front door. As her eyes adjusted to the deep shadow around him, she drank in his features and the expression on his face.

The man looked as if he might have laughed once, but did no more. He was one of those men who was a puzzle that begged to be solved. Despite the remoteness in him—or maybe deepened because of it—he was temptation personified.

But not to her, a woman sworn to put all her passion into her business and the coming Christmas. A woman who had sworn that the White Pond Inn was going to be *enough* for her, who could not trust herself to make a good decision about men if her life depended on it. No one, after all, had *looked* like a better bet than Peter.

Her intriguing visitor's eyes moved from her to the wreath on her door, taking in the sprigs of white pine interlaced with balsam and grand fir, taking in the gypsophila and tiny white bells, the glory of the homemade white satin bow. Finally, his gaze paused on the little wooden letters, red, inserted in the wreath, peeking out from under a sprig of feathery cedar.

*Believe.*

His expression hardened and his gaze strayed to the rest of her porch, glancing off the holly wound through the spindles, the red rag rugs, the planters filled with spruce boughs and red berries.

If she was not mistaken, it was contempt that darkened his eyes to pitch before they returned to her face.

*Slam the door*, she instructed herself. *Whatever he has come here for, you don't have it. And he doesn't have one thing you need, either.*

She reminded herself, sternly, of rule one: independence! Emma already knew, many thanks to her mother—a lesson reinforced by the good doctor—that a man was the easiest way to lose that sense of independence, that sense of owning your own life.

But the weather was providing a cruel reminder that she did not always make the rules for her life. Now she was given another such reminder.

Because, in a breath, closing the door on him was no longer an option. A tiny whimper drew her attention, finally, from the mesmerizing black ice of his eyes.

She was astonished to see that nestled into the huge expanse of his shoulder, made almost invisible by utter stillness and a black blanket that matched his coat, was a baby.

It turned its face from his shoulder, and gazed at Emma with huge blue eyes, a living version of a doll she had wrapped earlier. The eyes that gazed at her with such solemn curiosity were as innocent as his were world-weary.

A girl, if the bonnet, a strangely lopsided concoction of dark wool, was any indication. Emma realized the hat was on the wrong way.

Despite the fact the visitor who had emerged from the storm looked so formidable, and so without humor, she almost smiled at the backwards hat.

But his words stole the smile and her breath.

"We need a place to stay."

Her mouth moved in protest but not a single, solitary sound emerged from it. Him? Stay here?

With all his attractions and mysteries being doubled by his protective stance with the beautiful baby?

"The highway patrol just told me to get off the road. It was going to close behind me."

*Say something,* she ordered herself, but no sound came out of her mouth.

"Hopefully," he said, "it will just be for a few hours. Until the roads reopen."

Impossible to say yes to him. Even his voice was dangerous—as unconsciously sensuous as melted chocolate clinging to a fresh strawberry. He was dangerous to a woman like her who had made vows about the course her life was now going to take. *No more begging for approval, married to the inn.* And yet here she was, wanting to snatch the Santa hat off her head *for him.*

So, impossible to say yes. And even more impossible to say no.

He had a baby with him.

And isn't this where the age-old story began? With no room at the inn?

She, who so desperately wanted to give everyone the perfect Christmas, turning away a stranger on the flimsy excuse that her need for predictability felt threatened by his cynical look and the dark mystery that clung to him like fog clinging to a dark forest?

By the treacherous little niggling of her own attraction? The part of her she would have sworn, even seconds ago, that she had completely tamed?

A primitive longing that if she indulged it, could turn her into her mother in a horrifying blink? Prepared to throw away everything—*everything*—for whatever it was that hard mouth promised.

She tried to reason with herself. He needed a place to stay. A few hours. That was hardly going to rock her world, mature business woman that she was now.

She pulled off the Santa hat.

His eyes went to her hair, something twitched along the firm line of his mouth, but then was gone.

"The highway patrol said you have the only accommodations in the entire Willowbrook area." The way he said it made her feel as if he would have stayed elsewhere if he'd had a choice.

A modern hotel, stylish and without character. In his eyes, she saw all her hard work judged harshly, dismissed as corny, not charming. She did not like it one bit that the judgments of a complete stranger could hurt so badly. For a moment she wanted desperately to tell him she did not let rooms in the winter, which she didn't.

But he had no choice. And neither did she. She was not sending that baby back out into the storm.

Despite the fact that none of the normal precautions were in place that protected her as a single woman running a business—the pre-visit information sheet, the credit card verification of ID—Emma felt only the danger of her attraction.

Something about the way he held the baby, protective, fierce, made her understand the only dangers he posed to her were emotional ones. But even if she were foolish enough to let forced proximity threaten her vows of independence, one look at his shuttered face assured her he would never be foolish.

She stepped back from the door, coolly professional. "I usually don't operate as an inn in the winter, but I can clearly see that this is an emergency."

If she hoped her aloof graciousness would give her the upper hand, she was mistaken. Scent swept in the door with him, the deeply masculine smells of soap and aftershave, the baby scents of powder and purity, quickly overpowering all the warm cookie and Christmas smells.

When she firmly closed the door against the weather, the ancient knob came off in her hand, making her feel not professional, and not gracious, either.

*Not now,* she warned the old house, stuffing the knob back in the hole, hoping he hadn't noticed.

But when she turned back to him, she could see he was a man who noticed everything. He would have noticed even if the knob had not popped back out of the door and landed with a clatter on the floor.

She bent and picked it up, thoroughly flustered. "I don't charge extra for the rustic charm," she said breezily, trying to ignore the cold air whooshing through the round hole in the door where the knob should have been.

No smile.

"Ah." He glanced around her front foyer, took in the small welcoming hallway tree, decorated entirely in tiny white angels, the garlands of white-bowed boughs that wove their way up the staircase and had, until seconds ago, filled her house with the sharp, fresh scents of pine and Christmas.

He stood directly under the sprig of mistletoe she had suspended from the ceiling, and that made her look at his lips.

And think a distressing thought, entirely inappropriate for an independent professional such as herself, about what they would taste like, and what price a woman would be willing to pay to know that.

*Too much. The price would be too much.* She was still reeling from her mistake in judgment about Peter. Guessing what a complete stranger's lips might taste like was just proof, as if she needed more, that she was still capable of grave errors.

He frowned. "If you don't operate as an inn at this time of year, do you do all of this decorating for your personal enjoyment?"

"I was expecting guests for the evening." She fought further evidence of her poor judgment—a ridiculous temptation to drop the professional facade and to unburden herself about the disastrous inaugural evening of Holiday Happenings. Though his shoulders looked broad enough to cry on, his eyes did not look capable of sympathy.

His next words made her glad she had kept her confidences. "Do you have any rooms without the, er, Christmas theme?"

"You don't like Christmas." She said it flatly, a statement rather than a question. Given his expression, it was already more than obvious to her he did not like Christmas. And probably not puppies, love songs or tender movies, either.

Which was good. Very good. So much easier to get through a few hours of temptation—of her own bad decision-making abilities—if the effect of those intoxicating good looks were offset by a vile nature.

*What kind of person doesn't like Christmas? Especially with a baby! He practically has an obligation to like Christmas!*

The baby gurgled, reached up from under the blanket and inserted a pudgy finger in her mouth.

Nothing in the man's expression softened, but the baby didn't seem to notice.

"Mama," the baby whispered, and laid her head on his shoulder in a way that confirmed what Emma already knew. Her guest might be cynical and Christmas-hating, but she could trust him with her life, just as that baby, now slurping contentedly on her thumb, did.

"Is she wanting her mama?" Emma asked, struck by the backward bonnet again, by the incongruity of this man, seemingly without any kind of softness, being with this baby. *Of course. A mother.* That made her safe from this feeling, hot and liquid, unfurling like a sail catching a wind. He was taken. Her relief, her profound sense of *escape* was short-lived.

"No," he said, and then astonishingly, a flush of red moved up his neck, and Emma saw the tiniest hint of vulnerability in those closed features.

He hesitated, "Unfortunately, that's what she calls me."

Again, Emma felt a tickle of laughter. And again it was cut off before it materialized, because of the unwanted *softness* for him when she thought of him being called Mama. It was a startling contradiction to the forbidding presence of him, ridiculously sweet.

Even though she knew it was none of her business, she *had* to know.

"Where is her mother?"

Something shot through his eyes with such intensity it sucked all the warmth from the room. It was more than sadness, for a moment she glimpsed a soul stripped of joy, of hope. She glimpsed a man lost in a storm far worse than the one that howled outside her door.

"She's dead," he said quietly, and the window that had opened briefly to a tormented soul slammed shut. His voice was flat and calm, his eyes warned her against probing his soul any deeper.

"I'm so sorry," Emma said. "Here, let me take her while you get your coat off."

But when she held out her arms, she realized she was still holding the broken door knob.

He juggled the baby, and took the doorknob with his free hand, his gloved fingers brushing hers just long enough for her to feel the heat beneath those gloves.

Effortlessly, he turned and inserted the knob in the door, jiggled it into place and then turned back to her.

His easy competence made Emma feel more off center, incompetent, as if her stupid doorknob was sending out messages about her every failing as an innkeeper.

"The coat rack is behind you," she said, and then added formally, as if she was the doorman. "Is there luggage?"

"I hope we won't be staying long enough to need it." He handed the baby to her.

*Me, too,* Emma thought. The baby was surprisingly heavy, her weight sweet and pliable as if she was made of warm pudding, boneless.

The wind picked that moment to howl and rattle the win-dows, and it occurred to Emma she might be fighting temptation for more than a few hours. It was quite possible her visitors would be here at least the night. Thankfully she thought of the crib she had found so that the babies who came Christmas Day would have a place to nap.

The baby regarded her warily, scrunching up her face in case terror won out over curiosity.

"How old is she?"

"Fourteen months."

"What's her name?" Emma asked softly, grateful for the baby's distraction against the man removing his jacket to reveal a dark, expensive shirt perfectly tailored to fit over those impossibly broad shoulders, dark trousers that accentuated legs that were long, hard-muscled beneath the fine fabric.

"Tess," he provided.

"Hello, Tess," she crooned. "Welcome to the White Christmas Inn. I'm Emma."

"The White Christmas Inn?" the man said, "you aren't serious, are you?"

"Didn't you see the sign on the driveway?" Just this morning, she had placed the word *Christmas* over the word *Pond,* the letters of *Christmas* just the teensiest bit squished to make them fit.

"I saw a sign, I assumed it was for the inn, but most of it is covered in snow and ice."

"The White Christmas Inn. Seriously."

He groaned, softly.

"Is there a problem?"

His answer was rhetorical. "Do you ever feel the gods like to have a laugh at the plans of human beings?"

Even though he obviously expected no answer, Emma responded sadly, "Yes. Yes, I do."

*The White Christmas Inn.*

Ryder Richardson had no doubt the gods *were* enjoying a robust laugh at his expense right now. When he had headed out on the road tonight, he'd had one goal: to escape Christmas entirely. He had packed up his niece, Tess, and that amazing mountain of things that accompanied a traveling baby, with every intention of making it to his lakeside cottage by dark.

The cottage where there would be absolutely no ho-ho-ho, no colorful lights, no carols, no tree, no people and especially no phone. He had deliberately left his cell phone at home. Ryder Richardson could make Scrooge look like a bit player in the bah-humbug department.

He was not ashamed to admit to himself he just wanted to hide out until it was all over. Until the trees were shredded into landscape pulp, the lights were down, there was not a carol to be heard, and he could walk along a sidewalk without hearing bells or having complete strangers smile at him and wish him a Merry Christmas.

Ryder looked forward to the dreary days of January like a man on a ship watching for a beacon to keep him from the rocks on the darkest night.

In January there would be fewer reminders and fewer calls offering sympathy. The invitations to holiday parties and dinners and events designed to lure him out of his memories and his misery would die down.

In his luggage, he had made a small concession to Christmas. Ryder had a few simple gifts to give Tess. He had a soft stuffed pony in an implausible shade of lavender, new pink suede shoes, for she already shared a woman's absolute delight in footwear, and a small, hardy piano-like toy that he was probably going to regret obtaining within hours of having given it to her.

He had not brought wrapping paper, and probably would not give Tess the gifts on December twenty-fifth, taking advantage of the fact that at fourteen months of age his niece was not aware enough of the concept of Christmas to know the difference.

This would be his year of reprieve. Next year,

Tess would be two at Christmas. It wouldn't be so easy to pretend the season didn't exist. Next year, she would probably have grasped the whole concept of Santa, would *want* things from Ryder. Would he be able to give them to her?

As he turned back from the coat rack, through the open archway from the foyer into the living room, he caught sight of the fire burning brightly in the hearth at the White Christmas Inn, the huge tree glowing, top to bottom, an ethereal shade of white.

Despite steeling himself against all things Christmas, the scene called to him, like the lights of home calling a warrior back to his own land. For a disturbing moment he felt almost pulled toward that room, the tree, the promise it held. *Hope.*

# CHAPTER TWO

*HOPE.* The word burned in Ryder's heart for a second or two, not bright and warm, but painful. Because that was what he was intent on quashing in himself. He was a warrior who had glimpsed the lights of a home he could never go back to.

The socks that hung from the mantel, cheerful, were what triggered the memory.

Without warning—for the memories always came without warning, riding in on a visual clue or a scent or a sound he could not control—a picture flashed in his mind of different socks on a different mantel nearly a year ago. Those socks, bright red, with white fur cuffs, had names on them.

Drew. Tracy. Tess.

Ryder could see his brother, standing in front of those socks, holding the tiny baby way above his head, bringing her down, her round belly to his lips, blowing, the baby gurgling, and Drew looking as happy as Ryder had ever seen his brother look.

A shudder rippled through Ryder, and he looked deliberately away from the socks that hung on the mantel of the White Christmas Inn, picked up the baby bag that he had dropped on the floor, shrugged it over his shoulder.

In a few days, a year would have passed, and Ryder's pain had not been reduced. A reminder about the danger of hope. There was no sense hoping next year would be better. There was no sense hoping life could ever be what it had been before the fire that had swept through his brother's house early Christmas morning.

"Get the baby," Drew had cried to him, as he'd stumbled out of the guest room, "I'll get Tracy."

Anyone who had not been in a fire could not understand the absolute and disorienting darkness, the heat, the smoke, the chaos intensified by the roar and shriek of it, as if the fire was a living thing, a monster, a crazed animal.

Somehow, Ryder had found the baby, and gotten her outside. Tracy had already been out there, in bad shape, burned, dazed, barely coherent. At first Ryder thought that meant his brother was safe. But then he'd realized Drew was still in there, looking for his wife, not knowing she was out here.

He'd raced back for the door, uncaring that flames roared out of it like it was the mouth of hell. He'd almost made it, too, back in there to find his brother.

But neighbors had pulled him back, four men, and then six, holding him, dodging his fists, absorbing his punches, their urgency to keep him out of there as great as his to go back in. He still woke in the night sometimes, coated in sweat, his heart beating hard, screaming his fury.

*Let me go. You don't understand. Let...me...go.*

When Ryder thought of that the fury was fresh. If anything, he added to it as time went on. How could he have failed so terribly? How could his strength have failed him when he needed it most? If he could have shaken off those men, made them understand...

Then, just three months ago, more heartbreak, an intensified sense of failure, as Tracy, all out of bravery, had quit fighting her horrible injuries.

If there was a feeling Ryder hated more than any other it was that one: *powerlessness.* He'd been as powerless to save Tracy as he had been to break free of the men who had kept him from his brother.

Ryder shuddered again. He had put a wall around himself, and instead of letting it come down as time passed, brick by brick he made it stronger. He was ravaged by what had happened, destroyed by it. He could function, but not feel.

He hated it that his armor felt threatened by the fact that, ever so briefly, he had *felt* what the room had to offer. Heard the word. *Hope*. And seen that other word on her front door.

*Believe*.

"Are you all right?"

"Yes," he said, keeping his voice deliberately cold, protecting the coating of ice that shielded what was left of his heart.

No, he wasn't. He had tried to keep Christmas, its association with his greatest failure, at bay. Instead, at the caprice of fate, here he was at a place that appeared to have more Christmas than the North Pole. If there were no baby to think of, he would put his coat back on and take his chances with the storm.

But then, if there were no baby to think of, he was pretty sure he would have self-destructed already.

"You looked like you saw a ghost," Emma said. "Apparently we have them here, but I haven't seen one yet."

She actually sounded envious that he might have spotted one.

"I don't believe in ghosts," he said curtly. Did she notice the emphasis on *believe?* Because that was the first in a long list of things he did not believe in. He hoped he would not be here long enough to share the full extent of his disillusionment with her.

"Well, I do," she said, a hint of something stubborn in her voice. "I think there are spirits around this old house that protect it and the people in it. And I think there is a spirit of Christmas, too."

And then, having made her stand, she blushed.

He looked at her carefully. Now that she had taken the hat off, he felt much less inclined to ask to speak to her mother. How old would she be? Early twenties, probably. Too young to be running this place, and too old to be believing nonsense.

He replayed her words of earlier. *I usually don't operate as an inn in the winter. I don't charge extra for the rustic charm.*

*I* not *we.*

She ran a hand through the dark, wild hair revealed by the removal of the awful Santa hat, a gesture that was self-conscious. Her blush was deepening.

Despite the shard of the memory stuck in his heart like broken glass, her hair tried, for the second time, to take down a brick, to tease something out of him. A smile? Only Tess made him smile. Though her hair was worse than Tess's, which was saying something. His hostess's hair, dark and shiny, was a tangle of dark coils, flattened by the hat, but looking as if they intended to spring back up at any moment.

He was shocked by the slipping of another brick—an impulse to touch her hair, to coax the curls up with his fingertips. He killed the impulse before it even fully formed, but not before he pictured how encouraging the wild disarray of her hair would make her sexy, rather than the adorable image the red socks and red sweater projected.

She was looking at him like a kitten ready to show claws if he chose to argue the spirit of Christmas with her, which he didn't.

If the way she held Tess and crooned to her was any indication, she was exactly as she appeared; soft, wholesome, slightly eccentric, a *believer* in goodness and light and spirits protecting her house and Christmas. Not his type at all.

Even back in the day, before *it* had happened, when he cared about such things, he'd gone for flashier women, whitened teeth, diamond rings, designer clothes. Women who would have scorned this place as hokey, and his hostess for being so naive.

Except, last year, a spectator to the domestic bliss his brother had found, Ryder had thought, briefly, *maybe I want this, too.*

But now he knew he didn't want anything that intensified that feeling of being powerless, and in his mind that's what being open to another person would do, make him weak instead of strong, slowly but surely erode the bricks of his defenses. What was behind that wall was grief and fury so strong he had no doubt it would destroy him and whoever was close to him, if and when it ever came out.

For Tess's sake, as well as his own, he kept a lid on *feelings*. He knew he had nothing to give anyone; somehow he was hoping his niece would be the exception, though he had no idea how she would be.

"You don't run this place by yourself, do you?" he asked, suddenly needing to know, not liking the idea of being alone with all this sweetness, not trusting himself with it, especially after that renegade impulse to tease something sexy out of her hair.

He hoped, suddenly, for a family-run operation, for parents in the wings, or better yet, a husband. Someone to kill dead this enemy within him, the unexpected sizzle of attraction he felt. Someone he could talk hockey with as the night dragged on, to keep his mind off how little he wanted to be here, and how little fate cared about what he wanted.

Ryder's eyes drifted to her ring finger. Red nail polish, a bit of a surprise, but probably chosen in the spirit of the season, to match the socks. How could he possibly be finding this woman, who stood for everything he was trying to run away from, attractive?

There was no ring on her finger, so he knew the answer to his question even before she answered.

"It's all mine," she said, and her chin lifted proudly. "I inherited the house from my grandmother, restored it, named it the White Pond Inn, and have been operating it on my own ever since."

"I thought it was the White Christmas Inn," he reminded her dryly.

"Christmas transforms everything," she said with grave dignity, "it makes all things magic, even my humble inn."

Well, she obviously *believed*.

"Uh-huh." He didn't want to get into it. He

truly didn't want to know a single thing more about her. He didn't want to *like* the fact that despite her corkscrew hair waiting to pop into action, and despite her falling-off doorknob, she was trying so hard to keep her dignity.

*Show me to my room. Please.* But somehow, instead, Ryder found himself asking, "What makes a young woman tackle a project like this?" He didn't add, *on her own,* though that was really his question.

Ryder was an architect. He and Drew had drawn up plenty of plans to restore places like this one. Underneath all the cosmetic loveliness, he was willing to bet the abundance of decorations hid what the falling-off door handle had hinted at. Problems. Large and small. Way more than a little scrap of a woman on her own would be up to.

"I'm a dreamer," she said, fiercely unapologetic, and again, in the way she said that, he caught sight of her pride and stubbornness. And her hurt. As if someone—probably a hard-hearted jerk like him—had mocked her for being a dreamer.

*Whoo boy.* He bit his tongue, because it was obvious to him this house did not need a dreamer. A carpenter, certainly. Likely an electrician. Probably a plumber.

Despite biting his tongue nearly clear through, his skepticism must have clearly shown on his face because she felt driven to convince him—or maybe herself—that the house *needed* a dreamer.

"I actually saw it for the first time when my grandmother got sick. My mother and she had been, um, estranged, but one of the neighbors called and asked me to come home to help care for her. This house was love at first sight for me. Plus, it had been in our family for generations. When Granny died, I inherited, and I had to figure out a way I could afford to keep it."

That was a warning, if he'd ever heard one. He did not like women who believed in love at first sight. As a man who lived in the wreckage of dreams, he did not like dreamers nor all their infuriating optimism.

Aside from that, the words told him an even more complete truth, whether he wanted to know it or not, and he didn't. He saw the glitter of some defense in her eyes that told him things he would have been just as happy not knowing.

*Hurt.* Clues in what she was telling him. Something missing in her family, that had filled her with longing? Despite the happy Christmas costume, there was a reason a woman like that took on a place like this. And he was willing to bet it had little to do with family heritage, and a whole lot to do with a broken heart. She had decided loving a house was easier than loving a person.

He heartily approved, though he wondered if a dreamer could be pragmatic enough to pull that off.

This ability to *see* people more clearly than they wanted to be seen, and certainly more clearly than he wanted to see them, was one of the things Ryder hated since the fire. He sensed things, often seeing *past* what people said, to some truth about them. It was a cruel irony, since he was desperately trying not to care about anything, that he could see things he had never seen before, things that threatened the walls and armor of the defenses that kept some things in him, and some things out.

Pre-fire, Ryder had been a typical man, happily superficial, involved totally in himself. Building a business with his brother, hanging out with his buddies, playing in a semi-serious hockey league, and never getting even semi-serious with any one woman. That had been his life: a happy, carefree place. A guy zone of self-centered hedonism.

He had never been deep. *Insensitive* probably would have described him nicely, blissfully unaware there was any other way to be.

Now, he could walk by a complete stranger, and see their tragedies in the lines around their mouths and the shadows in their eyes. It was as if he had become a member of a secret club of sadness. *Not* seeing had been a blessing he had not appreciated at the time.

A little more than a year ago, Ryder certainly wouldn't have ever been able to spot the hurt hiding in the shadows of Emma's eyes. He realized, uncomfortably, that even with those shadows, her eyes were amazing.

A part of him, purely masculine, acknowledged that physically Emma was exquisite. Her features were small and perfect, her nose snubbed up a touch at the end, her lips formed plump bows of sensuality. And he was not sure he had ever quite seen that shade of eye color before, soft gray-green, moss and mist.

Despite the outfit—was it deliberately chosen to hide her assets? Another thing he probably would not have guessed pre-fire—he could see she was delicately curved, unconsciously sensuous.

Annoyed with himself, he realized it was the first time since the fire he had allowed the faint stir of attraction toward a member of the opposite sex to penetrate his barriers.

Strange it would be her. The women he had been attracted to in the past were as superficial as he was. He had liked women who wore clingy clothes, and push-up bras, who glittered with makeup and jewelry, and who intoxicated with expensive scents.

Emma had probably wiggled by his defenses simply because he would have never thought to erect that particular wall against someone like her: makeup-free, tangled hair, lumpy jeans, grandma sweater. And defiantly set on letting him know she *believed*.

Still, regardless of how she had done it, it had happened. That faint stirring of something, that felt like life. Trying to call him back.

To a place, he reminded himself sternly, that was gone.

He shut down what he was feeling, quickly, but he could not shut down the acknowledgment that it had been a first. He did not feel ready for firsts: to laugh again, to feel again.

Because somehow even contemplating the possibility of firsts, of returning, felt like some kind of betrayal, as if it minimized who Drew and Tracy had been and what they had meant to him. And maybe because it would require him to do what could not be done: forgive himself.

So, in a different lifetime, when he had been a different man, Ryder might have followed that thread of attraction to see where it would lead.

But he already knew Emma was hurt, had already seen secrets in her soft eyes that she probably would rather he not have known.

And the man he was now was so damaged that he knew he could only hurt her more. His hardness felt as though it would take all that was wondrous about her—such as this childlike delight in Christmas—and curdle it, like vinegar hitting milk.

It was all the smells in here, pine and pumpkin, all the decorations, her ridiculous hat making her look like an emissary from Santa, that were bringing up these uncomfortable thoughts. For the most part, Ryder was successful at warding off the worst of it.

Still, that all this had flooded in within moments of entering this place troubled him. He would probably be better off sleeping in his car than taking refuge here.

He'd known as soon as he stepped under the roof of her porch that this place posed a peculiar kind of danger to his armored heart. As if to confirm that suspicion, he had spotted the letters, peeking out from under the boughs of the wreath.

*Believe.*

The sign had made him want to head back to his car, find shelter elsewhere. *Believe in what?*

If he'd been by himself, he would have gone back to the car, found a pub, preferably with a pool table and a big-screen TV, to while away the hours in before the road reopened.

But he wasn't by himself, and the fact that he wasn't changed his ability to choose.

Every single decision Ryder made had to be run through the filter of what was best for Tess. Obviously it wasn't a place with a pool table, however comforting he would have found a rowdy male environment.

What was best for Tess? In the long run? He knew people wondered if he could possibly be the best guardian for her. Some of the bolder ones had even hinted that the most loving thing to do would be to find her a real family, a mother who could actually get a comb through her hair, who would enjoy the intricacies of those silly, frilly, small dresses.

But his brother and Tracy had wanted him to have her. He'd been stunned that they'd had a will, that they had appointed him guardian.

Despite the fact he knew himself to be terribly flawed, Ryder could not ever let her go. Tess was what was left of his brother. He was fierce in his protection of her. He hired a nanny who looked after the baby details—hair, baths, clothes—but Mrs. Markle had abandoned him for Christmas to be with her own family.

His initial awkwardness with the baby had quickly given way to absolute devotion. What was left of his heart belonged firmly to that little spark of spirit that represented all that was left of Drew and Tracy's great love for each other.

"I can show you to a room, or take you through to the kitchen to get something to eat first."

Tess had nursed a bottle in the car, but could use something solid. But Ryder realized he was also starving. And exhausted from fighting with the roads. If he had something to eat and a nap, he would be ready to leave here the second there was a break in the weather and the roads reopened.

"Something to eat sounds good." He could feel his own caution, as if even agreeing to have something to eat was tampering with forces he was not ready to tamper with.

"It must have been a nightmare out there," his hostess said, still lugging Tess, leading him down a narrow hallway that ended in a swinging door. She gave it a push with her hip.

"A nightmare," he agreed. "Hell, only the cold version, decorated in white." *Something like her inn.*

She didn't miss the reference to white decorations, and he saw her take his comment like a blow, as a personal insult. Too sensitive. Was that why she'd been hurt?

"Nothing against white decorations," he said curtly, his insincerity just making everything worse.

*Vinegar and milk,* he told himself.

He wanted to say he wasn't hungry, after all. Wanted to retreat to a room, hoping it wouldn't be too overwhelmingly Chrismasified, but the truth was, now that he was not battling his way through terrible conditions, he was ravenous.

And even if he wasn't, the baby had to eat something out of one of those little jars of mash he carried with him.

His initial relief that the kitchen was an oasis of "not decorated" evaporated. The smells were intense in this room, as was the atmosphere of country cheer and charm: sunshine-yellow walls, white cabinets, old gray linoleum floors pol-ished to high gloss. But, like the door handle falling off, he could see hints of problems, frost on the inside of the windows, a tap dripping.

A huge plank harvest table dominated the room and was covered in platters and platters of cookies.

On a closer look, there were cookies shaped like trees, and cookies frosted in pink, Santa cookies, and chocolate-dipped cookies, gingerbread men and gingerbread houses.

"You weren't kidding that you were expecting guests," he said. "How many?"

"I was hoping for a hundred."

He shot her a wary look at the disappointment in her voice. "You were expecting a hundred people here tonight?"

"The opening night of Holiday Happenings," she said, and he did his best to remain expressionless at how horrifying he found that name. She took his silence, unfortunately, as an invitation to go on, even though her voice had begun to wobble.

"There's a pond out back. There was going to be skating. And bonfires. A neighbor was going to bring his team of horses. Clydesdales." Something was shining behind her eyes.

He thought, again, of the kind of women he had once dated. Five-star meals, gifts of diamonds, evenings that ended in hot tubs. Not Holiday Happenings kind of women.

Emma's disappointment was palpable. He hoped, uneasily and fervently, she wasn't going to cry. Nothing felt like a threat to him as much as a woman's tears. Tess already knew, and used it to her advantage at every opportunity.

"Sorry," he said, gruffly, whether he meant it or because he hoped saying something—anything—could curb her distress, he wasn't sure.

"Things will be back to normal by tomorrow," she said, "Holiday Happenings is going to happen."

This was said fiercely as if she was challenging him—or the gods—to disagree with her. He wasn't going to, but the gods seemed to enjoy a challenge like that one.

It was Tess who took Emma's mind off her weather woes. Apparently the baby was tired of looking at the embarrassment of riches around her, and tired of the adult chatter.

She began squealing and pointing at various cookies and nearly wiggled herself right out of Emma's arms.

"WA DAT."

"Want that?" Emma guessed, mercifully distracted. "She's hungry."

"Or could squeeze in a cookie after demolishing a ten-course meal," he said, thanking Tess for evaporating the tears that had shone so briefly behind those eyes.

"Can she have one, daddy? Or does she have to have healthy stuff first?"

He frowned. Let it go? He wasn't going to be here long enough for it to matter, was he? Correcting her meant revealing something more of the private life, fresh with tragedy, that he kept so guarded.

On the other hand, revealing the fact he was not Tess's father seemed safer than returning to the possibility the weather could ruin her plans for Holiday Happenings.

If he never heard the words *Holiday Happenings* again, he would be just as happy. It was worth it, even if it revealed a little of himself.

He realized he had not introduced himself.

"I'm Ryder Richardson," he said, not trying to disguise his reluctance, "I'm Tess's uncle. Her guardian."

"Oh."

It asked questions, none of which he intended to answer. He stuck out his hand, a diversionary tactic to stall questions and to keep her mind off her failed evening.

She juggled the baby, and took his hand. As

soon as he felt her hand in his, he knew he'd made a mistake. Her hand slipped inside his, a perfect fit, softness intermingled with surprising strength.

He felt the *zing* of the physical contact, steeled himself against it.

She felt something, too, because she froze for a moment, stared up into his eyes, blinked with startled awareness. And then she pulled her hand away, rapidly.

His eyes went to her lips. Once upon a time, a long time ago, when he was a different man in a different life, he had known other diversionary tactics. Most of them involved lips. His and hers.

Now as profoundly committed to taking his wandering mind off lips as he was to taking Emma's mind off personal questions and the weather, he held out his arms, and Emma gave Tess back to him.

Babies were the grand diversion when it came to women. One look at Tess's hair should take Emma's mind irrevocably off her crushed hopes for the evening, and maybe off that sizzling moment of awareness that had just passed between them.

He propped Tess on the edge of the plank table, removed the blanket, pulled Tess's little limbs from the car coat he'd had her in. Last he fumbled with the ridiculously hard-to-reach snap on the stupid snow hat that he had put on the baby out of a sense of wanting to do the responsible thing before they left on their road trip.

*That was the worry part. A snow hat inside the car. In case.* Well, that, and to cover the mess of her hair in case they stopped anywhere along the way. The cop might have even looked at him differently if he had spotted the baby's hair.

*If you can't even look after her hair, how can you be trusted with the larger picture?*

"I hate this hat," he muttered, though what he really hated was that question.

"Why's that?"

"It never seems to go on right."

"Ah." It was a strangled sound.

Ryder shot her a look. She was smiling, biting back a giggle.

He glared at her. He disliked merriment nearly as much as Christmas, especially when it was at his expense and made him feel self-conscious about his baby skills. "Is something funny?" he asked, annoyed.

She held up a finger, letting him know that soon she would be in control of herself. Really, she looked like an evil elf, gasping. The more she tried to stop laughing, the more she couldn't, as if his dis-approval was making her nervous. Which was good.

"You…have…it…on…backwards."

He could look at it in a different way. Not that she was laughing at him, but that he'd succeeded. The sparkle of tears were gone from her eyes, replaced, that quickly, with the sparkle of laughter.

Only he hadn't really succeeded. Because he could clearly see she didn't look like an evil elf, after all. The laughter chased some shadow from her eyes, making them even prettier, and the smile made him even more aware of the sensuous lilt of those puffy lips.

He'd been here less than ten minutes, long enough to know he hated the White Christmas Inn and everything about it.

Ryder looked away from her, frowning. He stepped back from Tess and studied the hat. "I'll be damned. It *is* on backwards. No wonder it was so hard to work with."

A respected architect and he couldn't get a hat on right. He was learning babies were an exercise in humility. Experimentally, he turned the head-gear around the right way, admired it, allowed a small whisper of pleasure at this tiny discovery.

"It was the placement of the pom-pom that threw me," he decided gravely.

"Of course," she said, just as gravely.

"Now I won't have to buy another hat," he said, allowing that little whisper of pleasure to deepen.

He saw Emma's look, and was astounded at how his pride was stung at her misinterpretation. "Not because I can't afford another one," he said sharply, "because you cannot imagine how terrible it is being the sole man shopping in the baby department."

Tess was crankily trying to pull that hat back off.

"It doesn't look like she likes hats, anyway," Emma said.

"Until she lets me comb her hair, she wears hats." He took the hat back off and stepped aside, letting Emma see for the first time what was underneath.

If she started laughing at him again, he was going to pick up the baby and head back into the storm, knock on the door of the first house in Willowbrook that had no Christmas decorations and beg for sanctuary from the storm.

But Emma didn't laugh. Her gasp of dismay was almost worse.

*Hey, it's not as if your hair is all that different.*

But Emma's hair *was* different from Tess's. Emma's curls looked as if she had *tried,* maybe too vigorously, to tame them. He felt that inexplicable urge to touch again, focused on his niece's hair instead.

Tess's white blonde hair did not look as if it had been combed since the day she was born, even though it had only been two days. Her hair looked like it belonged to a monster baby.

It formed fuzzy dreadlocks and tortured corkscrews. There was a clump at the back that looked like it might house mice, and two distinct hair horns stood up on either side of her head.

"No nanny for the last two days," he explained, feeling the deep sting of his own ineptitude. "And in Tess's world, Uncle is not allowed to touch the goldilocks."

Emma looked skeptical, as if he might be making up a story to explain away his own negligence.

"I know," he said dryly. "It's shameful. A twenty pound scrap of baby controlling a full grown man, but there you have it."

Emma still looked skeptical, so he demonstrated. He reached out with one finger. He touched Tess's hair, feather-light, barely a touch at all.

The baby inhaled a deep breath, and exhaled a blood-curdling shriek, as if he dropped a red-hot coal down her diaper. He removed his finger, the shriek stopped abruptly, like a sentence stopped in the middle. Tess regarded him with her most innocent look.

"Ha," he said, moved his finger toward her, and away, shriek, stop, shriek, stop. Soon, he stopped as soon as her mouth opened wide, so she was making O's and closing them, like a fish.

Emma snorted with laughter. Not that he wanted to get her laughing again or explore the intrigue of shadows that danced away when she laughed, and flitted back when she didn't.

Again, he wondered what he was doing. He had not wanted Emma to cry. He wanted this even less. *Firsts.*

There was something tempting about being with someone who did not know his history, as if he could pretend to be a brand-new man. He contemplated that, being free, even for a moment a man unburdened, a man with no history.

But he wasn't those things and Ryder hated himself for thinking he should be free of the mantle he carried. His brother had died because he was, quite simply, not enough.

The fact that Emma could tempt him to feel otherwise made him angry at her as well as at himself, as irrational as that might have been.

# CHAPTER THREE

INSTEAD of moving toward the temptation, the *pretense*, of being a man he was not, Ryder mentally reshouldered his burdens, and stopped playing the little game with Tess, but not before he felt that small sigh of gratitude that his niece did bring some lightness into a world gone dark.

"Can she have a cookie?" Emma asked, coming back to her original question.

"I'll try her with a little baby food first." He dug through the bag, and a bottle dropped to the floor. He watched it roll downhill, another indicator the house was hiding some major problems.

Which were, he noted thankfully, none of his concern. He fetched the bottle back, and got out a jar, which he heated in the microwave for a few seconds.

But, of course, the baby food proved impossible, Tess wiggling around in the high chair Emma had unearthed and focused totally on the cookies that surrounded her. She swatted impatiently when he tried to deliver pureed carrots to her.

"Certified organic, too," he said, finally quitting, wiping a splotch of carrot off his shirt. "She had a bottle in the car a while ago, so go ahead, give her a cookie."

Unmindful that the baby was now covered in carrots, including some in the tangle of hair he was not allowed to touch, Emma swooped her up from the high chair.

"Which one, Tess?" Emma asked, stopping at each plate, letting his niece inspect.

Tess chose a huge gingerbread man, picked a jelly bean off his belly and gobbled it up.

"You must be hungry, too," Emma said to him. "I can't offer anything fancy. I have hot dogs for Holiday Happenings."

No! After all his work at distraction, they were right back to this? The shadow in her eyes darkened every time she mentioned her weather-waylaid event.

"If you'd like a glass of mulled wine or hot chocolate, I have several gallons of both at the warming shed."

Several gallons of wine sounded terribly attractive.

An escape he did not allow himself. Tess needed better.

"A couple of hot dogs would be perfect." He watched Tess polish off the jelly-bean buttons and take a mighty bite of her gingerbread man's head. Disappointment registered on her face as she chewed.

"YUCK." Without ceremony she spat out what was in her mouth, tossed the headless gingerbread man on the floor and reached for a different cookie.

Emma thought it was funny, but these were the challenges in his life. What was best for Tess? Was she too young to try and teach her manners? Did he just accept the fact she didn't like the cookie and let it go? Or by doing nothing was he teaching her the lifelong habit of smashing cookies on the floor?

*Serial smasher.*

Ryder rubbed at his forehead. He could convince himself he did okay on the big things for Tess: providing a home, clothing, food, a lovely middle-aged nanny who loved his niece to distraction. But it was always the little things, cookies and bonnets, that made him wonder what the hell he was doing.

People had the audacity to hint he needed a partner, a wife, a feminine influence for Tess, but to him the fact they suggested it only meant he had become successful at hiding how broken he was inside. What little he had left to give he was saving for Tess, and he hoped it would be enough.

Suddenly he felt too tired and too hungry even to think.

Or to defend himself against the thought that came.

That he was alone in the world. That all the burdens of the past and all the decisions about the future were his alone to carry and to make.

The warmth of the White Christmas Inn was creeping inside him, despite his efforts to keep it at bay, making him feel *more* alone.

Emma had said Christmas transformed everything and made it magic, and she had said there were spirits here who protected all who entered. But the last thing he needed was to be so tired and hungry that her whimsy could seep past the formidable wall of his defenses.

So what if he didn't have what most people were able to take for granted? So what if life was unfair? He already knew that better than most. So, he didn't have someone to ask about the baby spitting out a cookie, he didn't have a holiday season to look forward to instead of dread, he didn't have a place to belong that was somehow more than walls and furniture. He had made his choice. Not to rely on anyone or anything, because he of all people knew that those things could be taken in an instant.

Loss had left him weakened, more loss would finish him. He had a responsibility. He was all Tess had left in the world. He wasn't leaving himself open to the very forces that had nearly destroyed him already.

Ryder Richardson needed desperately to be strong for the little girl who had fallen asleep in Emma's arms, one mashed half-eaten cookie still clutched in a grubby fist.

He felt his strength returning after he ate the hot dogs and about two dozen of the cookies. But inside he felt crabby about this situation he found himself in. He had made himself a world without tests, and he felt as if he was being tested.

Make that *crabbier.*

"Thanks for the meal," he said, formally. "If you could show me our room, Tess needs to be put in a bed, and I need to check the weather."

"I don't quite know how to break this to you," whatever she was about to break to him delighted her, he noticed with annoyance, "but the only way you'll be checking the weather from your room is by sticking your head out the window."

For a moment he didn't quite grasp what she was saying. And when he did, the sensation of crabbiness, of his life being wrested out of his control, intensified.

No television in the room. No escape, no way of turning off everything going on inside him. He considered the television the greatest tool ever invented for numbing wayward feelings, for acting as anesthetic for a doubting mind.

"People come here to get away from it all," she said cheerfully.

"To feel the magic," he said, faintly sarcastic.

"Precisely," she said happily, he suspected missing his sarcasm deliberately.

"You have a television somewhere, right?"

"Well, yes, but—"

"No buts. Lead me to it. Or face the wrath of man."

She didn't seem to find his pun funny at all. And he was glad. He really didn't need to experience Emma's laughter again. Especially if he was going to stay strong.

*The wrath of man.* Funny. Except he meant it. And there was something in him, something fierce and closed, that reminded Emma of a warrior. There was no doubt in her mind he would lay down his life for the baby that so obviously held his hardened heart in the pudgy pink palm of her hand.

The baby had clearly—and gleefully—demonstrated her power with the hilarious hair show.

But whatever moment of lightness he had allowed himself then was gone from Ryder's face now. He was practically bristling with bad temper.

It would be a foolish time to let him know that television was not part of Emma's vision for the White Pond Inn, and it certainly didn't fit in with its incarnation as the White Christmas Inn.

But she had already told him she believed in spirits and magic, risking Ryder's scorn because she had vowed, after Peter, there would be no more trying to hide who she *really* was from other people, no more giving opinions that they wanted to hear.

What an expert she had become at reading what Peter wanted from the faintest purse of lips, giving that to him, making him happy at her own expense. How many times had she swallowed back what she really wanted to say so as not to risk his disapproval, his patronizing suggestions for her "improvement"?

"I consider the inn a techno-electro-free zone," she said, and could hear a certain fierceness in her own voice, as if somehow it was this man's fault that even after she had nearly turned herself inside-out trying to please Peter, he had still searched for someone more suitable. And found her.

"Techno-electro," he said, mulling over the word, which she was pretty sure she had just invented.

"Television is not on the activities agenda, not even on the bad-weather days."

"I'm dying to know what you do on the bad-weather days."

Even though he clearly wasn't, she forged on, determined to be herself. "I bring out board games, and a selection of jigsaw puzzles. I always have tons of books around. I encourage guests to shut off their cell phones and leave the laptops at home."

She crossed her arms over her chest, daring him to find her corny while almost hoping he would. Because if he judged her the way Peter had judged her she could dismiss the somewhat debilitating attraction she felt for him.

She realized she was a little disappointed when he didn't even address her philosophy.

"Since I'm here by the force of fate, instead of by choice, you're going to make an exception for me."

It wasn't a question, and he was absolutely right. He had not come here looking for what her other guests came here looking for. He was not enchanted, and he had no intention of being brought under the spell of the White Christmas Inn.

Which was good. What would she do with a man like that under her spell?

"I do have a television in my room," she admitted reluctantly.

What she didn't admit to was the DVD player. They were guilty pleasures she indulged in when she was just too exhausted to do even one more thing. There was always something to be done when you ran an establishment like this: windows to be cleaned, bedding to be laundered, floors to be polished, flower beds, lawns, paint-touchups. And that was just the day-to-day chores and didn't include the catastrophes, like the time the upstairs bathtub had fallen through the floor.

Sometimes, it was true, on those bad-weather days while her guests played games, she watched a growing collection of romantic movies. She saw them as a replacement for emotional entanglement, not a longing for it.

"Your room? That's the only television in the house?" The thought of entering her bedroom clearly made him as uncomfortable as it made her.

The very thought of those dark warrior eyes taking in the details of her room made her heart beat a fast and traitorous tempo. Her room matched the theme of Christmas: white, though that was how her room was year-round. The walls were the color of rich dairy cream, there was a thick white duvet on the gorgeous bed, an abundance of white pillows in delicious rich textures and fabrics.

When she walked in, the room always seemed soft to her, as comforting as a feather pillow.

But when she saw it through his eyes, she wondered what he would see. And the thought came to her: virginal.

A warrior and a virgin.

She nearly choked on the renegade thought, told herself she had been reading a few too many of the romance novels, more replacements, so much safer and more predictable than real-life romance. She kept a nice selection in tidy stacks on her bedside table, right beside the much-watched DVDs.

But it would make her feel altogether too vulnerable for him to see that, since he might misinterpret her fascination with a certain style of book and film as longing rather than what it was.

"I'll go get the television for you. You'd be more comfortable watching it down here than in my room." And then she blushed as if discussing her room was akin to discussing her panties. Which might be lying on the floor, one of the relaxed slips of the single life.

"I can carry it for you."

"No, no," she protested, too strenuously, "it's tiny."

"That figures," he said, still grouchy, having no problem at all being himself. Which was grouchy and cynical and Christmas-hating. It really balanced out the formidable attraction of his good looks quite remarkably.

"Make yourself comfortable." She handed the sleeping baby back to him, dislodging the cookie from the fist first. "Go into the great room. Through there. I'll be down in a sec."

She hoped her room would have the calming effect on her that it always did. But it didn't. There were no panties on the floor, of course, because she liked the room to look perfect, but even still, instead of being her soothing sanctuary, her sea of textured white softness seemed sensual, like a bridal chamber.

She realized she had been reading too many books, watching too many glorious movies, because totally unbidden her mind provided her with a picture of what he might look like here, lying on that bed, naked from the waist up, holding his arms out to her, his eyes holding smoldering welcome. She shivered at the heat of the picture, at the animal stab of desire she felt.

*Your mother was a wild child,* Tim had told her sadly, when she had been crushed by Lynelle's absence at her own mother's funeral. *It was like an illness she was born with. Nothing around these parts ever interested her or was good enough for her.*

Peter's mother had not warmed to Emma when they had finally met on that disastrous Christmas Day last year. Emma had felt acutely that when Mrs. Henderson looked at her, she disapproved of something. Make that everything.

"Stop it," Emma ordered herself sternly. Just because you had a wild child in you didn't mean you had to be owned by it, the way her mother had been. It was not part of being herself. In fact, it was something she intended to fight.

So she swept the romance novels off the bedside table and shoved them under the bed. Then, realizing it could just as easily be another symptom of make-yourself-over-so-other-people-will-like-you, as of fighting-the-wild-child, she fished them back out and stood holding them, not sure what to do.

This is what a man did! Disrupted a perfectly

contented life. She set the books on the table and planted the DVDs right on top of them.

Ryder Richardson was not coming into this room. Why was she acting as if he would ever see this? He was a stranger, and despite the harsh judgments in Mrs. Henderson's eyes, and despite her mother's example, Emma was not the kind of woman who conducted dalliances with strangers, no matter how attractive they were. No matter how attractive their helpless devotion for a baby.

Still, despite the fact Emma was definitely not conducting a dalliance, she quickly divested herself of the long johns under her jeans. They were not making her feel just bulky, but also hot and bothered.

*Wait, maybe that was him!*

Despite the fact she'd ordered herself not to, she spent a moment more trying to do something with hair made crazier by the Santa hat.

"Tess and I would tie for first place in the bad-hair-day contest," she told herself, combing some curl conditioner through her hair. The flattened curls sprang up as though she had stuck her finger in a socket, not exactly the effect she'd been looking for.

On the other hand, she was not conducting a

dalliance, so the worse she looked the better, right? She was hardly a temptation!

And never had been. When Peter's old girl-friend, Monique, had reentered the picture, he had gone back to her.

And blamed Emma! Her attention to the inn had caused him to be unfaithful. It hadn't been his fault, it had been *hers*.

She left the room, that memory fresh enough that no member of the male species was going to look attractive to her! Then she had to go back for the television she had gone up for in the first place.

Trying to look only composed, *indifferent,* neither a wild child nor a woman scorned, she moved into the great room, placed the TV on a small rosewood end table and plugged it in.

She needn't have worried about her hair. Or about being seduced by a warrior. Or about giving in to her own impulses.

A typical man, from the moment that television was plugged in, Ryder was totally focused on it. He made no effort to hide the fact he was appalled by its size.

"That isn't a TV," he grumbled. He moved his chair to within a foot of it, the snoozing baby a part of him, like a small football nestled in the crook of his arm. "Oh, wait, it is. Imported from the land of little people, the only place on earth that is known to make a seven-inch screen." He held out his hand, and Emma slapped the remote into it.

"Nine," she told him.

He turned on the TV.

"Color," he commented with faked amazement. "Quite a concession to the times, Emma. Quite a concession."

Well, at least he hadn't even noticed the hideous, pathetic effort she had made to fix her hair.

Ryder began grimly switching from channel to channel.

"You should have televisions in the rooms," he said, not lifting his eyes from the set. "Men like that. A lot."

"Actually, I know that."

He gave her a skeptical look, as if somehow she had managed to give him the impression she was the least likely person to know what men liked. A lot.

Her hidden wild child *did* know. Maybe if she had let that wicked woman out now and then, instead of trying so hard to be circumspect, Peter would still be hers.

"Well," he said, with a hint of sarcasm, "why pander to what people like, after all? Never mind good business."

*Is it that clear to him, on the basis of our very short acquaintance, that business isn't exactly my strength?* Should she put in television sets next year? She hated herself for even thinking it! For letting her judgment be so influenced!

"I want people to engage in the experience I offer," she said, aware she was arguing as if she was making a case before the Supreme Court. "The White Pond Inn is about old-fashioned family time. Games in the parlor. Fishing at the pond. Hikes. Reading a book in a hammock. Watching fireflies."

How wholesome. Not a hint of wild child in that!

But she might as well have spared herself the effort. She had lost his interest. He settled Tess on the long length of his thigh. The baby, her face smudged with cookies, and her hair tangles intact, sighed with contentment in her sleep. She settled onto his leg, her padded, frilly rump pointed in the air, her legs curled underneath her tummy, her cheek resting on his knee. In moments, a gentle little snore was coming from her.

Ryder's one hand rested on her back, protective, unconsciously tender. It would have made a lovely picture to go with Emma's decor, except for the fact that his other hand had a death grip on the remote control.

And then there was the unlovely scowl that deepened on his face as each channel reported the same ominous weather.

The storm was not projected to end until the early hours of morning.

Even then, roads reopening were going to depend on highway clean-up. One channel showed a clip of a road outside Fredericton. The scene showed devastation, the road completely blocked by sagging power lines, by trees broken and splintered by the weight of the ice on them.

Ryder snapped off the television. It looked to Emma as though he wanted to hurl her channel changer through the screen.

"Where were you going?" she asked wondering at his desperation to be out of here. "Is someone waiting for you tonight?"

"No," he said. "No one's waiting." It said something about his life—starkly lonely, not that anything about him invited sympathy. Except the baby sprawling along the muscled length of his upper thigh.

"Where were you going?" she asked again.

Nothing about him invited her questions, either, and yet something made her ask them anyway. The truth was she wasn't going to be invisible ever again. Not even if that was safe.

"We were going to my cottage on Lake Kackaticka."

Emma frowned. She was familiar with the lake and the community of upscale cottages that surrounded it. At this time of year it was pretty much abandoned. A few year-round residents looked after the cottages, but the summer people stayed away. It was cold and dreary around the lake in the winter.

"Who goes there in the winter?"

"No one," he said, making no attempt to disguise his satisfaction.

"How long were you going for?"

He shrugged.

"The weekend?"

He shrugged again, and she suspected the truth.

"You weren't going to spend Christmas there, were you?"

"Yes, I was, not past tense, either. Yes, I am."

"Alone?"

"Not alone. Me and Tess."

"But what kind of Christmas would that be for her?"

He looked at the sleeping baby, doubt

crossing those supremely confident features, but only for a moment.

"She has no idea that it is Christmas."

It was his right to parent that baby however he wanted, Emma told herself sternly. He was her guest. It really wasn't her place to argue with him. On the other hand, it wasn't as if she'd invited him here, or called down the weather personally to inconvenience him.

She didn't think pandering to his bad temper was a good idea, and besides she was committed to expressing her opinion after a year and a half of biting her tongue for Peter's convenience! And look where that had gotten her!

She'd already voiced her thoughts several times tonight, and apparently there was no stopping her now. In fact, she felt an obligation to render her opinion for the sake of Tess!

"That's the saddest thing I've ever heard," she told him.

He glared at the empty screen of the TV, then picked up the channel changer and turned the television back on, deciding it was interesting after all. "That just shows you've been sheltered up here in your fairy-tale world. You don't know the first thing about sad."

There was no point saying anything more. She

could tell in the set of his jaw that he was the stubborn type who never would admit he was wrong or change his mind.

And yet there was that little ghost girl again, the one who'd been disappointed by every single Christmas, who insisted she knew everything there was to know about *sad* and how dare he insinuate otherwise?

It must have been the ghost girl who couldn't let it go.

Emma said, sharply, "You're depriving Tess of Christmas, that's not just selfish. It's mean."

The announcer on TV picked that moment to say, voice over a map covered with red lines of road closures that it would be three days before travel resumed on some of those roads.

Ryder Richardson swore under his breath.

"I suppose the baby doesn't know any better than that, either," Emma said.

"You know what? I need you to show me to my room." He stood up, not bothering to shut off the television, lifting the baby with graceful unconsciousness as he stood, tucking her sleeping head into his shoulder. To himself he said, almost musing. "It couldn't get much worse than this, could it?"

But Emma, dedicated to airing her views,

wasn't letting it pass. Just this afternoon she had been a woman totally content with herself and her circumstances. Totally. And now wild-child and woman-scorned, and wholesome-experienced-innkeeper were all wrestling around inside her in a turmoil because of him, and she found she resented this intrusion on her life.

"No," she agreed coldly, "it couldn't."

But it did.

The lights flickered, dimmed, flickered again, and then the room was plunged into darkness. The television went out with a sputter, the embers from a dying fire threw weak golden light across them.

"It just got worse, didn't it?"

His voice in the darkness was a sensuous rasp that wild-child *loved*.

"Yes, it did," she said coolly.

"Do you ever get the feeling the gods are laughing at you?" he asked, not for the first time that night.

"Yes," she said sadly, "I do." Was now a good time to break the bad news to him? "The furnace is electric."

Her eyes were adjusting to the darkness. The firelight flashed gold, on the perfect planes of his face. Wild-child sighed.

It took him a moment to get what she meant.

"Are you saying the only source of heat in this falling-down old wreck is that fireplace?"

"Falling-down old wreck?" she breathed, incensed, pleased that woman-scorned was taking charge, getting the upper hand. "How *dare* you?"

It felt so good to say that! To stand up for herself! She wished she would have said that to Peter, at least once.

But no, not even when he'd told her, so sheepishly, while still making it *her* fault he and Monique had been seeing each other, what had she said?

*I understand.*

"Your front bell sounds broken, the door handle did come off in your hand, there's frost on the inside of the windows, and when I dropped the baby's bottle it rolled *down* the floor."

"Which means?" she asked haughtily.

"Probably your foundation is moving. The floor isn't level."

All her work on creating pure Christmas charm, and he was seeing *that?*

"Do you always focus on the negative?" she snapped. How much did it cost to fix a moving foundation, anyway?

"I do," he said without an ounce of apology, even though he followed up with, "Sorry."

"You aren't sorry," Emma breathed. "You're a miserable selfish man who is intent on spoiling Christmas not just for yourself, but for your niece and anyone else who has the misfortune to cross paths with you."

"Well, aren't you glad I won't be around to spoil it for you?" he said smoothly, completely unabashed by his behavior.

"Huh. With my record, you probably will still be around Christmas Day. Spoiling things."

Silence, the light softening something in his features, an illusion, nothing more. But when he spoke, there was something softer in his voice.

"What does that mean, with your record?"

*Don't tell him,* she ordered herself. *Don't.* But another part of her, weary, thought *Why not? What difference does it make?*

"It means I've never had a Christmas that wasn't spoiled. So why should this one be any different?"

Silence. She'd left herself wide open to his sarcasm, so thank God he was saying nothing.

Only when he did speak, she wished he'd chosen sarcasm.

"You've never had a good Christmas?" He

seemed legitimately astounded. And legitimately sorry, for the first time. But then his customary skepticism won out. "Come on."

She remembered last year, excited as a small child, arriving at Peter's parents' home. No, not a home. A mansion. A picture out of a splendid movie. The trees on the long drive lit with white lights, every window of the house lit, she could see the enormous tree sparkling through the window.

And that had been the beginning of a Christmas that *looked* exactly like the Christmases she had dreamed as a little girl, but that *felt* like an excursion into hell.

"Have you?" she asked Ryder, tilting her chin proudly, knowing his answer. There was only one reason people hated Christmas, wasn't there? They'd given up trying to make it something it could never be.

Maybe it was time for her to surrender, too, to forget trying to change her fortunes, to abandon that little girl who wanted something so badly. Maybe it all was just an illusion. Christmas had become a corny, commercial package, a dream that no one could ever make a reality.

Maybe the truth was that it was a terrible time of year, laden with too much stress and far too many expectations. Maybe it would be a good time to plan a vacation to Hawaii. It probably would have been a whole lot easier to talk her mother into celebrating Christmas in Hawaii than it had been to convince her to come here.

*A trip to Hawaii would be possible after a successful year of business. Maybe I'll give in and add televisions, after all. If the foundation doesn't collapse.*

After a long time, he surprised her by saying, quietly and with obvious reluctance. "Yes, I have. Had good Christmases."

She could feel him shifting in the dancing light of the fireplace flames. He came way too close, and peered down at her.

He shifted the baby into the crook of his elbow, and with his free hand he did the oddest thing.

He touched her hair.

"We'll be out of your hair in no time," he said solemnly, as if he had touched it only to make that point. "I won't wreck your Christmas, Emma."

She saw something desolate in his eyes, and was taken aback by the realization that he was trying to protect her from that.

"If you've had good Christmases, don't you want that for Tess?" she asked, quietly. "I had a mother who thought Christmas was a nuisance. It was awful."

And maybe it wasn't just Christmas, but parenthood in general, that her mother had found bothersome.

That's what had made Emma so eager to please, to prove somehow she was a good person. Worthy. Was she still trying to prove that? Was that what Holiday Happenings and Christmas Day Dream were really about?

She *hated* that she was questioning the purity of her motivations.

"Emma, I'm doing my best," he said quietly. "Just leave it."

But she couldn't. "And what if your best just isn't good enough?"

"Don't you think I ask myself that every day?"

She studied him, saw the torment in his face, went from being angry with him and with herself and with Peter and her mother and the world, to feeling something far more dangerous. Empathy.

"If you've had good Christmases, why do you hate it so much now?" she asked him.

The pause was very long, as if he considered telling her something, fought with it, won.

"Emma, I'm just passing through. I'm not leaving my burdens here when I go."

He said it almost protectively, as if they would

be too heavy for her to handle. He was right. They were strangers.

That was not changed by the fact he had touched her hair.

Or by the fact that he had an adorable baby.

It was not changed by the fact that they were marooned here by the storm, like shipwreck survivors on a desert island.

He had his baggage and she had hers, and he was right not to share it, to keep his boundaries high. It was a reminder of what she needed to do, as well.

"I'll find a flashlight," she said, moving away from the emotional minefield they were treading so lightly, realizing the only thing they had to share was how to get through a night without electricity.

She sighed. "If the power stays out, in very short order this room will be the only truly warm one in the house. I have a crib upstairs, and we can haul a mattress down here for you. I'll sleep on the couch."

"I hope the power is going to come back on," he said.

*So do I, but the way my luck is running, I doubt it.* "I'll show you where the crib is."

Moments later, Emma, holding the sleeping

baby, was watching him take the crib apart. Despite her resolve that they be nothing more than strangers, she couldn't help but admire how comfortable he was with tools, the man-thing.

It had taken her the better part of an afternoon to put that crib together, studying instructions, putting A into B. He had the whole thing dismantled and downstairs in a matter of minutes.

While he was reassembling the crib, Emma went back upstairs to get a mattress off the bed in the room closest to the staircase.

"Tess didn't even know I'd moved her," he commented, coming up behind her.

"She sleeps like a log."

"I'm envious," he said. A man who carried burdens so heavy they affected his sleep?

*Don't pursue it,* she told herself.

"It's already chilly up here," he said.

"Well, you know these old wrecks. The insulation is in about the same shape as the foundation."

"I said I was sorry."

"No," she said firmly. "I have a tendency to be way too sensitive. I know there's lots wrong with the old place. It's foolish to love her anyway."

"What *do* you have for insulation?"

A pragmatic question. He didn't want to know

anything about what she loved. She didn't blame him. She didn't want to know what he loved, either.

A lie. She did. Despite all her resolve, both wild-child and woman-scorned were supremely interested in what a man like him loved.

The baby was obvious, of course.

She stuck to her resolve and the relatively safe topic of her old house. " I found old newspapers in the walls when I redid the bathroom." She didn't mention how the tub falling through the floor had necessitated the renovation before she really had the funds to do it. "New insulation is on my to-do list."

"Big list?" he asked, conversationally.

But Emma already felt foolish enough for blurting out about her Christmases. She was saying nothing else to him that could be interpreted as self-pitying.

The insulation fell into that category. If she was going to borrow money, wouldn't that have been the sensible choice? New insulation? A new roof?

Oh, no, dreamer that she was she had been spending money on gifts for needy families, and redoing this bedroom in preparation for her mother's visit.

Was she still trying to prove herself worthy? Emma shut the thought off fast and focused on problems she could solve.

If she didn't become more prudent, next year she would probably be heading the "needy" line, not jetting off to Hawaii!

She had gambled everything on the success of Holiday Happenings. How many days of her Christmas moneymaker could she lose before she was in real trouble?

"Oh," she said, breezily, not letting any of those concerns leach into her voice, "it's a big list, but nothing I can't handle."

She was trying to regain ground as a complete professional.

They were in the room at the top of the steps that she called the green room. Once it had been her grandmother's, stuffed from top to bottom with clutter, a dusty-rose wall-to-wall carpet covering the beautiful aged hardwoods.

Now, in preparation for her mother's arrival, it was the most beautiful room in the house. The carpet had been ripped out, the faded layers of wallpaper stripped. The room had been restored to historical correctness and decorated in her mother's favorite color. It was her loveliest room, and Emma felt it not only showcased her abilities as a competent and professional innkeeper, but would convince her mother that White Pond was not such a bad place.

*And that her daughter isn't such a bad person?*

Where were these thoughts coming from? Still, she glanced at Ryder to see if he was suitably impressed, and saw he was looking at a huge crack in the wall that was opening above the window. That figured.

She really didn't want to hear what *that* meant, so she directed the flashlight beam to the focal point of the room, a beautiful antique four-poster with a lace canopy, layered with luxurious silk bedding and pillows in subtle shades of green.

"Nice piece of furniture," he said. Trying to gain ground for his "old-wreck" remark? Not wanting to let her know what the crack meant, either? Feeling sorry for her because she had never had a good Christmas?

She had shown dozens of guests to their rooms and never felt like this before.

As if the bed was a strangely intimate piece of furniture, and she was tempting something to be in here alone with him.

"It's not really a nice piece of furniture," she said, trying to sound as if she was not strangling. "The first night I put guests in it, it broke."

She had meant it to sound funny but it sounded pathetic, lost her any ground she had gained at presenting herself as a competent professional. Instead, she felt her own failing.

But he didn't notice. "Hmm. That sounds interesting. What were they doing?"

That strangling sound in her throat intensified. She refused to answer him or even look at him. Wild-child had a few ideas about what they might have been doing, but Emma was ignoring wild-child. She redirected the flashlight beam and hurried to the bed.

"Do you think we can just leave it made up?" She didn't wait for her answer, lifted a corner of the mattress, struggled to swing it off the bed frame and retain her grip on the flashlight.

"Stop it," he said. "You take the bedding and light the way for me. I'll get the mattress."

"I can clearly see if I let you get away with bossing me around once, you'll turn into a complete horror."

"As if I'm not already," he muttered. "Emma, I'm being reasonable. The mattress is too big for you."

"You are looking at a woman who refinished every inch of flooring in this place by herself. I've knocked down walls. I've repaired plumbing. I've been up on the roof. I've—" *failed to pay the bills, failed to impress my mother, lost my fiancé over this place...*

He held up his hand before she could rush on with her list. "Stop," he said dryly. "I'm having a heart attack thinking about it." But he was obviously thinking about it, because that familiar scowl creased his brow. "I hope you didn't put those Christmas lights on the peak of the roof yourself."

Tim had already given her a very thorough lecture about that. She wasn't listening to another one.

"I'm just making the point—I can handle my end of the mattress." She turned the flashlight beam on the floor so he couldn't see her face, which was blushing as if she had said something about sex. *Couldn't I have worded that differently?*

"Why do I have a feeling that what you think you can handle and what you really can handle are two entirely different things?"

"Because you're a chauvinist pig?" she asked, keeping her voice deliberately sweet, glad he couldn't see her face because his statement could sum up her knowledge of sex, too.

"Gee, and a minute ago I was worried you were going to fall down the steps and have the mattress

and me land on top of you. Now I'm thinking if
you fell, could you at least bite your tongue?
Preferably off."

"You charmer, you."

Was a desert-island camaraderie developing
between them? Wild-child was jumping up and
down at the desert-island possibilities.

"At least let me take the end that's going down
the stairs first."

"No," she said stubbornly. Woman-scorned,
who didn't need a man taking charge of anything,
took over. She picked up the foot of the mattress
and began dragging it along the floor, leaving
him with no choice but to pick up the other end.
She was trying not to grunt as they headed for the
stairs, but the mattress was an awkward bundle,
hard to get a grip on, heavier than she had thought
it would be.

As it turned out, he'd been right about the
bedding, too. They should have made two
separate trips. Because as they neared the middle
of the stairway, the silk caught in the holly on the
railing.

She paused to untangle it before it pulled the
whole garland down or tore the silk. She dropped
the flashlight, and they were in darkness.

It happened fast after that.

"Wait a sec—" she cried as she felt the mattress pressing against her. But it was too late. The mattress squeezed by her, sweeping her along with it. Emma grabbed a fistful of something before being plunged downward into complete darkness.

# CHAPTER FOUR

"ARE you okay?" Ryder called.

Emma couldn't answer at first, the wind knocked temporarily out of her.

"Are you hurt?" he asked again. She could hear him trying to get past the mattress that blocked the stairs.

"Fine," she managed to get out before he made a hole in the wall, bumping against it like that. The walls were admittedly flimsy in an "old wreck" of a house like this.

She couldn't help it. Emma began to giggle and then to laugh. But he mistook the muffled howls of her laughter for cries of pain and came hurtling down to her. Predictably, he got caught up where the mattress blocked the step, and he crashed down on it beside her.

They lay there, side by side, on the mattress

that blocked the staircase. Their legs and feet were up the stairs, their heads and backs on the floor of the foyer. They were only faintly illuminated by the shadows the firelight in the next room was throwing against the wall.

The laughter died in her throat as Emma became aware of how solid he felt beside her, how his presence here in the house during the storm was somehow reassuring.

Even if he was an ass who thought her house was a wreck and who was going to deprive Tess of Christmas.

"Emma, are you okay?"

"I'm fine," she assured him again, though as she drank in the scent of him she wondered how true that was. "Are you?"

She felt him get up on his elbow, stare through darkness made only a little less black by the slight light leaching in from the other room.

He lay back down, sighed. "I guess I'm okay. Providing jest for the gods tonight. So, did one of your spirits push you down the stairs?"

"Oh, no, just made sure the mattress was there when I hit the floor."

"Ah."

Was his cynicism slightly tempered? Ryder

had altered his position slightly, and Emma could feel the solidness of his shoulder touching hers, make out the strong line of his nose, the sensuous curve of his mouth.

"I want you to know I'm not the kind of girl who ends up on a mattress with a guy on such a short acquaintance," she teased, trying to reduce with humor the tension she felt in her belly.

"I already guessed," he said softly.

And her humor left her. What did that mean?

"Remember when I said I didn't think things could get any worse?" Ryder asked softly.

"Yes?"

"Around you they can. And they do."

"I know," she agreed, "The White Christmas curse."

"Maybe it's not a curse," he said softly. "Maybe it's magic, just like you said. And I'm not sure which I'm more afraid of."

And then he was laughing. It was a rusty sound, self-deprecating and reluctant, as if he had not laughed for a long, long time and did not particularly want to laugh now.

For all that, it was a sound so lovely, so richly masculine and so genuine, that it made her want to stay in this place, on a mattress jammed half on the stairs and half off, with this man beside her for as long as she could, to rest a moment in this place that was as real as any place she had ever been before.

Woman-scorned *tsked* disapprovingly.

Well, why not laugh, Ryder thought? His situation was absurd. He was trapped at a place dedicated to Christmas corniness, the power was out, the storm raged on. He could hear it rattling the windows and hounding the eaves. He was lying in the pitch darkness on a crashed mattress, with Emma so close to him he could smell the scent of lavender on her skin.

Life was playing a cosmic joke on him, why not laugh?

Why keep fighting this? He was stuck, she was stuck, they were in this together, whether he liked it or not. The powerful surge of intensity he was feeling toward her was only because of the crisis nature of the situation. People in situations like this tended to bond to each other in way too short a time.

He could not act on that. Maturity was being required of him. A certain amount of cooperation was going to be needed to get them through this, but nothing more.

There was no sense railing against the unfairness of life. He'd already done that, and it made no difference. It never changed what was, it only made the experience more miserable than it had to be.

"I'm sorry," she said, her voice still light with laughter. "I should have listened to you. I should have taken the bedding off, let you take the mattress, followed meekly behind—"

"Oh, yeah," he said, "I can certainly picture you in the meek position. Submissive, even. Would that be before or after you strung lights on the roofline and knocked out a wall or two?"

"Hmm," she said, pretending thoughtfulness. "Let's make it before. I might be too tired after to be properly meek."

Then they were laughing again, and he noticed her laughter was sweet, uncomplicated, real, like when Tess laughed.

"I'm sorry, too," he said, finally, "for taking out my frustration at having my plans interrupted on you. And for calling your house an old wreck. It isn't really. It's a Victorian, probably built at the very end of the eighteen-hundreds or in the early nineteen-hundreds."

"How do you know that?"

"I'm an architect. Though I have to admit, I avoid old-house projects like the plague. People are never realistic about what it's going to cost to restore an old building."

"Don't you think old buildings are romantic?" she asked.

Given the startling intensity between them, he did not want to discuss anything about romance with her.

"Not at all," he said. "You get in and the walls aren't square, the floors aren't level, the fifty-year-old addition is being held up by toothpicks. I prefer new construction, and my real preference is commercial buildings."

She was silent for a bit, and he hoped she was contemplating getting out of this old place before it ruined her financially, but naturally that wasn't what she was contemplating at all.

"We could start over," she decided.

"Could we? How?"

"Like this." Her hand found his in the darkness. And shook it. "Hi," she said, "I'm Emma White, the meek, submissive owner of the White Christmas Inn."

Her hand was soft in his, and again he felt something when he touched her that went beyond the sizzle of chemistry. Quiet strength. He turned his head to see her in the faint shadows being cast by the fireplace in the other room.

"I'm Ryder Richardson," he played along, despite the fact he knew this was a somewhat dangerous game, that he was incredibly aware of the loveliness of her hand and her scent.

Still, he was reluctantly amazed by how good it felt to play along with her, to let go of his legendary self-control, just a little bit.

She was silent for a while. "Do you think," she said hesitantly, "just in this new spirit of cooperation, you could tell me what a really good Christmas feels like? You said you'd had good Christmases. Just so I know exactly what to do for the Christmas Day Dream."

She was moving him further and further behind enemy lines.

"Come on," he said, "you have some good Christmas memories."

Her silence nearly took what was left of his heart.

Ryder was amazed to find his carefully walled world had a hole in it that she had crept through. He was amazed that he *wanted* to go there, to a good, good Christmas, to share it with her, to make it real for her, but for himself, too. To relive such a wonderful time proved to be a temptation too strong to resist, even as he wondered if he was going to regret this later.

"You wouldn't think this would be the best Christmas ever," he said, slowly, feeling his way cautiously through the territory that had once been his life, "but when I was twelve my dad was out of work, the only time I ever remember that happening while I was growing up."

He told her about how his dad and his mom had snuck out every night into the backyard and shoveled and leveled and sprayed the garden hose on sub-zero nights until they had a perfect ice rink to unveil to him and Drew on Christmas morning.

He and his brother had woken up to second-hand skates that didn't fit, and instead of turkey they'd had a bonfire in the backyard and cooked smokies and marshmallows.

They had skated all day. Pretty soon all the neighbors had drifted over, the neighborhood boys unanimously voting the Richardson brothers' skating rink as the best gift of the year. At midnight there had still been people around the bonfire, kids skating, babies sleeping.

"And then, our neighbor Mrs. Kelly, who sang solos at all the community weddings and funerals started singing 'Silent Night,' and everybody gathered at the bonfire and started singing, too." Ryder's parents had been dead now for more than a dozen years, but as he talked about them, he could feel their love for him and Drew as if it had all happened yesterday.

Maybe she had been right about ghosts living here. His parents had always been determined to make the best of everything. *Life gives you lemons, you make lemonade,* his mother had always said. He wondered what they would think of him, and how he was coping with the lemons life had handed him.

And suddenly reliving that memory didn't feel fun anymore and already he felt regret, and felt the shadows pulling at him, trying to take him back.

Fast forward to spending last Christmas Eve with Drew and Tracy, opening his gift from them. A gag gift, as always, a huge stuffed marlin, possibly the ugliest thing Ryder had ever seen, mocking the deep-sea fishing trip he and Drew had taken off the coast of Mexico earlier in the year. Was that the last time he had laughed, really laughed, until tonight?

*Come on, stay,* his brother had said, at the door, "Silent Night" playing on the stereo inside the house. *We'll put you in the guest room. You can watch Tess open her presents tomorrow.*

Since Tess had been a cute and occasionally smelly little lump of a person at the time, incapable of opening her own presents, and probably oblivious to what they contained, Ryder had failed to see the attraction of that. He could clearly see the baby was going to have no appreciation whatsoever for the signed football he had gotten for her.

But he had stayed, something about the magic of family being stronger than any other kind of magic.

It was the last night he had ever experienced joy. It was the last time he had laughed. Until tonight.

And he did not feel ready to invite those kinds of experiences into his life again. He had built his barricades for a reason—he was not nearly done beating himself up for his failure to save them all. But also to keep this out: longing for what could not be, ever again.

A man had to be whole, unencumbered, to welcome experiences like those into his life. He was not that man. The easygoing young man he had been only a year ago was scarred beyond recognition.

And knew he would not be that man again.

Emma seemed to sense his mood shifting, changing, even though she could barely see him. He let go of her hand abruptly. She felt the faint tensing, his energy drawing away from her. She tried to draw him back.

"Would you like to hear about Christmas at the inn?"

He wanted to tell her no, to grab back the things he had just told her, but that seemed too sour, even for him, and it seemed to be going against the new spirit of cooperation he had promised, so he grunted instead.

She took the grunt as interest, and she told him about Holiday Happenings and her neighbors helping her get ready, about the skating and the sleigh-riding, the craft sales, the wreaths, the amount of food they hoped to sell.

"I hope it's as wonderful as the night you just described to me," she said, "if it happens. What am I going to do with four thousand hot dogs if it doesn't?"

"Four thousand?"

"I always think big," she said ruefully. "I was thinking if a hundred people showed up every night for ten days and each ate two hot dogs, I would need two thousand. And then I started thinking, what if two hundred people showed up every night? Or what if a hundred and fifty showed up, but a few of them were teenage boys?"

Her math and her hopeless optimism were giving him a headache. Or maybe that was the thinly disguised worry in her voice.

"You already bought everything?" he asked. Despite the fact he'd commanded himself not to encourage her with in-terest, to stop this, he hated that she'd apparently invested more than she could afford to lose in singlehandedly bringing the Christmas spirit to Willowbrook.

Now, no one was coming.

At least not tonight. "You still have nine days to recoup your losses," he said. But he wasn't sure if he believed it. What if the storm lasted longer, or if it was like 1998 and the Atlantic seaboard was shut down for days? What if the power didn't come back on for weeks?

Just because he was stranded here with her, lying on a mattress with her, that didn't make it his problem.

*He didn't care.* No, that wasn't the whole truth. He didn't *want* to care.

"Where are the hot dogs now?" he asked reluctantly.

"Freezer."

"If the power doesn't come on by tomorrow, you could put them in a snowbank."

She said nothing.

"It'll be okay," he said. Hey, he'd get home and send her a check to cover her hot dogs.

"It *has* to be," she said, and he didn't like what

he heard in her voice one little bit. As if her whole life depended on Holiday Happenings working out.

"What do you mean it *has* to be?" Ryder knew from experience you had to be careful about throwing challenges like that at fate. It had a way of never giving people what they thought they wanted.

She told him about inviting the needy families, the gifts under the tree, the perfect Christmas Day she had planned for them.

He could feel himself closing his eyes, trying to steel himself against her *goodness*.

Suddenly she went silent. "Look at me chattering on and on," she said, embarrassed, probably figuring out that being stranded gave the illusion of camaraderie, but it didn't really make him worthy of hearing her dreams, sharing her confidences.

Why had he allowed himself to be sucked into this?

*Not just alone,* a voice answered him, *lonely*.

He hated that admission, the weakness of it. He had failed his brother and his sister-in-law. He *deserved* to feel the way he felt.

Still, something in him that was still human said to her, and meant it, "It's good that you believe."

There was that word again, creeping around the edges of his life, looking for a way to sneak past his guard and into his heart.

So it would be ready to break again.

*I don't think so,* he said to himself.

"Oh," she said, and laughed self-consciously. "I didn't mean to sound like that. Saint Emma."

"Don't forget—of the meek and submissive school of saints." Giving in, just a little bit, to that temptation to play with her.

But giving in a little bit was probably just a forerunner to giving in a lot. And in the end she was going to get hurt. He needed to pull back from this *now,* not just to protect himself. To protect her.

He got to his feet, hesitated, and then reached back a hand for her when the mattress was thwarting her efforts to get up. The momentum of that tug pulled her into the length of him. He could feel her slightness, her softness, the delicious hint of curves. The enveloping lavender scent of her that would make it so easy to lose his head.

The devil told him not to bother being a better man, not to bother protecting her. It told him to outrun the terrible loneliness reliving his memories had stirred up inside him.

She was an adult. Kiss her. See what happened.

He could almost taste her lips when he thought of that. A wanting, compelling, tempting, tantalizing, swept through him.

More than a year since he had connected with another human being.

But not her, he told himself sternly. You could not kiss a girl like Emma White without thinking it all the way through. Following an impulse could have far-reaching ramifications.

Emma wanted to be fiercely independent, knocking down walls and climbing all over the roof by herself. She wanted to send the message, *I don't need a man.*

But she struck him, with her Christmas fantasies, with her wistfulness, with her desire to bring something to others, as not just old-fashioned and decent, but romantic. Emma was the type of woman who might think a casual kiss meant things it did not mean. She might think that he wanted to get to know her better or was looking for a mommy for little Tess, a future that involved her.

The truth was Ryder Richardson did not look to the future at all.

Ryder just got through every day to the best of his ability. And that, he told himself sternly, did not involve doing damage to others. And how could he not damage someone like her? *Vinegar and milk,* he reminded himself.

"I'll get the mattress pulled into the great room, if you want to go find some bedding to make up the couch."

"Yes, boss," she said.

The temptation rose again. To play along with her. But this time he said nothing in response to her jesting.

In fact, he made up his mind he was leaving at first light.

*You'd leave a woman alone with no power?* a voice inside him asked.

*For her own good,* he answered it back.

But maybe she had been closer to the truth than he wanted to admit when she had called him mean and selfish.

It was himself he was protecting, not her. Protecting himself from these uncomfortable feelings, something thawing in him that allowed him to see his world as too stark, too masculine. Too lonely.

But getting to know someone was a minefield that rarely went smoothly, especially now that he carried so much baggage, so many scars, so much damage.

What started with a curious kiss could all blow up and leave her with another Christmas in shambles.

Not one good Christmas memory? How was that possible? And yet he could tell she was honest to a fault, and that if she could have dredged one up, she would have.

He dragged the mattress into the living room, rearranged the bedding, stoked the fire. The thought of sharing this room with her for the night seemed uncomfortably intimate given his vow not to encourage anything between them.

She came back down the stairs, loaded down with bedding, the duvet a plump eiderdown, whiter than a wedding night and just as sensual.

"Where's the woodpile?" he asked, looking everywhere but at her lips, needing a moment's breathing space.

She told him, and he put on his shoes and grabbed the flashlight. He went out the back door into the storm to her woodshed. The night, bitter and dark, the flashlight beam, frail against the wicked slant of white sleet, were in sharp contrast to the cozy intimacy inside, but Ryder welcomed the wind, the sharded sleet on his face slapping him back to reality. The sleet was freezing as it hit the ground, forcing him to focus intensely to keep upright, especially once his arms were loaded with wood.

He made five or six trips to the shed, filling the wood box beside the fireplace. Each time he came in, he would think *enough,* but the picture Emma made cuddled up on the couch inside her quilt, her hair every which way, would make him think *not one good Christmas,* as if he could or should do something about it. And that would send him back out the door, determined to cling to his vision of life as a cold and bitter place.

But going out into the weather again and again turned out to be one of those impulses he should have thought all the way through.

His clothes were soaked. He made one more trip—out to his vehicle, to bring in the luggage he had not wanted to bring in. *Another surrender,* he thought, shivering. The old house only had one bathroom, upstairs, and it was already cold. He noticed the tub seemed new, and the flooring around it did, too. He inspected more closely.

Her tub had fallen through the floor at some point in recent history. This place was way too much for her, and he killed the fleeting thought that she needed someone to help her. He hurried into a pair of drawstring plaid pajama pants, a T-shirt.

When he came back down, he noticed she was in pajamas now, too, soft pink, with white-and-pink angels on them, flannel, not, thankfully, the least bit sexy. Her blanket was a soft mound of snow on the couch, but she was up doing something at the fire.

He saw then that she was pouring steaming water from a huge cast-iron kettle she had put in the coals of the fire. She came to him with a mug of hot chocolate.

It was just a little too much like a pajama party, and he had talked enough for one night. Yet chilled to the bone because of his own foolishness, he could not refuse. He took the mug, wrapped his hands around its comforting heat. He took a chair across from her as she snuggled back under her blanket, one hand coming out of the folds to hold her hot chocolate.

*Home*.

The scene, straight out of a magazine layout for Christmas, had a feeling of home about it: fire crackling, baby sleeping, the pajamas, the hot chocolate, the tree in the background.

"Is it hard?" she asked softly. "Looking after Tess? How long have you done it for?"

That was the problem with letting his guard down, telling the one story. For a whole year he had avoided any relationship that required anything of him, even conversation. It was just too hard to make small talk, to pretend to care. Being engaged with another human being felt exhausting and like a lie.

His failure had killed his brother. Hardly a conversation starter, and yet how long could he know someone before he felt compelled to tell them that? Because that had become the biggest part of him.

But now that he had confided one deeply personal memory to her, it was as if a hole had opened in the dam that held his loneliness, and the words wanted to pour out of him.

"I was appointed her guardian three months ago." Ryder did not want to tell her the circumstances, Tracy's long fight ending, nor did he want to tell her how hard those first weeks had been. Thinking about them, loneliness and longing threatened to swamp him again.

But his voice was carefully neutral when he said, "I have a nanny. That helps. She's an older lady, married, her own kids grown up. She misses children." So much easier to talk about Mrs. Markle than himself.

But Emma persisted. "And when she's not there?"

"There's the hair thing," he admitted. "I do pretty good at everything else. The first few diaper changes I felt like I was scaling Everest without oxygen, but now it makes me feel oddly manly. Like I look at other guys and think, *I can handle stuff you can't even imagine, pal.*" He was still aware he was hiding in humor, but Emma's appreciative chuckle made it seem like a good tactic, so he kept going.

"Shopping for her is a nightmare. It's like being at a pigeon convention. You've never heard so much cooing. It's like I'm transformed from six-foot-one of highly-muscled, menacing man to this adorable somewhat helpless teddy bear."

"You do have kind of a menacing air about you, Ryder." Her eyes slid to his arms to check out the muscle part. He was pretty sure she wasn't disappointed. The gym was one of the places where he took it all, sweated it out, pushed himself to a place beyond thought.

"A much-needed defense against cooing, not that it works in the baby store. I go in for a new supply of pajamas with feet in them, the entire extent of Tess's wardrobe, and women come out of the woodwork. I get shown little diaper covers with frills and bows on them, and white dresses that Tess would destroy in thirty seconds flat, and the worst thing of all—hair paraphernalia."

"I noticed you bought the little diaper cover."

"I know," he admitted. "I get the hair junk, too, and more ridiculous shoes than you can shake a stick at, too."

"Ah, the boots with the penguins."

"I learned to just let them load me up, and I can get out of there quicker."

"Maybe underneath the menace, they see something else."

He could tell her. He could tell this stranger about his last year in hell, leave his burdens here when he walked away. It was pushing away at the damaged dam within him, wanting out.

Instead he said, coolly, "Something else? Not that I'm aware of."

"Hmm," she said with patent disbelief. He bet if he met up with her in the baby department, she'd be cooing along with the rest of them.

"Maybe they see a man doing his best in a difficult situation. Maybe they admire the fact you said yes to being put in that situation."

"It's not like I had a choice."

"I bet you did," she said.

"Not really."

"No, because a man like you would only see

the right choice, and never even realize there was another one."

He snorted. "You don't know me well enough to say that." But another voice, Tracy telling him the night before she married his brother, *You and Drew are the rarest of finds. Good men.*

That was before he had failed his brother and her.

Was there anything left of a good man in him? If there was, why would he even consider leaving Emma here, alone, a woman without power?

Self-preservation.

"You must have had the choice to walk away," Emma said. "I think when you hold that baby, you can't hide who you really are. That's what makes you irresistible—"

He looked into her eyes for a moment, almost felt his heart stop beating. If she found him irresistible they were both in deep trouble.

But she finished her sentence, "—in the baby department."

He felt his heart start beating again, but was warily aware his reaction to how she had finished that sentence was mixed. Part relief, more regret.

He was not sure he liked the way this was going, because if she prodded him now, he had the horrible feeling he would spill all, tell all. He had done enough spilling for one night.

He gulped down the hot chocolate, set it on the table beside him, got up and stretched deliberately.

"I'm done in," he said, much more polite than saying I'm done talking, since he'd made a mental agreement with himself to have a truce with her.

Emma said, "Quit fighting it."

For a horrible moment he thought she had read his mind, seen his weakness, but instead, she said, "Go to bed, Ryder."

It would have been much less awkward if bed wasn't right there in front of her, but it was what it was. He crawled in between the sheets of his mattress on the floor and was amazed by how comfortable the bed was, how strangely content he felt despite the restless directions his thoughts had taken tonight.

He kept his eyes closed as he heard her settling on the couch, discouraging himself from looking at her and feeling those unwanted desires.

A desire to connect with another human being.

One over the age of two.

*Ha,* he told himself sternly. He would be ready to reconnect when pigs flew.

"Good night, Ryder," she said softly. "Sleep well. I'm glad you're here."

Was she feeling the illusion of home, too? Despite all her proclamations of independence was she feeling safer having a man in the house with that storm raging outside and no power?

But then she added sleepily, "I would hate to think of you and Tess out in that storm somewhere."

He didn't rationalize with her, didn't point out to her if they were out in that storm somewhere they wouldn't be here. She would not even have known they existed.

Instead he thought about it: she was glad they were here *for them,* not for herself. And she was putting on this big Christmas event for others, not for herself.

Who was doing anything for her this Christmas? The homeless and the needy were coming here, what about her own family? Was she as alone as he was?

"You're not going to be alone, are you?" he asked, even though he had ordered himself not to. "On Christmas?"

"I told you. Fifty-one confirmed guests."

He heard something, knew she was holding back.

"A guest isn't family," he said.

"And my mother is coming."

"That's good." He wanted to probe something, an uncertainty, he'd heard in her voice, but that was enough of tangling his life with hers.

Troubled by those thoughts, way too aware of her proximity and the soft puffs of her breath as she fell asleep, he finally surrendered, too. But he slept like a cat, alert, one eye open, gauging the fire and the storm noises outside.

Finally, relieved, Ryder noticed gray light seeping into the room through the heavy closed drapes. Morning at last. The fire was embers again, and he could tell by the chill in the room the power was still not on.

He sat up and checked the baby, still asleep.

And then his eyes drifted to Emma. She was wrapped up like a sausage in the feather duvet she had brought down from upstairs, her dark hair sticking up in sharp contrast to it.

In her sleep, her brow was deeply furrowed, as if she could not let go of some pressing worry— probably hot dogs, or bathtubs falling through the floor—and Ryder could feel the concern for her aloneness. The sloping kitchen floor and that crack above the window in that room upstairs meant something was going on with the foundation. The door chime hadn't sounded right, either, and could be an indication of a bigger problem somewhere. This place was obviously too much for her, even before Holiday Happenings—and try as he might he couldn't quite shrug it off.

Sometime during the night he had cemented his decision to leave here.

Because he had laughed.

Because he had given in, ever so briefly, to the temptation to be a different man. Because you could begin to care about a woman like Emma even if you didn't want to.

Because he had hoped for something when the word *irresistible* had tumbled so easily off her lips, and despite the fact she had clarified what she meant, those mist-and-moss eyes had said something else.

He got up quietly, added wood to the fire, went to the window and lifted the drape. For the first time he noticed the difference from last night. It was quiet, now, eerily so, no wind. He noticed the snow and rain had stopped and the horizon was tinged with the indigo blue of a clear day. In the growing light he could see broken branches littering her front yard. A huge limb had missed his vehicle by inches.

The trees dripped blue ice, and the power line coming up to her yard was nearly on the ground it was so heavy with the rain that had frozen on it.

But the storm was over.

He had to go. But where, with all the roads closed?

Anywhere.

Other travelers had to be stranded. Churches were probably offering temporary shelter, recreation centers. Roads never stayed closed for long. He was sure they would reopen today, probably within hours now that the storm was over.

He went into her kitchen, the floor freezing on his bare feet, but he opened drawers until he found a screwdriver. He was fixing the front-door handle when Emma woke up.

"Morning."

He turned and looked at Emma. She was stretching, her hair sticking straight up.

She pulled back the duvet she had slept under, he could see the pajamas, pink flannel, little pink-and-white angels on them.

"The storm's over," he told her.

She cocked her head, listened. "Ah," she said, "the sweet sensation of survival."

"Your yard is a mess."

She came and stood beside him, surveyed the destruction being revealed by the growing morning light. Her shoulders drooped. "The pond probably looks the same way. How am I going to get that cleaned up for Holiday Happenings?"

"I don't know," he said.

She looked annoyed. "I was talking to myself, not expecting you to volunteer. And you don't have to fix the door, either." She made a grab for the screwdriver, but he held it away from her.

"If you could refill that kettle and put it on the fire, I can heat something up for the baby. Not to mention get a coffee into you. Sheesh. Prickly."

She turned from him abruptly, and then Ryder noticed it wasn't angels on her pajamas at all.

Pigs flying.

And then the baby screamed. Not her normal wakeup crabby cry but an animal shriek of pain and panic.

He set down the screwdriver and raced back into the great room, frightened that Tess had tried to climb out of her crib and had fallen.

But she stood at the side of her crib, screaming and jumping up and down, fixated on the fire.

He went and scooped her up, tucked her in tight to his shoulder, swayed with her.

"Shhh, baby," he said, and then not knowing where the words came from, only that he needed to say whatever would bring her comfort, he said, "Shhh. Mama's here."

And for a man who did not believe such things, he did feel as though Tracy was there, in some way, helping him soothe the baby, because Tess quieted against his shoulder, but refused to be put down, and would not even look in the direction of the fireplace.

Would a more sensitive person have realized the fire was going to traumatize the baby?

He felt the burden of his inadequacy, and then he realized Emma was watching him, a tender little smile on her lips and tiny tears sparkling in her eyes.

"I'm leaving," he said, before she admired him too much, before he became like a junkie, unable to live without that look on her face.

It was a look that erased his insecurities about not being sensitive and not being good with hair, a look that said, as clearly as if Emma had spoken, that she thought he was enough.

He rested in that for a moment, in the relief that someone thought he was enough for this child.

But then he steeled himself, reminded himself Emma did not know the whole story, and said again, more firmly than before. "I'm leaving."

# CHAPTER FIVE

RYDER told himself he wasn't just being mean and selfish, either. Tess was terrified of the fireplace and the fire within it, her tiny body trembling against his chest, her fist wrapped in his shirt so he couldn't get away from her.

He couldn't stay here with her. Even now, he was being very careful to use his body as a shield, placing it between Tess and the fire.

"Is Tess okay?" Emma asked. "What happened?"

"The fire scared her."

Thankfully, Emma accepted that explanation without asking him to elaborate. Her eyes went to the window where he'd opened the drape. Sunshine was beginning to spackle the walls.

"Is that wise? To leave? You should at least wait to hear what condition the roads are in. They could still be closed."

She had no electricity. He wasn't going to "hear" anything here. But he could tell it was not a rational explanation that she wanted.

Trying to take the screwdriver from him had been a token effort. Emma wanted him to stay, as if she had already formed some kind of attachment to the man who could least be trusted with attachments.

"The roads are never closed for long," Ryder said. Hopefully. The 1998 ice storm had been called the storm of the century for a reason: such storms happened once a century.

Of course, it was a new century now, and so far his luck had been abysmal.

"It's not as if you have urgent business," Emma said, and that furrow in her brow deepened as she turned worried eyes to the baby. "Your cottage isn't going anywhere."

But, of course, he did have urgent business. He had to reclaim the bastions that had had cracks knocked into them last night, he had to repair that hole in the wall she had slipped through. Even repaired, it would be a weak place now, and she knew where it was. If he stayed, she might slip through it again.

"I appreciate the shelter from the storm, Emma."

He appreciated more than that: the refuge, for a moment when he had laughed, and for another when he had remembered Christmas past, from the storms within himself, the glimpse of what it would be to be a different man, to have that feeling of home again.

But he wasn't ready and there was a possibility he never would be. People could only get hurt if he tried.

"We've imposed long enough."

She looked as though she had something to say about that, but she bit her lip instead.

"If you'll provide me with a bill, I'll finish getting Tess ready. I don't suppose you accept credit cards?"

Breaking it down to a business deal. Reminding her it was a business deal. Despite the mattress thing. Despite him sharing a memory with her of a long-ago Christmas that shone in his memory. Magic.

Despite knowing she had never had a good Christmas.

She looked insulted. "I'm not taking money! Hot dogs for supper and a bed on the floor! No, consider your stay at the White Christmas Inn my gift to you, humble as it was."

Ryder didn't want to accept a gift from her. He

hated it that she was offering one. Was she intent on giving that Christmas spirit to everyone, even those completely undeserving? Who would not make Santa's *nice* list?

But she had that mulish look on her face, and he wasn't going to argue. He'd mail her a check when he got home after Christmas. No, an anonymous money order because she'd probably be stubborn enough not to cash a check with his name on it.

Even if by after Christmas she'd mortgaged the place to pay for her hot dogs, and her falling-down house, and her fantasy Christmas day for the needy.

So, he'd make sure it was a darn generous check.

"Speaking of hot dogs," he said. "Don't forget, if the power stays out much longer, you'll have to take them out of the freezer."

*What a hero,* Ryder told himself cynically, *leaving her without power, but making sure to dispense hot-dog-saving advice before departing.*

A sound broke the absolute silence of the morning, a high-pitched whining engine noise. A snowmobile.

It was now full light out. The landscape outside the inn looked like a broken fairy tale, trees smashed, lines dangling, but everything coated in a thin shimmering sheet of incredibly beautiful blue-diamond ice.

A snowmobile pulling a sled came around the corner of the house. A man drove the snow machine; the sled had a woman and two little girls in it

"My neighbors," Emma said, and a smile of pure delight lit her face. "The Fenshaws. That's Tim driving, his daughter-in-law, Mona, and his two granddaughters, Sue and Peggy."

Relief washed over Ryder. She wouldn't be alone, after all. She had people who cared about her. Cared about her enough to be here at first light making sure she was all right.

He was free to leave.

The Fenshaws didn't so much come into the house as tumble in, laden with thermoses and a huge basket wafting the incredible smell of homemade bread. Flurried introductions were made.

The girls, perhaps nine and eleven, spotted Tess and put the baskets they were carrying down.

"A baby," they breathed in one voice.

The older one, Sue, came and took Tess from him with surprising expertise, put her on her hip, danced across the foyer to her mother.

"Look, Mom. Isn't she the cutest thing ever? Oh, I can't wait to comb her hair!"

As tempting as it would be to stay for that, and to sample whatever was in those baskets, now would be the perfect time to make his getaway, leaving Emma amongst all this energy and love.

"Actually, Tess and I were just getting ready to leave," Ryder said, amazed by his own reluctance, knowing, though, that that very reluctance was telling him it was time to go. He had to bite his tongue to keep himself from reminding her about the hot dogs again.

"Were you now?"

The man, Tim, weathered face and white hair, was kicking off his boots inside the front door. He rounded on Ryder and eyed him, taking in the pajamas and the mattress on the floor in the other room in one sweep of his gaze which was deeply and protectively suspicious.

"We got stranded by the storm," Ryder said, pleased by the older man's suspicion rather than put out by it. He was happy Emma had someone this fiercely protective of her, someone to look out for her. It relieved him of a burden he had taken on without wanting to. "But we're leaving now."

Tim had one of those faces Ryder could read.

Loss was etched there, and yet calm, too, as if Tim had made peace with what was, didn't even consider asking the world to take back its unfairness and cruelties.

"You think I'd arrive on my snowmobile if the driveway was open?" the man said. "Trees all over the thing."

Ryder stared at him. He'd been so anxious to go he had not seen what was right in front of him.

"You better have yourself some grub, son, and then we got us some work to do. You look like a city boy. You know how to run a chain saw?"

Ryder wanted to protest being called son. He wanted to rail against fate keeping him here when he was desperate to get out.

"We'll eat in the living room," Mona said, as if it was all decided. "It'll be too cold in the rest of the house."

"Tess doesn't like the living room."

But he was ignored and Tess, clearly enamored of the little girls, only cast a suspicious look at the fireplace before taking her cue from the other children and allowing herself to be put in the place of honor at the very center of the picnic blanket they were laying out on the floor.

The basket was unpacked, and soon they were

tucking into homemade bread and jam, steaming mugs of coffee.

The magic seemed to be deepening in this place, as the two little girls fussed over Tess… and over him.

"This is my doll," Peggy told him, wagging a worn rag doll in his face. "Her name is Bebo."

"Uh, that's an unusual name."

"Do you think it's pretty?"

It rated up there with *Holiday Happenings* on his ugly-name list, but he couldn't look into that earnest face and say that. Considering it practice for when Tess would be asking him such difficult questions, he said, "I think it's very creative."

Peggy frowned at him, not fooled. "I don't know what that means."

"It means pretty," he surrendered, and shot Emma a look when he heard her muffled laugh.

The attention of the little girls made him feel awkward. Mona said to him, softly, "My husband, Tim junior, is in the Canadian Forces. The girls seem to crave male attention. I'm sorry."

Ryder was sorry he'd made his discomfort that visible. He was glad he was leaving as soon as the driveway was cleared. He was no replacement for a hero. Not even close. "It must be very difficult for you."

She lowered her voice another notch, as Tim senior left the room to check the water pipes. "It's hardest on him. He lost his wife a while back and seems to age a year for every day Tim is gone."

Losses. Ryder had read the elder man's face correctly. This family was handling their own fears and troubles.

"Do you have power at your place?" Ryder asked, chang-ing the subject. He tried to sound casual. In actual fact, he hoped the fresh-made bread meant the Fenshaw house had power because he would feel better if Emma went there when he left.

"No," Mona said. "I have a great old wood-burning stove, the kind the pioneers had. You can cook on it, it has an oven. It's fantastic. It heats the whole house, though the house isn't as large as this one."

Again, there was the sense of *needing* to go, the momentary helpless frustration, and then surrender.

He wasn't going anywhere until they got the driveway cleared. He might as well enjoy the mouthwatering bread, the homemade jams, the hot coffee. He might as well enjoy the innocence of those children, the fact that they liked him without any evidence that they should.

"Would you like to hold Bebo?" Peggy asked him.

He heard Emma laugh again as he tried to think of a diplomatic response, and then she rescued him by saying, "I'd like to hold her, Peggy."

*"Me,"* Tess yelled, and Peggy surrendered her doll to the baby even though Tess was covered in jam.

Of course, surrendering to enjoyment was like surrendering to the magic that was wrapping itself around him, trying to creep inside him. Somehow as he filled up on breakfast and giggles, he became aware something was changing. He felt not *trapped,* somehow. Not ecstatic, either, but not trapped.

"Water's fine so far. What do you think we start clearing first?" Tim asked Emma, coming back into the room. "Pond or driveway?"

"Driveway," Emma said.

And Ryder might have appreciated how practical she was being—since no one could even get to the pond without the driveway, except that she looked right at him, and smiled sunnily. "Mr. Richardson is anxious to go." She didn't say it, but she might as well have, *And we're anxious to have him leave.*

He felt stung. Because for some reason he had

thought she was anxious to have him stay. But she wouldn't look at him, and he remembered he had seen heartbreak in her devotion to this house.

His leaving was what was best for everyone, some sizzle in the air between him and Emma was not going to pass if it was tested by too much time together.

"Let's see what I remember about using a chain saw," Ryder said, and got up when Tim moved to the door.

At the door he saw the older man pause, smile at the commotion. "Look at them girls with that baby. It's like Christmas came early for them."

Ryder looked back, and his heart felt as though a fist was squeezing it. Tess waddled back and forth between the two girls, Peggy's doll in a grubby death grip. The girls clapped and encouraged her every step.

The sense of his own inadequacy, from which he had taken a quick break, languishing in the warmth of Emma's approval, came back with a vengeance.

Ryder felt, acutely, the thing he could not give Tess.

This.

Family. She needed the thing he was most determined not to leave himself open to ever again.

He wondered if Emma was right about there being only one right decision, or if only the most selfish of men would think he could possibly know what was best for that baby, think that he could give her everything she needed.

Not because it was what was best for her. But because he loved her. Hopelessly and helplessly and she was all that was left of his world.

Tess normally kept a sharp eye out for any indication of a good-bye. When he left for work in the mornings, she would arch herself over Mrs. Markle's arms in a fit of fury. But this morning, covered in jam from her fingers to her ears, she did not seem to notice he was preparing to leave her in the care of strangers.

He was relieved that she was not making a fuss about the fireplace, either, though every now and then she would cast it a wary look, then look to the girls to see if they noticed the fire-breathing monster in the room with them.

It wasn't really as if he was leaving her with strangers. Somehow in one night Emma was not a stranger, and he seriously doubted the Fenshaws remained strangers to anyone for more than a few seconds.

He turned away from the play of the children and went out to his car to retrieve the boots and gloves he had packed for the cottage because Tess loved to play in the snow. He didn't even go back in to put them on, refusing to subject himself to the warmth of that scene again. He slid his winter clothes over what he was wearing.

Tim put him to work straight away.

Two huge trees and several smaller ones had fallen over the driveway. Branches littered the entire length of the road.

Ryder soon found himself immersed in the work of cutting the trees, bucking the branches off them. The pure physical activity soothed something in him, much like the punishing workouts he did at the gym.

Plus, working with a chain saw was tricky and dangerous. There was no room for wandering thoughts while working with a piece of equipment that could take off a limb before you blinked.

Out of the corner of his eye, he saw Emma leave the house and come down the driveway to join them.

"They kicked me out. Mona said I can't even be trusted in a kitchen with full power, but I think the truth is they wanted the baby to themselves. Pigeon convention in full swing."

It was only a mark of how necessary it was that

he leave that he appreciated how carefully she had listened to him last night.

"Oh, and I buried the hot dogs in a snowdrift outside the back door."

Emma was dressed casually, in a down parka, her crazy hair sticking out from under a red toque. She had on men's work gloves that made her hands look huge at the ends of her dainty wrists.

"Tess okay with you leaving?" he asked her, idling the chain saw, worried that the incident with the fire could be repeated now that both he and Emma had left the house.

But Emma reassured him. "Tess appears to be having the time of her life. They've heated up some water. Mona is showing Sue and Peggy how to bathe a baby. They're using a huge roasting pan for a tub, in front of the fire. I nearly cooed myself it was so darned cute. I told them to take some pictures for you. I can e-mail them to you. After."

After. After he was gone. Setting up a little thread of con-tact, making his leaving not nearly as complete as he wanted to make it. He wanted to leave this place—and all the uncomfortable feelings it had conjured up—and not look back.

"Watch for the ice," he told her, not wanting to encourage her to send him pictures. "Every now and then it breaks off the wires or the trees and falls down like a pane of glass."

"You watch out, too," she said.

"For?"

She scooped up a handful of snow, balled it carefully, hurled it at his head. It missed and hit him square in the chest.

*Don't do it,* he ordered himself. Despite her acting as if she was as eager for him to leave as he was to go, she was looking for that hole in his defenses again. Intentionally or not?

Despite his strict order to himself, he set down the chain saw, idling, scooped up a handful of snow, formed it into a solid ball. She was already running down the driveway, laugh-ing, thinking she'd escaped.

He let fly the snowball. It missed. And for a moment, with-out thought, without any kind of premeditation, without analysis, he was his old self again, just an ordinary guy who couldn't stand the fact he'd missed. He scooped up another handful of snow, went down the driveway after her. She laughed and scooted off the road, ducked behind a tree. His snowball splatted against it.

"Na, na," she said. She peeked out and flagged her nose at him.

He let fly again, she ducked behind the tree.

Splat. He scooped snow, moved in closer, she darted to another tree. A snowball flew out from behind it, and hit him squarely in the face.

It was a damned challenge to his manhood! He wiped the snow away and made ammunition. When she showed herself again, he let fly with one snowball after another, machine-gun-like. He thought she'd run, or better, beg for mercy, but she didn't. She grabbed an armload of snow, ran right into the hail of his fire and jammed the white fluffy stuff right down his pants!

He burst out laughing. "You know how to put out a fire, don't you, Emma?"

"Were you on fire?" she asked, all innocence.

No. Not yet. But if he was around this kind of temptation much longer he was going to be.

He shook his head, moved away from her, ordered himself again to stop it. But he didn't. "Watch your back," he warned her.

But she just laughed, moved past him down the driveway. He went back to his chain saw, still idling, and stopped for a moment to watch her pulling branches off the road, blowing out puffs of wintry air as she applied herself to the task.

He frowned. She was tackling branches way too big for her.

"Save your breath," Tim said, following his

gaze. "If you tell her it's a man's work she'll be trying to find her own chain saw. Stubborn as a mule."

But he said it with clear affection.

"It runs in her family." That was said without so much affection.

*Don't ask,* Ryder said. He hoped to begin the process of disengaging himself, but somehow he had to ask.

"What's her family like?"

"There's just her and her mother now that her grandmother died." He hesitated, stared hard at Ryder, weighing something. "Lynelle ain't gonna be takin' home the Mama of the Year award."

"But she's coming for Christmas, right?" Why did he care? Why did it feel as if it relieved him of some responsibility? He had to get out of here. He was not responsible for Emma's happiness. How could he be? He couldn't even be responsible for his own anymore. He was broken. Broken people couldn't fix things, they could only make them worse.

"Humph," Tim said crankily, "Emma's mother, Lynelle, doesn't give a lick about this place, never will."

"It's not about the place," Ryder said, aggrieved. "It's about her daughter."

Tim looked troubled, and Ryder could clearly see in his face he wasn't sure if Lynelle gave a lick about her daughter, either, though he stopped short of saying that.

"Ah, well," Tim said. "You can't choose your family."

Since Tim clearly didn't feel that way about his own family, it was a ringing indictment of Emma's. Ryder had fished for more information about Emma, but now he was sorry for what he'd found out. She was as alone as he was. Maybe more so. She didn't have Tess.

Tim's revelations made Ryder see Emma's need to make a perfect Christmas in a new light. It was as if she thought that if she could create enough festive atmosphere, help enough people, she could outrun her own pain and loneliness.

In a way, he and Emma were doing the very opposite things to achieve the same result.

Troubled, he focused on the tasks at hand, but despite working steadily they had made almost no headway on the driveway by noon. A bell rang, and Ryder realized Mona was calling them for lunch, and that he was famished.

"Mama!" Tess crowed when she saw him. She was seated in her high chair in front of the fire, both little girls standing on chairs beside her, pa-

tiently working combs and gentle fingers through
Tess's wet hair. She had obviously had a bath,
been dressed in fresh onesies from her baby bag,
and was proudly sporting a pure white Christmas
bow in the center of her chest.

Emma came in behind him stomping snow off
her boots.

"Isn't that cute?" she asked. "She looks like a
pint-sized queen commanding her attendants."

He kicked off his own boots, walked in and inspected Tess's 'do. The worst of the tangles were
out of her hair. Experimentally, he reached out
and touched.

Tess screeched.

The older girl said sternly, "Tess, that is
enough of that!"

And Tess stopped, just like that. He touched her
hair again, and the baby gave her captors a sly
look and made a decision. She cooed, "Mama."

"He's not your mama, silly," the older girl, Sue,
said again. "Papa."

"I'm her uncle."

"Uncle," the child said, not missing a beat,
pointing at him. "That's your uncle, Tess."

"Ubba."

Three months he'd been trying to coax his
niece to call him anything but Mama.

And he hadn't been able to.

Girls, women, knew these things. They knew by some deep instinct how to deal with babies. How to raise children. What did he know of these things? How could he ever do this job justice?

Really, in the end he just wanted to know he was doing a good enough job, and for one moment Emma had made him feel that way. Made him feel that he didn't have to be an exquisite baby hairdresser, or nominated for guardian of the year.

In Emma's eyes in that moment this morning when he had rescued Tess from her fire-breathing dragon, he had felt certainty. His love for the baby was enough.

Or was it? What about moments such as these that his brokenness, his unwillingness to reengage in the risky business of loving others would deprive Tess of?

And he wondered, even if he never gave Emma his e-mail address, just how completely he was going to be able to leave this behind.

Peggy, the smaller of the girls, approached him while they ate.

"Would you like to see my drawing?"

"Uh, okay."

She handed it to him. A little blobby baby, obviously Tess because of the hair, smiled brightly in front of a Christmas tree.

"That's very nice," he said awkwardly. "I like the way you did Tess."

"It's before we fixed her hair." Peggy beamed at him as if he had handed her a golden wand that granted wishes. As if he was *enough*.

Then he had to admire Sue's drawing, too. Sue had drawn a picture of a man in a uniform in front of a Christmas tree.

"That's my dad," she said.

Something about the way she said it—so proud, so certain her dad could make everything right in her world—made him ache for the moment he had not made right and could never bring back. It made him ache for the moments of fatherhood his brother was never going to have, for the moments Tess was never going to have. His sorrow fell over the moment like a dark cape being thrown over light.

It was light that Emma, with her innate sense of playfulness, her ability to sneak by his defenses with falling mattresses and flying snowballs was bringing to his world.

He got up quickly, without looking at Emma, went outside and back to the soothing balm of hard, physical, mind-engaging labor.

* * *

"No Holiday Happenings again tonight," Emma said, as they finally reached the base of her driveway. They had spent the whole afternoon clearing it. It was now late in the day, the sun low in the sky, a chill creeping back into the air.

She was so aware of Ryder, the pure physical presence of the man, as he stood beside her surveying her driveway where it intersected with the main road. The sun had been shining brilliantly up until a few minutes ago, and he had stripped down to his T-shirt. His arm muscles were taut and pumped from the demands of running that chain saw. She could smell something coming off him, enticing, as crystal-clear and clean as the ice falling off the tree branches and telephone wires.

From the way he'd been dressed when he arrived last night, she had assumed he was a high-powered professional, and he had confirmed that when he had told her he was an architect. But seeing him tackle the mess in her driveway, his strength unflagging, hour after grueling hour, she had been awed by the pure masculine power of the man.

The way he worked told her a whole lot more about him than his job description. Even Tim, whose admiration was hard-won, had looked over at Ryder working and when Emma went by with a load of branches, had embarrassed her by saying, a little too loudly, "That one's a keeper."

So she'd said just as loudly, "And what would *you* keep him for?" But then she'd been sorry, because Tim missed his son, and could have used another man around to help him with his own place, never mind all that he had taken on at hers.

Ryder was leaving as soon as he could. And that was wise. She realized he was right to want to leave. She realized it was in her best interests for him to go. Something was stirring in her that she thought she had put away in a box marked Childish Dreams and Illusions after the devastation of Peter's fickleness.

Now she stared up the main road. It was as littered with debris, broken boughs and fallen trees as her driveway had been. In the far distance, she listened for the sounds of rescue, chain saws or heavy equipment running, but she heard absolutely nothing.

"I guess Tess and I aren't going anywhere today," Ryder said.

She cast a look at his face. He looked resigned, like a soldier who had just been told he had more battles to fight. It wasn't very flattering.

But the way his gaze went to her lips was, except

that he took a deep breath and moved away from her.

Emma watched him go, and despite the fact she was exhausted after the hard day of physical labor, she felt a little tingle of pure awareness that made her feel alive, and as though her life was full of possibilities.

*Stop it,* she ordered herself. *Be despondent! No Holiday Happenings for the second night in a row? And the road closed. For how long?* She needed to get that bus ticket to her mother.

It was a disaster! A harbinger of another Christmas disaster.

And yet, despite the fact this year was shaping up about the same way, the road to her inn obviously impassable, something inside her was singing! And it wasn't wild-child, either, though she had definitely perked up at the way Ryder had looked at her lips moments ago.

No, it was another part of her, singing because of flying snowballs and the way he had looked so awkward and adorable studying the girls' drawings.

The rational part of her knew that saying goodbye would be the best thing, but how quickly her own life—Holiday Happenings, even her Christmas-day celebrations—were taking a backseat to rationality.

That was her weakness, and it ran in the family. After watching her mother toss her life to the wind every time a new and exciting man blew in, Emma had done the very same thing with Peter! She had tried to make herself over in the image Peter Henderson had approved of.

She had been amazed when Peter—wealthy, handsome, educated, sophisticated—a doctor and her boss, had asked her out. To her, he had been everything she dreamed of—stable, successful, *normal,* from a stellar family.

Only, it hadn't been very long before she discovered that keeping up with appearances, which, admittedly, had impressed her at first, was an obsession with him. His shoes had to be a certain make, his ties were imported, his teeth were whitened. Looking good, no matter how he was feeling on the inside, was a full-time job for him.

And it hadn't taken very long for him to turn his critical eye on her. *You're not going to wear that are you?* Or *It would have been better, when you met Mrs. Smith, if you said you enjoyed your Christmas charity work instead of telling her that dreadful story about the homeless man.*

And Emma had gone overboard trying to please him, worn herself out, lived for the praise and approval that never came.

Despite his pedigree, it had all started to remind her a little bit of her relationship with her mother: she was looking for things the other person never intended to give her.

The truth was that she'd been glad when her grandmother had needed her, glad that she had a place to go, glad to escape from the demands of the role she had to play for him.

When she'd finally invited Peter to White Pond Inn, halfway through the renovation, thinking he would love it and see what a beautiful summer place it could make for them once they were married, he had hated it. He had told her, snobbishly, with *hostility,* that she was trying to make a silk purse out of a sow's ear.

That was something else he had in common with her mother, who hated this place so much she hadn't even come back for Granny's funeral.

And then the final blow—by telephone, the coward! Monique was more suited to his world. It was Emma's own fault for going to the inn. For putting her interests ahead of his.

How had the love of her life, the man who was her dream, turned out to be a snobby version of her mother? To both of them, their interests came first. They didn't even hesitate to divest themselves of anyone or anything that asked something of them, that wanted a return on an investment. And Emma had bought into it for so long, telling herself real love didn't ask for anything. It only gave, never took, exhausting and unrewarding as that was.

Why did Emma think Lynelle would come for Christmas when she hadn't even come to her own mother's funeral?

*She'll come,* Emma told herself. *She said she would come.* But a promise in her mother's world was not always something you could take to the bank. The doubt was going to be there until the moment her mother stepped off the bus.

And Emma felt guilty about her lack of faith in Lynelle.

"Emma, Emma, Emma," her mother had said, annoyed, the last time they'd spoken and Emma had pressed for an answer about Christmas. "Where *do* you get that sentimental streak from?"

As if somehow Emma was in the wrong for wanting her to come.

"Okay, okay, *okay,*" Lynelle had finally said, irritated. "I'll come. Send the damned ticket. Are you happy now?"

"Hey," Ryder said. When had he come back beside her? "Don't take it like that. The road could be open tonight." And then, softer, "Please don't cry."

Which was when she realized she was crying! She swiped at her cheeks with a mittened hand. "I'm not crying," she said stubbornly. "I poked myself in the eye with a branch."

She held out a branch to show him, but he looked right past it and right past the words.

He cupped her chin in his gloved hand, slipped the glove off his other hand with his teeth, brushed the tear from her cheek. She saw the struggle in his face, knew he wanted nothing more than to walk away from her pain.

And she knew she was seeing something he tried to hide when he didn't walk away, or couldn't.

"Come on," he said, throwing a casual brotherly arm over her shoulder, guiding her away from the road, "you'll have a good Christmas this year. Meanwhile, let's see what that miracle worker Mona has planned for supper."

As soon as he walked in the door, Sue and Peggy, who had apparently lugged Tess around all afternoon, were on him as if he were a favored uncle. They handed over Tess, who now sported several more bows, somewhat reluctantly.

"Mama," she said.

"No, Tess," Sue said sternly.

"Ubba?" Tess guessed.

"Yes!" The gleeful girls danced around as if Tess had scored a touchdown. Ryder stroked Tess's combed hair, and Tess didn't even howl a protest.

"Me preffree," she declared to her uncle. "Har."

"She means she's pretty," Sue translated officiously. "'Cause of her hair."

"Pretty," Ryder said thoughtfully. "No, I don't think so."

All three girls looked shattered at his pronouncement, but the smiles started when he said, "Um, no, pretty isn't good enough. Lovely?" He seemed to think it over, regarded Tess, then shook his head. "Gorgeous. Beautiful. Stunning. Dazzling."

"Creative!" Sue crowed, and he smiled.

And then he lifted his niece up with that easy masculine grace, dangled her over his head, her little legs waggling with glee, and then he swooped her down and blew a kiss onto her belly.

Emma could have watched him play with the baby forever. But even thinking that word in close proximity to him seemed to be inviting danger, so she deliberately turned her back on the scene and went in search of Mona. Mona was on the back porch, assembling the bundles of balsam and fir and spruce that went into wreaths.

"The road's not open," Emma said, glad to have this moment alone with Mona. "I'm not sure we need any more of those. We probably won't be able to sell what we have."

She took a deep breath, "I appreciate you and Tim and the girls spending the day, but I'm not sure about tomorrow. If Holiday Happenings doesn't happen soon, I'm not going to be able to pay you."

Mona gave her an insulted look. "We came as your neighbors and your friends today, not as your employees, and we'll be here as long as you need us."

Emma could feel those awful tears burning in her eyes again.

"Besides, you know how I love this house and it's good to keep busy. It keeps all of us from thinking about Tim. Two more Canadian soldiers were wounded yesterday."

And then Mona's eyes were full of tears, too, but she quickly brushed them aside. "Let's have supper at my place. I can cook on the wood burner. I took out chicken this morning. Plus the whole house will be nice and warm from the woodstove."

The thought of so much warmth—physical and emotional—was more than Emma could refuse.

But Ryder refused with ease, closing something in himself that had opened during the snowball fight. "Tess and I will stay here," he said. "I've got food for her. I can have a hot dog for supper."

Emma knew something about all this bothered him: the children, the family, the moments of playfulness, the togetherness. She could see that he deliberately planned to turn his back on it. She refused to beg him to come, which woman-scorned was very pleased about. Emma knew he was posing a danger to her. She could see that by coming to the inn she had deliberately removed herself from all those things that, after Peter, she was ill-equipped to handle.

But Mona was having none of it. "You are not having a hot dog for supper after the kind of work you did today."

Ryder still looked stubborn.

Peggy came and took his hand, shook it vigorously to make sure she had his full attention. "Tess *has* to come to my house. I want to show her my dollhouse that my daddy made."

"I could use another man," Tim said, clearly having to overcome his pride to ask. "The pump won't be working, and I'll need to haul water from the creek."

Emma was not sure which of those arguments won him over, but she was aware of the sweet sensation within herself of *wanting* to be with him and to spend more time with him, and being glad she didn't have to reveal any of that by convincing him herself.

Somehow they all managed it in one trip, Mona on the snowmobile behind her father-in-law, Ryder, Emma, girls and baby squashed onto the sled.

Ryder went in first, Emma between his legs, the baby on her lap. She had to push hard into his chest to make room for Sue and Peggy, who squeezed in practically on top of her and the baby.

The extremely crowded ride the short distance to the Fenshaws' should have been uncomfortable. Instead, it felt incredible. It wasn't just because she was so close to him, though she could feel his heart beating through his jacket, feel the steel of his strong legs where they formed a V around the small of her back. It was the whole picture, the baby and the girls shouting with laughter as their grandfather picked up speed, the snowmobile cutting a smooth path through the snow.

It was the party atmosphere the Fenshaws insisted on creating, as if closed roads and downed power lines were exactly the excuse they'd been looking for to spend some time together.

It was the feeling of family that Emma had yearned for her entire life.

The house Mona had come to share with her father-in-law when her husband was away was as old as Emma's but more rustic. Inside was as humble as out; it was a true farmhouse, more about function than fashion, especially since Tim had lived here on his own after the death of his wife.

Wall art ran to framed school photos of the girls, and a large picture of Tim, Jr., in his military uniform, smiling shyly at the camera.

There was nothing "up-country" about the Christmas decorations, either; they were a happy mishmash of fake silver and gold garlands, a scrawny tree nearly falling over under the weight of pine-cone decorations obviously made by Sue and Peggy, the table centerpiece a skinny Santa Claus made out of a paper towel roll and cotton batten.

And yet, the feeling of Christmas and of family was perfect.

Peter would have hated every single thing

about this house, and he would have called the decorations tacky.

But when she slid Ryder a glance to see how he was reacting, she saw him take in the humble home, something reluctant and oddly vulnerable in the dark of his eyes.

How could it be, that just twenty-four hours ago when she had seen him those dark, dark eyes had made her think the devil had come to visit?

Could he have changed that much in twenty-four hours? Or had she?

# CHAPTER SIX

EMMA watched with admiration as Mona, unfazed by the lack of electricity, stoked the cookstove, lit coal-oil lanterns, warmed water for washing, set her old coffeepot on the stove and began to get chicken ready to fry in an old cast-iron pan.

The men hauled water, a hard job that left them soaked in their own sweat and the water that sloshed from buckets. When they were done, Mona gave them a scrub basin filled with the warm water, and dry shirts and shooed them into the back porch off the kitchen. She gave Emma a potato peeler and pointed at a mountain of potatoes.

Unfortunately, from where she stood at the table peeling, Emma had a clear view through the open door to the porch. Her mouth went dry as Ryder stripped off his wet shirt. He was one hundred-per-cent-pure man. He had incredibly broad shoulders, his chest was deep and smooth, his pectoral muscles defined, his abdomen a rippled hollow. His pants hung low over the slight rise of his hips.

Emma felt a fire in her belly. Around Peter she had always striven to feel cool and composed. Even their kisses had been stingy and proper.

Nothing could have prepared her for the pure primal feeling she felt now.

How could she be a brand-new woman— totally devoted to her inn and her independent life—with someone like him around?

*He's a temporary distraction,* she told herself. But did that mean she could look all she wanted? Was it something like those chocolate oranges that came out only at Christmas? You had to give yourself permission to enjoy them while they were around?

Embarrassed by her own hunger and curiosity, Emma forced herself to focus on the potato she was peeling, but she just had to slide him one more little look. Who knew how long before she would see something like this again?

Ryder Richardson was built as if he had been carved out of marble. The male strength and perfection in every hard line of him was absolute.

He took the washcloth, dipped it in the water, soaped it and then ran it along the hard bulge of his forearm, up his arm to the mound of his biceps.

She hoped she hadn't made a noise! Because he looked up, caught her looking and his gaze rested on her, heated, knowing. He continued what he was doing, but he held her gaze while he did it. She looked away first, her face feeling as if it was on fire.

She didn't look up again, scowling with furious concentration at the potato in her hand.

Then he was beside her, filling her senses in yet another way, the soapy scent of him as sensual as silk on naked skin.

"Wow," he said, his voice husky, "not much left of that potato."

Despite her attempt at concentration, despite the fact she had not looked away from that spud for a single second, she had whittled away at it until only a sliver of it remained in her hand.

"You should go check on Tess," she said, throwing that potato in the peeled pile and picking up another, trying to get rid of him. Only he wasn't falling for it.

"I can hear her laughing. She's obviously okay."

He picked up a paring knife, sat on the stool

beside her, took off a potato peel in one long coil, his hands amazing on that knife, his movements, despite the strength in those hands, controlled and fine.

It was very easy to imagine hands like those doing things and going places—

"Pay attention," he said, as if he *knew* she was looking at his hands, and thinking totally wicked thoughts about where she would like them to be. "Don't cut yourself."

She glanced at him, saw a teasing smile playing across his face. The scoundrel knew exactly what effect he was having on her!

Probably because he'd had it on about a million women before her.

"Ouch," she said. She'd nicked her finger.

"Tried to tell you," he said smugly. But then he set down his potato and his knife and lifted her hand.

She who had always disdained the word *swoon* and the kind of woman who would do it—certainly not an independent innkeeper—could feel something in her melt and slide.

"It's nothing," she said, trying to take her hand away.

He held fast. "I'll finish up, if you want to go take care of it."

"I said, it's nothing." Her voice was high and squeaky, and it had an unattractive frantic quality to it. She yanked her hand away, picked up another potato to prove a point, though, at the moment, she was so addled she wasn't quite sure what that point was.

Her hand was *tingling*.

He sighed, exasperated. "You've got to know when to quit, Emma."

That was a problem for her, all right. Because she should quit this right now. She should set down her paring knife and go join the girls and Tess in the other room. She could hear them trying to play cards and keep the cards out of Tess's clutches at the same time.

But good sense did not prevail. She did not quit. Instead she said, boldly, "Maybe I'll let you take care of it for me later."

And when he was silent she glanced at him and saw he was now concentrating furiously on his task.

Whatever was going on was mutual.

Which made a wholesome farm dinner, platters of perfectly browned chicken, wedged potatoes, a simple salad, seem fraught with hidden dangers—the touch of his hand while he passed the salt, his leg brushing hers when he got up to get something that Tess had dropped on the floor.

Ryder's presence, her aching awareness of him, made her feel as awkward as a teenager on her first date, as if she was just learning to chew food and how to use a knife and fork.

"Mona, you cooked," Emma said after dinner. "I'll clean up. You go visit with the girls. Relax."

*I need a break from this man, from the intensity I feel around him, from the awareness of his scent and his eyes and the way his chest rises and falls when he breathes.*

"I'll help," he said.

*Great. Hide the knives.*

Why was he doing this? Maybe because he was helpless not to do it, the same as she was? Maybe because he wanted to be close to her, the temptation of the faint but growing sizzle between them a warmth too hard to walk away from if you were chilled from the inside out?

Emma did not miss the look on Tim's face. Not in the least judgmental as he looked between the two of them, but satisfied somehow.

Alone in the kitchen, Ryder took a tea towel and wiped the dishes she washed.

"Tell me what made Christmas so bad for you," he said.

"Oh, I wish I had never said that. It was silly. A moment, that's all."

A moment of trusting another person with your deepest disappointment.

The truth was the Christmases of her childhood had been chaotic, full of moves, Lynelle's new men, not enough money, too much adult celebration.

And that shadow seemed to have fallen over the Christmases of her adult life, too.

"One year my new puppy had died, another I ended up in the hospital with pneumonia."

And then last year, when she had so been looking forward to her first Christmas with Peter's parents, practically quivering with expectation, she had been devastated by the reality.

Not that she was going *there* with this man!

"Just normal stuff that happens to everyone," she said. "I'm too sensitive. Everyone says so. Sorry." *Especially my mother. Repeatedly.*

"Emma," his hand was on her shoulder.

There was that *tingling* again.

"You don't have to apologize for being sensitive. The world could use a whole lot more of that. It's people like you who make everything that is beautiful."

Emma stared at him, thinking it was the loveliest thing anyone had ever said to her. If she got nothing else for Christmas, would that be enough?

"Hurry up," Sue said, appearing out of the living room.

Ryder's hand dropped off her shoulder but the tingle stayed.

"Hurry up. We have enough people to play charades. You two and me on one team, Mom and Grandpa and Pegs on the other. Come on!"

Ryder's silence made Emma look at him. She could clearly see some battle in his eyes. He did not want to play charades.

He didn't say, *I don't want to.* He said, "I can't."

Sue stepped across the floor, took his hand and tugged. She looked up at him with enormous eyes. "Pleeease?" she whispered.

His face looked not as if he were deciding whether to play charades, but as if he was a warrior deciding whether to pick up his weapons or lay them down.

In the end he could not refuse Sue, was incapable of hurting her, and Emma had the sensation of seeing who he really was.

"Who gets Tess?" Ryder asked the little girl, only Emma sensed the surrender, and how hard it came to him.

"We're letting her think she's on both teams," Sue whispered solemnly.

Emma had never played charades, family games not being high on her mother's list of priorities, but the girls were experts on the game, and took great pleasure in explaining her responsibilities to her.

After several rounds, Tess fell asleep on the couch. It was Emma's turn. A little nervous, she drew a card from a bowl. *Love Story.* Okay. Who was the joker who had put that in?

She didn't want to try and act out anything about love with Ryder in the room. And how was she supposed to get that subject across with only her limited acting abilities?

Reluctantly, she made the motion the girls had showed her.

"Movie," Sue and Peggy crowed together, Peggy apparently forgetting whose team she was on.

So far so good. Taking a deep breath, Emma crossed her hands over her heart, smiled, and swayed in what she hoped was a swoon, something she was newly experienced at. She blinked her eyes.

"Giraffe?" Sue said doubtfully.

Ryder snickered. Emma glared at him and drew a large invisible heart with her hands.

"Giraffe that has swallowed something large.

Like a potato. Only not one Emma peeled," Ryder suggested.

Everyone seemed to think he was hysterically funny. He was grinning slightly and she saw that once he had been this man: full of mischief and fun. The grin made him look young, made her think how somber he looked most of the time. What had happened to him? Obviously whatever it was made him the worst possible man to feel attracted to. He was wounded. So was she. That was a bad, bad combination.

Despite knowing that, she went from feeling reluctant and awkward to wanting to make him laugh. She threw herself into her performance, going on bended knee before him, clasping her hands in front of her, blinking dreamily.

"A giraffe with eye problems," Ryder said.

"Would you forget the giraffe?" she cried.

"You're not allowed to talk, Emma!" Sue reprimanded her.

"Yeah," Ryder said. "Whoever heard of a giraffe that talks?"

Emma was exasperated that he would get a talking giraffe out of her practically prostrating herself in front of him with love.

Could she fall in love with him? Given time? Luckily they didn't have time. Then again, how much time would you need to fall hopelessly in love with a man like him? And it would be hopeless. The remoteness that never quite left his eyes, not even when he laughed, was warning her off, trying to tell her something.

Still, he'd walked into her life twenty-four hours ago, and his appeal was, unfortunately, outweighing the warning, swaying her against her will. She thought of the exquisite tenderness on his face when he had soothed Tess this morning, when he had said to the baby, *Mama's here.* She thought of his clumsy awkwardness with the girls, of the way he pitched in to help, of the seamless way he had joined in with the Fenshaws and with her. Emma thought of him telling her about his best Christmas, the light that had come on in his face, she thought of him chasing her down the driveway armed with snowballs. Did all this mean that if he stayed another day she would lose her good sense completely?

"Good sense is my middle name," she muttered a reminder to herself.

"You're not allowed to talk!" Sue reminded her, hands on her hips, frowning.

Emma got off up her knees. Naturally she didn't expect Sue to get her acting out love, but he was being deliberately obtuse. Despite the fact that good sense was her middle name, Emma skipped across the living room, a woman obviously in the throes of love, picked an imaginary daisy, tore imaginary petals off it, *he loves me, he loves me not.*

*"The Birds,"* Ryder suggested dryly, though he was obviously enjoying himself at her expense!

She glared at him, blinked again, blew him a kiss, wrapped her arms around herself and hugged, doing her best dreamy look.

"You love him!" Sue crowed.

And Emma felt herself turn bright red. Of course she didn't love him. She barely knew him! And the little she did know did not bode well for loving him. But she thought of the way he'd been unable to refuse Tim's request for help or Sue's plea for him to play the game with them, and she wondered about herself and her strength and the temptations of another twenty-four hours.

Though surely in these circumstances, seeing how people coped with disaster and with life being wrested out of their control, you knew a lot more about them sooner than under normal circumstances.

Emma decided she better move on before she embarrassed herself completely. She motioned that she was doing the second word, pretended to be turning the pages of a book.

"You're reading," Sue guessed. "A book. A story."

Emma clapped her hands, thrilled to have gotten that part over with so fast.

*"Love Story,"* Ryder guessed, and then gave a shout of laughter, as if his own enthusiasm had taken him by surprise.

Emma realized, staring at him, that what she needed to do was not think about the future or project her romantic nature onto it. She needed to remember the past, and how her ability to fill in the blanks had brought her nothing but grief. With Peter. And with her mother.

She needed to remind herself what grief felt like and to know that the unfathomable darkness that swam in the man's eyes promised her more of it.

"I have to go," she said, leaping to her feet, re-membering guiltily her *true* love now, her house. "I have to put more wood on the fire at my place or the water will freeze for sure. But Ryder can stay."

"No, I'll go with you."

Something shivered along her spine. "No, it's fine."

"I'm not letting you go over there by yourself."

Emma could tell Tim approved of that. The independent woman in her was strangely silent.

"Let Tess stay the night here then," Mona said, as if it were all settled, "there's no sense waking her up and sending her into the cold."

Ryder hesitated.

"Okay," he said, reluctantly, obviously weighing out what was better for Tess.

Emma was newly taken by his tender protective attitude toward Tess. It probably wasn't good to be heading over there, just the two of them, feeling like this.

*So* aware. Her shoulder still tingling from where he'd touched it an hour ago! Woman-scorned told her to go home and throw out every one of those romantic movies she'd been collecting. They had obviously filled her head with nonsense.

"There's an extra snowmobile in the shed next to the house," Tim said. "My son's. Take it over."

For a moment, all the laughter was gone from the room, and Emma could feel how much this family wished Tim, Jr., home.

"I'll be over first thing. We can get started on the pond," Tim decided. "We should at least be able to clear a section of it for skating."

"I'll bring breakfast," Mona said.

And then Emma and Ryder were outside, the moon full and bright above them, the air crystal-cold and clear, the stars sparkling, close enough that she felt she could reach out and put one in her pocket.

Ryder did up his jacket against the brisk breeze that was blowing. "There's something incredibly admirable about those people. Father, husband, son called to war, power out, roads closed, they just handle everything with a certain calm courage. I admire that."

"I think you handle crisis about the same way."

He looked at her. "That's where you're wrong," he said. He went to the shed, got the snowmobile out of it and then mounted it and patted the seat behind him.

She climbed on, trying to keep the dangerous awareness somewhat at bay by grabbing onto the bar behind her.

"Hold on tight."

So she did, wrapping her arms around him, burrowing her cheek into the strong curve of his shoulder. Surrendering.

They surged through the night, her hands wrapped around his belly. He opened up the throttle and she was sucked even closer into him.

The cold air, the glory of the night and him.

She felt exhilarated. Free. As if there had been no moment before this one, and there would be none after. Her senses gave her mind, always too busy, a much-needed rest. Her senses dismissed the caution she was trying desperately to resurrect.

And maybe he felt that way, too. Because of what he said next.

"Do you mind if I take the long way home?" he shouted over the roar of the engine.

She honestly didn't feel that she cared if they ever went home. This felt oddly like home. Being with him. Feeling his warmth and his strength penetrating through his jacket, feeling the play of his muscles as he guided the snowmobile around debris, picked a route that snaked through fallen trees up the ridge behind both her and Tim's places.

The world was a place of sharp and almost mystical contrasts, the cold sting of night air on her cheeks in contrast to his warmth, the beauty of the moon making the broken trees glitter silver, the forest where she had walked many times damaged now and seeming like a place she had never been before, a place that could hold equally promise or destruction.

He stopped at the crest of the ridge and cut the engine. The silver, black and white vista below them was beautifully silent. They could see the dark silhouette of her inn, Tim's place looking brighter with the yellow glow from the oil lamps lighting his windows. Beyond that, they could see Willowbrook.

"You could almost imagine it was the little town of Bethlehem," she said, the town looking so pretty and peaceful.

He snorted but not with the same amount of derision as he would have done so last night.

"The lights are on in the town," he noticed. "They have power there. And look, you can see headlights moving on the road west of it."

It could take days for those things to happen here, but it was still a reminder that this was all temporary, an illusion of sorts, that would come to an end.

He turned and looked back at her, and then he took off the thick snowmobile glove and scraped his thumb across her lip.

She leaned into it, something flashed through his eyes and he moved his hand away, faced forward, put the glove back on.

He shook his head, and his voice was remote. "I think for both our sakes I should take you back to Fenshaws'. I can look after things at your place by myself tonight."

"You go back and stay at Fenshsaws'," she said, thinking *I'm as bad at this as I am at charades*. How could he not understand what she wanted? Or worse, understand exactly what she wanted and reject her?

"You can drop me off," she said stiffly. "The inn is my responsibility and I'm not turning it over to you."

"If you knew how badly I wanted to kiss you right now," he said softly, "you'd go back to Fenshaws'."

She totally forgot that good sense was her middle name.

"Would I?" she challenged him.

"Yeah," he said roughly, "you would."

"I think you're wrong. I think I'd kiss you back."

He sighed, his breath harsh, impatient. "Emma, let's not complicate things."

He was right. He would be a terrible complication in the world she was building for herself. It was too soon for this. He was being the reasonable one.

But that's not how she acted. Instead, she got off the snowmobile and went around to the front of it, facing him. She leaned into him, took his face in her gloved hands, pulled his face to hers and brushed his lips with her own.

The first time she had seen him, last night, under the mistletoe, she had wondered what his lips would taste like. Now she knew, and they did not disappoint. Like the other contrasts of tonight, his lips were like ice and fire, steel and silk.

For a split second the force of his will was enough to resist her. And then it collapsed, and his lips accepted the invitation of hers, his hand curled behind her neck and pulled her deeper into him.

To Emma, it felt as though the stars fell from the sky, as if the snow around them turned to fire, as if her heart had been bound in chains and broke free of them.

She had a moment of intense clarity, as if she had lived in a fog, and the sun shone through.

It felt as though every experience of her entire life had led her to this moment, had made her ready for this moment. It felt as if every bad thing and every betrayal had made her deeper and stronger, building her into a woman capable of understanding what she tasted in him. He was not the remoteness in his eyes, nor the coolness in his demeanor. He was not his shields and not his armor. The touch of his lips told her what was behind those things.

He was the man who tackled those endless physical jobs that had to be done as a result of the storm with the inner toughness and fortitude that gave glimpses of the true spirit she had just tasted.

He was the man who said yes to a little girl who wanted him to play charades even though the part of him that guarded his own preservation had wanted to say no.

He was the man who braved the baby department of a store out of a capacity to love that that ran so deep and so true it made her shiver with awe and longing.

He was a man who could make a woman who knew better question what she knew and hope she was wrong.

"Why *not* complicate things?" she whispered against the softness of his lips, amazed at her own imprudence, but so certain of what she had felt, glimpsed, tasted.

His truth.

"Because," he said, his voice hoarse, "I'm not a man who can give anything to anyone. You need to know the whole truth before you decide whether or not to complicate things."

"I don't believe you," she said, because she knew the truth in him that she had just tasted.

"I've seen what you give to Tess." She touched her lips to his again, but he turned his face from her.

"Please," he said, his voice hoarse.

"Trust me with the whole truth, Ryder."

Silence.

"Is there someone else?" she asked, shocked at how devastated that possibility made her feel. Of course he had someone else. Look at her history. Look at Peter!

No, look at him! He'd probably met someone in the baby department.

"No, there's no one else."

Relief, pure and exhilarating, shot through her.

"It's something. Not someone."

"You can tell me, Ryder. Trust me."

He was silent for so long, she thought he might not speak, that he would refuse her the gift of his trust, that he would just start the snow machine and go.

He was obviously having some kind of battle with himself. And she was amazed when he lost.

His voice low, he said, "Emma, I can't love anyone, any-more. Not ever again."

She was tempted to say she wasn't asking him to love her. She wanted a kiss on a moonlit night. But there was something about the ravaged look on his face that stopped her. She needed to hear what he had to say.

And more importantly, he needed to tell it, it was a demon that ate him from the inside out.

"You want more than I could ever give you," he said roughly. "You deserve more than I could ever give you."

"How do you know what I want?"

"Don't even try to tell me you're the kind of girl who could ever kiss a man lightly, without knowing exactly where it was going and what happens next."

"I'm not a girl," she said, but her protest sounded half-hearted. "I'm a woman. An independent business woman."

"Don't even try to tell me you aren't the kind of *woman* who dreams of a man and of babies of your own."

"I have my inn," she said. "That's enough for me."

"No, it isn't, Emma. You want a place like that one down there," he nodded toward Fenshaws', "and you want to fill it to the rafters with laughter and love."

"I don't," she said stubbornly, trying to ignore the longing his words caused in her, the pictures that crowded her mind. How quickly a woman like her could put a man like him in the center of each of those pictures.

"If you don't, you should, because that's what you deserve, Emma."

"It's not what I want," she said, trying for a firm note.

"Uh-huh," he said skeptically.

"I gave up on the romantic fantasies," she insisted.

"When?"

She hesitated. "I had a broken engagement last year."

"If you tell me it happened at Christmas, I'm going to believe the curse."

She actually smiled a little, until he said, "I figured as much. A broken heart somewhere in the recent past."

"Excuse me?" How pathetic was that? That she was telegraphing her broken dreams to every stranger who showed up at the door?

"No single woman takes on a place like the inn without having had romance problems."

No, not every stranger, just a man who saw everything. Right from the beginning she had known that about him. And now he saw she was falling for him, even before she'd completely admitted it to herself. And he seemed to be seeing that, too.

It was humiliating. "I did," she said. "I gave up all my romantic illusions. I gave my life to the inn."

"Like a nun giving her life to the church," he said dryly.

"Yes!"

"Except for the kissing part."

She was silent.

He laughed, but it wasn't a pleasant sound. "No, you didn't give up your longings, Emma. You just wanted to. Your dreams shine in your eyes in unguarded moments, like tonight when you were part of that family down there. They will come right back when the right man comes into your life. Was your fiancé a jerk?"

"He was a doctor."

"I didn't ask what he did," Ryder said sharply, "I asked what he *was*. I've met lots of doctors who were jerks and lots of construction workers who weren't."

"Okay," she said, miffed, "he was a pompous, full-of-himself jerk, who thought he could mold a poor girl from the wrong side of the tracks into perfect wife material. And I was supposed to be grateful for it! Of course, when perfect wife material, pre-made, reappeared in his life, he ditched me."

She was astounded she had said that, and astounded by the clarity with which she could suddenly see her relationship with Peter.

"He never saw you at all, did he?" Ryder asked softly. "He missed it all. The determination, the love of life, the mischief, the generosity. Not to mention a not-bad giraffe impression."

"He would have hated every minute of tonight, and especially the undignified giraffe impression. I didn't realize it at first, but he never saw me, he saw what he wanted me to be. He saw that I didn't use my fork correctly, and that I wore white slacks after Labor Day, but that I had the potential to be *fixed*."

"Oh, Emma."

"But at least he never refused to kiss me!" Unsatisfying as that experience had been— Peter's kisses perfunctory and passionless— Ryder didn't have to know!

"I'm going to tell you why I won't kiss you. Not because I don't want to—Lord knows I want to—but because there is a hole in me nothing can fill, Emma. Nothing, not even the sweetness of your kisses."

He took a deep breath, shuddered, closed his eyes and after a very long time he spoke, his voice ragged.

"A year ago," he said, "on Christmas day, my brother died in a fire. His wife Tracy was badly injured, she died three months ago."

It was as if every ounce of beauty had drained from the night, and left only the cold.

"Tess's mom and dad," she breathed, shaken. "Oh, no."

He held up a hand stopping her, stopping her sympathy from touching him.

But he didn't stop her hand from resting on his chest. She could feel he had started to tremble and that made her want to weep.

"I was there. My brother, Drew, asked me to get Tess out. He was going back in for Tracy. Only, somehow, Tracy was already out, and he was in that inferno looking for her. I had gotten Tess out, and I tried to go back for him. Some neighbors held me. They wouldn't let me go."

The trembling had increased under her hand, she pressed harder against his heart.

"I wasn't strong enough," he said, his voice cracking. "I just wasn't strong enough. If I could have shaken them off, I would have gotten him. Or I would have died trying. Either would have been better than what I live with now."

She wanted to tell him how wrong he was, but she bit her lip and pressed her hand harder against the brokenness of his heart, knowing he *needed* to get this out. This absolute fury with himself, the lack of forgiveness, the sense of failure.

"I loved them," he said softly, and she heard that love in the fierce note in his voice. "I loved my brother. He was like the other half of me. We did everything together. And I loved Tracy, the woman he had chosen to be his wife.

"I failed them." The tremble from his heart had moved into his voice. "I failed the people I loved the most. And I failed myself. A long time ago I believed in myself. I believed I focused my physical strength and the strength of my will on what I wanted and it happened.

"Now I know that's not true, it's just a lie people tell themselves."

She said nothing, keeping her hand on his heart, trying to absorb his pain, to take it from him.

But it was so tragically easy to see he could not let it go.

"It took everything I had when they died. Everything. I can't love anybody anymore. Maybe never again. It tore the heart out of my body."

She did not tell him she could feel his heart beating in his body, strong, just where it was supposed to be.

Finally, the trembling subsided, and she could feel his breath, deep and even. She spoke, softly.

"It took everything except Tess," she said, a statement, not a question. Her heart seemed to swell with warmth when she thought of that, that he had found the strength to come out of his pain enough to get Tess.

"Yes, except Tess."

"I'm so sorry, Ryder." The words seemed fragile, too small for the enormity of his pain. And yet she felt deeply moved and honored that he had told her this, trusted her with it. And she saw so clearly what he could not see. His strength had not failed him at all, he was coming into his strength in ways he refused to recognize.

"Now that you understand," he said, grim, distant, picking up the armor he had laid down in those exquisite moments of absolute trust in her, "I'll take you back to Fenshaws', and I'll look after the inn."

She knew that would be the easiest thing for him, and probably for her, too. He had told her he had nothing to give, and she knew she should believe him.

But it was Christmas.

And if there was one message about Christmas that rose above all the others, holy, it was that one.

The joy in it was not in receiving, but in giving.

That was true of Christmas and of love. He had trusted her with this, and she planned to be worthy of his trust.

And so she said, gently, "No, Ryder, I'm not going back to Fenshaws'."

# CHAPTER SEVEN

RYDER frowned at her. He could have sworn she understood. They could not follow the flames of attraction that were burn-ing hot between them. He'd made it clear he had nothing to give her. Nothing.

"Why?" he demanded.

She looked at him and said softly, soothingly, "Because I'm not leaving you alone with this."

*Alone.* The word hung in the air between them. His truth. He had been alone with this for 354 days.

"Understand me," she said quietly. "I'm not going to talk. I know I cannot do or say anything to change the way you feel, to fix it, but I'm just not leaving you alone with it."

Others had tried to come into his world. He had not allowed it. But no one else had made this promise—that they would not try to fix it, would not try to make him feel better. Just be there.

He wanted to say no to her. To drop her off at the Fenshaws' despite her protests. But she had that mulish look on her face and would probably just walk back across the snow, through the moonlit night.

So that he would not be alone.

And suddenly Ryder realized the thought of not being alone with it, even for one night, eased something in him. He had nothing to give her. But she had something to give him, and he was not strong enough to refuse her gift.

He started the machine, felt her arms wrap around him, her cheek press into the back of his shoulder.

And felt something else, exquisite and warming. *Not alone.*

That feeling was intensified an hour later as they lay in the same room, separated only by air and a few feet of space, the fire throwing its gentle golden light over them, crackling and hissing and spitting.

"That's why the fire bothered Tess this morning," she said, her voice coming out of the darkness, like a touch, like a hand on a shoulder. "Does it bother you? The fire?"

So many things bothered him. Couples in love, children riding on their daddy's shoulders, Christmas. But fire?

"No. What happened at Tracy and Drew's house was a fluke, a short in a Christmas-tree bulb. The tree went up after they'd gone to bed. Their smoke detector had been too sensitive, going off every time they cooked something. Drew disconnected it. He meant to move it to a different location, but he never did."

He wanted to stop, but the new feeling of not being alone wouldn't let him. "One small choice," he said, "seemingly insignificant, and all these lives changed. Forever. If only I could have gone back in there, things could have been so different."

She was silent for so long, he thought she would say nothing. But finally she did.

"But what if the difference was that Tess had been left all alone in the world? What if she hadn't had even you?"

This was a possibility he had never even considered. Not once. And maybe that was part of what happened when you weren't alone anymore. The view became wider. Other possibilities edged into a rigid consciousness that had seen things only one way.

Ryder had imagined he could have pitted his will and his strength against the fire that night and saved them all. But Drew had possessed every bit as much strength and will as he had. And he had failed to save himself.

So, what if they had both failed, both died that night, Tracy struggling for life, Tess ultimately left alone? Left to complete strangers who would never understand that her eyes were the exact same shade of blue that her mother's had been, that that faint cleft in her stubborn chin had come through four generations of Richardsons so far?

And might go on to the next.

Because Tess had survived. And so had he.

"Ryder," she said quietly, "I know it was a terrible night, more terrible than anyone who has not gone through something like that could ever imagine. I know it is hard to see the miracle."

"The miracle?" he said, stunned.

"You survived, and because of you, Tess survived. Because you saved her, your brother's arrow goes forward into the future. Tess," she said softly, "is the miracle. Tess is the reason it isn't only a day of sorrow."

He felt his throat close as he thought of that. It was as if a light pierced the darkness. This whole year had been so fraught with emotion and hardship, with traps and uphill battles, that he had become focused only on the bad things. They had overwhelmed his world and his thoughts so much that Ryder had not once stopped to contemplate the one good thing—Tess.

Tess, who had coaxed laughter out of him when he had thought he would never laugh again. Tess, who had made him go on when he would have given up long ago. If not for her.

His journey in the darkness had been threatened by the dawn ever since he had arrived here at the White Christmas Inn. The first ray of sunshine—full of hope, and celebration— touched him.

Tess had lived.

"Thank you," he said gruffly to Emma, aware that if you ever allowed yourself to love a woman like her, she would constantly show you things from a different angle. Life could seem like a kinder and gentler place.

"You know what I would like to do?" she said, after a long time. "I would like to take down every single thing in this house that causes you pain. The trees, the mistletoe, the garlands, the wreaths. Everything."

"You weren't going to try and fix it, remember?" He could not help but be touched that she would give up her vision of Christmas to try and give him peace.

"Still…" she said.

He looked over at her to see if the mulish look was on her face, but all he could see was loveliness. The desire to kiss her again was strong, even though he'd sworn off it for the good of them both.

"No, Emma, I think it would be better for me—and Tess—if I tried to see the miracle. If I tried to see things differently. Before I go."

There. The reminder that he was leaving this place. Before he fell in love with Emma.

But he could not deny that something had already happened. He was a different man from the one who had knocked on her door during a storm such a short time ago. He felt something he had not felt for almost a year.

Peace. Because he'd gotten things off his chest? Because he was determined to see things differently?

Or because of the way he was feeling about her?

. "I'm leaving," he said again. "As soon as I can." For whose benefit was that tone of voice? Her? Or for him?

She did not protest or try to talk him out of it.

Emma just said, quietly, "Ryder, until you go, I won't leave you alone with it."

He knew she meant it, and he knew he was not

going anywhere for a while, that he was still at the mercy of the roads. Despite the fact he knew he should fight it, he could not. Instead, he felt an intensified sense of peace, of being deeply relaxed, fill him, and then he slept like a man who had been in battle and who had finally found a safe place to lay down his head and his weapons. A man who didn't know when the next battle would be, but who appreciated the respite he had been given.

He awoke the next morning to the arrival of the Fenshaws and Tess. Ryder felt deeply rested.

New, somehow, especially when he took Tess into his arms and she gave him a noisy kiss on his cheek.

"Ubba," she said, and then sang, delighted, "Ubba, Ubba, Ubba," clearly celebrating the miracle he had not completely recognized until now.

They had each other.

"Tess, Tess, Tess," he said back, and swung her around until she squealed with laughter. His eyes met Emma's and he felt connected to the whole world. And to her.

And despite the fact he was stranded, he surrendered to the experience, maybe even came to relish it.

\* \* \*

Over the next few days Ryder would become aware that telling Emma his darkest secret had consequences he had not anticipated.

He felt lighter for one thing, as if by sharing he had let go of some need to carry it all by himself.

Now that Emma knew completely who he was, he felt understood in a way he had not expected. Accepted for who he was and where he was.

He found himself telling her his history in bits and pieces, about growing up with his brother, the mischief they had gotten into, the gag gifts at Christmas, the competitiveness over girls and sports, how they had helped each other through the deaths of their parents. It was as if he was recovering something he had lost in the fire: all that had been good was coming back to him.

And slowly, Emma opened up to him. Watching her become herself around him was like watching a rosebud open to the sun.

She shared, with humor that belied the hurt, the sense of inadequacy she had grown up with, the secondhand clothes, the Christmases with no trees, her mother's rather careless attitude toward her only child.

Emma had grown up feeling as if she was a mistake, and she shared how it had made her want desperately to do something good enough to be recognized, how, finally, it had made her vulnerable to a false love.

She told him about her failed engagement, her last disastrous Christmas.

"So, there I was, so excited I was wriggling like a puppy as we arrived at Peter's parents' house for Christmas day," she admitted. "I hadn't met them before, and it felt as if I had passed some huge test that I'd been invited for Christmas.

"Honestly, the house was everything I could have hoped for. It was like something off a Christmas card—a long driveway, snow-covered trees decorated in tiny white lights. The house was sparkling with more tiny white lights. Inside was like something out of my best dream of Christmas—poinsettias on every surface, real holly garlands, a floor-to-ceiling Christmas tree, so many parcels underneath it that they filled half the room.

"Everything looked so right," she remembered sadly, "and felt so wrong. As soon as Peter opened the car door for me there were instructions on what to say and how to say it. Don't tell them I got the dress on sale. Don't ask for recipes. Don't ooh and aah over the house as if I was a hick from the country.

"His parents were stuffy. His mother asked me questions about what schools I'd gone to and fished for information about my family. His father didn't even acknowledge it was Christmas and barely seemed to know I was there. He kept leaving the room to check the channel on the television that runs all the up-to-the-minute stock information.

"We opened gifts before dinner. It was awful. Robotic. These people had everything, what did they care about more? His mother looked *aghast* at the brooch I'd gotten her, his father was indifferent to the cigars Peter had recommended I get him, Peter hardly glanced at the electronic picture frame I'd filled with pictures of us.

"And then there were their gifts to me. Peter got me a diamond bracelet. He called it a tennis bracelet, as if anyone would play tennis in something like that! When I saw it, I felt crushed, as if he didn't know me at all. I never wear jewelry, had told him I didn't care for it. I got a very expensive designer bag from his mother and father. Nobody had put any thought into anything. It was like an obligation they'd fulfilled.

"And the worst was yet to come. Dinner. Served by a poor maid, and prepared by a cook. Naturally, I earned the *look* from Peter when I asked why they were working Christmas day. Then, his mother announced, casually, *slyly,* that

Monique had been calling all day hoping to speak to Peter.

"I knew that was his old girlfriend. I'd worked in his office while he was going out with her. She was everything I wasn't. She'd ditched him to go to France.

"And he didn't even try to hide how excited he was that she was back.

"Naturally, when I called him on his excitement later that evening, I was being unsophisticated. I was the hick. He could have friends other than me!

"Maybe it was the pleasure he took in calling me a hick that made going home to my grandmother so irresistible."

"I think you just wanted to get away from him," Ryder deduced, not trying to hide his irritation with Peter. "He would have killed you quietly, one put-down at time. Why did you accept that as long as you did?"

She smiled sadly.. "Ah. The great put-down. That's all I've ever known."

And he vowed right then and there that for as long as their time together lasted, put-downs would never be part of the way he communicated with her. He wanted to snatch back every careless word he had said about her dreams and the inn, but instead, he took her hand, kissed the top of it, a gentleman acknowledging a complete lady. "Their loss," he said quietly.

And the way the sun came out in her eyes made him kiss her hand again.

There was no shortage of work while the road remained closed, and the hard work was as amazing an antidote to his pain as Emma. Until the road reopened and the power came on there was more work to do every day than ten men could have handled. It was back-breaking, hand-blistering work, and it was just what he needed. It was what he had tried to achieve with punishing workouts at the gym and never quite succeeded. Not like this. Exhaustion.

Utter and complete.

He crawled onto that mattress at night and slept as he had not slept since the fire.

To add to that, he had a sense of belonging that he had not had since the death of his brother and then his sister-in-law had ripped his own family apart.

Tim, Mona, the girls formed an old-fashioned family unit, their love fluid rather than rigid, the circle of it opening easily to include Ryder and Tess, just as once it must have opened to take in Emma. It was a plain kind of love: not flowers and chocolates, not fancy Christmas gifts, or dramatic declarations.

It was the kind of love where people worked hard toward a common goal, then ate together, laughed over simple board games. It was a love that toted a demanding baby with it everywhere it went, as though there was nothing but joy in that task.

What had really happened when he had told Emma he was broken beyond healing?

It was as if the healing had begun right then.

It was as if he had given Emma permission to love him in a different way—one that did not involve kisses—and that love—steady, compassionate, accepting—was stronger than the kisses could have been. Building a foundation for something else.

But what? Maybe it was as simple as building the foundation for one perfect day.

Was there such a thing as a perfect day?

People thought there was. They tried to find those days on beaches in tropical countries in the winter. They tried to have them on the day they got married. They tried to create that day on Christmas in particular.

Who would ever have thought a perfect day looked like the one he had had on the second day after the storm? By late afternoon, all of them, Mona, the girls, Emma and Ryder had cleared a ton of broken limbs off the pond, Tim pushing it to them with his tractor shovel, clearing snow in preparation for skating. Tess shouted orders from the little sled they all took turns pulling her in.

An army emergency team arrived on snowmobiles to let them know they were close to having power restored, and the roads would be reopened within twenty-four hours.

Ryder did not miss the stricken look on Emma's face and her quick glance toward him, but he understood perfectly what she felt.

They had built a world here separate from the world out there and their own realities. They had built a family of sorts, one filled with the things people wanted from family and that he suspected Emma had never had: a sense of safety and acceptance.

But when the roads opened and the power was restored, they were all, in their own ways, moving on, leaving this place that necessity had created. The sense of belonging and of meaning was going to be hard to leave.

Especially since Ryder had no idea if he was taking this new sense of peace with him or leaving it here.

"Enough," Mona cried, as the light was fading

and she dragged one more branch to the fire. "Enough work!"

Hot dogs rescued from a snow drift appeared and buns, more mugs of hot chocolate were served from the huge canning pot Emma had wrestled from the warming shed down to the side of the pond where they were burning branches.

After he'd eaten enough hot dogs to put even his teenage self to shame, he noticed Mona sorting through the skates she found in the warming shed. "Come on, girls, let's go skating!"

And soon all the Fenshaws, including Tim, were circling the pond, graceful, people who had probably skated since they were Tess's age. They were taking turns pulling Tess, still, and he could hear her squeals of delight as they picked up speed, as the sled careened around the edges of the pond behind the girls.

And then Ryder noticed Emma putting away things, stirring the hot chocolate, sending the occasional wistful glance toward the frozen pond.

"How come you have so many skates?" Ryder asked. "Are you renting them at Holiday Happenings?"

"No, people are bringing their own. But there will be a few here for people who don't have them or forget. And the kinds of families who are coming to the Christmas Day Dream probably don't have skates. I tried to collect as many different sizes as possible, so everyone can skate."

"Including your size?" he asked, seeing her cast another wistful look at the pond.

"Oh, I don't skate. I've never even tried it."

Wasn't that just Emma to a T? Giving everyone else a gift, but not taking one for herself?

"How is it possible you haven't tried skating?" he asked. "You must be the only Canadian in history who has never skated."

"Ryder," she said, "not everyone had the childhood you had. My mother didn't have money for skates."

He saw suddenly the opportunity to give Emma a gift, humble as it was. He would teach her the joy of flying across an icy pond on sharp silver blades, give her the heady freedom of it. He would give her something from a childhood she had clearly missed.

He sorted through the skates, found a pair that looked as though they would fit her.

She sat on a bench and put them on, and he sat beside her, lacing up a pair that had looked as though they would fit him.

"No," he said, glancing at her. "You have to

lace them really tight." And then he knelt at her feet and did up her skates for her.

Her eyes were shining as he rose and held out his hand to her. She wobbled across the short piece of snow-covered ground from the bench to the pond.

"You are no athlete," he told her fifteen minutes later, putting his hands under her armpits and hauling her up off her rear again, but then he remembered she had heard nothing but negatives about herself all her life. "Though I'm sure you have other sterling qualities."

"Name them," she demanded.

"World's best giraffe imitation."

The laughter in her eyes, true and sweet, the shadows lifting, rewarded him for this gift he was giving her.

"Hard worker," he went on, "passable cleaner-upper of baby puke."

"Stop! I can't learn to skate and laugh at the same time."

"Smart. Funny. Cute. Determined. Brave. Generous. Compassionate. Wise."

"You must stop now. I'm having trouble concentrating."

But he could tell she was pleased. It was time for Emma White to have some fun, even if it was true that she had not an ounce of natural-born talent in the skating department. She walked on the skates, awkwardly, her ankles turned in, her windmilling arms heralding each fall.

"Can you relax?" he asked her.

"Apparently not," she shot back, and then she dissolved into giggles, and the arms windmilled and she fell on her rump again.

He got her up, glanced at the shore of the pond. They had moved all of fifteen yards in as many minutes.

"Watch the girls," he told her sternly. "Watch how they're pushing off on one leg, gliding, then pushing with the other leg."

She pushed tentatively, fell.

"We're going to go," Mona said. The sun had completely gone from the sky, the ice on the pond was striking as it reflected the light of the huge brush fires they had lit around it. "We'll take Tess home again for the night. Brrr, it's getting too cold out here for her."

And then the giggles and shouts and laughter faded as they moved further and further away until Ryder and Emma were completely alone.

He didn't feel cold at all. He felt warmer than he had felt for nearly a year.

"You want to take a break?" he asked Emma. She had to be hurting.

"No."

There it was. That fierce determination that let him know that no matter what, she would be all right. When he left.

The road was going to be open tomorrow.

And knowing that, and that it was his turn to *give* to her, something in him that had held back let go. Enough to tuck his arm around her waist and pull her tight into him.

It was time for her to skate. He thrust off on one leg, and then the other, steadying her, holding her up, not allowing her to fall. There was something so right about holding her up, about lending her his strength, about the way she felt pressed into his side.

"Oh," she breathed, "Ryder, I'm doing it."

She wasn't. Not at first. He was doing it for her. But then he felt the tentative thrust of her leg, and then another.

"Don't let me go." The end of the pond was rushing toward them. "How do I turn? Turn, Ryder!"

And he did, taking her with him, flying across the ice, feeling her growing more confident by the second.

"We're like Jamie Salé and David Pelletier," she cried, naming Canada's most romantic figure-skating duo.

He laughed at her enthusiasm. "This year, White's Pond—2010, Whistler," he said dryly. "You might have to learn to lace up your own skates, though."

She punched his arm. "I can't believe I'm still on the ground. How can you feel like this without flying? Let me go, Ryder, let me go."

And he did. She took her first tentative strokes by herself.

He watched her moving slowly, and then with growing confidence. At first he called a few instructions to her, but then he let her go completely. She had about as much grace as a baby bear on skates, falling, skidding, picking herself back up almost before she had stopped, then going again, arms akimbo, blades digging into the ice.

And then, just like that, joy filled him. It came without warning, sneaked up on him just as those memories did. Only this time he felt young again, and carefree, like that boy he had once been on his mother and father's backyard rink.

He whooped his delight, thrust hard against the ice, surged forward. He flew down the length of the pond, raced the edges of it, skidded to a halt in a spray of white ice, turned, skated backwards at full speed, crossed his legs one over the other, and then raced around the pond the other way in a huge, swooping circle.

He moved faster than a person without wings or a motor should be able to move, delighted in his strength and the clear cold and the freedom. He delighted in knowing her eyes followed him.

He knew he was showing off for her, did not care what it meant. He raced down the ice to where she stood, swooped by her, snatching her toque off her head, challenging her new skills.

Game as always, Emma took off after him, those curls gone crazy. He teased her unmercifully, skating by her, making loops around her, swooping in close, holding out the hat, and then dashing away as she reached for it.

And then she reached too far, and slammed down hard. She lay on the ice silent and unmoving.

"Emma?"

Nothing. He rushed over to her, knelt at her side. What if he had hurt her? What if he had pushed her too hard? She was brand new to this, and if she was hurt badly there was no place to take her.

They weren't wearing helmets. And she wasn't tough. Her skull could be cracked open. She could be dying. He, of all people, knew how it could be all over in a blink. How you could be laughing about a stuffed marlin or a snatched toque one minute, and the next minute life was changed forever. Over.

Cursing his own foolishness, not just for playing with her, but for letting himself care this much again, he leaned close to her, felt her breath warm on his cheek.

And knew, from the panic that hammered a tattoo at his heart he had come to care about her way, way too much. And he also knew he could not survive another loss. That was why he had built such strong walls around himself.

Because he knew. He could not survive if he lost one more person that he loved.

And, as he contemplated that, her eyes popped open and, with an evil laugh, she reached out and snatched her toque from his hand, slammed it back on her head, and managed to grab his before she clambered to her feet and skittered away, taking advantage of the fact he was completely stunned by the revelation he had just had.

He wanted to be angry at her for frightening him, and for the realization he had just had. But how could you be angry with her when the laughter lit her eyes like that, when her cheeks glowed pink?

"I'm laughing so hard I can barely skate," she shouted at him.

*Give yourself to it. One night. To carry these memories deep within you once it's gone.* "I hate to break it to you, but you could barely skate before."

"Not true," she said, spreading her arms wide and doing a particularly clumsy stumble down the ice. "Jamie Salé, move over."

"Somehow, I don't think Jamie has anything to worry about!"

He caught her with ease, tugged at her wrist, turning her around to face him on the ice.

Was it that momentary fear that she had been hurt that made him so aware of how he felt?

Not saying a word, for some things were without words, he let the laughter between them fade and the mood between them soften until it glowed as golden as the pond reflecting the firelight.

*One night.*

"Though if you want to be Jamie, you have to learn how to do this."

And then, he laced one hand with hers and put the other on the small of her back, pulling her in close to him. He danced with her. He, a hockey player who had never danced on ice in his life, took to it as if he had been born for this moment.

To the music of the crackling bonfire, and blades scraping ice that had turned to liquid gold, he danced with her. Her initial uncertainty faded as she just let him take her, gave herself over to it, surrendered to his lead.

They covered every square inch of that pond, his eyes locked on hers, and hers on his.

And then it was over, the fire dying to embers, the chill of the night penetrating the sense of warmth and contentment they had just shared.

It was time to end it. Not just the dance, either.

He pulled her hard to him, kissed her forehead where her curls had popped out of her toque and whispered to her, "Thank you, Emma."

She looked at him, stricken, and he knew she had heard not *thank you,* not heard *thank you* at all.

Emma had heard what he had really said. That all this was too scary for him. What he had really said was good-bye.

He could see that she wanted the road open tomorrow—indeed, her business needed the road open. And she wanted the road closed, this cozy world kept intact.

The magic had been building every day that road was closed, and it had culminated in this: for a few short days he had felt young again, carefree, as if the world held only good things.

For a while, here at the White Christmas Inn, Ryder had been free from that place of pain he had lived in. At first he'd been free for minutes, and then for whole hours at a time. Today, he had experienced a day that had been nearly perfect, from beginning until end.

Ever since Ryder had told Emma the source of his deepest pain, everything had felt different between them. He had revealed the brokenness of his soul to her. He had done so out of absolute necessity, and he had done so to back both of them off from the attraction they were feeling.

He was not available. As not available as a man who was married. In a way, he was married to his sorrow. It was his constant companion, particularly with all things Christmas reminding him, triggering memories and his overpowering sense of failure.

He had come a long way, but he did not feel he had come nearly far enough to accept what he saw in her eyes. She was falling in love with him.

He found himself looking at her now, on that skating rink with the firelight dying around them, the way an art lover would look at a painting. With a kind of tender appreciation for who she was and what she did.

When had he stopped hoping for, planning his

escape? When had he started dreading the opening of the road, because he was committed to a decision he'd already made?

The decision never to love again.

And, despite that decision, and despite the fact this was good-bye—or maybe because of it—he could not stop himself from tasting her lips one last time, as if he could save something of her, hold it inside himself, a secret source of warmth when he returned to a world of coldness.

She tilted her head back, met him halfway, and his lips touched hers. He was not sure what kind of kiss he intended—sweet farewell, perhaps—but he did not have the kind of control to execute that kind of kiss.

From the instant of contact, when he tasted her hunger, felt the passion that lurked just below her calm surface, something in him unleashed. The part of him that wanted things he could not have rose up to greet her, urgent and fierce. Instead of having an experience he could save, he found himself having an experience he did not want to end.

Instead of the kiss saying a chaste good-bye, her answering fire consumed him and filled him. His hands tangled in her short hair—he knew a startled *ah* of satisfaction that it felt exactly as he had known it would—and his lips claimed her and branded her, even as hers claimed him and branded him. He found his hand at the back of her neck, pulling her closer, wanting to go deeper, wanting *more*.

Her tongue danced with his lips, the edges of his teeth, tangled with his tongue, and he thought he would melt from the inferno she was creating. It felt as if the ice could be banished, as if he could be alone no more—

He pulled away from her, but it took every ounce of power he had left. His armor, made of steel, had melted like butter before her.

And he didn't want her ever to know that.

"We should go back to the house. I'm going to go start packing my stuff—" His voice was rough with determination that hid his weakness from her. "—tonight, so that Tess and I will be ready to go as soon as the road opens tomorrow." He hoped to slip out quietly, no long-drawn-out good-byes.

"Stay," she said quietly. "Ryder, stay for Christmas."

"Your neediest family?" he said sourly, trying to be what he had been before, a man who could chase others away with his bitterness, trying not to let her see what had just happened to him.

She said nothing.

"I don't need your pity," he said sharply, trying again.

"In case you haven't figured it out by now, I don't pity you," she said just as sharply. "If you can't do this for yourself, do it for Tess."

"No." He kept it short. If he engaged her in discussion she might think she could convince him to stay. "I *have* to go."

Even without the heat of kisses, the ice was melting from around his heart. Deciding to give into her had been his undoing. How could you not care about her?

Despite his every attempt not to, he was falling as in love with Emma White as she was with him.

Ryder Richardson knew that was impossible. He knew that you could not fall in love with someone in such a short period of time.

But he also knew that love was not logical, and that it defied the rules people tried to make around it.

How could this be happening to him? He who knew the exact price of love, he who knew he would be destroyed if he rolled those dice again and lost?

Better not to take a chance at all than to risk so much.

There was Tess to think of, too. How could he ever be what Tess needed if he left himself open to being destroyed by the fires of love again?

He had to go now. While he still had the strength. Before the magic took him completely and did the worst thing of all.

Made him believe.

Just as the letters buried in her wreath had promised that first day.

The next day, the road opened before it was light out.

Emma listened to the snowplow down on the main road. Ryder had packed up the night before, just as he had said he would.

Now, as Ryder tried to get her ready to go, Tess was having a full-blown melt-down, struggling against the implacable strength of her uncle's arms.

It would serve him right, Emma thought, if she just stepped back and let him deal with it. But she couldn't. She had to try and ease Tess's distress, and that of Sue and Peggy. The Fenshaws had arrived with Tess and their baskets of food and their hearts full of good cheer, just as Ryder was packing the car to leave.

Now they were all in the front doorway of her

house, except Tim, who had taken one look at Ryder's packed bags, sent him a look of disgust and stomped off.

"Shh, sweetie," Emma said, trying to get the hat on Tess's head, "please don't. It's going to be all right. Everything will be fine."

In her heart she felt this was patently untrue.

Sue and Peggy were both sobbing quietly, clutching their mother.

"I don't want Tess to go," Peggy cried, a little girl who had already said good-bye to her father this year, and was having trouble with one more good-bye. But it was obvious Ryder and Tess were going. Ryder's face remained impassive and determined.

He took the hat from Emma's hand, stuffed it into his own jacket pocket.

"Let's not drag this out," he suggested, cool and remote, once again the man who had arrived on her doorstep with his devil-dark eyes and wearing his cynicism like a cloak.

He turned and walked out the door and down to his car, the engine already running, the ice and snow scraped off it.

The sad little entourage followed him outside. Tim, who had been standing on the porch, his hands thrust into his pockets, rejoined them, held out his hand.

"Good luck, son," he said quietly, his eyes searching Ryder's face. He seemed to find something there that gave him something to believe in, because he nodded. But he was the only one who found it, because as Ryder and the baby reached the car, Peggy broke away from her mother and thrust Bebo into Tess's hands.

Emma, hanging on by a thread, bit her lip at the act of selfless generosity from one so young.

The screaming stopped for a blessed second, and then started more intensely than before. Tess threw Bebo, previously beloved to her, on the ground, and arched herself over her uncle's arm with such fury that anyone less strong might have been taken off guard and dropped her.

Emma found something to believe, too.

That another Christmas would be ruined. No matter what happened now—if Holiday Happenings had a thousand people a night show up, if the Christmas Day Dream was a complete success, if her mother showed up beaming more love than the Madonna, it felt as if it didn't matter, it couldn't erase this horrible scene and it couldn't even touch the place going cold inside her.

Because he was leaving. And if he was leaving—his heart hard to Tess's shrieks of protest and the heart-wrenching tears of Peggy and Sue—he was not looking back once he left here.

It would be so much easier to accept that if she had not laughed on that mattress with him, held his broken heart under her fingertips on that moonlit night, if she had not given so much of herself into his keeping, if she had not seen his soul last night when they had skated, danced across that golden ice connected to one another, free, joyous.

All that was gone from his face now, as if he regretted what he had allowed himself to feel as much as she had rejoiced in it.

"Good-bye, Emma." With finality.

She wasn't giving him the satisfaction of saying goodbye.

"Thank you for teaching me to skate," she said, instead. It took every ounce of her pride to choke out the words without crying.

And, for a moment, some regret did touch his eyes, but then he turned from her and put the baby in her car seat, ignoring her flailing fists and feet and her cries.

*"Tess NOT go."*

Sue picked up Bebo off the ground, wiped a smudge of snow tenderly from the triangle nose and then reached in the open door and shoved the doll back into Tess's arms. She stepped back from the car and wailed.

Emma watched in a daze as Ryder shut the door, glanced at Tim, accepted Mona's quick hard hug, and then turned and looked at her.

What did she expect?

Nothing.

Expectations were clearly her problem, the reason she always ended up disappointed by Christmas. And by life. And by men.

He did not even hug her. He had said his good-bye to her last night on that skating rink.

He lifted a finger to his brow, a faint salute, his eyes met hers and he looked quickly away.

No sense thinking she had seen anguish there. No sense at all.

"I hope your mother comes for Christmas," he said, and then his eyes went to Tim, who had taken a sudden interest in scraping the snow away from his feet with the toe of his boot. He frowned.

As if her mother coming for Christmas would absolve Ryder of something.

"She'll be here Christmas Eve. Now that the roads are open, I can send her the bus ticket this afternoon."

He nodded, relieved. She glanced at Tim who

was now looking into the far distance, hands in his pockets, rocking on his heels.

Right until the moment his car turned at the bottom of the driveway that he had helped to clear, and then slipped from view, Emma could feel herself holding her breath, hoping and praying he would change his mind.

"Emma," Tim said uncertainly, "I don't think you should get your hopes up about—"

She held up a hand. She didn't want to hear it. *Don't get your hopes up. About Holiday Happenings. About your mother. About him.*

That was her curse.

Not Christmas.

Those damn hopes, always picking themselves up for one last hurrah, even after they'd been dragged through the mud and knocked down and shredded and stomped upon.

Emma turned and walked away from the Fenshaws, her shoulders stiff with pride. It wasn't until she saw the damned Believe letters in the wreath that she closed the door, sagged against it and cried like a child.

# CHAPTER EIGHT

'SNOWMAN?' Ryder asked Tess.

She did not look up from Bebo, her new best friend. Ryder had given her the much newer lavender soft-stuffed pony the day they arrived here at the cottage. Why wait for Christmas? He had needed the distraction then.

He now saw it had been a ridiculous effort to win back her affection. The pony lay abandoned under the couch with the pink suede shoes.

He'd given the shoes to her five minutes after the pony hadn't worked, a desperate man. She had kicked them off in a fit of anger and had not looked at them since.

He sighed, watching her. Tess was sitting on the floor, talking soft gibberish to Bebo, sporting monster hair again, refusing to allow him to touch it.

Anyone who thought a baby was willing to forgive and forget didn't know Tess.

They had been at his lakeside cottage long enough that the accusing look should have left her face by now. He had lost track of days, and counted them now on his fingers.

Tomorrow was going to be Christmas Eve.

"Let's go outside and build a snowman," he said again, thinking she might not have heard him the first time. Building snowmen had been her favorite thing at home, before the White Christmas Inn had become part of her reality.

"Tess NOT go." She slammed on the toy piano to make her point. He had also given her the piano in an effort to distract her from her fury with him. It hadn't worked any better than the pony or the shoes. She didn't play with it, but used it as emphatic punctuation to her anger with him. The tone of the piano was awful and reminded him of Emma's doorbell.

He should have fixed that before he left.

Ryder told himself to stop pleading with the child and take charge.

He could bundle her up into her snowsuit, wrestle her boots onto her feet, put her hat on the right way and take her outside, build the snowman, hope to distract her from his treasonous act of removing her from the Fenshaws, from "Eggie and Boo," from Emma and from the White Christmas Inn.

It would take an hour or so out of a day that seemed to be stretching out endlessly, despite the fact the cottage had a forty-two-inch plasma television set and a satellite that got four hundred channels. He had not found one single thing to watch that could hold his attention, and Tess was suddenly not interested in her old favorite cartoons.

What had he ever been thinking when he had thought coming to the cottage would be a refuge?

Over the last few days, Ryder was discovering he hated it here. He had bought the cottage last summer, a place his brother had never been, no memories. A pleasant place in the heat of the summer, with water sports, along with the satellite dish, to add to the distraction quotient.

But there seemed to be no escaping the dreariness in the winter.

The decor and furnishings, which had come with the cottage, were modern and masculine. The paint was a neutral frosty white, the furniture ran to sleek black leather, the finishes were stainless steel. The art was large abstract canvases, meaningless brush strokes of red. At the time of purchase, it had all looked sophisticated to him, clean and uncluttered.

Not cold and impersonal, a showroom not actually intended for people to live in. Of course, the cold could be because of the endless damp billowing off that lake.

Or from the way he felt inside.

Like a cold-hearted bastard. *Not just selfish, but mean.* Ask Tess. Ask those little girls who had sobbed as he was leaving. He couldn't even look at that rag doll without being filled with self-loathing.

Little Peggy had been able to overcome her own distress enough to think of someone else first, to try and bring comfort.

That final scene filled him with shame.

Looking around the ultra-modern bareness of the cottage, Ryder missed the inn. He missed doorknobs coming off in his hands, and the imperfection of the sloping kitchen floor. He missed the fact that everywhere you looked inside or outside that inn, there was something that needed doing.

Not like here.

Unbelievably, he missed all that Christmas clutter, the hokey cheer of wrapped packages and angels in trees, white poinsettias and red cushions. He missed the way the tree smelled, and he found he especially missed the crackle, the warmth, the coziness of the real fire.

He had a gas version here, throwing up phony-looking blue flames behind a stainless-steel enclosure, not beginning to touch the chill.

He missed getting up in the morning and having that sense of urgency and purpose.

He missed Mona's cooking, and the quiet companionship and wisdom of Tim, he missed the girls fussing over Tess and jostling for position to show him their drawings and tell him their stories.

Who was he kidding? Certainly not the person he wanted to kid the most. He was not even beginning to kid himself.

He missed Emma. He missed her quirky hair and the ever-changing moss-and-mist of her eyes. He missed her laughter and the mulish set of her jaw. He missed her voice, her ability to have fun, the seemingly endless generosity of her heart.

He missed the subtle scent on her skin, and her hand brush-ing his at unexpected moments, and he could not get the taste of her mouth out of his mind.

He missed how, against all odds, she held on-to hope.

Most of all he missed how he had felt. *Not alone.*

Instead of that he had chosen this. A cottage so dreary and cold that he could not seem to warm it up no matter what he did.

Or maybe it was himself he could not warm up.

That time, the night before she had married his brother, when his sister-in-law had said to him with such honesty and affection, "You and Drew are the rarest of finds. Good men," now seemed like one of the things he had lost to the fire.

He did not feel like a good man anymore.

A good man would not have left the White Christmas Inn, putting his selfish need to protect himself above the heartbreak of a shrieking baby and two little girls who had the maturity to know that even when you hurt, you still gave, you still tried to make the world better instead of worse.

A good man would not have left Tim to be the sole man to try and get that place ready for the crowds that would be descending on Holiday Happenings.

And Ryder knew there were crowds, because the only call he'd made since he'd got here was to the PR firm that handled all his company's advertising. He'd had to go and use the pay phone at the Lakeside Grocery and Ice Cream Palace because he'd so stubbornly left his cell phone at home.

Patrick had promised he would call in all his favors to make sure everyone within a day's drive of the inn knew about what was happening there, and knew what the proceeds were going to.

"Wow," Patrick had said before he hung up, "what a great way to shake off the blues from the storm and get back in the Christmas spirit. I'm going to take my wife and kids out. And what would you think if I suggested people arrive with an unwrapped gift for the families that will be spending Christmas with her?"

"Perfect," Ryder had said.

But it didn't feel perfect at all. It didn't take away one bit of the guilt he was experiencing.

Because all Emma had wanted was one Christmas that felt good, and he had walked away from her.

It wasn't him she wanted, precisely, he tried to tell himself. It was that feeling of family. He thought of his parting words, hoping her mother came for Christmas. As if that absolved him in some way.

Absolved? He didn't owe her anything!

But a good man would have stayed, not protected himself.

"Well, I'm not a good man," he said out loud.

Tess shot him a look that clearly said *You aren't kidding*.

He remembered Tim suddenly not being able to look at him when Emma had said she would be sending the bus ticket that day, that her mother would arrive for Christmas Eve.

He scowled. Tim didn't think Lynelle White was going to come home for Christmas with her daughter. And, after all Emma had confided in him, could Ryder possibly believe Lynelle would show up?

Ryder could barely stand the thought of one more disappointment for Emma. A phone call. He'd just check. That was all.

He wrestled Tess into her coat after all, but not to go and build a snowman. As soon as he tucked her into the car seat, she started to sing happily. Anticipating a return to the inn.

"I'm not going that far," he said grouchily. "I'm just going back to the pay phone. And that will teach me to leave my cell phone at home, too!"

At the Lakeside Grocery, while watching Tess in the car talking happy nonsense to Bebo, he inserted his credit card in the phone. And then he had to sweet-talk a very cranky operator to get her to check every directory in two provinces before he found the name he was looking for. Thankfully, Lynelle still had the last name *White*.

Finally, determined but his fingers numb from the cold, he called the number he had found.

A raspy voice answered.

"May I speak to Lynelle White please?"

No answer at first, but he could hear loud voices in the background.

"And who wants to speak to her?" The voice became cagey, loaded with suspicion. It sounded like there was a party going on. Not the nice kind, with Christmas music and tinkling glasses. The kind where fights broke out and bottles got smashed.

It occurred to him the words were slurred around the edges.

"Is this Lynelle?" he asked.

"Yup." There was the distinct sound of a match being struck, followed by the long slow inhale.

He suddenly wasn't sure what to say. *Go spend Christmas with your daughter. Tell her you're proud of her. Make a fuss over the inn. Make a fuss over her. Help her have that one good Christmas.*

"My name's Ryder Richardson. I—"

He needn't have worried what to say, because Lynelle didn't let him finish. "Look, buddy, whatever you're selling, I don't want it." And then she said a phrase he'd heard on plenty of construction sites and slammed down the phone.

He took the dead receiver from his ear, stared at it for a moment. Then, slowly, Ryder replaced the receiver in the cradle. He knew there was no sense calling back.

He knew why Tim had looked away when Emma had said she would send the ticket. And he knew why Emma had never had a good Christmas.

From that extremely short encounter, he knew everything about Lynelle, Emma's mother, that you could know.

And he knew she wasn't going to anyplace called the White Christmas Inn for the holidays. In all likelihood, a bus ticket cashed in was what the background noise was all about.

A girl from the wrong side of the tracks, Emma had confided in him, telling him about her botched engagement, bowled over by the attentions of a doctor, probably for no more reason than that the doctor *wasn't* from the wrong side of the tracks.

Standing there in the cold outside the phone booth, it became very clear to Ryder that he and Emma had something in common.

They both longed for a Christmas that could never happen.

His hopes destroyed by death.

Hers just plain unrealistic.

But at least he'd known what it was to be surrounded by a family's love at Christmas.

That's what it was all about for Emma, he realized. All the decorations, all the holiday happenings, all the Christmas Day Dream.

She still hoped.

Despite life giving her all kinds of evidence to the contrary, Emma stubbornly clung to a belief that life was good, people were good, that given enough chances they would eventually do the right thing.

*Believe.*

And he wondered if he could be the man his sister-in-law had thought he was, a man he had once been. A man who believed, when all was said and done, in himself. It was not the immature belief that he could just use his strength and his will to create the world he wanted, but the deeper belief that when life didn't go his way and didn't give him what he wanted, he could count on himself to be strong enough, and to forgive himself when he wasn't.

If he was such a man, he would go back there,

and turn hope into belief, then he would be the man he had once been. Better, maybe. A man worthy of Emma.

But that was one big *if*.

It was nearly ten o'clock, the night before Christmas Eve. Emma could finally abandon her post by the parking lot where she had been collecting admission and stamping hands.

She hurried to the warming shed, where Mona gave her a frazzled look.

"Emma, could you go to the house and see if there are any more of the chocolate-dipped short-bread cookies in the freezer? I sold out the last of them that we had here. And if you could put a few more of the wreaths out, that would be great."

Emma hiked up to the house, and looked at the long line of cars parked all the way down the driveway. For hours, people had been walking up from the main road, the closest parking, carrying brand-new toys and teddy bears, paying the admission happily.

"Where did you hear about it?" she asked the first family to arrive, the first night Holiday Happenings had finally opened, after they told her they had driven up from Ontario just for this.

"Oh, it's on the radio." And then they'd given

er an extra twenty to help with expenses for the Christmas Day Dream. They actually called it by ame!

"Lovely idea," the mother had said. "Exactly what I want my kids to know about Christmas." And then, "Would you mind if I peeked around inside the house? We're always looking for these charming little out-of-the-way places to spend a few days in during the summer."

They heard it on the radio? Emma hadn't been able to afford a radio ad. She'd put up some posters and run a few ads in the classified sections of a few New Brunswick papers. Her budget had not allowed for more than that, certainly not for Ontario.

And who was telling them to bring an un-wrapped gift for the Christmas Day Dream?

How did they even know about the Christmas Day Dream?

Now, the day before Christmas Eve, they had gone through all four thousand hot dogs and run out to buy more twice. When she checked the freezer, she found there were no chocolate-dipped shortbread cookies left, and there were no wreaths stored on the back porch.

Emma delivered the bad news to the warming shed, where Mona was being rushed off her feet selling a dwindling supply of crafts and cookies. She had long since given up on selling hot dogs. All the supplies were out with a cup beside them and a sign that said By Donation. The donation cup was overflowing.

*My cup is overflowing,* Emma said to herself, watching the skaters skim across the pond, hearing the jingle of the horse bells as they pulled the big sled around the torch-lit trail that circled the pond.

But, looking at her pond, it was as if all the skaters disappeared and she could just see two, herself and Ryder.

If her cup was overflowing, why did she feel so empty? This was her dream come true. The fortunes of the White Christmas Inn had been turned around. Her bills were paid. The storeroom off the front hall was filled to bursting with toys and gifts.

The chartered bus to bring people for the Christmas Day Dream was paid for, Emma had enough money to get each family a supermarket certificate for a month's worth of groceries after Christmas was over. Three huge turkeys were thawing for the feast, Mona had volunteers making pies.

Holiday Happenings had succeeded beyond her

vildest dreams. Tonight a news crew had come 'rom Fredericton, which meant tomorrow, Christmas Eve, could be the inn's biggest night so 'ar.

Her success didn't feel the way she thought it vould at all. She felt oddly hollow, empty lespite the fact Holiday Happenings had suc-:eeded beyond what she had ever dared to lream for it.

Maybe the truth about all her ruined Christmases was that no matter what happened, hey could never meet her expectations.

What she really wanted was not Christmas. Not skaters on ponds and perfect gifts piled high under the tree, not turkey and stuffing and carols sung around a crackling fire.

Maybe what she really wanted was what Christmas had stood for a long time ago, before trees and packages and music and trinkets had all cluttered the message.

Love.

And that was what had eluded her again and again.

After everyone had gone home, Emma wearily climbed the stairs, and went down the hall to her room, feeling so alone.

She hesitated and opened the door to the green

room, ready for her mother's arrival tomorrow night on the eight o'clock bus.

Emma went in and sat down on the bed. The little ghost of the girl she used to be came and sat down beside her.

"We're going to have a good Christmas," she promised her. "Finally."

And in the quiet of that moment, without the crush of skaters and the gallons of hot chocolate she was amazed that she believed it.

Suddenly, she knew that's what it was all about Holiday Happenings, the Christmas Day Dream—it hadn't been about giving to others though that's what it looked like from the outside

Inside herself, Emma knew the truth. It was really all about her. Every single thing she had done, including insisting her mother come, had been about her, about her trying to be good enough, trying to shore up that terribly shaky self-esteem.

She had been trying desperately to create something that never was with all the Christmas hoopla, with taking on the house, with creating that perfect room for her mother. She had been looking to repair what was inside herself by making a perfect picture outside herself.

The only time she had ever felt the magic she

wanted from Christmas was on the pond skating with Ryder. It had not been the wild-child who had skated with him. Not the woman-scorned. Not the independent-woman-innkeeper.

It had been Emma. Just Emma. And with that had come a feeling of freedom, of finally being seen and appreciated for who she really was.

And Ryder had still walked away from that. From who she really was. It was devastating. So much worse than Peter's abandonment, because Peter had walked away from a role she played, not who she was. In retrospect, he had done them both a favor, released her from pretense.

That first night Ryder had come, she had told him bravely, proudly even, "Christmas transforms everything. It makes all things magic."

And now she realized something magic *had* happened. It didn't have to do with Christmas, but with love. Falling for Ryder, she had put away the masks and found out who she really was, become who she really was, and even if Ryder had walked away from that, she wasn't going to.

She was going to give herself the gift she had looked for from everyone else. Love. Surprised, for it had come when she least expected it, Emma felt the exquisite sense of peace that she had looked for her entire life.

# CHAPTER NINE

RYDER couldn't believe the cars. The parking lot was full. There were cars parked all along the driveway, and halfway to Willowbrook.

"Don't people have better things to do on Christmas Eve?" he asked grouchily, finding a place, finally, to squeeze his car in where he wouldn't have to walk too far carrying Tess to get to the house and the pond.

But he wasn't really grouchy. As soon as he had turned into that driveway he had felt as if he was coming home.

Tess was babbling happily, Bebo held firmly in her clutches. He'd finally realized it wasn't exactly gibberish. It was Boo and Eggie she was talking to. When she said Emma, *Um-uh,* it sounded like *Mama.* She said those three names over and over again, running them together, in a little melody of joy. She was still humming excitedly as they got out of the car, as she strained in his arms, looking.

He went up the front steps. There was a basket on it, with a sign. Admission by Donation. The basket was overflowing.

He wandered through the house, allowed the sensation of homecoming to deepen.

"Um-uh, Boo, Eggie," Tess cried.

But it was obvious the house was empty.

"Burglar heaven," Ryder said out loud. How like Emma to just trust the whole world—her house open, the basket of money on the stairs. "At least she doesn't have a television anyone would want," he said to Tess, heading out the back door.

He followed the Christmas-lit pathway to the pond. Throngs of people skated, swirling in bright patterns over torch-lit ice. The sounds of the laughter and conversation of those gathered around the bonfires drifted up to him.

It was a Christmas-card-pretty scene. Emma must be loving this.

He moved through the crowds at the warming shed, and suddenly Sue and Peggy burst out of a little cluster of people around the bonfire, looking taller on their skates.

"Tess!"

Tess went shy. "Boo, Eggie," she whispered,

and then leaned out of his arms, offering Bebc back.

The shyness was momentary.

"DOWN," she ordered, and her best friends each took a hand and patiently walked her down to the ice and her little sled, sitting nearly where they had left it.

Mona, harried inside the warming shed, looked at him, looked again, and then as beautiful a smile as he had ever seen lit her face.

"Isn't this great?" she shouted. "Welcome back."

"It's great," he agreed, but he felt as if he could not wait a moment longer. "Where is Emma?"

"I haven't seen her for awhile. If you do see her, could you tell her I need some more ginger-bread? That's about all we have left."

"Will do. The girls have Tess."

"I'll watch out for her."

Ryder focused on the pond. Surely with all the things that needed to be doing, Emma wouldn't be out there skating? He remembered her delight in her newfound skill. Then again, maybe she would be. Maybe, he frowned, she had even found someone to dance with her. But, no, as he searched the throngs, he did not see a familiar red toque with crazy curls protruding around the edges of it.

He did see Tim bringing the big team of horses around the pond, steam coming out their nostrils, poofs of snow exploding around their huge feet. The harness bells jingled. He went to meet him.

Tim pulled up beside him, jumped down, helped each person off the sleigh.

He turned and regarded Ryder not with surprise, but with approval, judging him a man who had done the right thing.

"She's not here," Tim said, not a doubt in his mind what Ryder had come back here for. And it was not Holiday Happenings.

Ryder felt his heart fall. Not here? But where—

"She left for the bus station in Willowbrook. At least an hour ago. The bus was supposed to be in at eight, so she should have been back by now."

Tim's eyes met his, something in them unspoken.

But Ryder heard him loud and clear.

He headed for Willowbrook breaking all speed limits. It seemed as though every residence and business in the tiny hamlet was in competition to have the finest Christmas display. The bus station stood out for its lack of Christmas attire, a gray, squat building with no cheer, inside or out.

Through the front plate-glass window, he saw Emma sitting in a row of hard chairs, the only one in the station except for a clerk behind the counter. The red Santa hat was on the seat beside her.

Seeing her there, so alone and so hopeful despite the fact it was now nearly nine-thirty, Ryder should have been able to tell himself that he had come back for her.

He should have been able to confirm he was a good man after all.

He had come just in time, to help Emma finally know what a good Christmas was.

He'd come back, a choice. Choosing to live, even if it meant risk. Last year, one year ago on Christmas, standing in the ashes of his life, he had made a choice not to live anymore, and to not forgive himself, ever, for what had happened there.

Now, standing here, he was aware of making another choice, this time to live after all. And finally, to forgive himself.

He'd come back here because he had started off on a road to one place ten days ago, and instead he had ended up somewhere else. And by some miracle the place he had ended up had turned out to be exactly where he needed to be, where he was meant to be.

Was it possible that all things, even the things

he had no hope of ever understanding, like two people gone too soon, lost too young, could have a meaning if his heart opened to them?

Watching Emma, he was so achingly aware of what she was hoping would come off the next bus.

And while she waited for it to get off that bus, watched the main door, the place the passengers came through into the bus depot, love would do what love did. The unexpected, the unscheduled, love would slip in the side door.

Hadn't it already? Hadn't it come to her in the form of Tim and Mona, and Peggy and Sue?

Hadn't it come to her on a stormy night nine days ago?

Ryder walked through the side door. A man in chains had entered her life nine days ago, but a free man went to join her now.

Emma watched the clock. One more bus at midnight. Chances were remote that her mother was going to be on it. There was no point sitting here, waiting for something that wasn't going to happen. She should really go back to Holiday Happenings, but she didn't feel like it.

It felt like too much chaos and too much noise, and as if the whole world was made of people who cared about each other and had families, except her. Still, she had herself, and all day she had felt a growing appreciation of what that meant.

"Hi," he slipped into the seat beside her.

Without even turning her head, she knew who it was, let his familiar scent fill her senses. She closed her eyes for a moment, breathing him in, then opened them and looked at him. Her heart began to pound when she saw something in his face she had not ever seen before, not even that night they had skated on the pond.

There was some kind of openness in him, she could see tenderness in the darkness of those eyes.

But of course, she could imagine all kinds of things! She had imagined her mother really meant she was coming.

And she had imagined learning to love herself would be enough, though with him sitting beside her it seemed not that it wasn't, but that loving herself was the stepping stone she had been missing in being able to love another.

"What are you doing here?" she asked. It felt as if she would give away the tiny bit of power she had left if she admitted how happy she was to see him.

"I thought we could start again." He took his glove off, held out his hand to her. "I'm Ryder Richardson, dumb jerk."

"How did you know I was here?" She didn't take his hand.

"Tim told me."

"I hope you aren't here because you feel sorry for me," she said stiffly.

"Why would I be sorry for you?"

"Come on, Ryder. Everybody knew she wasn't coming, except me. Hopeless dreamer. Everybody knew I was trying to rewrite history with all of it. None of it, not even Christmas Day Dream, was ever about giving to those other people. It was always about me trying to repair something that can't be repaired. You can't rewrite the past. It's done. You don't get to do it over, no matter how hard you try. I have a new goal now. To love myself in spite of all of it."

It felt as if she had to be very brave to say that.

"Ah."

"Why do you say it like that?"

"Because I think you'll find loving you is the easiest thing in the world. Speaking from experience."

For a moment she couldn't believe he had said that, so he said it again, leaving no room for misinterpretation.

"I love you, Emma."

When she looked in his eyes she saw it was true.

He was offering her what she had never had. A shoulder to lean on. But more. Acceptance. Connection. Love.

"You know," he said softly, "right until the minute I came through those doors, I was convinced I had come back here for you. Now I can clearly see that's not true."

"It's not?"

He shook his head. "I came back for myself, Emma."

"You did?"

"I came back to save myself. I can't change what happened, either. Changing myself into someone untouchable and bitter hasn't changed what happened."

His voice grew unbelievably gentle. "Maybe it's time for both of us to move forward. Instead of trying to fix what's done, we need to build the future, not rebuild the past."

His voice was low. "Emma, I don't want to be lonely anymore. Or bitter. Or closed. That's no way to honor the gift of love my family always gave me. My mom and dad, my brother Drew, my sister-in-law Tracy. I need to be the man they expected me to be when they made up a will that gave me guardianship of Tess.

"I need to be a man," he said softly, "who can

show a girl who has never had a good Christmas just what that feels like."

Her tears came then, and he reached out and caught them with his thumb.

And Emma was amazed that she didn't give one hoot what Christmas felt like. Nothing could hold a candle to the way she felt right now. Nothing.

Not even the most perfect Christmas in the whole world.

And maybe it was because she let go of it, that it finally, finally happened.

Christmas became a dream.

With Ryder right beside her, the next morning as the bus pulled up, they welcomed fifty-one guests to the inn.

How shy and awkward those poorly dressed people looked as they got off the bus and looked toward the house.

And how quickly that awkwardness melted away as the unofficial greeting "elves," Tess, Sue and Peggy, rushed forward to meet the children and to shoo them toward the house that smelled of the turkey that had been in the oven since early this morning.

Mona had a hilarious game set up, an ice breaker, that helped everyone meet each other and get to know their names. Then there was buffet breakfast laid out at the dining-room table.

Soon they were all crowded into the great room, plates empty, coffee and cocoa mugs full, the laughter and warmth flowing easily, the children quivering with anticipation at what was under the tree.

Tim handed out gifts until the room was awash with paper and shouts of glee and exhilaration. There were new snow boots and warm jackets, fuzzy pajamas, mittens and hats. There were toys for the young children—dolls and fire trucks—and electronics for the older ones, portable DVD players and personal stereos.

"Not bad goodies for the techno-electro-free zone," Ryder teased her.

After the gifts, there were skating and sleigh rides, and then after naps for the younger ones, a dinner feast fit for kings.

Then they gathered around the fire once again. Strangers just this morning, they were a family now. A family of babies and old people, teenagers and young moms and dads. Mona had more games, and it was nearly midnight as they all began to reboard the bus, the children clutching their favorite toys, packages being loaded into the cargo hold under the bus. There were hugs and expressions of gratitude and tears.

Mona and Tim packed up the girls, and Tess was put to bed in a crib in the green room.

Emma and Ryder were alone in front of the fire.

"I'm exhausted," she told him, stretching out her legs. "And exhilarated. It was better than anything I planned."

He touched her hair, ran his fingers through it.

"You know the weird part?" she said, quietly, "it wasn't really Holiday Happenings. And not even today, as beautiful as it was."

He nodded. "I know, Emma."

"You do?"

"Yeah. It's this, what we're feeling right here, right now, isn't it?"

"That's it exactly," she said. "Exactly. When I stopped *expecting* the world, overlaying reality with my dreams, it was as if I could enjoy it for the very first time."

And that feeling didn't go away because Christmas had, and neither did Ryder. He stayed.

She woke up most mornings with a kink in her neck from falling asleep on him.

And she woke up eager for the next day, to see what love brought.

A touch of hands, a moment stolen to share a

hot dog, an afternoon while the Fenshaws kept Tess.

Ryder and Tess left on New Year's Day.

And that was when the romance began in earnest. He sent flowers. He e-mailed. They talked on the phone as late into the night as they had every day since Christmas.

He came for the weekends, but more and more Emma went to the city, aware that she had missed the city and loved it. Sometimes they would take Tess with them as they explored little coffee shops and antique markets, other times they left her with Miss Markle while they went to the theatre, or out for a quiet grown-up dinner.

The passion between them grew until it flared, white-hot. Every touch, every look, a promise.

But it was Ryder who would never let the passion culminate.

"Hey, I have to be an example for Tess. I don't want her to think it's okay to give in without committing."

For Emma's birthday, in the spring, Ryder gave her an engagement ring, and asked her to marry him.

In the summer, at White Pond Inn, they married, a quiet, small outdoor ceremony with the people they cared about most in the world. Tim, Sr., was there, and so was Tim, Jr., in his uniform. Mona and Sue and Peggy had on matching burgundy dresses.

Tess, in a snow-white dress that somehow had a big smudge down the front of it, was supposed to be the flower girl, but she sat down on her way up the grassy aisle beside the pond, and started picking dandelions and couldn't be persuaded there was something more interesting than those little yellow flowers.

And to Emma it didn't matter. She had given up expectations. And perfection.

And yet, when she saw Ryder waiting for her at the end of that aisle, she stepped around Tess and kept going. She didn't once look to see if Lynelle had made it after all.

They were writing their own history now. Beginning today.

And Emma could clearly see that it was not Christmas that transformed everything; it was love. And it was love that made all things magic.

And that the man waiting for her, with such a tender light in his dark eyes, was all the perfection she ever needed.

# EPILOGUE

TWENTY-TWO gallons of hot chocolate.

Ten of mulled wine.

Four hundred and sixty-two painstakingly decorated Christmas cookies.

And it was not going to be nearly enough.

"If you lift that kettle of hot chocolate, I'm throwing you over my shoulder and taking you home," Ryder told Emma, irritated.

"I love it when you're masterful," she said, clearly not seeing how serious the situation was.

"I'm not joking, Emma."

"Ha. As if you could pick me up right now."

"I could," he said threateningly. He still felt this thrill when he looked at her and used the word *wife*. This woman had come into herself so completely it nearly made him dizzy that she had chosen to love him. Emma was sassy, confident, radiant, strong, on fire with her love of life. And of him.

"Okay, okay," she said. "Tim, could you get this hot chocolate for me? Ryder has decided I'm delicate."

Tim, Jr., came over and lifted the pot of warm liquid easily. "You *are* delicate," he told her sternly. "Keep an eye on her, Ryder. I don't trust her as far as I could throw her."

"And that would not be very far," Emma said giving her huge belly a satisfied pat.

The truth was Ryder had tried to talk her out of White Christmas at the inn this year.

The doctor had told them to expect a New Year's baby. What if they got snowed in, like the year they met?

But Emma had gotten that mulish look on her face and he'd known there was no sense arguing with her. He'd call a helicopter if they got snowed in. He had his cell phone with him, just in case.

Besides, there would have been no living with Tess if he had cancelled their yearly Christmas trip to White Pond Inn.

She was four now, a young lady who knew her own mind. He looked for her—Emma had dressed her in neon pink so they could spot her in the crowds. She was down on the pond, in her new skates, shuffling along between Sue and Peggy. This year, their little sister, born about nine months after Tim had returned home from his tour of duty—was in the sled being pulled behind the girls.

"Don't take this the wrong way," Tim said, following Ryder's gaze to the four little girls on the pond, "but I hope that's a boy in there."

"Chauvinist," Emma accused him, but her eyes twinkled with the shine of a woman well-loved.

"Healthy is good enough for me," Ryder said.

He decided, as long as he could keep an eye on Emma and keep her from lifting anything too heavy, it was good to have come to White Pond this year after all.

She had sold the White Pond Inn to Mona and Tim shortly after she'd agreed to marry Ryder. The younger Fenshaws didn't run it as a bed-and-breakfast, the inn was now their family home. But every year they held Holiday Happenings, though Mona, Ryder thought thankfully, had renamed it Home for the Holidays. The Christmas Day Dream event had gotten bigger, and it was called Coming Home for Christmas.

Ryder suspected they kept both activities going mostly for him and Emma.

Because, as the friendship had grown between the two couples, they'd learned about each other's histories and heartbreaks. The Fenshaws knew this was always going to be a hard time of year for Ryder, a good time to stay busy, to give to others.

"You don't have to," he'd said to Emma when she had announced she planned to sell. Tim, Jr., wanted the inn not to run as a bed and breakfast, but to farm, as his father farmed, and his grandfather had farmed before that.

Ryder had not been looking for a brother, just as he had not been looking for love that night a storm had stranded him.

But in Tim he'd been given a brother anyway.

"No," Emma had said firmly, "the house and land need what they have to give. It's falling down and in need of the kind of repairs Tim can give it and I can't. Mona has always loved that house. Tim is home now."

"If you want it, I'll fix it up for you as a wedding present."

"Ryder," she said, smiling at him. "You don't seem to get it. I don't need it anymore. It was like my dreams, falling down and in need of repair. I wanted White Pond to give me a family, and a feeling of belonging. But I have a better dream now, and I know better than to think a house can make you *feel* things."

And the way she looked at him when she said that made him feel, not ten feet tall and bullet-proof, but as if he was enough.

"Mama, Papa, look at me."

Tess's voice rose high over the sounds of the crowd and he and Emma both turned to look.

Tess's pronunciation of Emma had been close to *Mama* all those years ago. And somehow he had become *papa*.

When he showed Tess the pictures of Drew and Tracy, they were Mom and Dad, and he was achingly aware of never wanting to take their place. At the same time he wanted to do a job that would make them so proud of him.

If Tess's level of confidence was any indication, he and Emma were doing just fine.

For a moment, watching Tess strut proudly across the ice, he felt the spirit of it all.

His brother and sister-in-law.

Christmas.

And he believed. He believed that things had a reason.

Once upon a time, he'd been a man trying to outrun Christmas, finding exactly what he needed en route to where he thought he was going, and had not been going there at all.

With each year that passed, Ryder was able to

see more clearly that the fire had taken things from him. But it had given him things, too.

It had put him on the road that had led him to Emma. And it had made him a man capable of feeling deeply for others, capable of forgiveness of failings. He was a better man than he had been before, worthy of love.

That made him wonder, sometimes, if he could find meaning in that, of all things, was there meaning in everything? Even in the things his mind, limited and human, could not grasp?

He was an architect, trained to think in terms of mathematical precision. But he knew, as an architect, that there was a place where planning and precision left off and inspiration began. Often inspiration came as the result of a problem that seemed insoluble, a hardship that did not seem as if it could be overcome.

The greatest buildings came from that place.

And maybe the greatest men and women did, too.

Look at Lynelle. How could someone like her produce someone like Emma?

His mother-in-law had chosen not to be a part of their lives at all. She did not come at Christmas; she said she would have come for the wedding if they'd held it anywhere but at White Pond.

But he didn't believe it. She was as indifferent to Tess and the coming baby as she had been to Emma.

But even his fury at that had been distilled by the love he lived in.

When he looked at Emma and saw her compassion for others, he knew it came from all those years when she had tried to win attention and approval from Lynelle that never came.

Emma showed him that good could come from bad, good people from bad parents, good things from bad situations. It was the fire that tempered the steel.

She showed him every day that love was not a destination he had arrived at, but a journey he had embarked upon. It was full of peaks and valleys, challenges and rewards, but most of all, it was stronger than anything else.

Christmas represented that.

It represented all the things that, for awhile, he had lost belief in.

Goodness.

Hope.

Faith.

Light.

"Papa!"

Life.

Suddenly, Emma's hand flew to her belly, and her eyes widened and then met his. She inhaled sharply and deeply.

"The books don't get you ready for how that feels," she marveled. "Do you think we're going to have a Christmas baby, Ryder?"

The calmness in her face, her absolute trust in him made him remember the other belief love had restored—his belief in himself.

A child would be born and he would be enough to welcome another life into this world, enough to accept the responsibility as well as the joy. It was another thing to celebrate during the season, his list of things to celebrate slowly outgrowing his things to grieve.

And wasn't that really what Christmas represented? An evolution of thought, man's belief that everything in the end had a reason, and that everything in the end was for the greater good.

Somewhere in the last years, with Emma and Tess making his good outweigh his bad, Ryder had realized he could surrender. He could trust himself, but know that when his own strength flagged, or was not enough, that was when the real miracle happened.

The truth was that something greater than him ran the show.

Isn't that what Christmas really celebrated?

The birth of a child that would bring a message to the world.

Love is the most powerful.

Love is the thing that cannot be destroyed.

And it went on and on, even after death.

It went on in a little girl down there a flash of neon pink, shouting "Mama! Papa! Watch me."

And it would go on in a new baby, a new life, a brand-new messenger of the power of love to bring hope and to heal all.

Despite her saying he couldn't possibly lift her, Ryder swept his wife into his arms and headed for the car. "Tim," he called, "she's going into labor."

"Stop it," she insisted. "Ryder, really! I'm too heavy. I can walk. It was only the first pain."

But the thing was, she didn't feel heavy to him at all.

She felt light. And he felt light. And all of it, the skaters on the pond, Tess, the Fenshaw girls, the laughter, the scrape of blades on ice, Tim racing toward them with a look on his face that reminded Ryder of the soldier he had been, all of it suddenly seemed as if it was swirling together, becoming one immense energy.

Ryder realized, suddenly, his heart swelling

until he thought it would break, that he really *believed*.

And in that shining second of pure love, his breath, his bone, his life, his whole world, became a reflection of the Light.

# Bestselling author Melanie Milburne writes for

# MEDICAL™

## The Doctor's Rebel Knight

### *Her rebel with a heart of gold...*

Dr Frances Nin has come to Pelican Bay in search of tranquillity...but motorbike-riding local rebel Sergeant Jacob Hawke gets her pulse-rate spiking! One glimpse of the heat in Jacob's icy blue eyes and Fran's fragile heart starts to bloom...

## On sale 1st January 2010

Available at WHSmith, Tesco, ASDA, Eason and all good bookshops. For full Mills & Boon range including eBooks visit **www.millsandboon.co.uk**

### *Praise for Melanie Milburne*

Her love scenes, no matter what genre, are never boring and I can't stop reading them!
—*Romantic Times BOOK Reviews*

I have come to love Ms Milburne's writing
—*Romantic Times BOOK Reviews*

# millsandboon.co.uk Community

## Join Us!

The Community is the perfect place to meet and chat to kindred spirits who love books and reading as much as you do, but it's also the place to:

- **Get the inside scoop from authors about their latest books**
- **Learn how to write a romance book with advice from our editors**
- **Help us to continue publishing the best in women's fiction**
- **Share your thoughts on the books we publish**
- **Befriend other users**

**Forums:** Interact with each other as well as authors, editors and a whole host of other users worldwide.

**Blogs:** Every registered community member has their own blog to tell the world what they're up to and what's on their mind.

**Book Challenge:** We're aiming to read 5,000 books and have joined forces with The Reading Agency in our inaugural Book Challenge.

**Profile Page:** Showcase yourself and keep a record of your recent community activity.

**Social Networking:** We've added buttons at the end of every post to share via digg, Facebook, Google, Yahoo, technorati and de.licio.us.

## www.millsandboon.co.uk

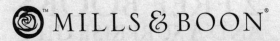

# 2 FREE BOOKS
## AND A SURPRISE GIFT

We would like to take this opportunity to thank you for reading this Mills & Boon® book by offering you the chance to take TWO more specially selected books from the Romance series absolutely FREE! We're also making this offer to introduce you to the benefits of the Mills & Boon® Book Club™—

- **FREE home delivery**
- **FREE gifts and competitions**
- **FREE monthly Newsletter**
- **Exclusive Mills & Boon Book Club offers**
- **Books available before they're in the shops**

Accepting these FREE books and gift places you under no obligation to buy, you may cancel at any time, even after receiving your free shipment. Simply complete your details below and return the entire page to the address below. You don't even need a stamp!

**YES** Please send me 2 free Romance books and a surprise gift. I understand that unless you hear from me, I will receive 5 superb new stories every month including two 2-in-1 books priced at £4.99 each and a single book priced at £3.19, postage and packing free. I am under no obligation to purchase any books and may cancel my subscription at any time. The free books and gift will be mine to keep in any case.

Ms/Mrs/Miss/Mr_____ Initials _____

_____

Surname _____

Address _____

_____

_____ Postcode _____

Send this whole page to: Mills & Boon Book Club, Free Book Offer, FREEPOST NAT 10298, Richmond, TW9 1BR